Joyous Noelle

ARABELLA H. WEISS

ISBN 978-1-63784-117-4 (paperback)
ISBN 978-1-63784-118-1 (digital)

Copyright © 2024 by Arabella H. Weiss

All rights reserved. No part of this publication may be reproduced, distributed, or transmitted in any form or by any means, including photocopying, recording, or other electronic or mechanical methods without the prior written permission of the publisher. For permission requests, solicit the publisher via the address below.

Hawes & Jenkins Publishing
16427 N Scottsdale Road Suite 410
Scottsdale, AZ 85254
www.hawesjenkins.com

Printed in the United States of America

Chapter 1

"Noelle, aren't you going to eat one? I'm starting to feel like a pig eating all the appetizers by myself," Valerie replied while dipping her mozzarella stick into some marinara sauce. Her thick, long raven-colored ponytail swayed gently back and forth behind her.

Noelle barely glanced over at her friend, quickly brushing a few tight blond curls out of her left eye. She slouched down in the booth, taking a sip of her soda while her piercing blue eyes remained fixated on the entrance. "I'm not really hungry… I'll just wait until we order the pizza when Paige gets here," Noelle replied solemnly.

Valerie sat upright across from her friend, readjusting her plum-colored dolman sweater before reaching over for another mozzarella stick. "Where is Paige? Isn't she supposed to be here by now?" Valerie asked, only half interested, while quickly finishing her mozzarella stick.

Noelle sat back in the booth and turned her attention toward Valerie. "Paige said she's coming. She's just running a little bit late. Something about Laurel needing her to do something else at work," Noelle replied, placing her focus back on the entrance of the restaurant.

Valerie took a sip of her soda and then rolled her eyes. "Ah yes, Laurel, the boss she complains about every time I see her and yet she still works for… Can't seem to figure that one out. At least you will never have to deal with Janice anymore," Valerie replied confidently before taking another sip of her soda.

Noelle sighed, turned, and gave her friend a somber look. "It's not like I had a choice—I was fired. But it doesn't matter anyway because Janice didn't hire me, her cousin Charlene did. I guess Charlene should have checked with her cousin to see whether or not I was *worthwhile* hiring to manage Janlene's. I doubt I would have been Janice's first or even last choice for being hired as manager. I don't even know why she would really care so much because Janice didn't want to run the business. She was only interested in the return on her financial investment…at least that's what I was able to grasp from bits and pieces of several overheard conversations. Laurel is different; she's a workaholic who expects her employees to work just as hard or even harder than she does. Paige doesn't complain about the long hours, only how demanding Laurel can be from time to time," Noelle replied while taking a sip from her soda.

"Why are you defending Laurel? Have you been listening to Paige at all when she complains? Oh, whatever…but even if Janice didn't want to run the business and was upset that her business partner had to retire early, that's no reason to make your life extremely miserable. You are incredibly hardworking. I don't know anyone else who would come to work on their birthday because there weren't enough workers. If I'm not supposed to work, I'm not coming in," Valerie replied, smirking.

Noelle rolled her eyes. "Well, considering that you employ yourself, you have the right to cancel appointments or close for that day…or any day for that matter. It's your business. You are free to make whatever schedule you want. As for working on my birthday, I was the manager and had responsibilities. Besides, I had nothing special planned anyway, and it was only for a few hours," Noelle replied, trying to defend her actions.

Valerie rolled her eyes. "You are way too easygoing and predictable. It's easy to know what you are going to do because you are always playing it safe and trying to avoid any conflicts," Valerie replied honestly.

Noelle gave her friend a stern look. "Oh, really? Does being responsible and dependable really make me way too predictable? Does planning everything out thoroughly make me look boring? Well, then I would much rather be boring, predictable, and reliable," Noelle answered back angrily.

Valerie cracked a smile as she took another mozzarella stick off the appetizer plate. "I think you're more upset about being fired than anything else because this wasn't something that was in your plans. You didn't expect nor *plan* for this to happen. Remember the first job I got fired from? It was the summer going into junior year, and I was working at the deli that was owned by the family of my mom's best friend. My mom and dad were so upset they grounded me for over a month—basically for the rest of summer vacation. I had to miss out on going to the beach with my cousins or any of my friends, including you, but it was worth it. At least that cranky old customer everyone referred to as the curmudgeon started to act nicer after I yelled at him. So it wasn't a total loss," Valerie replied, smiling.

Noelle shook her head and rolled her eyes. She was then quickly startled by a gentle tapping on her left shoulder, causing her to turn to her left to see a slender redhead with grayish-blue eyes, fair complexion, and freckles looking a little bit flustered.

"Am I late? I'm so sorry. Laurel needed me to stay late and finish some of the inventory and make some phone calls, and then I got stuck in traffic… I tried some of the back roads to get here faster. Well, here I am. How are you doing, Noelle?" Paige asked, almost speaking a mile a minute, not taking a breath in between words. Noelle smiled and nodded but could barely understand half of what Paige had just said. Valerie looked over at Paige with a perplexed expression on her face before responding.

"Huh…can anyone understand what she just said? Paige, maybe next time you could try to say it again, this time in a speed audible to humans," Valerie remarked sarcastically.

Paige gave Valerie a sarcastic smile while she immediately turned her attention back to Noelle. Noelle was distracted, fidgeting with the buttons on the sleeves of her three-quarter length lavender-and-silver pin-striped dress blouse. She wasn't making much eye contact with either of her friends at that point.

"I'm not thrilled, but I think it was inevitable. I was just hoping that she would have at least waited until the end of the year or maybe next semester before I finally graduated with my master's degree. This wasn't the way it was supposed to be. The timing is all wrong," Noelle replied, letting out a dramatic sigh.

"Some things are just out of our control, Noelle. You cannot plan everything no matter how hard you try," Valerie said sharply. Her tone was harsh but honest. Although Valerie could come off as a little too harsh sometimes, nobody could ever accuse her of being dishonest.

Paige could sense the tension in the air and wanted to try and diffuse some of it while cheering up her friend. "Hey, is this mental telepathy or what? We are all wearing some shade of purple. This is totally cool!" Paige remarked with a bright smile. She placed her beige hobo purse down on her right side next to Noelle in the booth.

Valerie looked at her with annoyance and confusion. "Do you also predict winners of horse races and lottery jackpots?" Valerie asked sarcastically.

Paige was biting her tongue to avoid vocalizing what she really wanted to say.

As much as Paige and Valerie both thought of Noelle like a sister, they could barely stand each other. Each meeting was always a tense and challenging situation. Noelle was becoming visibly annoyed and losing her patience as she didn't invite her two closest friends to get into another fight when she needed them to be there for her. Valerie would always have a snide remark, and Paige would always take everything too personally. Being friends with Valerie for so long, Noelle knew to take everything with a grain of salt—the same philosophy she used while growing up with her brother. It made her life so much easier.

"Let's order some pizza," Noelle interrupted to change the subject. She looked out for their waitress who seemed to be busy going back and forth between several other tables.

"What's the waitress's name? Maybe I can get her attention," Paige offered.

Noelle looked at Valerie for the answer to that question. Valerie sat there for a minute before replying. "I think it's Karley," Valerie muttered out while squinting her eyes as though that would somehow help her to remember.

"She's tall and has dyed blond hair," Noelle chimed in, describing the waitress who brought their menus and their sodas.

Paige looked around and waved to a tall blond waitress who resembled what Noelle just described. The waitress saw them waving and quickly rushed over to their table.

"I'm so sorry, everyone. Someone called out sick tonight, and it seems like everyone decided to go out for dinner. I mean, it's a Thursday evening. It's not that people don't go out, but not like this. I mean, I almost thought there was a holiday that I missed." Karley laughed nervously. She took her wrist to move a few loose strands of dyed blond hair off her visibly flushed forehead.

"Maybe nobody felt like cooking tonight?" Valerie joked. Karley laughed, but Noelle still appeared distracted, allowing her eyes to wander around the restaurant as though she was searching for something. Realizing that the waitress wanted to take their order, Noelle tried to gather her thoughts together, quickly shifting her attention to the menu in front of her.

"I guess it's time to order," Noelle said, staring at her open menu.

Karley nodded and quickly took out her pen and notepad. "What can I get everyone?" Karley asked eagerly.

Noelle, Valerie, and Paige all looked at one another and discussed briefly about pizza toppings before Paige replied.

"Large pizza with extra sausage and peppers. Can you also bring me a large cola?" Paige replied, looking at both Valerie and Noelle for their approval or any last-minute comments.

"Sure! Is there anything else you need? Maybe refills on your sodas?" Karley asked quickly. Both Valerie and Noelle nodded.

Karley took away one of the appetizer dishes and left the other plate with only a couple of roasted potato skins on it. Paige reached over and took one, while Valerie eyed and took the other one. Paige was annoyed.

"Could you have left them both for me? Maybe I'm hungry too," Paige replied irritably.

Valerie looked at her nonchalantly. "Well, next time get here quicker…first come, first served," Valerie remarked sneeringly.

Paige took a moment to calm herself down to prevent an argument with Valerie before she turned toward Noelle. "So what exactly happened, Noelle? I mean, I know you got fired, but your text messages were kind of cryptic. It didn't seem like you at all," Paige asked, concerned.

Noelle's face lowered as she felt ashamed and discouraged. "What is there to say? I got fired last Friday. I went to work that morning and immediately started brewing several pots of coffee and making sure everything was stocked up like usual before quickly rushing over and helping out with the long line of customers, burning my thumb in the process. After the customers left, I started working on the weekly inventory when Janice called me into her office. The conversation started off somewhat civil but quickly escalated as she accused me of being irresponsible and unable to handle taking care of the store. She told me to leave and that I was fired," Noelle replied, the agitation starting to grow on her face.

"You being irresponsible? That's probably one of the most ridiculous things I have ever heard," Valerie chimed in.

Noelle sighed deeply. "Yeah, my vision for the store was not what she had in mind. I don't know what she meant, but over the past few months, she had accused me of wasting time with frivolous stuff and overspending on supplies, which was amazing because she cut the budget down for our…their inventory and still expected none of the customers to complain. Customers get mad when we run out of cups and their favorite coffee flavor is out of stock." Noelle shook her head in disgust.

"Noelle, don't be so hard on yourself. You were doing your job the best you could with what you had," Paige tried to cheer her friend up.

"I should have seen this coming. I should have started putting out résumés a few months ago. I knew when Charlene left, things were not going to be the same. Now here I am a couple of weeks from the start of the fall semester totally unemployed…and now behind on my goals timeline." Noelle sulked. Valerie and Paige looked at each other as if one of them had the right words written on their faces to say to their friend.

"Janice sounds like one of my old bosses, Sheila, but at least I got to give her a piece of my mind before I was fired. I wouldn't have wished her on anyone." Valerie's face tensed up.

Noelle looked over at her with a look of fatigue and frustration. "Sure, I could have chosen that route, but I actually cared about keeping my job through graduate school. Besides, your situation was completely different from mine. Sheila took credit for that entire bedroom makeover you did during your internship. Janice never took credit for anything that I did, but she had absolutely no problem blaming me for everything that went wrong with the store." Noelle sighed again.

"The bedroom was actually the last straw… She did the same thing with a couple of other projects that I worked on too. Honestly, you were probably gonna get fired anyway. In the least, you could have let out some pent-up anger before you walked out. It would have been very cathartic," Valerie replied, smiling.

Noelle shook her head in disbelief. Paige noticed the growing tension and wanted to try and diffuse the situation by switching topics.

"How did Janice end up in charge? Whatever happened to Charlene?" Paige asked inquisitively. Noelle hesitated for a moment.

"I don't know everything, but Charlene had some minor health problems when she opened Janlene's with her cousin Janice. Somehow, her condition either became worse or she became sick with something else. She had been slowly pulling away from the store for months. It started off as just one day off a week and then eventually increased to a few days. With the more time she missed, the more responsibility was being placed on my shoulders. At one point, I was literally running the whole store by myself. Janice barely came in. She only started to come back after Charlene had to 'retire,' as she put it," Noelle explained.

Before Noelle could say another word, Karley approached the table with a large tray with their pizza. Valerie and Paige moved the empty appetizer plate away from the middle of the table to make room.

"Okay, do you need anything else? There are napkins in the holder at the end of the table. I will be back in a little while to see how everyone is doing," Karley said in a rushed tone while she ran toward another nearby table. Paige took the first slice and immediately took a bite. Valerie glared at her because that was the slice she wanted.

"First come, first served," Paige replied back to Valerie with a smirk.

Valerie clenched her teeth but couldn't keep from cracking a smile knowing that Paige actually got even with her. "Touché." Valerie smirked as she took a slice of pizza and began to eat.

"So what are you going to do now? Are you going to just take some time off from work? I mean, you haven't really had a vacation since I met you," Paige asked in between bites of her first slice of pizza.

Noelle shook her head adamantly. "Take a break? That's insane! It's not part of my plan! This is kind of a detour…one that I didn't want to go through. But I still have bills, and I still want…need to continue working through graduate school. Books alone are so expensive, and then there's gas and food…and…," Noelle continued speaking while reaching over for a skinny slice of pizza.

"Noelle, you can't plan everything. Sometimes things don't work out the way you want them to. Remember what happened to me? I had all the aspirations to work as an interior decorator for a big company right after college, and I ended up being a party planner with an occasional dining room makeover." Valerie sighed.

"Valerie, you do event planning and interior decorating together. That makes you unique. You even told me it was a blessing in disguise you ended up back in New Jersey because your parents allowed you to use their garage for free until you built up enough business to go out on your own," Noelle replied, perplexed at her friend's response.

Valerie's face grew serious. "I didn't say that I regret how things worked out for me. I honestly like doing some of the party planning events. The anniversary parties can be really sweet, and the family reunions can be heartwarming and memorable. You know that my family is so big and spread out I haven't even met some of my extended family, and I have cousins I haven't seen since before I started school. I'm twenty-seven. Think about how long ago that is! Thank God for technology to allow us to keep in touch a little easier…but that's not the point. My point is that things did not work out the way I had originally planned. I thought maybe working in the industry for a few years at a company would help me form some connections while I saved up money to start my own business. Well, you know that didn't quite work out. The only job I was offered was part-time, and although it would have been a great opportunity, I couldn't even afford rent working part-time. But looking back, I think even if I was offered a full-time position, I would have been really miserable because I would still have restrictions and limitations working for someone else. Having my own business allowed me to do things the way I wanted to, and I will never regret that," Valerie replied honestly.

Noelle was a bit baffled by her friend's point of view. It completely dismissed her personal philosophy up to that point. "Your situation was different. You knew you eventually wanted to open a business. It just happened faster than you had anticipated. I have never wanted to own or open my own business and cannot foresee myself changing my mind in the future. I don't want to deviate from what I know and have been doing. I was good at it, and I was comfortable, and I had it all planned out," Noelle protested angrily.

Valerie rolled her eyes and took another slice of pizza.

"Maybe what Valerie is trying to say is to try thinking outside of the box. You know, you have so much experience, and you are a really good worker. Why not try a different perspective or career path?" Paige suggested but was not sure how Noelle would take it.

Noelle shook her head adamantly again. "Think outside the box? What is that supposed to mean? People fail because they do something totally unplanned and careless. I will not be one of those people! I have worked way too hard for way too long to just throw in the towel and do something else. That would make all my hard work mean nothing up until this point," Noelle replied angrily. Her voice started to get louder.

"Calm down, Noelle. We're not arguing with you. It's just... what is left for you to do? I mean, ever since I met you...what, six years ago...you have worked in coffee shops. That's all you know. You can't go much further. Maybe you need to try a different direction, or you could just take some time off and rest," Paige suggested before finishing her second slice of pizza.

"There is a lot I can still do and a lot I can still learn. I don't know everything. Besides, I have been at home for nearly a week, and I don't know what to do with myself. It's been so long since I had time to watch television. I don't even know any of the current sitcoms. I really feel like I'm out of the loop everywhere." Noelle sighed.

Valerie just shook her head because she knew that no matter what she or Paige said, Noelle was not listening or maybe just not ready to listen.

Paige attempted a different strategy. "Have you applied to any other coffeehouses?" Paige asked casually. Valerie half-listened while eating her second slice of pizza.

"Yeah, I have a few résumés sent out to all the coffee shops within driving distance in both New Jersey and New York. It's the end of the summer and the beginning of the school year. So I might need to wait a little bit longer to hear back." Noelle continued to pick off small pieces of her slice of pizza. She began to perk up a little bit more after responding.

"How far is the driving distance?" Paige asked curiously while reaching for another slice.

"I would say forty-five minutes. Ideally, thirty, but I can't be too picky. I want to make sure that I will be able to make it to class on time," Noelle replied quickly as her facial expression began to soften.

"What are you going to do if those jobs don't work out? I mean, you always plan. Is there a backup plan?" Paige asked, deviating a bit, which definitely made Noelle feel uncomfortable and agitated. She didn't want to hear about that right now.

"I will cross that bridge when I get there, but I am sure that at least one of them will hire me. I mean, with all my experience and my flexible schedule, how could I fail at this?" Noelle asked, trying to appear confident.

Valerie said nothing, and Paige tried to hide her doubt from Noelle. Paige tried changing the subject yet again but this time to try and encourage her friend and lighten everyone's mood.

"So how about dessert? I know that some chocolate layer cake always cheers me up when I am feeling kind of down." Paige perked up, looking at the end of the table to see if there was a dessert menu.

"Sure, I'm in. I'll restart my diet tomorrow." Valerie laughed as she finished her second slice of pizza and took a drink from her soda.

"Aren't you always on a diet?" Paige asked, trying not to sound rude.

Valerie laughed. "Yeah, I try, but it usually fails. I try to eat pretty healthy, but I will never be a size 3, and I'm okay with that," Valerie replied, referring to her hourglass figure.

"Sure, why not? Chocolate can fix anything," Noelle muttered out after finishing her slice of pizza.

"Oh, but you cannot forget the coffee. Dessert is just not the same without the coffee." Paige smiled because she knew of her friend's love for coffee. Noelle rolled her eyes and sighed.

"Oh, of course, can't forget the coffee…the same thing that brought me happiness for so long has left me unemployed and miserable," Noelle muttered out in disgust.

Paige and Valerie looked at each other and sighed while they tried to get their waitress's attention. They knew that it would take more than one evening out and dessert to cheer up their friend.

Chapter 2

The rich, sweet aroma of the blend of garlic and spices intensely grabbed Noelle's attention as she closed her bedroom door. She quickly walked down the stairs, allowing the sweet aroma to drag her toward the kitchen. Noelle leaned against the doorframe with her eyes closed as she slowly breathed everything in. Her mother stood very still, slowly stirring a large pot of stew for several minutes before she looked over and realized her daughter had been standing there.

"Oh, Noelle, I didn't see you there," her mother replied with a startled smile.

Noelle smiled back. "Yeah, how much television can I watch per day? I don't even remember the last time I actually watched anything. I don't know any of the new sitcoms. I feel totally out of the loop." Noelle sighed.

"Well, enjoy the extra rest you are getting. You've been working hard for so long maybe it's time to take a moment to stop and smell the roses and enjoy life," her mother suggested with her two dimples becoming pronounced as she smiled back at her daughter.

Noelle's face tensed up. "Mom, I do take time to 'smell the roses,' but I have so many other things that need to get done that are far more important. Right now, I need to find a job. I'm graduating from college with my master's degree next year, and I want to be totally prepared for the workforce," Noelle replied agitatedly.

Her mother shook her head gently and walked back toward the stove to stir the contents of another pot. "I'm not here to argue with you, Noelle. I am just saying it's okay to take a moment off every so often and relax. College is a time to enjoy yourself a little bit," her mother explained calmly.

"I had fun. I went out for pizza with Valerie and Paige last week. It was fun. We got a couple pieces of chocolate layer cake too. They were huge," Noelle replied, trying to sound more enthusiastic than she really felt.

"That's not exactly what I was talking about. But how are Valerie and Paige doing?" her mother asked while removing a pot of boiling water from the stove and pouring it into a colander in the sink. It wasn't until after that Noelle noticed that her mom made egg noodles.

"They're doing okay. Valerie is waiting for the holidays to start so her business will start picking up, and Paige is working a lot of hours like always," Noelle replied flatly.

"Well, that's good." Her mother went back to stirring the pot of some type of strew.

"You know what was strange? They both agreed on something together. They both said that I spend way too much time planning everything and that I have to just let go and learn to adapt to change." Noelle started laughing. Her mother raised her eyebrows but didn't say anything at first.

"Oh, really? Do you think that maybe they might have a point?" her mother asked casually.

Noelle stood up straight and started to glare at her mother. "Seriously? Mom, not you too," Noelle groaned.

Her mother sighed, unable to try and reason with her daughter at least to help her see a different side to her situation. "Do you want to do me a favor? Can you set the table for dinner?" her mother suggested, changing the subject to avoid an argument.

"Now? In the kitchen?" Noelle looked a little confused because it was only about three in the afternoon.

"No, in the dining room. You can use the fancy dishes from the cabinet," her mother instructed, trying to multitask.

"Mom, what's going on?" Noelle seemed a little intrigued.

"Well, I know that it's been a little tough the last couple of weeks, and your birthday is tomorrow, so this is an early birthday dinner. Your father is picking up the cake. It's an ice cream cake, not homemade like l usually make for you and your brother. I…we were hoping this would cheer you up." Her mother looked over to her daughter lovingly, yet concerned.

Noelle felt ashamed for starting an argument with her mother.

"Mom, I'm sorry. I think I'm just under more stress than I realized. It was different when things were working out the way they were planned." Noelle lowered her eyes to the floor.

"Honey, sometimes the only way to get you to change direction is to hit a roadblock. Maybe this is a roadblock that will open up the door for something better because it will make you take a minute to think about what you really want. Right now, try not to think too much about that." Her mother smiled at her daughter.

Noelle nodded and walked into the dining room. "How many dishes?" Noelle yelled from the dining room.

"Five. It's me, your father, Chris, you, and Ally," her mother replied quickly.

"Oh, Ally is coming! Great, I haven't really seen her all summer. I know she is working a lot of hours, but it's still kind of quiet without her." Noelle's smile grew wide at the possibility of seeing her potential future sister-in-law. Sometimes she actually liked Ally more than her own brother.

"Yes, I made sure Chris wouldn't forget to tell Ally," her mother announced.

"What are you making? It smells like stew, and you made egg noodles, but this isn't what I'm used to you making when it's still hot outside," Noelle commented.

"It's your favorite, and it is your birthday. I think you should probably go upstairs and change as soon as you have finished setting the table. They should be here soon," her mother replied, looking up at the clock.

Noelle nodded. "Okay, I'll try to be down as fast as I can."

Noelle basically ran through the kitchen into the small hallway and up the stairs toward her bedroom on the left. She was a little frazzled searching through her closet. She picked out a nicer pair of jeans and a short-sleeved cream-colored sweater set out of her closet. She searched in her closet for the matching cream-colored flats but couldn't find them, so she put on her favorite and very comfortable black flats. Noelle pulled her tight blond curls into a high ponytail, leaving a few loose strands on the sides of her face. She smiled, and both of her dimples illuminated in her mirror. As soon as she heard the front door open, she ran downstairs to see who had arrived.

"Happy birthday, Noelle." Her father smiled while walking through the front door holding a big cake box.

"Dad, my birthday is tomorrow." Noelle laughed.

"Yeah…well, today is your party, and I might not see you tomorrow because you're starting school for the semester. Plus, your mom will get mad if I forget," her father joked.

"I heard that Charlie." Her mother put her hands on her hips and stared at her husband from the middle of the kitchen.

Her father smiled and lowered his eyes while he carried the cake box into the kitchen and placed it on the kitchen table. "Need to leave the cake on the table to defrost in time for dessert. I'm going upstairs to get changed. Chris said he'll be here soon," Noelle's father said quickly as he left the kitchen and hurried up the stairs.

Noelle walked back into the kitchen. "Do you need any help, Mom?" Noelle asked, looking around.

"Um…you can put the salad on the table. It's in the refrigerator on the second shelf," her mother replied while adding a few more ingredients into the stew.

Noelle walked toward the refrigerator to get the salad and quickly placed it on the dining room table, which was now fully set for dinner. Noelle looked at the table admiringly while her mother interrupted her thoughts.

"I hope your brother is on time today. I swear he would be late for his own…" Her mother looked annoyed but stopped herself from saying something else.

"Well, if Ally is with him, then he should be on time." Noelle remained calm.

"You know, you are five years younger than your brother and about ten years more mature." Her mother shook her head and went back to stirring the pot of stew on the stove.

Noelle walked back toward the dining room to take out the dessert plates and coffee cups from the hutch and place them on a small empty table near the opposite wall. She was disrupted by the sound of the front door opening and slamming shut and two familiar voices talking pretty loudly down the small hallway toward the kitchen. Noelle walked out of the dining room back into the kitchen to greet her brother and his girlfriend.

"But, Chris…" Ally's voice sounded whiny and raspy as though she had been yelling previously. Chris looked like an average-height husky yet very muscular football player type-build with bright baby-blue eyes, thick wavy light-blond hair, a blond goatee, and sun-kissed light-olive complexion. He was wearing a light-blue golf shirt and a pair of khaki pants. Ally was slightly shorter than him with long blond hair, a deep tan, and very slender. She wore a pink spaghetti-strap handkerchief dress with matching pink heeled sandals, a pink sweater, and a pink purse.

"Not now, Ally…" Chris turned around to face her for a moment with a very serious look on his face. His mother felt awkward being in the middle of their disagreement, but he paid no attention to anyone else's perceptions.

"Birthday girl!" Chris yelled with a bright smile on his face. Noelle walked over to him, and he gave her a big hug. She tried to ignore what appeared to be habitual behavior from her brother and his girlfriend.

"Chris, my birthday is tomorrow," Noelle reminded him flatly.

"Yeah, but I'm usually late every year, so being early might be a good thing for once." Chris laughed.

"Noelle!" Ally ran toward Noelle to give her a great big hug.

"So great to see you! I haven't really seen you at all this summer. I guess retail was really busy this year," Noelle commented.

Ally gave Chris a harsh sideways glance before turning her gaze back to Noelle with a bright almost-fake smile. "Yeah, you know clothing stores are really the worst to work in during the summer, especially for teenagers and young adults. Everyone wants to buy a new outfit. Last couple of weeks have been really hectic because of back-to-school shopping. I'm so thankful I get discounts on all my clothes… I wouldn't be able to afford my wardrobe if I didn't," Ally explained.

"Why do you spend so much of your spare time shopping? Then you complain there isn't enough time in the day to do everything. It doesn't take me that long to go shopping for some clothes while still having enough time left over to get everything I need done. Women can really complicate things," Chris muttered out loud, somewhat off topic. Ally gave him a dirty look.

"Chris, you as a guy can get away with wearing the same thing four hundred times over, and most people wouldn't say anything. If a girl wears the same thing two days in a row, it's the talk of the town. This coming from someone who doesn't care at all about fashion," Noelle replied, a little snarky.

Chris ignored it and walked into the dining room to take a seat. "Is there anywhere that we can sit, or are there seating arrangements?" Chris asked, already sitting with his back facing the kitchen.

"The chair near the head of the table is for your father, and I sit next to him. The rest of the seats are up to the three of you. There are four chairs to choose from," their mother instructed them.

"I guess you want to sit next to Ally." Noelle smiled casually while walking back into the dining room.

"You can sit next to her. I sit near her all the time. You can have some fun talking to her too. My ear needs a little bit of a break," Chris replied coldly.

Noelle's eyebrows went up as that was very odd behavior from her brother. Ally looked away, trying not to show anyone that her eyes were starting to get misty. She reached down into the pocket of her pink cardigan to pull out a tissue and gently wiped her eyes to keep her mascara from running down her face.

"You can sit next to me. We have a lot of catching up to do." Noelle grabbed Ally's arm and pulled her toward the two chairs facing the kitchen. Noelle took a seat across from her mom, and Ally took the seat across from Chris. Even though it seemed as though Chris wanted to avoid sitting near Ally, she was seated right across from him. Chris tried to avoid Ally as he was looking around at everything and everyone else.

Their father walked into the dining room wearing something similar to his son. They resembled each other, and sometimes Noelle wondered if that was what her brother would look like in twenty or thirty years, but she could never imagine her brother with the same beard. Chris would look like a real lumberjack. Sometimes Noelle wondered looking at her mother if that was what she would look like in twenty or thirty years too, which was a possibility. However, Noelle's cooking and baking skills would never be even close to her mother's ability.

Their mother walked into the dining room a few minutes later with a huge casserole dish full of egg noodles and a beef stew with vegetables.

"Smells delicious, Mrs. DeGarmo," Ally said politely.

"Thank you, Ally. I just hope it tastes as good as it smells." Mrs. DeGarmo took a seat down at the table next to her husband.

"Can we just serve ourselves? Or do we need to wait for anyone?" Chris asked impatiently. Mrs. DeGarmo pursed her lips and started to bite her tongue from saying anything to her son. Although Chris's personality could come off as rude at times, something appeared to be very different this afternoon. He was never this tense or short-tempered.

"Yes, unless you prefer that I serve everyone instead," Mrs. DeGarmo offered. Noelle shook her head adamantly against that idea. She wanted her mom to relax.

"Let's eat!" Chris yelled with a bright smile.

Noelle rolled her eyes as she took the first scoop of food and put it on her plate. Chris hurried and took the serving spoon from his sister to serve himself. Even though Chris and Ally were sitting close by to each other, he gave the serving spoon to his mom instead, intentionally avoiding Ally. Mrs. DeGarmo looked annoyed but remained calm as she gave Ally the serving spoon to take some for herself. Noelle waited until everyone had some food before she started to eat.

"This is delicious, Mom." Noelle took a couple of bites in quick succession.

"Great dinner, Mom," Chris replied, stuffing his face.

Ally looked embarrassed. "Chris, slow down. You're making a pig of yourself," she whispered loud enough for everyone else at the table to hear.

"If I want your opinion, I will ask for it. Until then, keep it to yourself," Chris answered back coldly. Noelle could feel a strong tension in the air, and now her parents could see it as well. Ally gave him another dirty look before trying to completely ignore him.

"I'm so glad that I was able to make it for your birthday dinner." Ally smiled brightly before she started to get a little weepy.

Chris rolled his eyes. "Are you really crying again? Wow, you will cry at almost anything, won't you? You know, I have to make sure that I buy an extra box of tissues because whenever we go anywhere, especially a movie, I can be prepared for when Ally starts to cry. That's why I call her Ally Waterworks." Chris was trying to make a joke, but it came out sarcastic and hurtful.

Ally turned her head to compose herself before looking back at Chris. "At least I am aware I have emotions. Sometimes I need to check your pulse to make sure your heart really isn't made out of stone and your blood isn't made out of ice," Ally yelled back bitterly.

Noelle and her mother looked at each other before her mother quickly interrupted. "Oh, I almost forgot. I made homemade honey wheat biscuits. They are on a baking sheet on top of the stove if anyone wants one," Mrs. DeGarmo stated, trying to diffuse the growing tension.

"Lorraine, you made the biscuits too?" Mr. DeGarmo's face lit up as they were one of his absolute favorite biscuits.

"Maybe I'll go get one. Would anyone like butter with theirs?" Chris asked calmly, looking around the table.

"Please bring the butter in here. Thanks, Chris," Mrs. DeGarmo replied, trying to smile despite the nagging feeling in her stomach.

"Ally, is everything okay with you two?" Noelle turned toward Ally.

Ally turned away for a moment to take a deep breath and try to prevent herself from bursting into tears before turning back to Noelle.

"It's…it's…" Ally's eyes started to tear up again.

Chris walked back into the dining room and placed the butter on the table. He looked up and shook his head. "Really, Ally? You can't even go for an entire meal without trying to drag all the attention on yourself." Chris rolled his eyes.

Ally picked up one of the biscuits off Chris's plate and threw it forcefully at his shoulder. Chris barely flinched, but it only seemed to agitate him more. Mr. and Mrs. DeGarmo looked at each other in total disbelief. Noelle thought this was a bad dream that she couldn't wake up from. Chris gave her a stern look, and both of them started to bicker before walking out of the dining room back into the kitchen, engaging in a full-fledged argument.

"You know, Allyson, I knew this was a bad idea to take you here today. I should have just come alone. Now you are helping to ruin my sister's birthday dinner just because things didn't work out for you the way you wanted!" Chris yelled.

"How dare you!" Ally shouted back.

"Dare what? Tell the truth? You have been in a horrible mood for the past three months, and it's been all my fault, right? Just like whenever anything goes wrong, it's always Chris's fault! Ally never does anything wrong!" Chris shouted.

"You are…you are the most selfish and brutish male I have ever met! I can't believe that I actually thought about a future with you. I guess we all make stupid mistakes!" Ally yelled back. The tears glistened in her blue eyes.

Noelle lowered her head as she heard their argument taking a turn for the worse. Chris and Noelle's parents just looked at each other while they heard Ally and Chris continuously arguing. Mrs. DeGarmo tried to change the subject, but the yelling from the kitchen continued to get louder, making it almost impossible to hear themselves talk or think.

"I'm tired of you getting upset with me and then crying to everyone who listens. How many people think that I'm this big ogre who treats you horribly? I mean, nobody knows that you are the biggest nag out there!" Chris yelled. His face was becoming pretty red as the tone of his voice indicated that he was pretty angry.

"I don't even know why I ever bothered going out with you! You have not changed. You never will…biggest overgrown child I have ever met!" Ally yelled as her eyes welled up with tears.

Chris started to pace away from her to calm himself down, but it wasn't working. "At least I'm not a walking waterworks that constantly needs to be coddled and protected. I'm your boyfriend, not your guard dog!" Chris yelled back.

Noelle was already trying to tune it out at this point.

"I'm going home. I shouldn't have come today!" Ally yelled.

Chris jingled his truck keys in his pocket.

"All right, I'll take you home," Chris replied, trying to calm himself down.

"No, I am not going anywhere with you. Stay here or go somewhere else…play in traffic…I don't care! I'm calling my cousin." Ally took out her phone and quickly dialed her cousin's phone number. "Hey, Whitney, can you pick me up? I'm at Chr—Noelle's house," Ally asked. She got off the phone, and Chris seemed to get angrier.

"So what, are you just trying to cut me out now? I forget one day, and you have been in a horrible mood ever since—even after I remembered and apologized. It's only an anniversary date, nothing dire—" Chris replied, seriously agitated.

"It is more than just a date! If you can't understand why I really got so upset, then you really are a lost cause and don't care! Ally shouted back.

"I'm sick of this." Chris shook his head.

"Well, I'm sick of you! I'm leaving." Ally picked up her small pink purse off the kitchen chair.

"You walk out of this house, don't think about ever coming back!" Chris shouted.

Ally turned around to face him after walking out of the kitchen. "No problem! I have no interest in ever coming back, especially to see you!" Ally shouted, stomping down the small hallway before opening and slamming the front door shut.

Noelle and her parents flinched at that sound. Chris stormed out of the kitchen into the small hallway toward the door of his basement apartment, quickly opening and slamming it shut behind him. After a few minutes, Noelle turned to her parents with a dazed look on her face. Her mother put her head in her hands for a moment and clenched her hands as though she was praying. Her father looked at his wife, concerned, but tried to change the subject so as to try and save Noelle's birthday dinner.

"Well, does anyone want coffee with their piece of cake?" Noelle's mom asked while bringing some of the dirty dishes with her into the kitchen. Noelle just sat at the table in shock. Mr. DeGarmo got up and got the ice cream birthday cake, placing it on the dining room table without the box. Noelle stared at the cake.

Bon anniversaire, Noëlle.

"Happy birthday, Noelle…yeah, what a great birthday," Noelle muttered to herself. "This has really been a great couple of weeks. I can't wait to see what happens next!" Noelle sat back down, resting her head in her hand until her parents came back, ready to have cake and coffee to celebrate her birthday and salvage what was left of her birthday dinner.

Chapter 3

"Hey, stranger, long time no see!" Rowena exclaimed excitedly. She was a little shorter and a little heavier than Noelle and had thick, wavy auburn hair with light-brown freckles all over her nose and under her greenish-grey eyes.

"Rowena, how are you?" Noelle asked while leaning on her notebook on top of her desk.

Rowena took out her notebook and a couple of different-colored pens, placing them on her desk. "Pretty good. Wasn't really looking forward to going back to school so soon. I kind of wish that summer vacation was just a little bit longer. Then again, I think I'd prefer to be in school rather than working around fifty hours a week." Rowena chuckled while taking out a small eyeglass case from her purse.

Noelle nodded as though she understood completely. "Yeah, homework and tests aren't the most exciting things to do, but it does pay off in the long run. Where were you working this past summer?" Noelle asked curiously, trying to continue the friendly conversation.

"Oh, I work at a bakery down the street from where I live. It's a smaller family business. I work full-time over the summer and winter breaks, and I'm on call during the semesters. They usually ask me to come in on the weekends, but it depends on what part of the year. They are always busier during the holiday seasons," Rowena replied, reaching into her bag for another pen.

Noelle tried to hide her eagerness and desperation to ask about a possible job at the bakery. She knew it would be a bad idea, so she let that idea slip away.

"What about you? Are you still working in that coffee shop? Was it Jolene's Coffee or something?" Rowena asked casually.

Noelle smirked as she wanted to keep her real feelings to herself for the moment. "Um, I'm kind of in between jobs right now. I need to put my focus primarily on finishing my degree. It's not always easy to find flexibility in jobs with fitting school into the equation," Noelle replied calmly, trying to hide any uneasiness she felt from still being unemployed.

"Absolutely right. College comes first. We'll be ready for the big jobs when we graduate, right, Noelle?" Rowena grinned from ear to ear.

Noelle forced herself to smile just as brightly. "Yeah, two more semesters and then off into the real world," Noelle added.

Rowena looked at her watch and looked around at the classroom before turning back toward Noelle. "Where is everyone? Are we in the wrong classroom?" Rowena started to get nervous.

"No, it's the right classroom. I triple-checked everything. After that one semester where I missed the first class because I was in the wrong classroom, I don't want that to ever happen again." Noelle's face began to tense up slightly.

"I can do better. One semester I ended up in the wrong building. I was so upset because there was another class in my supposed classroom. I was right about the classroom number and which floor the class was located on, but the class itself was something totally different than what I registered for. Then I double-checked my schedule and saw I was in the wrong building. I ran like my hair was on fire to the correct building, just arriving to watch the students leaving. Thankfully, the professor was still there." Rowena laughed while reminiscing.

Noelle didn't find it funny, but she pretended to laugh along with her. "Where is Fallon?" Noelle asked, looking around the classroom.

"Oh, she won't be in class today. She said she got stuck at work, so she asked me to get a syllabus for her. She'll be here next week. I think this is the only class she's taking though. She said she's getting more hours at the office where she works and may not want to take on too much homework, but she could still change her mind. You know Fallon." Rowena laughed.

"Yeah, she's the complete opposite of you. Please don't take this the wrong way, but it's hard to see how you two are such close friends," Noelle confessed.

Rowena nodded and smiled. "Don't worry. Everyone tells us the same thing, but she's not my friend. She's my cousin. We pretty much grew up together and went to the same schools since sixth grade. We have our differences but always managed to get along really well. We both have brothers, so she's like the sister I always wanted. It's really strange. We didn't go to the same colleges or even picked the same majors but somehow ended up in the same graduate program. Life is funny sometimes." Rowena shrugged it off as though it didn't matter.

Noelle couldn't really understand the nonchalant attitude toward life's unexpected journey. No matter how hard Noelle tried, she couldn't look at life's journey as some spontaneous adventure because those always blow up in everyone's faces. She glanced at the doorway of the classroom and saw students starting to rush into the classroom quickly to take a seat. It was almost six o'clock, and nobody wanted to be late for the first class.

A familiar face with short ebony curly hair tapped Noelle on the shoulder while she took a seat behind her.

"Hey, Noelle," Keisha whispered as she unpacked her schoolbag. She was slender, a little taller than Noelle, and always displaying her simple yet chic and sophisticated fashion sense while carrying a bright smile that reflected her continuous optimism.

Noelle's face lit up at the sight of her friend. "Hey, Keisha," Noelle replied before all the lights in the classroom were turned on. The brightness made Noelle blink to readjust her focus. She cupped her hand over her eyes to try and help adjust to the brightness, then sat for a moment rubbing her eyes.

Their professor walked slowly into the classroom with his dress shoes clicking against the floor. He walked toward the front of the class and placed his beat-up leather briefcase on top of it. He looked to be about average height and almost completely bald from the back. His wardrobe looked like it needed to be desperately updated from the early 1970s. When he turned around to face the class, he exposed the best part of his ensemble—a wild authentic 1970s polyester shirt with a matching bow tie. A few students chuckled lightly but tried to remain calm as nobody knew what type of personality he had. He turned around to write a few words on the blackboard. Then he turned back around to face the class.

"Good evening, class. My name is Professor Summerfield. How is everyone tonight?" Professor Summerfield asked, looking around the class. A lot of the students nodded.

"We're here," a couple of students answered.

Professor Summerfield smiled. "I can see that," Professor Summerfield replied mildly sarcastically. A couple of students giggled at his unusual approach to everything so far and wondered if he was weird or eccentric.

"Okay, so this is intro to entrepreneurship. It's an elective. Just need to make sure that everyone is in the right class before we begin," Professor Summerfield continued. Several students took out their schedules to make sure they were in the right class. Everyone remained in their seats.

"Everyone is in the right class?" Professor Summerfield looked around in amazement. "This must be my honors class. Every semester, without fail, there's always at least one student in the wrong class. Now I'm not trying to be mean. One semester when I first started teaching—quick story—I walked into the classroom, and I knew I was running late. Well, the classroom was full, and there was no professor. I walked right in, introduced myself, and started discussing about business ownership and consulting projects. I spoke for at least thirty minutes before one student raised his hand and asked if this was extra information because it wasn't listed under the course description. I found out that I had spoken for thirty minutes in a German literature class. Needless to say that a few students were very excited that they got to learn two subjects for the price of one." Professor Summerfield chuckled after the story.

One student raised his hand.

"Can you speak German?" Owen asked seriously.

Professor Summerfield chuckled. "No, I actually was speaking in English. That would have explained the bizarre looks that I got probably because they weren't just expecting discussions of literature but also discussions in German. The whole point of the story is to put you at ease. Learning is a process, and we all make mistakes. Whether it's entering the wrong classroom or, in my case, teaching in the wrong classroom, that stuff happens, but we learn from them. Only thing you can do is move forward being wiser and more experienced," Professor Summerfield explained calmly.

One student raised her hand.

"Yes, oh, please tell me your name when I call on you because I'm still learning about everyone, and I don't want to have to call everyone student 1, 2, 3, or 'Hey you,'" Professor Summerfield replied sort of deadpan. His personality was a little quirky, but he came off as being genuine at the same time.

"My name is Amanda. I'm confused. Is the point of this class to make mistakes? I thought it was a business class." Amanda looked perplexed.

"No. But I know one thing about students is the fear of making mistakes or getting any answer wrong because they are afraid it will impact their grade, but this is the time to experiment a little bit and try out different scenarios and ask questions so when you are out in the real world, you are better prepared for it," Professor Summerfield explained. He looked around and could see a sea of confused faces before him.

"My name is Rowena. What does this have to do with entrepreneurship?" Rowena asked impatiently.

"Okay, let's try this another way. Who can explain entrepreneurship to me? Can anyone define it?" Professor Summerfield looked around the classroom.

"Call me Jeff. Opening a business?" Jeff guessed while slouching back in his chair, allowing his long shaggy hair to cover his eyes.

"Not quite. Anyone else?" Professor Summerfield kept looking around the class.

Another student raised her hand.

"Um…I'm Sally. It says, 'One who organizes, manages, and assumes the risks of a business or enterprise,'" Sally read from her small handheld dictionary.

"That's the definition. It's correct. By the way, dictionaries are a great thing to keep with you during this class—just a pointer for the semester. But what does that mean?" He continued to look around to a class of bewildered faces. He stood there for a moment until someone else raised her hand.

Noelle figured she couldn't do any worse. "Does that mean it's a person who pursues new ventures or businesses? The person with the ideas and the drive?" Noelle guessed, figuring she was wrong.

"That's a good way to put it. And your name is?" he asked.

Noelle's face became flushed as she realized she forgot to introduce herself. "It's Noelle…sorry," Noelle replied quickly, feeling a little embarrassed.

"So using Noelle's explanation of what entrepreneurship is, how does that apply to this class? I mean, what are we supposed to be doing here? It's not like capital or money just falls out of the sky," Professor Summerfield joked.

The class was still looking at him a little confused.

"I'm Sally. Does this mean that we will be learning about ways to pursue new business ventures and ideas? That sounds like a lot for one semester," Sally replied, looking overwhelmed.

"Yes, it really can be. There are complete bachelor's and master's programs dedicated to just focusing on entrepreneurship. This class is just meant to get your feet wet. I'm sure even by the end of the semester, you will have some questions, but the purpose is to give you a brief foundational understanding of the concept and the process." Professor Summerfield took a seat on the front of the desk.

"Will there be a lot of reading and writing for this class? Some of our other classes want us to memorize all foundational principles and everything. Oh, I'm Owen," Owen asked, also looking a little overwhelmed.

"So this class will be a little bit different than your other classes. You will be required to take a midterm and a final exam, along with a reflection paper at the end of the semester and a large end-of-the-semester project, which counts for 30 percent of your final grade," Professor Summerfield explained.

A lot of the students in the class were looking around bewildered and overwhelmed. Another student raised her hand.

"Hi, I'm Keisha. What type of final project, Professor?" Keisha asked with her pen ready to jot something down in her notebook.

"So after teaching this class for several years, I have discovered that the best way to teach this subject is through a hands-on approach. In other words, you will be developing your own businesses this semester. Each week, you will be given an assignment for each of the ten steps in opening a new business. These assignments don't have a specific length, but they need to be long enough to explain and support your answers to the questions. So, for example, the first assignment, which is the easiest, will be you brainstorming an idea for your new business. The best suggestion I can give you is to choose a topic that you are interested in and are comfortable with. For example, if you go to the gym a lot, perhaps you would be interested in opening a gym or something involved with health and fitness. These are only suggestions." Professor Summerfield explained while noticing a student who was sitting in the first seat in the first row near the door with her hand raised.

"Do you have anything to explain this more thoroughly?" She asked anxiously.

"Your name again?" Professor Summerfield asked.

"Me? It's Kendall," Kendall replied, nervously and a little embarrassed about forgetting to state her name.

"Kendall, can you please come up and hand out the syllabi? You can give them to the first person in the row and have them pass them back." Professor Summerfield took out a pile of papers and placed them on the corner of his desk. Kendall picked them up from the desk and started to pass them out.

"Professor, it's Jeff again. Are there any restrictions to the business ideas?" Jeff asked with a boyish grin on his face.

Professor Summerfield looked at him blankly. "There are a list of restrictions and guidelines in the syllabus, but I will say this. Anything that is considered overtly or even covertly controversial or inappropriate will not be approved," Professor Summerfield stated empathically. He continued to look blankly at Jeff, who gave off the vibe of a class clown and also an instigator. Future classes would help answer that question.

"Owen here. Professor, would you be willing to give us examples of what to stay away from just so we don't take the wrong topic?" Owen asked genuinely. Jeff sat there completely still, waiting for the professor to answer his question.

"Again, there is a list of restrictions and guidelines in the syllabus to follow for brainstorming your ideas for your business venture; however, if you are still unsure, please talk to me before or after class, or just pick another business idea. I am flexible with accepting business ideas, but within reason—they must be both practical and set in reality. If your business requires a rocket ship to get to, for example, it probably won't be accepted. Are there any other questions?" Professor Summerfield replied calmly with his signature deadpan expression.

"Thank you, Professor." Owen nodded while jotting some notes down. Jeff didn't say anything.

"Nobody needs to be nervous about this project. You aren't actually going out and getting a business license and signing a lease for a store. This is a hypothetical approach to the whole process. You get to see what opening a business involves while not actually needing to do the work in real life. Remember, you are not being graded on whether or not the concept will succeed or not because that is a very complex answer. I can tell you from personal anecdotes from real-life business owners who did everything correctly and they still didn't succeed, while others made many mistakes early on and flourished. I will have real stories to support these situations—both bad and good—in future classes." Professor Summerfield could see as the students began looking over their syllabi that they began to relax.

"Professor, does the weekly assignments have to be typed or can they be handwritten?" Keisha asked.

"For the weekly assignments, I will accept either one. Of course, if I can't read it, I will not grade it. So if you have messy handwriting, I would suggest typing it to be on the safe side. For the essays and the final project, everything needs to be typed. I will not accept handwritten for those. Any other questions?" he asked while looking around the classroom.

Everyone looked at one another while making small notes on their syllabi.

"No," a few students answered.

"Okay, well then, you can leave. If anyone has any questions, I'll be staying after class for a little while. If not, you are free to go. Have a great weekend, and see you next Tuesday." Professor Summerfield happily looked around at the class.

"It's Rowena. Professor, what about attendance?" Rowena asked while getting out of her seat while watching some students already leaving the class.

"Oh, I knew I forgot something. That's my fault. I will give everyone the benefit of the doubt and mark everyone present today. However, attendance will be taken starting next week," he replied, watching most of the class run out quickly.

A couple of students walked up to their professor's desk to ask some questions. Noelle quickly threw her books into her schoolbag and picked up her nearly empty thermos.

"Hey, Noelle, where did you park?" Keisha asked, walking up right behind her.

"Oh, I'm in Lot 7A again. I even got to class a little earlier too." Noelle looked disappointed.

"Oh, I got a spot in Lot 3A. I guess arriving at school late worked out great. Someone was leaving, and then I was ready to park and run to class. The traffic was horrific. I'm glad that I only have another semester left here. I like this college, but I should've picked one in New York closer to me." Keisha lowered her eyes.

"I was the opposite. I wanted to go far away to graduate school, and here I am, still going to school locally. It's not like I want to leave New Jersey, but I kind of wanted to branch out a little bit by now," Noelle joked.

"Shorter commutes and being closer to home are better. I'm speaking from experience. Other than that, how are you? There were a few times I meant to stop by your job to get an iced coffee for me and Gil, but I never got a chance. I was working so much this summer." Keisha pulled her schoolbag over her shoulder as they walked through the corridor of Delaney Hall.

"Honestly, I'm not working there anymore," Noelle replied, a little embarrassed.

Keisha's mouth dropped. "Why? What happened? I mean, didn't you practically run that store?" Keisha asked, nearly stunned.

Noelle stopped for a moment before turning to her friend. "Personality conflicts," Noelle replied succinctly.

Keisha nodded as though she understood completely. "Well, I'm sure there is a better job out there, one that has your name written all over it," Keisha replied optimistically.

"Thanks. I could use as much positivity as I can get. I'm starting to become a cynic." Noelle appeared disappointed with that feeling.

"Remember, when a door closes, another door opens. Maybe it wasn't the timing you were expecting, but things don't happen on accident. There's always a reason. God works in mysterious ways," Keisha replied philosophically.

Noelle stood there for a moment as those words hit her pretty hard. "Maybe you're right. Anyway, I have to go this way. I'm parked in Lot 7A," Noelle replied, walking toward the left side of the walkway.

"It's been great seeing you! See you on Thursday night. You are in that class, right?" Keisha smiled brightly, pivoting toward the right toward Lot 3A.

"Yeah, I think it's financial management or something, but I'm in that class. I'll see you on Thursday night." Noelle waved as she started to walk away.

Keisha nodded and waved before turning around to walk toward her car.

Noelle stopped for a moment with a deep gnawing feeling of worry that she would never find a job. She hoped the next job interview would let her know where to go.

Chapter 4

Noelle got out of her fifteen-year-old light blue sedan, making sure she had her résumé and her purse in her hand before closing the car door. She stood up to straighten her black dress pants and her short-sleeved beige dress blouse embroidered with several mini coffee cups. It wasn't a blouse that she liked to wear often, but she believed that it might bring her some luck while going on this interview. She had practically no luck with any of the previous interviews over the past couple of weeks, and some potential jobs didn't bother to call her back at all. Noelle was so ecstatic that Java Planet had called her back and scheduled an interview. It was located in an area she was familiar with, being not too far from her previous job as manager at Janlene's but far enough to not share many of the same customers. Even though this interview might have been for an assistant manager, which was a demotion, Noelle was positive that with all her diverse experience and customer service skills and her excellent ability to make an irresistible cup of coffee, she would be a shoo-in.

Noelle pulled open the front door and looked around the planet-themed coffeehouse. She had never seen a coffeehouse that used so many dark and bold colors in decorating, but everything seemed to blend together nicely. She briefly wondered what Valerie would think of the store's interior decorating since that was her field of expertise. Noelle looked around and saw several customers sitting and talking with friends and family while a few students were working on homework assignments. Noelle felt comfortable as this was a familiar environmental setting. She walked up to the counter, momentarily looking at the cashier's indigo-colored aprons with big orange letters spelling out Java Planet. She wasn't impressed with the color combination, but everything was neat and organized. A short barista with hazelnut-colored eyeglasses turned around from setting up the coffeepots to make more coffee and walked over toward the cash registers.

"Can I help you?" the cashier behind the counter asked, standing in between the two cash registers.

"Yes, I'm here to see the manager. I have an interview. She's waiting for me. My name is Noelle," Noelle replied.

"Oh, okay. Jessalynne is in her office right now. She should be out soon. Can I get you something while you are waiting?" the cashier asked enthusiastically.

Noelle looked up at the menu and nodded. "Sure. I think I'll have a medium caramel latte with no sugar and skim milk. Do you have any chocolate chip cookies?" Noelle asked.

The cashier looked at the refrigerated case. "We have a chocolate candy cookie. It's good," the cashier replied, still very upbeat. Noelle nodded. She picked up a cookie sealed in a package and handed it to Noelle.

"How much?" Noelle asked, opening her wallet.

"It's $6.15," the cashier responded.

Noelle was a little surprised at the price but knew it was a little more expensive in New York than New Jersey, so she handed her the exact amount while throwing in a dollar worth of quarters into the tip cup. Noelle took her cookie and walked down to the pickup station, which was very similarly set up like at her old job. There was no one else before her, so she just picked up her latte and went to go sit down at a corner table that the cashier had previously pointed toward. Noelle took out her cell phone to make sure she didn't miss any phone calls or text messages and then turned the ringer off so she wouldn't be bothered during the interview. She tried to take a sip of her latte, but it was too hot, so she took a piece of her cookie instead. Not what she had in mind, it reminded her of something that she would want to eat when she was in grammar school, not as an adult, but she shrugged it off. Noelle looked around at people coming and going, and still there was no one walking toward her small table in the corner. She was hoping that the cashier didn't give her wrong directions. Noelle was extra nervous because this had been one of several job interviews she had been on since she was fired from her previous job. No matter how things seemed to be working out, Noelle kept herself positive.

Then out of the corner of her eye, she saw a medium-height, slender woman wearing an indigo apron with JAVA PLANET in bold gold letters walk out from behind the counter. She looked around for a moment before one of the baristas pointed her in the direction where Noelle was sitting. The woman nodded and walked toward Noelle.

"Noelle?" the woman asked with a pleasant voice.

"Yes," Noelle replied, smiling and getting up while extending her hand toward the woman.

The woman smiled brightly and reciprocated the handshake. "I am the manager here. My name is Jessalynne. Most call me Lynne, but either name is okay. Would you mind if we sat here and talked? My office is a bit cramped, and after sitting in there for hours doing scheduling and payroll, I need some fresh air," Jessalynne replied, laughing, while she took a seat.

"Oh, sure, no problem. I remember doing payroll and scheduling. I felt like I was living in a closet. Thankfully, I'm not claustrophobic." Noelle laughed nervously. She wasn't sure if Jessalynne had found that funny or not.

"Oh, I don't know what I would do then." Jessalynne sighed. "So you did payroll and scheduling? I don't remember seeing that on your résumé. I hope I was looking at the right one," Jessalynne commented while looking around for something, as though she misplaced or forgot something.

Then Noelle realized she didn't hand her a hard copy of her résumé. "Here, I'm sorry," Noelle quickly handed Jessalynne a copy of her most recent résumé secured in a clear folder.

"It's okay. I know you sent me one, but it's probably lost in my office along with a few other things like my favorite coffee cup. So tell me a little bit about yourself," Jessalynne replied, looking over Noelle's résumé.

"Well, I have worked in three different coffeehouses. I was hired at Coffee Clubhouse, and I worked there from summer '97 to spring '99. I started as a part-time barista and worked up to being a full-time barista. Then from spring '99 to summer '03, I worked as an assistant manager of Coffee-n-Cookies. From summer '03 to summer '06, I worked as manager of Janlene's. I have extensive experience with ordering supplies and inventory, payroll and scheduling, and even some interviewing." Noelle tried to condense everything quickly.

Jessalynne's eyes widened as she continued to look through the résumé. "Well, this is a very impressive résumé. You worked as an assistant manager for over three years and three years as a manager. According to this, you were pretty much running the coffee shop for a period of time?" Jessalynne inquired.

Noelle took a deep breath. "Well, it didn't exactly start out that way. I wasn't supposed to do that originally. I was hired to take care of customers and ordering supplies and helping the baristas…employees. My boss was to take care of all the office work. However, if I needed to leave or eat, she would come out and help take care of some of the customers. Then she started having some health problems, and she went from being at work five to six days a week to two or three. She started showing me everything, and then I just started to run the entire store. It was only supposed to be temporary until she got better, but her health didn't improve much." Noelle lowered her eyes.

Jessalynne focused her eyes on the résumé. "That's too bad to hear. I mean, it was a benefit for you, but it's too bad that your boss got sick. Do you mind me asking what happened? Why aren't you working there anymore? Was there a problem with all the extra responsibilities? I'm sure that was overwhelming, especially not being in the job description." Jessalynne looked at Noelle with a concerned look. She was trying very hard to read Noelle's facial expressions to see if she was missing something more from her story.

"No, I was actually doing pretty well balancing everything. I was working seven days a week some weeks, but I didn't mind it. The stuff needed to get done. Plus, I had some great baristas working for me that would take care of all the customers while I was in the office. I think it was more a personality conflict with the other boss." Noelle left it at that.

Jessalynne nodded as though she completely understood without hearing the words. "Well, tell me why, with all your experience, you would be willing to be demoted to being an assistant manager again? According to your résumé and what you just told me, you are more than qualified for my job, maybe even more qualified than me. I can't, in good conscience, allow you to take a position you are clearly overqualified for." Jessalynne put the résumé down and looked at Noelle genuinely.

Noelle's face grew long. "I miss the bold and sweet aroma of coffee and working around it—but mainly I miss working. But honestly, not many businesses are really looking for a manager, and the few that were all told me I was way overqualified to work for them. It was suggested that I should try being a district manager or something. I'm a student. I can't take on a job like that right now…maybe after I finish with school." Noelle tried to hold back her disappointment, but it was becoming evident in her voice.

"It would be a demotion of responsibilities, and it could even be a little boring for you. There is no crossover. Even before I go on vacation with my family, I take care of the payroll and scheduling so everyone still gets paid and doesn't have to worry when they are supposed to work. You would be very bored, plus it's a significant pay cut from what you were making as a manager," Jessalynne said.

"The pay doesn't matter. I don't mind a pay cut. Besides, it's better than what I am making now, which is zero," Noelle tried not to sound like she was pleading.

"Noelle, even if the pay cut doesn't bother you, what about the fact that you will be stagnant, possibly even regressing? Your situation is almost like a fifth grader being sent back to second grade. Sure, the fifth grader can do the work and probably do it excellently but would be easily distracted and underchallenged. I can't, in good conscience, place you in that situation. You deserve something bigger, like another manager position or even higher," Jessalynne replied honestly. She could see the disappointment all over Noelle's face.

"What am I supposed to do? This is the last coffeehouse within driving distance for me that was actually hiring." Noelle sighed again. She didn't want to respond like this, but she was really at a loss. This place was her last shred of hope.

Jessalynne took another quick look at her résumé before saying anything. "According to this, every time you got a promotion, you went to work for a new place. Maybe this is a sign that you need to take another step forward. Even if I was willing to overlook the fact that you are way overqualified, I would be doing a disservice to you by hiring you for this job. You need something else…something much better," Jessalynne replied.

"I don't know anything else. I tried office assistant, receptionist, salesclerk, and secretary and the ones that contacted me all said I didn't have the right skills even though I had a lot of knowledge from my previous jobs. I don't fit anywhere, and I apologize for going off on a tangent. This is totally unprofessional of me. It's just frustrating." Noelle sighed. She tried really hard to fight back the mistiness building up in her eyes, but it was a struggle since there were so many disappointments.

"Noelle, there's a job out there for you. At each job you had, you excelled and moved forward, which is what you are supposed to do. I wish it were here, but I would be holding you back. All I can say is good luck with everything." Jessalynne got up and extended her hand toward Noelle.

Noelle questioned whether or not she wanted to shake her hand but knew that being cordial was the right decision because Jessalynne had been nothing but pleasant to her. The honest part was what Noelle wasn't ready for. "Thank you for your time," Noelle muttered out while picking up her cookie and her latte.

"Don't give up. Sometimes things will work out when you least expect it. Please don't undervalue your accomplishments. You will be a wonderful addition to someone's business. Good luck with everything." Jessalynne smiled as she took a copy of Noelle's résumé back to her office with her.

"Thanks," Noelle mumbled as she turned toward the front door of Java Planet and walked out back to her car. She opened her car door and threw her cookie package and her purse on the passenger's seat and placed the latte in her cupholder. She sat down in the driver's seat, closed the car door, and leaned her head against the steering wheel, letting out a loud sigh. She wasn't sure how to feel anymore. There was a part of her that wanted to just start crying—crying over frustration and desperation. It seemed like nothing that she was doing was working. She was doing everything she was supposed to do—actively researching job openings, sending out résumés, and going on interviews—yet she felt like she always kept hitting a wall or some type of roadblock. It was time for her to try something new and perhaps outside of the box. It was just that Noelle had no idea where to go from there. This was the first time no amount of planning or preparing could solve her problem. She needed a new solution, which just might push her out of her comfort zone.

Chapter 5

"Hey, Noelle." Keisha waved excitedly to Noelle from her seat. Noelle, who was usually pretty upbeat, was feeling disillusioned and confused. She was trying very hard not to let anyone else see how she was really feeling. "Hey, Keisha," Noelle replied, taking a seat at her desk, placing her schoolbag on her lap, and slowly unpacking all her books and pens for class.

"How is the project going? I'm so stumped as to what topic to pick. I mean, there are so many things I could pick, but I have no idea. I think opening a business is very complicated," Keisha responded quickly.

Noelle barely looked up from her schoolbag, her blond curls swaying back and forth below her shoulders. "I don't know… This semester isn't exactly starting off the way I had planned or expected," Noelle mumbled.

"Maybe you plan too much," Keisha replied honestly.

Noelle didn't turn to face her friend because she was getting pretty annoyed at everyone who kept telling her that she plans too much.

"Hi, Noelle." Rowena waved as she took a seat across from her. A tall, slender female with the same color of hair as Rowena walked in right behind her and took a seat in front of Noelle. She was dressed in a very bohemian-style ensemble.

"Hi, Noelle, how are you? How was your summer?" Fallon asked, turning around in her seat.

Noelle smirked. "Hi, Fallon. How's everything going? I thought you were only taking one class this semester?" Noelle asked flatly.

"Life is great! Sorry I missed Tuesday night's class. Ro tells me he's quite a character. Yeah, I was originally going to only take one class but then realized it would push my graduation further back. I want to finish my degree." Fallon laughed.

"Yeah, that's one way to describe him." Noelle laughed.

"I'm looking forward to meeting him next week," Fallon exclaimed.

"Oh, cuz, I have something for you." Rowena took something out of her folder and started a pretty in-depth conversation with Fallon about the syllabus from Tuesday night's class.

Noelle looked away and turned her attention back to Keisha. "Keisha, do you know anything about our professor?" Noelle asked curiously.

"Yeah, I heard she likes to give a lot of homework, but I also heard that Professor Summerfield is a very hard grader, so I guess we have our semester cut out for us," Keisha replied, taking a pen out of her purse.

"He's a tough grader? He seems like he gives lots of work, but that he was a fair grader or even easy grader." Noelle looked kind of panicked.

"From the professor reviews, he's tough, but if you do what you are supposed to do, you should be okay. He's a stickler for knowing terminology and understanding and applying concepts. Good thing that the fall semester is shorter than the spring semester." Keisha pretended to wipe sweat away from her forehead.

"What kind of grader is this professor?" Noelle asked anxiously.

"I don't know, but I read her exams are very difficult. Guess we should form a study group this semester," Keisha suggested.

"Sure, we'll figure something out…maybe even get some extra classmates to join," Noelle added.

"Great idea. The more heads, the better," Keisha mumbled out.

Noelle looked at her strangely. "I think it's two heads are better than one." Noelle giggled.

"I like mine better, but Gil is always teasing me that I get it wrong. He's a great guy…accepts my quirks." Keisha beamed.

Noelle forced a smile. It was not that she wasn't happy for her friend; it was that finding love and a happy relationship always seemed to really elude her. Just another thing to be completely frustrated over. "I hope there's a guy out there for me like that," Noelle muttered under her breath. Keisha didn't hear what she said but nodded at her friend anyway.

The class got quiet as a shorter woman wearing a pantsuit walked into the classroom with a leather briefcase. Her very thick raven hair was pulled back into a tight bun as her subtly tanned features glowed under the florescent lights.

"Good evening, class. My name is Professor Kalpana Devi-Smith. You can call me Professor Smith or Professor Devi-Smith or just plain old professor. Whatever you feel most comfortable using," Professor Kalpana Devi-Smith said in a much more forceful voice than anyone would expect for her small stature.

"Good evening," the students muttered out, half asleep.

Professor Devi-Smith started laughing. "Yeah, I know, without my nightly cup of coffee, I would probably be as sleepy as all of you are right now. I know a lot of you are not looking forward to taking financial management in the evening or maybe even at all, but I promise this class will be more hands-on and interesting than you're expecting. There will be a lot of work, and I have high expectations, but if you keep up the pace with me, everyone will be fine. Okay, can someone take out a piece of paper and start a sign-in sheet? It's easier for me because I'm still learning your names. This will only last a few classes at most," Professor Devi-Smith replied quickly while one student in the first row took out a sheet of paper and began to pass it around.

This was a little strange because the students were all scattered around the classroom appearing more like a zigzag maze. Professor Devi-Smith took a pile of syllabi and placed a handful in front of each row before walking back toward the front of the classroom and started writing something on the blackboard. The students in the first seat passed them back to the students sitting behind them and over to the students who didn't receive one or were sitting by themselves.

"Excuse me, Professor, but according to this, we don't have just a midterm and a final exam but also midterm and final papers. I want to clarify that the papers and exams are the same assignment or different ones?" Sally asked a little nervously and hopeful she was misreading the class requirements.

"No, you did read that right. It won't be due on the same day but the same week. You will also have a final project and pop quizzes and biweekly graded class assignments," Professor Devi-Smith replied.

The class groaned. Noelle looked down at her syllabus and almost refused to open her textbook. Between her two classes, it now felt more like five classes of work.

"Ahh," a couple of students groaned.

"Listen, I know it sounds like a lot, but it is beneficial. Everything has a purpose. You want to make sure when you build a foundation that it's strong and wide, not weak and narrow. We cover a lot of material. Okay, so the exams are not cumulative, but they do build off each other, and I will expect you to know basics for both the midterm and final exams. As for the papers, when we get closer to the due date, I will explain them more. So, class, open your books to page 2, which is the first page of chapter 1," Professor Devi-Smith replied while turning around to write a few more terms on the blackboard.

Noelle sat there for a moment before taking out her textbook and her notebook with a pen. She slouched to the side and just stared at the blackboard. To her, this was the perfect ending to a completely stressful and crappy week. Their professor stood still at the blackboard for a moment thinking about something before turning to face the class.

"How about everyone gets into groups? Lemme see, there are eighteen…nineteen…twenty students. Okay, so that would be six groups of three and one group of two. Do I really only have two guys in my class this semester?" Professor Devi-Smith looked in disbelief.

"There are actually three of us. Orlando couldn't make it to class tonight. He'll be here next week," Owen explained.

"Okay, so you two can be the group of two, and the rest will be in groups of three," Professor Devi-Smith replied, looking around the classroom.

Keisha and Noelle turned and agreed to be in a group together. Everyone else seemed to find a group to latch onto, except for one blond girl from the other side of the classroom. She looked a little long in the face. Keisha noticed her and waved for her to come over. She grabbed her bag and rushed over to sit near them.

"Hi, I'm Sally. I was afraid that I would be sitting alone… or with the two guys," Sally joked as she pulled up a desk to sit in between Keisha and Noelle.

"I'm Keisha, and this is Noelle. Yeah, we can't have anyone sitting alone," Keisha declared.

"This is what I get for taking a year off from the program. A lot of students I started with graduated last semester." Sally lowered her eyes.

"Don't worry. I don't even think we know everyone in the program, and we started with some of these students," Noelle replied casually.

"So what are we supposed to do?" Sally asked.

Noelle looked up at the board. "Looks like we are supposed to answer questions on the bottom of page 5. I wonder if she needs everyone to write down the answers," Noelle pondered.

"Class, everyone needs to help answer the questions, but only one person needs to write down the answers. I would choose the one with the nicest handwriting," Professor Devi-Smith joked.

Noelle and Keisha looked at each other before Sally took out a piece of paper.

"I have neat handwriting, plus I don't mind writing. I'm an English lit undergrad. This is actually normal for me," Sally joked.

"How did you end up in a business master's program?" Keisha asked curiously.

"Well, it's kind of a long story, but basically, teaching didn't quite work out for me. So I had actually planned on maybe being an English tutor or something close to that. My boyfriend suggested opening my own business, but I don't know. So that's how I ended up in a graduate business program. I'm not sure what's going to happen in the future, but I'm learning a lot of stuff," Sally spoke pretty quickly.

"Is that what you are going to do for your project? For Tuesday night's class?" Keisha asked. Noelle just sat there half-listening, half-daydreaming about what she would be doing after class.

"Well, I was kind of stumped, but I think English grammar and literature tutoring business. I also thought about essay writing or correct grammar instruction. It's something I am passionate about and was on my mind before," Sally answered, seemingly confident with her choice.

"Well, I was really stuck too. I mean, I have a business undergrad with a minor in Spanish. I took a break, and then I went back to school for my master's degree. I wanted to do something with international business, but I don't know anymore. Things have changed, and I don't like the idea of traveling a lot. I already have an hour commute each way to work and almost an hour commute to school in opposite directions." Keisha sighed.

"What kind of work do you do?" Sally asked curiously.

"Oh, I am a coordinator for home health care. It's exhausting but rewarding," Keisha replied.

"How about your own home health-care business? I mean, you can add that you are bilingual, and that might be helpful to more clients," Sally suggested.

Keisha sat there and thought for a moment before turning to Noelle. "What do you think, Noelle?" Keisha asked excitedly.

"Oh…what…um…I think that is a good idea. But do you speak Spanish fluently?" Noelle asked curiously.

"Not exactly. Gil's been trying to help me. He thinks it's cute how hard I try," Keisha gushed.

"Isn't this pretend? I mean, it doesn't mean whether or not you are actually fluent but that your intent is to offer bilingual services," Sally explained.

Keisha nodded. "That's a great idea! Thanks, Sally." Keisha hurried to write it down before she would forget.

"What about you, Noelle? Have you figured out what you want to do?" Sally asked.

Noelle sat there for a moment and shook her head. "I have no idea. I thought about a lot of things, but I think I've been so preoccupied with trying to find a job that I can't think straight." Noelle's face showed extreme stress. She rubbed her temples to try to avoid developing a headache.

"Oh, I guess the interviewing hasn't gone quite as well as you thought. Don't give up. I found my job after months of applications being sent out. On the bright side, I got a whole summer off to enjoy before I started working full-time." Keisha smiled encouragingly.

"What kind of work did you do before?" Sally asked curiously.

"I worked as a manager of a coffee shop," Noelle replied quickly.

"That's pretty cool! I always thought that job was so nuts. Trying to take care of all the right orders while paying extra close attention to specialty orders that are health-related like no caffeine or dairy products while running the entire store," Sally replied in awe.

Noelle nodded. "It's not a big deal. I think you get used to it after a while. Plus, the regular customers who have special requests eventually become memorized. I guess it helped that I really liked what I did. It's funny. When I was looking for my first job, I wasn't looking for anything specific. It wasn't something I planned. I applied for a bunch of jobs, and it was the coffee shop looking for a part-time barista that hired me. I guess the rest is history." Noelle chuckled.

"How about a coffee shop? You know, like a small coffeehouse type of setting?" Sally suggested.

A smile grew slowly on Noelle's face, because as much as she didn't want to admit it, that was a great idea. "You know, that might not be a bad idea," Noelle replied.

Keisha turned to Sally. "How do you do that? I mean, you seem to just be able to help people figure things out so quickly," Keisha observed.

"I don't know. I think it's because I talk a lot. It's funny, for as much as I talk, my boyfriend is so quiet. Sometimes I think he thinks I talk too much." Sally laughed.

"They love us anyway." Keisha smiled.

Noelle smiled but really wanted to try and change the topic so she wouldn't have to think about being single and lonely. "What time is it? We should probably start answering the questions. They are due by the end of class," Noelle warned, getting a little anxious.

"Oh, wow, it's already ten to seven. Okay, how many questions are there?" Keisha asked.

Sally looked at her book. "It looks like seven, but two of the questions have multiple parts. We could break it up or just work together with the ones that are there," Sally replied.

"How about we break them up? And then if any of us get stuck, we'll go back to work on it together," Noelle suggested.

"Great idea. I'll take the first two, Noelle can take the next two, and, Sally, you can take the next two. We'll all answer number 7 together. That way, it's even," Keisha suggested.

"I'm glad I found this group. You two are so cool," Sally replied while starting to work on her questions.

"Yeah, we're cool until midterms and finals. Then we're all hot messes," Noelle replied flatly. For some reason, Sally and Keisha found that hilarious and just started laughing.

"If the coffee shop thing is taken, maybe I can always add comedy club owner," Noelle joked. The three of them started laughing together before getting to work on their class assignment.

Chapter 6

Noelle stood in front of her full-length mirror while she finished buttoning her pink plaid vest over her cream-colored short-sleeved T-shirt. She looked in the mirror to make sure that her jeans were wrinkle-free. She was reaching up to pull her blond curls into a ponytail when she was startled by a noise coming from her desk.

Ring...ring...ring...
Ring...ring...ring...

Noelle walked toward her solid white desk with matching white chair and saw a phone number light up on her cell phone. It didn't look familiar, so she thought maybe it was a wrong number. She thought about waiting to see if there was a voice mail to decide whether or not it was important. The phone stopped ringing, and there was no voice mail, so Noelle turned around to face the mirror again before her phone started to make buzzing noises. That was a sign she had a voice mail. She quickly picked up her phone and checked her messages. As she listened, her face grew from reluctant to hopeful.

"Oh, it's a potential job. I have to call them back right now," Noelle instructed herself as she listened to the voice mail again to quickly write down the phone number and extension. Noelle quickly dialed the number back and waited for someone to answer.

"Hello, this is the voice mail of Carol Simmons, director of HR. Please leave your name, number, and a short message stating why you are calling, and I'll get right back to you," the message said.

"Hello. This is Noelle DeGarmo. I am returning your phone call. I recently applied for one of the secretarial positions. You can call me back at any time on the same phone number. It's 201-555-2332. Have a great day!" Noelle hung up the phone but kept it in her hand tightly to make sure she wouldn't miss the phone call again. She took a seat on her pink shag carpet with her back toward the end of the bed. She looked down and saw the phone was ringing again.

"Hello," Noelle replied somewhat enthusiastically.

"Hello, is this Noelle De…Garma?" an older female voice asked.

Noelle rolled her eyes at the mispronunciation. She always believed her last name was pretty easy to pronounce because it was phonetical, pronounced the way it looks.

"Yes, this is she," Noelle replied calmly. She got up from sitting on her pink shag carpet to move toward her desk in case she needed a piece of paper and a pen to write anything down.

"Okay, great. My name is Carol Simmons. I called earlier and left a message. I'm sorry I missed your call. I was on the phone. Thankfully for the invention of answering machines," Carol said lightly.

Noelle smiled but tried to maintain her composure from getting too anxious. "That's okay. I didn't recognize the phone number, so I let it go to voice mail. I've had a couple of memorable experiences picking up wrong numbers…" Noelle trailed off.

"I can imagine. Anything with customer service always has its stories. That is why I am calling. It's in reference to the secretarial job that you recently applied for. I know you haven't sent a résumé yet, but you filled out a job application and sent it in. You'll need to send a copy of your most recent résumé before the actual interview. Right now, I have your application in front of me, and I have some follow-up questions that need clarification," Carol replied kind of ambiguously.

Noelle was a little perplexed as she had never had a job interview start like that, but she knew things were changing and were being handled differently now. She decided to go with the flow—anything if she could get hired for a job.

"Oh, okay, sure." Noelle finally started to feel optimistic. She figured maybe Jessalynne was right about reaching a plateau in the previous field she had worked in, and maybe now was the time to pursue a brand-new field.

"I see you worked in customer service. What type of industry did you work for? What were some of your responsibilities?" Carol asked quickly.

"Oh, well, I have spent my entire work career so far in customer service primarily in regard to coffee and food," Noelle replied confidently.

Carol fell silent for a moment. "Oh, I see. You worked in the food industry. That's good. Do you have any office experience? I know many of those jobs have back offices or managerial responsibilities," Carol replied, sounding a little more engaged.

"Well, my last job, I was manager. I also was responsible for payroll and scheduling of employees. Trying to maneuver vacations could be really tricky," Noelle made a small joke. Carol didn't seem to find any humor in it.

"Well, in HR, we take care of all those things—days off, leave of absences, sick days, vacation days, and sometimes scheduling depending on how the departments are with staffing," Carol replied matter-of-factly.

Noelle was a little confused because she had never heard that before, but then again, she had only worked in one industry and still felt wet behind the ears.

"Oh, I see. How about any experience working in an office setting? Have you experienced working in an office setting while working in the coffee shop?" Carol asked, starting to sound more distant.

Noelle could tell a change in Carol's tone, but she ignored it. "Well, part of my many managerial responsibilities were to take care of payroll and make the weekly store schedule. But no, I wasn't responsible for paying the bills or actually running the office. However, my old boss did put me in charge of inventory and made me responsible for ordering supplies from time to time. I used to get so annoyed when the computer system would go down right before I was trying to order supplies," Noelle replied, still trying to remain confident.

Carol fell silent again. "Oh, okay. It says also that you are a business major. When do you expect to graduate?" Carol asked, a little bit more engaged than a few minutes earlier.

"I completed my bachelor's in business administration, and I am currently finishing my master's in business administration on track to graduate in the spring," Noelle replied quickly.

"Oh, well, congratulations. Hard work does pay off," Carol chimed in.

"Yeah, it wasn't an easy task balancing school and work, but I managed to do it," Noelle replied confidently.

"You left off typing speed on the application. Do you have any idea what your typing speed is?" Carol asked curiously.

"Not really. It's fast enough to get my assignments done on time," Noelle was trying to lighten the tense mood again.

Carol fell silent yet again. "That's not a number. We usually require our secretaries to be able to type at least seventy-five words per minute with less than a 2 percent error rate. We actually prefer no error rate but understand things can happen from time to time, including keys sticking on a keyboard and inaudible recordings and illegible dictations," Carol replied flatly.

Noelle's mouth dropped. She didn't even think she could do thirty words per minute with less than a 2 percent error rate. "I know I can't type that fast, but I am a really fast learner and would be willing to go to training classes or to school to learn to become a better typist." Noelle was trying very hard to remain confident but could feel this conversation wasn't going the way that she wanted it to go.

"I'm sorry. We need our secretaries to be able to step right into the job and be able to do the basics, including filing, faxing, and typing. A lot of memos and paperwork go through these offices, so the faster the typing, the more efficient this business runs." The distance in Carol's voice grew even stronger.

Noelle knew what this meant. "Is there anything else at your business that is currently looking to hire anyone?" Noelle asked, trying to avoid sounding desperate.

"I'm sorry, Noelle. Right now, we are only searching for secretaries to replace a couple who have moved up in the company. We are also hiring an office manager and a financial analyst, neither of which you currently qualify for. Maybe after you graduate and get some other experience under your belt, you can call us back, and we might have an opening for you," Carol replied indifferently.

Noelle tried to keep her disappointment hidden deeply. "Thank you very much for your time," Noelle replied while she rested her head in the palm of her left hand while still holding the phone in her right hand.

"Good luck with your job search," Carol said quickly before hanging up.

Noelle sat up and hung up the phone. She stuck her tongue out at the phone in frustration but soon realized that wasn't the way to handle anything. She couldn't help that she wasn't qualified to do anything except work in a coffee shop. Noelle was really starting to wonder if this careful planning she had been doing for years had actually helped place her into a box that she couldn't get out of. It seemed right now the only thing that was working in her favor was finishing her master's degree, but there was no way to know for certain if her degree would help her get a job in the future or if it was a big waste of money and time.

She got up and looked around her room to see if there were any other job listings in the newspaper that she had been looking at weekly since she was fired. Noelle took out a neon yellow highlighter and sat on the floor where the newspaper was laid out. She carefully read through the job postings. Initially, she was being optimistic about the first few because she knew those were not for her, but as she continued down the columns, she realized that many of the same jobs that were listed, she had already applied for. Even a couple that had told her that they weren't hiring were now in the newspaper looking for help. Noelle could feel her fists tense up with pent-up frustration, but her face grew long as she started to lose hope in being able to find another job. She had already sent out dozens of résumés for dozens of jobs. There were no more coffee shop jobs that were available, at least that she would be able to commute to without relocating. She tried every type of office job—mail room clerk, mail room assistant, receptionist, customer service operator—and all of them either didn't get back to her or told her she wasn't what they were looking for.

She put her head in her hands while she pushed the newspaper off to the side of the room. She really didn't feel like doing any homework but never felt comfortable just doing nothing. Even though graduate school would help her to supposedly secure a better-paying job in the future, what Noelle really needed was a breakthrough right now. If only there was someone out there willing and able to help her or just take a chance on her. At this point, all she could do was hope and pray that someone or something would extend an olive branch.

Chapter 7

Noelle slowly walked up the stairs and down the small hallway toward a closed door with big black block letters spelling Career Services. Feeling very anxious, she readjusted her black dress jacket and matching black pants so that they were neat and wrinkle-free. She double-checked her collar to make sure it was laying neatly around the top of the jacket. She wanted to look her very best to leave a memorable impression. She took a deep breath before reaching down to open the door. She looked around and saw a few students sitting in the waiting area. Noelle noticed a window straight ahead and proceeded to talk to someone.

"Hello. I'm here to see Ms. Rutkowski," Noelle said politely.

"Take a seat. She's with someone. She'll be with you shortly. What is your name?" the woman behind the desk asked while pushing her reading glasses up over her nose.

"It's Noelle…um…Noelle DeGarmo," Noelle replied, a little startled. She looked down to see if the receptionist had a name because there was no plaque or name tag.

"Okay, take a seat. Your name will be called when she's available," the woman replied, still trying to push her reading glasses over her slender nose.

Noelle nodded while clutching her purse in one hand and a copy of her résumé in the other hand. She took a seat near the door. She looked around and didn't recognize anyone. Everyone looked either older or younger than her, and nobody seemed particularly friendly, but then again, Noelle thought perhaps everyone there was too preoccupied with trying to get a job. Noelle took out her phone to make sure the volume was off so that it wouldn't go off when she was talking to Ms. Rutkowski. Her phone went off once at the wrong time, and ever since then, she was very careful to double- or triple-check to make sure it was off. She looked over and saw a couple of people leave as one of the doors opened, and someone walked out. Noelle looked up and wondered if that was Ms. Rutkowski but realized it was an older male in a pair of dress pants and a short-sleeved dress shirt with a bow tie. Noelle lowered her head so as not to attract too much attention while placing her cell phone away. She picked up one of the latest fashion magazines and started to look through it slowly. She tried to remain alert but started to get a little lost in some of the pictures of the latest fashions, causing her to be quickly startled when her name was called.

"Noelle DeGarmo," the same middle-aged woman called out from behind the counter. A few students online looked at each other while Noelle quickly got up from her chair near the door. She picked up her purse and walked toward the front window.

"I'm Noelle," Noelle replied, looking at the same woman sitting down with a pile of paperwork all over her desk and still fighting with her eyeglasses. She looked up and nodded at Noelle.

"She'll see you now. Just make a left and go all the way down the hallway and make a right. It's the second door on the left," the same middle-aged woman instructed her to do.

Noelle nodded and quickly moved through the doorway to walk down the hallway and tried not to peep into any of the other offices before she ended up at Ms. Rutkowski's office. Noelle gently knocked on the doorframe.

A woman with very short graying hair and thick red-rimmed glasses looked up from her computer screen. "Come in and take a seat," Ms. Rutkowski instructed. She spent a couple of minutes finishing typing something before taking her glasses off and giving Noelle her full attention.

"Did I come at a bad time?" Noelle blurted out nervously.

Ms. Rutkowski shook her head. "No, I just had to make sure I sent that email out as soon as possible. What can I do for you today?" Ms. Rutkowski asked while leaning on her elbows and giving Noelle her full attention.

Noelle took a seat across from her but couldn't help thinking she seemed a little unusual. "Well, I'm currently looking for a job. I called yesterday and was told that you handle helping students find employment on campus," Noelle explained with a glimmer of hope.

Ms. Rutkowski leaned back in her chair, revealing her bright leopard-print blouse. Noelle bit her lip.

"Are you looking for work study? Because if you are, then you are in the wrong office. That would be financial aid," Ms. Rutkowski replied quickly.

Noelle lowered her eyes, a little discouraged. "Um…actually, for some reason, I don't qualify for work study. Maybe I made too much money last year…I'm not sure. I was told that when I was filling out some paperwork for school loans for this semester. I was told that you are responsible for job placement on campus or through campus. I'm not really sure how this works." Noelle started to stumble on her words a little bit.

"Oh, I am mainly responsible for internships and apprenticeships. I try to get students into as many paid internships as possible, but sometimes even an unpaid internship can be like gold on a résumé after graduation," Ms. Rutkowski explained.

"Oh, I wasn't looking for an internship. I'm not even sure if I qualify," Noelle replied, a little confused.

"What level are you? Are you undergrad or grad?" Ms. Rutkowski asked while sitting up and shifting over to her computer screen.

"I'm a graduate student…in business," Noelle replied. The expression on Ms. Rutkowski's face said everything that Noelle was afraid to hear but she sat there anyway.

"I can double-check if there is something, but for graduate students, they are usually rare. I deal with mainly undergraduate students. However, I can keep checking for you throughout the semester to see if something comes up. Sometimes things are posted later than the beginning of the semester," Ms. Rutkowski offered.

Noelle nodded. "That would be great. Thank you. I appreciate it." Noelle tried to force a smile.

"Here, write down your name and phone number, and I will give you a call if anything comes up," Ms. Rutkowski offered.

Noelle took the paper and wrote her first and last name and her phone number.

Ms. Rutkowski smiled as she took back the piece of paper. "Ah…another southpaw." Ms. Rutkowski laughed.

Noelle was a little distracted because she wasn't used to anyone taking notice of the fact that she was left-handed. "Yeah, most don't notice." Noelle laughed.

"Sometimes it's the smaller details that really paint the bigger picture," Ms. Rutkowski said a little cryptically.

Noelle was confused about the reference but nodded and smiled anyway as she got up. She had no idea how profound that statement would prove to be in the future.

"Thank you for your time, Ms. Rutkowski." Noelle smiled as she turned around to start leaving.

"Wait, Noelle." Ms. Rutkowski got her to turn around for a moment. "Sometimes places around campus individually hire. I can't guarantee what type of job it would be, but the cafeteria has contracted vendors that are sometimes looking for people. You can always try looking there. It is something at least."

Noelle smiled and nodded. "Thank you. I never even thought about that, and I go to the cafeteria at least twice a week. I might make a stop there before I leave campus today," Noelle replied excitedly.

"Good luck, and I'll be in touch!" Ms. Rutkowski shouted before going back to staring at her computer screen and visibly typing something quickly.

Noelle took a slow walk through the hallway before leaving the office building. She stepped out onto campus again and looked around at all the students and professors rushing across campus to get to class on time. She walked down the pathway toward the student union where the cafeterias were located. She stopped for a moment to smell the fresh flowers that someone was holding next to her. Noelle had no idea where the flowers had come from because she rarely saw or smelled flowers on campus but wondered if this was a sign that she was going in the right direction. Her philosophy was always simple: if it's not planned out thoroughly or planned out properly, it's open to not working out at all. This was one reason she never really believed in signs; they always seemed to be too illogical and impractical. However, after some of her failed romantic relationships and even previous platonic friendships, she started to definitely believe in red flags. So why would it be a stretch to possibly believe in signs?

As Noelle pulled the door open to the student union, she was relieved to see that the lunch crowd was already gone. There were a few students here and there, either leaving with a sandwich or a muffin in one hand and coffee or tea in the other with a textbook or newspaper under their arm. Noelle wasn't really hungry because she ate a late big breakfast, but she was always open to getting a cup of coffee. She walked into the smaller cafeteria as they usually had a better selection of coffee and was usually fresher than the larger cafeterias. She walked slowly through the doorway and initially stopped at the small pastry section. Although the double chocolate chip muffin probably wasn't the best choice, it was a sort of reward for the stress she had been under. She quickly walked toward the back counter where there were three large commercial-sized coffee pots filled with either different flavored coffees or hot water for hot chocolate and tea. Noelle carefully scanned the types of coffees available. After a few minutes of carefully pondering flavors and sizes, she settled on a medium hazelnut with skim milk. However, when she was searching the small cooler for skim milk, there was nothing. Noelle noticed a woman walking around in the back and tried to get her attention.

"Excuse me," Noelle called loudly but gently. The woman turned her head and motioned to wait a moment. Noelle nodded and waited until the woman came back over.

"Can I help you with something?" the frazzled woman asked, blowing her sandy-brown bangs out of her flushed face.

"Yes, I just wanted to know if there was any skim milk. There is none in the dairy case." Noelle tried not to sound like one of the rude customers she used to deal with.

"Yeah, we just got a shipment, but I'm short-staffed. Someone quit, and someone else is out sick, so I'm doing shipment by myself. If you want to wait, I could probably get to it in about ten to fifteen minutes," the woman replied, pushing a few more strands of short sandy-brown hair out of her face.

"It's okay. I can use regular today. It's not a big deal. The skim milk is just my attempt at trying to keep the weight off," Noelle joked.

"Yeah, you're better than me." The woman laughed before turning back around.

Noelle, out of impulse, decided to ask a question. "Are you looking for workers?" Noelle asked randomly.

The woman quickly turned around excitedly. "It's part-time and an hourly wage, but yes, at least through the fall semester," the woman replied.

"Well, I have a little experience working with coffee, and I'm looking for a job, so is there an application?" Noelle asked very eagerly.

"Yeah, let me grab one." The woman reached under the counter to grab an application form.

"Here, you can bring it back when you are able to. I am looking for someone who can work definitely Fridays and Saturdays. If those days aren't good, I'm sorry, I can't hire you," the woman replied bluntly.

Noelle was a little taken aback by her brash response but ignored it. "Yes, that's fine with me. The only times I'm not available is at night on Tuesdays and Thursdays," Noelle replied quickly.

"Great! We close at five here, so unless there is shipment or something big going on, there won't be any conflicts," the woman replied.

Noelle smiled.

"And your name?" the woman asked.

"Noelle," Noelle replied, smiling.

"I'm Selby. Nice to meet you. Fill the application out as soon as possible, and hopefully, you'll be working with us soon." Selby smiled and turned around to continue working on the shipment.

Noelle put the application in her bag while she went to go pay for her muffin and coffee. She walked over to the cashier and quickly handed her a $10 bill and waited for change. She took a seat down at one of the small empty tables and quickly pulled out a pen to start filling out the application while drinking her coffee. Noelle couldn't seem to write fast enough for herself. She had never filled out an application so quickly, but this was the most amount of hope that she had in over a month. This wasn't her dream job, but it was convenient and was doing something that was already habitual to her. Noelle knew she had to be careful when filling out the form because adding in that she was a manager or assistant manager might actually work against her like it did for other jobs she applied for. Java Planet was still making her upset even though deep down a part of her knew that Jessalynne was right in what she said. In the least, this job would help her cover her basic expenses without forcing her to delve too much into her savings account. She left the section for work experience as minimal of just working as a barista. She didn't like being dishonest but felt like the end justified the means. Noelle threw her unopened muffin into her bag and put her pen into one of the small compartments in her schoolbag before getting up with her cup of coffee and her application.

"Excuse me, Selby. I finished the application," Noelle called out as she saw Selby still working on the shipment.

Selby was startled by the sound of Noelle's voice but quickly walked toward the counter. "Wow, that was fast. I mean, that's good, but usually, students take a couple of days to fill these things out." Selby marveled.

"It's probably because they were running late to class. I remember those da...semesters...those semesters," Noelle corrected herself because she didn't want to be known as a graduate student either. She never really liked lying and was usually terrible at it, so she figured avoiding the topic altogether would be the best way to go. Noelle had learned from previous job interviews that having additional education could also prove to be a real disadvantage for her. Who would think that working hard to try and do better could also hinder the process of moving forward? It truly felt like a catch-22. Noelle could not figure that out no matter how hard she tried.

Selby took a quick look at the application and started to smile. "Well, looks like you won't have to be completely trained with the basics, which is a good thing for me because that's hard to try to do with everything else," Selby replied, still looking over the application.

"Why is it so hard to find help here?" Noelle pondered out loud.

Selby shrugged. "Maybe the pay is too low. It's a little more than minimum wage, but there is no opportunity for overtime, and it's only full-time hours toward the end of the semester when the hours increase because of extended library and campus hours. The only other thing is maybe students don't want to spend more time at school than they have to." Selby laughed.

Noelle nodded in agreement. "Makes sense. I think the last thing college students want to do is spend more time at school than necessary, but maybe there are exceptions," Noelle replied casually.

"Well, I would hire you right on the spot, but I have to talk it over with my supervisor. She does all the hiring. I just manage the coffee corner and take care of all the shipment. That's the fun part. Only positive is that I don't have to listen to customers complain about the coffee and stuff." Selby let slip out a little bit of her real personality. Noelle figured that she was just overtired and frustrated from being the only one working there, but for some reason, it burned in the back of her mind. As a manager, Noelle would never say that because one of the reasons she loved her job was dealing with some of the same friendly and generous customers on a daily basis. Her goal was to make all the customers happy or at least try to remedy their problems.

"That's not a problem. I put down my cell phone number, so it's the best way to reach me," Noelle replied quickly.

"So you are available all day both Friday and Saturday, right?" Selby wanted to double-check. Noelle nodded.

"Yeah, I'm available anytime except Tuesdays and Thursdays," Noelle said quickly.

"Must be nice that you could schedule all your classes into just two days," Selby remarked.

Noelle didn't realize it, but she inadvertently told Selby that she was an undergrad. For fear of being called a liar or being called overqualified, Noelle just played along with it. "Yeah, I guess I just got lucky this semester, but the homework, that's another topic." Noelle rolled her eyes.

"Okay, great, you'll be hearing from me." Selby put the application in a folder and then went back to doing the shipment.

Noelle smiled brightly and left the cafeteria in a better mood than she had felt in a little while. She was starting to wonder if perhaps things were going to start moving in the right direction for her. She didn't know if things were working out, but she was certainly hoping this was a good sign.

Chapter 8

"Good evening, class! I have finished grading all your assignments from the first week. I know I'm a week behind, but don't worry, you will have everything you need when you start putting together your final projects. I have left comments on several of your assignments. Now please don't be upset if you see something negative. Remember, this is a learning process. For anyone who has some corrections or suggestions or comments, you are welcome to rewrite your assignment for a higher grade. The higher grade will be recorded," Professor Summerfield said.

A couple of students raised their hands.

"Professor, that means that the lower grade doesn't count, right? I'm afraid that I really didn't understand or complete the assignment correctly. I don't want it to be negatively affecting my grade." Rowena sulked.

"The higher grade is counted. If you have any questions on how to correct anything from your homework assignments or even just discuss your business idea or anything else related, you can see me before or after class or even during my office hours listed on the syllabus," Professor Summerfield replied subtly.

"How much do these assignments count for?" Kendall asked.

Professor Summerfield looked at her with his traditional deadpan expression. The light shining brightly off his balding head made his bright orange-and-yellow bow tie look illuminated, making him appear more like an entertainer or a gameshow host rather than a college professor. "It is written down on your syllabus...in the section marked Grading. I think it's 25 percent of your whole grade, but remember that it's worth much more because your final project is based off these assignments. So if you are having problems with them, you will also struggle with the final project," Professor Summerfield warned.

"Is there extra credit?" Jeff asked.

Professor Summerfield's expression spoke volumes. "We are only in the third week of the semester," Professor Summerfield replied, unfazed, while looking around at the rest of the class. "Okay, are there any other *substantial* questions? If not, we will be moving on to the next step of the business process."

"Is there a specific length the assignments are supposed to be, or is it just how long it takes for the assignment to be completed?" Fallon asked, still a little bit confused because she missed the first week of class.

"No, because everyone's responses will be different. Some students tend to write a little longer, while others write shorter. What I am looking for is that the question...questions...in the assignment are answered fully. The more textual support that you add will not only strengthen your argument but also increase the length of your response," Professor Summerfield replied while being met with a sea of groans.

"We were supposed to add textual support?" Kendall became distraught.

Professor Summerfield looked around the classroom. "Everything I just said is written in your syllabus. However, the assignment that you are getting back tonight is from week 1. That was your business idea. You didn't need to use textual support, but if you did, you will receive credit. Last week's assignment, which is due today, is the type of business plan you are looking at utilizing. That should have been supported through some type of textual support. I will allow you to correct your homework assignments today in class and will collect them at the end of class. If you already used textual support, you don't need to do anything." Professor Summerfield looked around the classroom. A couple more students raised their hands.

"Do we have to use the textbook, or can we use any source to support our reasons and arguments?" Noelle asked inquisitively.

"Noelle, right?" Noelle nodded nervously as she saw the class staring at her. "I prefer using the textbook, but if you find a better outside source, that would be fine too. Even better is using one of each. You don't need a paragraph as a source, only a few words or a sentence or two. Enough to support your argument."

Noelle could feel her face blushing as she looked around the rest of the class not understanding why he knew her name and seemed to not know other students' names. Noelle felt a light tapping on her shoulder.

"Noelle, how does he already know your name?" Keisha asked, a little concerned.

Noelle shrugged her shoulders, leaned back, and turned her head slightly to respond. "I have no idea. I hope this doesn't mean I did pretty poorly on my homework assignment. The bad ones always seem to stick out like a sore thumb," Noelle whispered with a solemn expression on her face.

"Okay, if that's all the questions, let's start this week's lesson. So the first week was a quick introduction, and last week was the business plan. This week is how to fund your new business. Remember that everything builds off each other. Without a great business plan, the chances of getting funded are much lower. If you were more thorough, there should already be a little bit of an introduction on how to fund your business," Professor Summerfield started.

"Is that $50,000 mentioned in the syllabus still the baseline?" Sally asked.

"Yes, you don't have to use all of it, or you could use all of it and still need more, but it's easier to have everyone in the class start with the same amount. There is a lot of information that will be packed into a little bit of class. So I will try to go into as much depth as possible, but with time constraints, it's difficult. For anyone who would like to learn more or have longer discussions, please feel free to visit me at my office hours listed on the syllabus. I love discussing this stuff for hours. Just ask my wife." Professor Summerfield chuckled. Some of the students followed suit.

"Was everyone's business idea accepted?" Jeff asked seriously.

"Yes, this is a rare class because all the business ideas were acceptable. However, a couple of you need to possibly consider renaming your businesses," Professor Summerfield instructed.

"Why?" Orlando asked.

"I don't want to specifically call anyone out, but there were a few names that were questionable because they could be misconstrued as something crude or inappropriate. Also, anyone who chose a name that is difficult to pronounce or too long to remember would probably want to consider renaming their business. Here's a hint. Sometimes short and corny is the best way to go," Professor Summerfield answered quickly.

Orlando nodded and quickly jotted down a note.

"If there aren't any other questions, let's start tonight's lesson—how to fund your new business. Remember, when you are calculating the total amount you need for your business, you need to subtract the $50,000 that I already allotted to everyone for the use of the project. I don't remember everyone's business idea off the top of my head, but I think most of you chose smaller businesses. That $50,000 would definitely be more significant to a smaller business owner than to someone who wants to open a luxury hotel. This week, you need to do a lot of research because you need to figure out what you need to run your business. This includes all equipment and rent and utilities. You get the point. It's okay if your amount is a negative number. The remaining will need to be covered through additional funding. We're going to discuss that in a moment," Professor Summerfield replied while looking around the classroom to make sure everyone is following what he was talking about.

"Negative number?" Kendall asked, confused.

"Okay, so let's say Wally—an imaginary classmate—is planning on opening a business for auto repair. He calculated all the necessary expenses that he would incur for his business, and it came out to $120,000. So he would deduct the initial $50,000 in savings, and he would be left with -$70,000. It's money that he will need for his business but that he doesn't have yet. So he's in the red, as they say in business," Professor Summerfield explained.

"Oh, wow, I get it now. So the $50,000 we have right now to use. Then we have to determine how much more our business would require to open?" Kendall asked, looking a little embarrassed by asking that question.

"Exactly. Remember, if you don't have the money to pay for something, you can't get it. That includes anything from rent to equipment to paying future employees. So do some research and get a general idea how much it would cost to open and run your type of business. I'm not looking for exact numbers. Approximates are fine. I would suggest rounding up because it's always better to have overestimated than underestimated," Professor Summerfield explained.

"Professor, what happens if there is nothing listed for something? Maybe an extra piece of equipment or something necessary to run a business?" Fallon asked, leaning back in her chair with her pen in hand, waiting to write down an answer.

"Remember that this is not real life. It's hypothetical. It's okay if the amount is not exact. You can leave that part out if you cannot find an exact amount or price, but if you need to include it or you prefer to include it, just give an educated guess. I don't mean to just pick a number out of a hat but to do some research for something similar and factor in that number. For example, if you are opening a restaurant and you can't find the exact cost of aprons, you can look up uniforms or aprons for businesses. Whatever that price range is, you can factor that into your project," Professor Summerfield explained.

"So you just need approximate amounts for opening the business?" Keisha asked, uncertain.

"Exactly. Nobody needs to be worried about this project. This project is designed to make you think, not to stress you out beyond repair. I'm glad that so many of you are taking this seriously. I'm looking forward to seeing your final projects," Professor Summerfield replied optimistically.

"So what other ways can you fund a business?" Rowena asked attentively, waiting to write something down in her notebook.

"Well, there are few different ways. One is through investors. Another is through business loans. A third one is through grants. There are several other ways to raise capital, but I will be keeping it simple for your projects. All three options have both positive and negative aspects to them," Professor Summerfield explained.

"What do you mean? Is one better than the other?" Fallon asked curiously.

"Neither one is better nor worse. It's more of a preferential thing for the business. A smaller business might be able to get along suitably with a business loan, but a luxury hotel would probably do better with investors. It's really about the amount of capital that is needed. Does that answer your question?" Professor Summerfield asked.

"I think so, Professor. Thank you." Fallon lowered her head and made a quick note in her notebook.

"Okay, if nobody else has any other questions, you can break into your groups. I'm allowing you to get into groups earlier so you can correct your homework assignments that are due tonight. For those of you who don't need to correct your homework assignments, you can go straight to tonight's class assignment. Turn to page 37 in your textbook for more in-depth explanation of different types of raising capital for your business. If anyone has questions, I will be walking around handing out your graded homework assignments from last week," Professor Summerfield instructed.

Many of the students started to gather up their books and personal items to move into groups. Sally waved to Keisha and Noelle and moved to the other side of the classroom.

"Hey, long time no see," Sally teased. Keisha and Noelle turned their desks to face each other.

"I'm still working on memorizing your names, so I might call out some of your names to avoid handing them back to the wrong student," Professor Summerfield stated seriously. He lowered his eyes toward his leather briefcase to take out a pile of papers. Most of the students became too engrossed in their conversations to notice him walking around. He managed to remember Owen and Jeff and guessed that Orlando was the third male student. After that, their professor became a little unsure and started to call out the rest of the students' names. He walked toward Rowena's group.

"Are you Rowena?" Professor Summerfield asked, still not completely sure if he remembered her name correctly. She nodded.

"This is Fallon. She wasn't here the first week," Rowena answered in place of her cousin.

"Did you complete the assignment?" Professor Summerfield asked, looking through his pile of graded assignments.

"Yeah, but I'm handing it in with this week's assignment. I did get approval from you for my business idea. I chose to pretend to open a dog groomer. I love my dogs." Fallon laughed.

"I remember speaking with you before class tonight. Are you okay so far with everything?" Professor Summerfield asked, concerned.

"Yeah, I think so. Luckily, I only missed the first week, but if any questions come up, I'll be sure to ask. I don't want to fall behind in these assignments," Fallon replied, a little worried.

"Rowena can help you because she seems to have a pretty good grasp on everything. However, you can visit me during office hours or even ask me when class first begins or after class. In fact, I might start that next week, spending the first five or ten minutes on *lingering questions* or *clarifying confusion*. I should trademark those phrases," Professor Summerfield joked.

Fallon and Rowena nodded and laughed. At times, their professor was very knowledgeable and great at explaining, and at other times, he appeared to be more like a quirky game show host. Definitely a unique experience for the class.

Their professor continued to walk around calling out names and placing homework assignments down on the desks of the students. When he got to Noelle's group, he called out Sally and Keisha's names but seemed much more certain with Noelle. After he left, Sally and Keisha lifted up their papers.

"Oh yeah, I got a B+!" Keisha exclaimed.

Sally looked at hers. "Oh yeah, me too!" Sally exclaimed excitedly.

"This is great. We got B+s. I'm hoping for at least an A– after submitting corrections," Keisha said excitedly.

"What did you get, Noelle?" Sally asked curiously. Keisha looked over at her too.

Noelle sat still for a moment before lifting up the paper from her desk and had the most perplexed expression on her face.

"Noelle, what's wrong?" Keisha asked.

"I don't have a grade. It says, 'See me after class.'" Noelle's face became flushed as she started to believe that she was in over her head.

"Oh, I wouldn't worry about it. Maybe there was something in your answer that he wanted to ask you about before he gave you a grade. You're a good student and very serious. He seems like he gives the benefit of the doubt to his students." Sally tried to console her friend's worries.

Noelle tried to smile, but her face grew long from stress. If she wasn't able to get a job, she needed to at least perform very well in school, at least that was what Noelle believed.

"So did everyone get a graded assignment back? Good. Well, it's a quarter after eight. If anyone wants to leave early tonight, you can if you completed everything. If you need to stay longer to make corrections to your homework assignment, feel free to stay until the end of class. I'll be at my desk for anyone who has questions or concerns," Professor Summerfield said to the class while taking a seat back at the desk and opening one of his grade books looking like he was making adjustments to some of the grades. He made room at the end of the desk for students to drop off their homework assignments due that evening.

Several students looked up at the clock and began to throw their books into their bags and rushed up to the professors' desk to either ask questions or drop off their homework assignments. A few students remained seated discussing some business-related topics while completing their assignments.

Keisha looked around and then yawned. "I know we could or should stay longer to work on next week's assignment, but I'm tired, and I need to go home. I've been up since really early this morning. This commute is becoming too much," Keisha groaned.

"Hey, it's only a few more weeks of this semester, and then after next semester, it's time to graduate." Noelle nudged her to remain positive.

"Yeah, you're right. Right now, I need to try and catch up on sleep." Keisha yawned again while putting her desk back in a straight line and putting her books away in her bag.

"I'm going to head out early tonight too. I could use a little more sleep too," Sally replied, putting her desk back in the row and putting her books away in the bag.

"Are you coming?" Keisha and Sally asked as they walked toward the classroom door.

"No, I have to talk to the professor. Don't worry. I'll see you two on Thursday." Noelle waved to them as she slowly put her desk back in the row and packed up her books to put in her bag.

"See you Thursday!" Sally and Keisha yelled while walking out of the classroom door.

Noelle put on her sweater jacket and gently threw her schoolbag over her shoulder while holding her homework assignments in her hand—the one due that evening and the one that was ungraded. She waited behind a couple of students who asked quick questions to the professor. After they left, Noelle walked up to the professor to ask about her homework assignment.

"Professor?" Noelle asked.

"Noelle, right?" Professor Summerfield nodded his head as though he did remember her.

Noelle still felt it was strange that he seemed to remember her name and not a lot of her classmates. He remembered the guys in her class because there were only three, and he remembered Rowena, but she asked several questions each class. Noelle barely talked during class unless it was related to group work.

"I'm a little bit confused. Everyone else seemed to get a grade, and I got a 'See me.' That made me think I was back in elementary school and did really poorly. Am I lost because I don't feel lost." Noelle seemed perplexed.

"No, you are definitely not lost. In fact, that was probably one of the best homework assignments that I had read in a long time.

You do have a grade, which I must have forgotten to write down, but I wanted to ask you something." Professor Summerfield lowered his voice so that the other students would not hear the whole conversation.

Noelle's eyebrows raised as her eyes lowered. She was feeling both confused and doubtful of herself. "Did I pick a topic already chosen? Did I choose a bad topic? I mean, I thought a coffee shop was a pretty safe choice." Noelle was still a little bit perplexed.

"Your answer was very in depth, and usually, I don't see something so intricate unless it's from a current business owner or a potential business owner. Do you have a business, or have you considered it at some point?" Professor Summerfield asked in the same tone.

Noelle was taken aback; this was something she had never even thought about for a career. "No, not in any way. It might be a little over the top because I am kind of an overachiever, but I also worked in coffee shops for several years before recently becoming unemployed." Noelle chuckled lightly.

"I'm assuming from your response the part about becoming unemployed wasn't completely voluntary," Professor Summerfield surmised.

"You can say that." Noelle stopped it at that.

He nodded as though he might have understood more than she alluded to. "One of my longtime friends—he was also a client of mine—I consulted on his business plan before he started his business. He struggled with working several different types of jobs, and he would always say, 'Sometimes the best boss you can have is yourself.'" Professor Summerfield seemed to be trying to plant an idea in the back of Noelle's mind, but she was still not totally receptive.

"At least you don't have to worry about being fired. I mean, being fired after being self-employed means you must really stink at your job," Noelle joked.

Professor Summerfield couldn't help but crack a smile at her comment. "Do you have your homework assignment?" he asked while taking out a purple gel ink pen. Noelle nodded her head and handed him the ungraded assignment while she reached over and placed her current homework assignment in the pile on the desk with the rest of the students' assignments. He quickly wrote a large grade on top of the assignment before handing it back to her.

Noelle's mouth almost dropped to the floor. "An A+? I didn't know that college professors give those grades out." Noelle marveled as she picked it off his desk and looked at it more thoroughly.

"Yes, some do. It doesn't really count any more than an A, but I like to use them because it shows exceptional work. I rarely use them, but this assignment…well, it deserved it. I am so really looking forward to reading the rest of your assignments and seeing it all come together for your final project. Do you have a name yet for your coffee shop?" Professor Summerfield asked.

Noelle shook her head. "I really didn't think too much about it, but the couple of names I have thought of so far haven't really stuck yet. I think I would rather spend the time just working on the actual development of the business than worrying about what to call it. Do I need a name yet?" Noelle asked, concerned.

"No, you don't need a name until…I think it's week 7 or 8. I have switched a couple of weeks around to make it easier for everyone. I just can't remember exactly because I was playing around with them for a couple of semesters, but it should be listed in your syllabus," Professor Summerfield reassured her.

Noelle nodded and smiled. "Thank you, Professor. Have a great weekend. See you next week." Noelle smiled as she placed her now graded assignment in her schoolbag. She quickly walked out of the classroom, making a left down the dimly lit hallway leading toward the back of the building and out toward the parking lots.

On the walk toward her car, she kept getting this reoccurring idea pop up in her head of starting her own business. Whenever she would seriously start to think about it, it just seemed so ridiculous that she had to erase the thought. As she got to her car and leaned against the driver's side door, she pondered for a moment about being a business owner. Then she quickly shook her head and started laughing before getting into her car to hurry up and drive home.

Chapter 9

Noelle reached behind to tie her apron a little bit tighter. This was the third time that day the apron came untied. It had happened at least a dozen times this past week alone. It was a minor problem, which she didn't think was worth complaining about, but it seemed to be one of many minor issues that she had been dealing with since she first was hired. Sure, Noelle was thrilled that she finally found a job, especially one that was in a convenient location and in a field that she knew very well, but something still felt off, almost like it might not be the right place for her. When she first met Selby and started working with her, things were great, but then the atmosphere started to change. Noelle initially thought it was the strain of constantly being understaffed, but she also worked as a manager and never reacted in the same way. There was a growing tension between her and Selby partly because of the stressful environment but also because every single suggestion fell on deaf ears. Even though she followed all safety procedures carefully, because they weren't exactly the way Selby instructed them to be followed, it was considered "deliberate disobedience." Noelle almost felt like she was living through a sort of déjà vu, but she consistently tried to ignore it because she still believed this job was her saving grace. It was a gift, and she wasn't going to look a gift horse in the mouth.

Noelle saw that there was a big milk spill on the counter and some spilled coffee near the drain. She picked up a small red rag out of a small red bucket of sanitizer under the counter to clean up and sanitize the mess. After cleaning one side, she went to turn around and was pleasantly surprised to see one of her classmates stop by.

"Sally!" Noelle called out happily but a little surprised. She almost never saw someone she knew at work.

"Noelle, I didn't know that you worked here. I rarely come in here, but if I knew, I would have tried to stop by more often to say hi." Sally beamed as her blondish high ponytail swayed back and forth.

"Yeah, I've only been here a couple of weeks. I was just looking for something part-time that was flexible around my class schedule and convenient to get to, and surprisingly, I was able to find this job right on campus. I work every Friday and Saturday, with sometimes a Monday or Wednesday. If I come in on a Tuesday or Thursday, it would probably be to fill in for someone. What are you doing here on a Friday? Were you at the library?" Noelle asked curiously.

"No, I thought about going to the library, but I spent a couple of hours there on Tuesday before class, and I think it's my limit for the week." Sally laughed. "Actually, I'm waiting for Jimmy to get out of class. He's still an undergraduate and has classes five days a week."

"Anything special planned with Jimmy?" Noelle asked seemingly interested.

"Well, I think Jimmy wants to go out to dinner, but I really don't want to go anywhere. I worked today, and I'm tired. I would be thrilled to order a pizza and just watch a movie at home. It's so great that he only lives down the street from me." Sally still beamed despite being visibly exhausted.

"That's amazing that you live so close. Was that planned?" Noelle asked curiously.

Sally laughed. "No, it was completely by chance. After I started college, my parents decided it was time to move to New Mexico as they were both able to retire early. I didn't want to go with them, so I moved in with my sister Kiersten. She has her own home and has an extra room. It really was perfect timing because her hours had been cut right before, so with my paycheck, I was able to help her cover all the bills. One evening after dinner, I went to walk my sister's dog, and Jimmy happened to be there walking his dog. He was so shy and quiet that he barely even made eye contact. I had to try to be a little more direct, which did work because he eventually asked for my phone number. The rest is history." Sally was still smiling.

"That's a great story...kind of gives me hope. I have some of the worst luck." Noelle started to feel sorry for herself.

"Noelle, don't give up. I didn't have the best luck either, and I was about to give up right before I met Jimmy. Now I'm glad I hung in there. I couldn't have asked for a better guy. If it can happen to me, it can happen to you too," Sally said encouragingly.

Noelle nodded, but she didn't want to continue with that conversation, so she changed the topic. "How is everything else going?" Noelle asked curiously.

"Ask me closer to midterms," Sally joked.

Noelle cracked a smile. "Is that good or bad?" Noelle asked, taking her friend's response a little too seriously.

"It's not bad. Financial management seems to be a little bit clearer cut but is more challenging. Entrepreneurship is a little more confusing but much more engaging, and he's kind of a comedian. I think Jeff makes it easier for him some days though," Sally joked.

"I think Jeff and Owen like to try and annoy the professor, but he's always one step ahead," Noelle added.

"But we should definitely have a study group for at least financial management. I don't think there's much you can do for the other class, but financial management is hard," Sally groaned.

"Yeah, I was talking to Keisha about that. She's completely on board with a study group. We can even invite other students," Noelle replied calmly.

"Please not Rowena though. Her cousin seems okay, but Rowena tries to act like the teacher's pet, and besides that, she was gloating that she got an A on the first and second homework assignments. She's trying to make herself look like an expert." Sally looked disgusted.

Noelle felt kind of in between because she was casually friends with Rowena but definitely understood what Sally was saying.

Rowena always had to get the best grade in the class and didn't allow others to forget that fact.

"I doubt that Rowena would want to be in a study group anyway, but she might be jumping ahead a little bit. There might be other students who are doing as well or better in the class than her. Some students don't like to share their grades with everyone on the planet," Noelle replied while tensing up her eyebrows.

"That's what I think too," Sally agreed.

Noelle looked around and saw her boss in the background and knew she needed to change the conversation before she got into another disagreement at work about her behavior. "So are you more of a tea drinker or a coffee drinker?" Noelle asked, moving toward the side to give Sally room to look at all the coffee flavors.

Sally stood there with her arms crossed, and her eyes focused very intently on all the different labels. It seemed to be a very difficult decision. "I like both. I am probably more of a tea drinker, but I do like coffee. I especially like flavored coffees," Sally shared while still looking seriously at all the flavors.

"Well, we have three flavors. There is French vanilla, which is probably the most popular; hazelnut, which is also common; and then the autumn blend. I'm not sure what's in it, but some have said it tastes and smells like apple cinnamon," Noelle explained.

"I think I will try a medium autumn blend. Do you have regular creamer? If not, regular milk is okay. I don't really like skim milk. I'll drink 1 percent because that's all that my sister likes using," Sally replied quickly while grabbing a medium-sized cup and filling it with the autumn blend and then reaching over for the regular half-and-half. She placed a lid on her coffee cup and was about to continue their friendly conversation before Selby leaned over the counter and interrupted them.

"Noelle, this is not a social gathering. This is your job! I have asked you to refill the dairy case because it was running low." Selby sounded angry.

Noelle turned to face her boss. "I already checked to make sure the dairy case was full. I even placed an extra half-and-half in there because it's so popular and we run out quicker. I double-checked to make sure that the temperature was correctly set to prevent illness. In addition, I sanitized all the counters and made two pots of fresh coffee," Noelle replied with an unfazed expression. Sally could feel the tension.

"That's not what I told you to do. Even if I did, you did it out of order. Remember, there is a certain protocol to follow with everything!" Selby's eyes became wild.

Sally started to feel very uncomfortable and tried to calmly slip away. "I'll see you in class next week. Nice to see you," Sally whispered as she picked up her coffee and muffin to walk toward the register to pay for them before leaving the cafeteria. Sally glanced over at Selby once more and looked away, feeling sorry for Noelle to be working with her.

"Maybe now you'll do what I told you to do. This is the biggest problem here…all the college kids always socializing with the customers. You have a job to do. You're not paid to socialize. You're paid to work!" Selby yelled.

Noelle was visibly losing her patience but still maintained her composure by biting her tongue from saying something she would later regret. "Yes, ma'am," Noelle replied back before mumbling under her breath. "Now I understand why you can't keep anyone here for longer than a couple of weeks."

"What did you say?" Selby demanded, knowing that Noelle had said something after her initial comment.

Noelle was trying to keep her mouth shut, but she was really struggling to keep it bottled up any longer. "I said I understand why nobody wants to stay here and work for you. You criticize everything I do, and even worse, you talk down to me as though I don't know what I am doing. I may not be a manager, but I am capable of taking care of my responsibilities. If I wasn't, then why did you hire me?" Noelle asked, her eyes narrowing as her frustration was beginning to mount.

"You better watch yourself," Selby warned her.

Noelle gave her a stern look back. "Watch what? What am I saying? I'm telling you the truth. I mean, since you hired me, you are still short-staffed as one of the other employees quit last week. So what are you going to do, give me another crappy job to do as punishment? Clean out the coffeepots again? Which I already did twice. Or throw out all the heavy garbage with coffee grinds by myself again? If I was manager, I would never treat my employees like you do. You make a simple job feel like a torturous punishment." Noelle was becoming annoyed.

Selby's face changed rapidly. She was no longer annoyed; she was just plain angry. "Pack up for today. Get out. You're done," Selby demanded.

Noelle took off her apron and threw it on the counter. "That's fine." Noelle didn't seem bothered by being asked to leave.

As Noelle walked around the counter to grab her purse and put her apron on the hook, Selby confronted her. "Clock out today and leave. Won't need you tomorrow or any day next week either," Selby started.

Noelle stood there a little bewildered. "Are you firing me?" Noelle asked, being caught off guard.

"Yeah, I really had high hopes for you. You were cordial and a good worker the first couple of days, and then you slacked off. Now you refuse to do any of the work that I tell you to do, and you have made my job more difficult. I don't need the additional stress, and you need a job that apparently requires no guidelines or restrictions. It's just so hard to find good employees these days. Instead, I get stuck with employees like you!" Selby yelled before she turned around and walked into her office, slamming the door shut.

Noelle took her purse, threw it over her shoulder, and stormed out of the small cafeteria. Her face was so red she couldn't see anything around her until she got several feet away from the entrance of the cafeteria. That was when it became obvious that she was back in the same position she was in over a month ago. However, this time, it felt much worse. Now she really would be blacklisted from being hired to work as a manager or even a barista at another coffee shop.

Noelle slouched up against the wall of the student union near a magazine rack and sighed loud enough for a few students walking by to turn their heads. She paid them no attention. Noelle pulled on her long-sleeved shirt past her wrist and fell down to the floor with her head resting on her knees. Now Noelle needed to think of something else. There was no more applying to every job out there because she tried that, and nobody hired her except for a part-time job, which made her life miserable from the first day of working.

So many thoughts circled around her head, from warnings and suggestions from friends and family and even a couple of strangers who recommended taking the semester off to just focus on school. Noelle couldn't allow that to happen because she was a workaholic, an overachiever, and couldn't just sit around and do nothing. The idea of taking just two classes this semester made her feel like she was accomplishing nothing. Noelle started the program part-time because she was working full-time and knew that would work out best for her, but now things had changed, and it was too late to switch to full-time status. Even if she was allowed to, the other two classes she needed weren't available until the spring semester when she was set to graduate. Noelle now needed to face the real possibility of being backed into a corner that she couldn't get out of so easily by trying to plan or stick to some safe and normal routine. She was overqualified in one field, while in other fields, she was not trained at all or was severely underqualified. She felt like she finally hit a fork in the road. The one path was familiar and a more play-it-safe planned route. The other was completely unfamiliar and out-of-the-box territory—two things that made her feel both anxious and very uncomfortable. She had the choice to either continue to follow through with the same goals and same philosophy as before or to try something completely new and totally outside her comfort zone. It had to be something that she couldn't actually plan out and also for her to boldly step in and move forward without looking back.

For the first time in Noelle's life, all the planning in the world wasn't going to fix her situation, but stepping out in faith and taking a risk just might.

Chapter 10

Noelle zipped up her hooded pink sweater jacket all the way up to her chin and pulled the hood over her ears. She couldn't believe the powerful arctic breeze sweeping across campus that Saturday morning. It made it feel more like the end of October instead of late September. She tried to walk against the wind but felt like she kept getting pushed back. However that didn't deter her in the least, it only made her want to fight harder to continue walking ahead. Eventually, once she got onto campus, the wind seemed to ease up a little bit, but the bitterness in the air seemed to linger. Noelle was thrilled that the library wasn't that far of a walk from the parking lot because she was starting to form goosebumps on her arms from the cold. As she approached the entrance of the library, she took off her hood and reached up to try and tighten her ponytail. Noelle didn't have a mirror, but she still didn't want to seem like she just rolled out of bed. Slowly walking through the front doors, she could see the library was nearly empty. She looked around and barely saw any students and only a few staff members. Noelle shrugged as she knew most students did not want to get up early on a Saturday to go to the library, at least not this early in the semester. She walked toward the reference desk where she saw a tall, slender female with dark hair and olive complexion with a bright, friendly smile.

"Good morning, I'm Esma. Can I help you?" Esma, a young library assistant, asked.

"Esma, that's a pretty name…sounds unique," Noelle commented before realizing how distracted and off topic she was. She would rarely ask immaterial questions or make random comments like that unless she was majorly sleep-deprived or didn't get enough of her morning coffee.

"Thank you kindly. Not many people ask. It's Turkish. How can I help you today?" Esma replied with a polite smile.

"I need some help with research for a class I'm taking. It's BUS 730," Noelle started to explain.

Esma nodded as though it sounded familiar. "Would this happen to be Professor Summerfield's class? Every semester, there are always a few students who come in here looking for information about business ownership, I think. I didn't realize there were so many different types of businesses to own," Esma replied inquisitively.

"Yes, it is, and that's why I'm here. I need information about opening a business. I need help with both business ownership and a specific type of business," Noelle replied, trying to remain hopeful that Esma could actually help her with her project.

"I will check on the computer for any reference books. Do you have a specific business, or are you still researching that part?" Esma asked as she frantically typed something into the reference computer.

"I was looking at food services or delis or even coffeehouses. I figured there might not be one specific book or chapter about that but maybe a combination?" Noelle was trying to make it sound like she was well versed in business.

Esma looked attentively at the computer screen before glancing up at Noelle. "Well, there's a reference book for business ownership. You can't check that out, but you can make photocopies. It looks like there is one book that might be available to borrow, but I'm not sure if it's in the library or not because its status isn't listed. It's coffee and beverage businesses." Esma glanced up from the computer screen at Noelle.

"Wow, that sounds great. If you can find it, I want to borrow it." Noelle's eyes widened.

"Okay, I will go look for these for you. In the meanwhile, you can take a seat at the public computers and do a search for yourself.

Right now, only printers C and D are working. You should be able to use any computer, but you might need to walk a little further to get what you printed out," Esma explained while multitasking looking for a pen and paper and quickly jotting down the information.

"Okay, thank you," Noelle said quickly while turning around to walk toward the public computers. Before Noelle could blink, Esma had already disappeared from behind the reference desk. She wasn't sure if she was moving extra slow that morning or if Esma was moving extra fast. Noelle shrugged it off as being overtired and not having enough coffee that morning and started to walk over toward the computers, sitting down at the third computer in the first row. There was nobody else sitting in that row of computers, but Noelle figured the extra empty seat could be for Esma if she actually was able to find anything.

Noelle sat down and immediately unzipped her jacket to take it off. She didn't know how long she would be in the library but knew it was starting to feel warm inside, and the computer was only going to amplify that feeling. She reached over to turn on her computer, which seemed to take forever just for the screen to light up. She was hoping it wasn't broken but remembered that some of the computers could be very slow. What usually took around five minutes to fully turn on could feel more like five years. In the meantime, Noelle looked around at the back rows to see who else was at the library that morning. In the row behind her, there was a student trying very hard to solve some chemistry homework, looking fiercely between the computer screen and his notebook. At the other end of the row, a girl looked to be researching for a project as she kept jotting down notes, typing on the computer, and running up to get piles of papers being printed out.

After several minutes, Noelle looked back at her computer screen and quickly logged on and clicked the Internet icon to start her search. Initially, Noelle convinced herself that she was doing research for her project alone, but the more and more information she began to find and read, the more she realized there was a pull toward the very wild idea of being a business owner. Every so often,

Noelle would seriously consider it and then start laughing to herself at the absurdity of it.

For someone who was adamantly against ever opening a business for herself, the doubts that kept that idea on the back burner started to fade away. Noelle couldn't explain it, but no matter how much she tried to rationalize the stupidity or the insanity of making a huge leap like that, especially at this point in her life, there was something constantly popping up that would start pushing her toward business ownership again. The only idea that made her laugh was something that Valerie used to say all the time. *At least when you own your own business, you can't fire yourself, because if you fire yourself from your own business, you are a lost cause.* Noelle started to giggle quietly to herself while Esma surprised her out of nowhere. Noelle shook the laughter out of her system so she wouldn't be looked at as weird.

"Excuse me. I found two reference books—this book that was not in the system and another book that I have never seen before that said it wasn't checked in. I think I'm going to have to go over inventory with Mrs. Chambers," Esma replied, placing the books on the table in between the second and third computers.

"Mrs. Chambers?" Noelle asked, looking confused.

"Mrs. Chambers is the head librarian." Esma laughed.

"Oh, I think it's too early on a Saturday, or maybe I didn't have enough coffee this morning. I feel like I'm being rude. I'm Noelle," Noelle replied, starting to look frazzled.

"Noelle, it's a little too early in the semester to be stressed. At least wait until midterms," Esma joked.

"I'm going to try. Oh, so I was able to find some stuff online too. I'm glad you were able to find those books," Noelle replied, looking relieved.

"Yeah, two of the books you could take out, but the other two, the reference books, you would need to make photocopies. But since there really is no one here and it's early in the semester, if you don't need a lot, I'll make the photocopies for you," Esma replied kindly.

"Oh, thank you so much. No, I probably only need a few pages. I really appreciate it," Noelle said appreciatively.

"No problem. I'll take these two books with me to the front, and you can look over these other two books and decide what you want photocopied," Esma replied quickly while getting up.

Noelle nodded and went to open up the books to the table of contents. She didn't really want to look through the entire books, so she just quickly took two pieces of paper and marked off the two chapters she wanted to be photocopied. Noelle made sure she printed all the information that she found online. She quickly logged off the computer and then picked up her schoolbag and the two reference books before walking over to printer C to pick up the pages of information she printed out. She double-checked to make sure all the papers were from her computer, and she tossed them into her schoolbag. She walked toward the reference desk, placing the two books on the counter.

"I marked off the two chapters that I need photocopied. They're only a few pages each chapter. Hope that's not too many pages." Noelle looked a little worried as she felt like she was taking advantage of Esma's kindness.

"That's fine, as long as they aren't that long. Okay, so you can sign these two cards while I go in the back to make some copies," Esma replied while walking into a small back room.

Noelle couldn't really see Esma, but she heard the laser and saw the bright lights from the photocopier reflecting off part of the door and the back wall of the small backroom. She shifted her focus onto one of the books she was going to borrow. She was really amazed that an entire book was written on opening a beverage shop with a couple of chapters specially dedicated to coffee. Noelle became pretty engrossed in the beginning of the chapter when she heard a small pile of black-and-white photocopied papers placed in front of her. She was visibly startled and lost her place in the book because she wasn't expecting Esma to be back that quickly.

"That was pretty fast," Noelle said, a little surprised. Esma nodded while pushing the two books she just borrowed toward Noelle's end of the desk.

"Yes, you should be all set. Just remember to bring them back in two weeks. I think you are eligible to check them out again, but just double-check in a couple of weeks. Is there anything else you need?" Esma asked, still pretty chipper.

Noelle shook her head slowly. "Thank you so much for all your help. Have a great rest of your weekend." Noelle smiled as she placed both books in her bag and walked out of the front entrance of the library.

Even though Noelle wasn't in the library for that long, she noticed what a huge change in the weather from when she first arrived. It was extremely brisk, breezy, and overcast, and now it was calm, warm, and beautiful. Although she had no plans on staying on campus, she felt too energized to just go home and hang out in her room. Noelle looked down at her watch and saw it was only eleven thirty. She decided to take a seat in one of the buildings but wanted to stay clear of the student union for fear of bumping into her now ex-manager. She looked around at the different buildings within walking distance and decided to go over to Rutherford Hall.

Rutherford Hall was a building she hadn't been in since she was finishing her undergraduate, but she remembered that there was a small lounge and vending machines nearby. The vending machines seemed like a good idea because she was getting a little bit hungry as she hadn't eaten much for breakfast that morning except a muffin and some coffee. Noelle pulled open one of the doors at the front entrance, which led right toward the small room with vending machines on the left and the entrance to the lounge just a little further up on the same side. She took out a few dollars from her pocket, scanning the limited selections in the vending machines, and finally deciding on a bottle of fruit punch and two bags of pretzels, placing the snacks in her bag while she walked into the lounge. There was a small couch and a bench and several chairs and tables. There wasn't much room for many students, but it was more than enough room for a couple of small groups to work on projects or study for an exam. Noelle stood in the doorway for a moment looking around at where the best place to sit was. She saw a small table with a chair near the corner of the room. Noelle thought it was perfect because she didn't need much room to work and didn't want to have to share her workspace with anyone else. It wasn't until after sitting down did she realize just how close her back was up against the wall. There was a bit of irony attached to that because it wasn't just literally sitting in a chair cramped up in a corner of a room but also metaphorically because her circumstances were pushing her to make a drastic, out-of-the-box decision. If she wanted anything to change, a bold decision might be the only option for her—something outside her comfort zone.

Noelle took out her bottle of fruit punch and a neon pink highlighter with her small pile of photocopied papers. She wasn't planning on writing a paper or even going any further about the crazy idea of opening a business, but she wanted to get a head start on next week's assignment. She wasn't completely sure if it was accurate because her professor said he switched a couple of weeks around, but the following week was supposed to be the location for the business. One thing she did remember from one of her other business classes was the importance of location. She opened up the bottle of fruit punch and took a drink before she started to read through some of the material. Noelle became so focused on what she was reading that she tuned everything else out. She didn't even realize when a small group of students walked into the room. They sat down pretty quietly but then started a conversation, which seemed to get louder with each comment.

"I really wish there was somewhere else to go on campus to study," the one girl with pink streaks commented, laying her head down on her arm resting on the table.

"Come on, Kara, this is the best place for us to go on campus. I mean, at least we can eat here," the guy replied.

"Ganesh, all you care about is eating," Kara complained.

Ganesh laughed. "So? Food is good. It helps the brain work better," Ganesh argued.

Noelle was trying not to pay attention to their conversation, but it was becoming harder and harder to focus on what she was doing. She continued to pretend like she was highlighting parts of her photocopies.

"You have not changed since high school," replied the other girl with short mousy-brown hair.

"Yes, I have, Jocelyne. I grew a few extra inches and maybe added a couple of extra pounds." Ganesh laughed. Both girls rolled their eyes and groaned.

"Okay, are we going to try and get some work done? That project for history class is due in a couple of weeks," Jocelyne asked, becoming anxious.

"Yeah, but first, allow me to go to the vending machines. I can't focus if all I'm thinking about is eating. Anyone want anything?" Ganesh asked while getting up from his chair and walking out the door toward the vending machines. Jocelyne and Kara started talking to each other but much quieter, so Noelle couldn't really hear what they were saying.

A few minutes later, Ganesh walked back into the room with a long look on his face and a small bag of chips in his hand.

"What's wrong?" Kara asked, concerned.

"This is all that's left. Isn't it too early for vending machines to be out of food?" Ganesh looked frustrated.

"The cafeteria has a much larger selection of food than the vending machines," Jocelyne suggested.

"Yeah, but it's the weekend, and the tables will probably be a mess. That's how I got a huge jelly stain on my notebook. The only benefit was, I was able to use it as a part of my Halloween costume last year. I scared a few people. I wish we had a place to go that was close to campus where we could get coffee and was opened late. Even better if they served food too," Ganesh complained while he slouched back in his chair.

"Yeah, I can definitely go for more coffee, and food is never a bad idea, at least some snacks. I've been up since six thirty this morning. I love this school, but the commute is really getting to me," Kara whined.

"How far is your commute?" Jocelyne asked.

"Well, it's like forty minutes without traffic, but with traffic, it's so much longer, almost like a nightmare." Kara sighed.

"You know, you can always apply to live at the dorm," Jocelyne suggested.

"Yeah, I was trying to save money, but I think next year, I'm going to apply so I can stay my last two years of undergraduate on campus," Kara replied calmly.

"That's if you get out in four years," Ganesh teased.

"Yeah, well, I'm a little more motivated than you!" Kara yelled back.

"I'm motivated. I just like to take the slower route. But if my parents heard that…" Ganesh flinched.

"Yours and mine both." Jocelyne laughed nervously.

"Hey, why don't we ask this young woman what she thinks? It's always good to get an outsider's opinion," Ganesh suggested, referring to Noelle.

Noelle's ears became alerted as she had a feeling he was talking about her.

"We can't go out and annoy strangers. Besides, she looks very busy!" Kara shouted at him.

"She's not a stranger. She's a fellow student. Maybe even a classmate somewhere. We might have already met somewhere else on campus and don't remember it," Ganesh suggested.

Noelle couldn't help but crack a smile but pretended not to hear anything.

"Excuse me. My name is Ganesh, and these are my friends, Kara and Jocelyne. Would you mind giving us your opinion about something?" Ganesh asked politely.

Noelle turned toward the three of them and nodded. "Hi, I'm Noelle…um…okay?" Noelle replied hesitantly.

"So do you think there are enough suitable places around campus to study that are also opened late enough and have the option to serve food and drinks? Or do you think there should be somewhere outside of campus that offers all those services?" Ganesh asked attentively.

Noelle looked at them strangely. "Well, the campus is usually open until ten or eleven p.m. You can go to one of the cafeterias to grab some food or something to drink. And if it's too late, there are always vending machines. Vending machines don't close…only the buildings when campus closes," Noelle replied succinctly.

Ganesh's eyes widened, and he nodded. "Well, yeah, but remember, the cafeterias on campus close earlier. Have you ever had a late class on the weekend? There's practically no place to get any type of food on campus except for vending machines. Trust me, vending machine food is something, but it does not supplement a real meal, and there are no coffee vending machines," Ganesh responded seriously.

Noelle sat there for a moment and really thought about what he said. It was true. She remembered several times during her undergraduate that she needed to eat a really late dinner after class or she had to veg out on "vending machine cuisine." She could sympathize with Ganesh and his friends as she remembered feeling the same way, but right now she had to push all of that to the back of her mind as there were much more important issues that needed her attention.

"Are you talking about a place off campus that would serve coffee and maybe snacks? Aren't there other places around here that would offer those things?" Noelle asked nonchalantly.

Ganesh looked at her seriously. "There are a few places, mainly fast food, that we can stop at and get something to eat, but there is no place to study or work on projects. Even if we chose a diner, which has the room to study, it's too noisy in there. We need a place that serves caffeinated beverages but also supplies a place where we could get a late snack or maybe a light dinner that has the space for studying and is quiet enough to concentrate on schoolwork. Unfortunately, there is really no place around here like that." Ganesh's face filled with disappointment.

"A coffee shop or even a tea shop would be perfect for me because I live far away, and the commute is rough. It's easier for me to stay longer on days that I have class than to come back and forth like five days a week. I also prefer to travel after rush hours," Kara explained.

"Where do you live, if you don't mind me asking?" Noelle asked curiously.

"Oh, Bleu River," Kara replied, propping up the back of her head by her right arm. She was angled to be able to see Noelle's face clearly.

"I know Bleu River. Had a couple of classmates in my undergrad from there. That's quite a commute. One of them tried commuting, and the other moved into the dorm freshman year," Noelle recalled.

"Yeah, that's my goal next year. I thought the commute would work out if I had all my classes on two or three days, but it's exhausting. That's why it would be great to have somewhere other than campus to go study or work on group projects," Kara explained.

Noelle nodded her head as though she completely understood. "You know, come to think about it. I heard the same complaint when I was an undergraduate. Not saying that there weren't places to go to or that campus was completely unaccommodating, but sometimes things run later than campus is open until, or there is a rush to get everything done. It's not always convenient to go over to other classmates' houses, because in college, students attend from different parts of the state. I didn't think too much about it because of my work schedule, but you are right. There should be an alternative," Noelle agreed.

"I know this is totally random, but I really like your name. It reminds me of the holidays, and Christmas is one of my favorite times of the year." Jocelyne smiled.

Noelle smiled sheepishly. "Thanks, but it's not always my favorite. I think I've heard way too many jokes over the years about my name and Christmas carols," Noelle replied a little bitterly.

"Don't listen to anyone else. I'm sure Christmas is an extra special time of year for you. Maybe you'll get some Christmas miracle this year," Jocelyne said completely out of the blue.

Noelle wouldn't have minded a breakthrough or a miracle. In fact, she would welcome it, but she really didn't want to wait three months for it to happen. She was feeling impatient. Noelle noticed Kara started to get up from her chair and pull her purse over her shoulder. Jocelyne followed her.

"Well, Noelle, it was a pleasure to have met you. I hope that we can bump into you around the campus sometime in the future. Maybe there will be a fun place to hang out outside campus by then." Ganesh smiled and waved as he picked up his empty potato chip bag and walked out of the lounge. Kara and Jocelyne waved and smiled as they followed their friend out of the study lounge. Noelle nodded her head as she watched the three of them leave.

For a brief moment, Noelle seriously considered the idea of opening up her own business. She understood how the students felt because she was and still is one of them. She also understood the coffee shop business inside and out, but it was one thing to work in someone else's business and something totally different to open up and run your own.

Chapter 11

Noelle arrived a little before two in the afternoon at Fairlight Oakes Realtors. As she pulled into the parking lot, the sky appeared overcast, leaving a feeling of gloominess in the air—a feeling that she had become very familiar with recently. She pulled up toward the building and parked adjacent to the front entrance. She knew that her appointment wasn't for another ten or fifteen minutes, but it didn't matter. It would give her some more time to really think about what she was doing there. She had convinced herself that this was the best way to help choose a location for her business project. Although Professor Summerfield didn't explicitly say to go and start looking at physical properties, he didn't say that there was anything wrong with it either. For some reason, Noelle felt she needed to go above and beyond for this class. She started convincing herself it was for her grades as she received A+s on the first three assignments. She knew that wouldn't continue, but the extra work for the better grade did tie in with her overachieving nature and wanting to be the best student she could be. Noelle thought that the better the grades, the better the distinction at graduation and possibly the better job after graduation. But was this really about getting the best grades and having an excellent GPA, or was it a distraction from openly pursuing a new and unexplored direction? Thoughts would occasionally circle around her mind about the distant possibility of opening a business, but she would always quickly dismiss them and place her focus back on something else, such as schoolwork or even finding another job. Although nothing had worked out until this point with finding a job, Noelle was now okay to be unemployed for at least the rest of this semester. She would rather be unemployed than work in another toxic work environment.

Throughout the whole process, no matter how much she tried to convince herself this was only for a project, a part of her would continue to resort back toward the idea of starting a business. It seemed completely impractical and unreasonable, especially since she was still in school and barely had enough in savings to take on that type of venture on her own. Despite how much Noelle would try to convince herself that this wasn't for her, a part of her kept drifting back toward that direction. It kind of worked in Noelle's favor that the several properties she had already seen with the realtor were not good choices. Some were too big; others too small. Some were way too expensive, while others had no parking and needed too many repairs. Factoring in all that for her project made her think that this whole idea of opening a business for real stemmed from a sense of boredom about having no job or social life outside school. She brushed it off as though these signs were demonstrating the whole concept was ridiculous, and this was all for her school project. Noelle tilted her head back and closed her eyes to take a short nap while she waited for the realtor to show up. She barely had closed her eyes before hearing a loud tapping on her window. She looked up and reached over to roll down the driver's-side window.

"Hi, Noelle, how are you doing? I'm sorry nothing has really worked out so far, but thanks for agreeing to not throw in the towel just yet," Yvonne replied with a bright smile in her warm Caribbean accent. She wore a sky-blue pantsuit with matching sky-blue heels, a white blouse, and a matching scarf.

Noelle shrugged her shoulders. "Oh, it's no problem. I know that when some people are searching for houses, it could take weeks or even months. I'm patient, just trying to go with the flow." Noelle pretended to not worry about anything. A part of her felt like she was wasting time, while another part of her thought it was a good learning experience. A sense of ambivalence kept following her around everywhere.

"Well, that's a great attitude. I mean, some clients would be so upset at this point. Sometimes I think it's a little bit of fate or luck for things to work out at just the right time," Yvonne replied softly.

Noelle froze for a moment as one of her friends had mentioned perfect timing, and for some reason, that really struck her hard. She tried to hide her shock. "Yeah, timing is everything," Noelle muttered out with a small smile.

"So there is one more listing I would like to show you. It's not too far, so you can just follow me. I know you said you have somewhere to go later on this afternoon," Yvonne replied.

Noelle nodded as she had remembered telling the small lie to give her a sort of escape route if things didn't work out too well and to help avoid her being pushed into signing a lease. Although she really couldn't imagine Yvonne acting like that, Noelle held everyone and everything at this point with a healthy dose of skepticism. The whole idea was to call up a realtor for educational purposes *only* and nothing more.

"So here is the address just in case you lose me while we're driving. It shouldn't take more than ten or fifteen minutes to get there," Yvonne replied, smiling.

Noelle nodded as she watched Yvonne walk back toward her bluish-gray luxury sedan. She buckled her seat belt and turned on her car to be ready to follow Yvonne out of the parking lot. Noelle didn't look at the address on the paper, but as they started driving, the roads became very familiar to her. She even knew some of the street names and intersections, but Noelle still couldn't figure out where they were going. Yvonne put her right signal on as they were approaching a wide driveway nearly surrounded by various trees and shrubbery on both sides of the driveway. Noelle followed Yvonne's car into the parking lot and what looked to be an old abandoned strip mall. Noelle parked her car, grabbed her purse, and quickly got out of her car. She reached into her purse to put her phone on silent mode so it wouldn't distract her. Nobody knew where she was or what she was doing, so she wouldn't be inundated with questions or comments from anyone. She walked up to the front of the building. Yvonne got out a couple of minutes later and met her at the front door.

"Okay, so this is in a residential area, which I think is one of your requests. There are a couple of colleges in both directions. I'm not sure how far, but no more than a few miles, and I think there are a couple of high schools down the street. One is public, and the other one is private…maybe a Christian academy. It's a very quiet area. Main Street doesn't get very busy, except maybe around rush hour, when people are driving home, but think about it, where isn't it busy during rush hour?" Yvonne asked, trying to build this place up.

Noelle didn't recognize anything, but she couldn't shake this feeling of déjà vu, almost like she had been there before. "Is this an old mini mall?" Noelle asked while Yvonne took out the keys for the store to open up the front door.

"It used to be a small strip mall…mini mall, but the stores started to close up starting in the early '90s. This store was actually the last to close," Yvonne replied while finding the right key and opening up the front door.

Noelle walked through the doorway first as Yvonne removed the key from the lock. It looked huge inside, much bigger than how it appeared from the outside, but it was so filthy. There was at least an inch of dust on the floor, and everything was either covered in an old sheet or exposed and full of dust and cobwebs.

"Someone forgot to pay the cleaning lady," Noelle muttered out loud.

Yvonne laughed out loud but secretly bit her lip as it didn't seem to be making the impression that she had hoped it would. Yvonne looked around the wall for the light switch and turned it on. Immediately there was a flicker. Noelle tensed up thinking something bad would happen, while Yvonne stood there very relaxed. After a couple of seconds, the lights went on, even though they were all dim.

"What is this place?" Noelle looked around, both disgusted and yet curious.

"Well, the listing has it as a luncheonette that closed around early 2000. It opened in the mid-1970s. I think 1976 to be exact, but I would need to double-check that at the office," Yvonne replied, allowing Noelle to look around and let everything sink in.

Despite looking filthy and uninhabitable at this point, Noelle could see some potential. It reminded her of some of the aspects of her previous jobs working in coffee shops, but this was better. She couldn't explain it, but there was something different about this place, which was making it stand out to her. "Why did the business close? How is the business environment around here?" Noelle asked, looking seriously at Yvonne.

"This area is unique because it is near residential areas, but this is zoned for businesses. So a lot of the customers that you would be getting would be from around this area. However, you can still get customers who travel through town or work around the area too. There are a lot of younger children…well, adolescents who could come in here and could get something to drink. This would be ideal for some college students," Yvonne suggested.

Noelle's face froze as she automatically thought about the conversation she had with the three undergraduate students in the study lounge. "What happened to the business? Why did it close?" Noelle asked again, looking around the store and then back to Yvonne.

"Oh, I don't know the whole story, but I think it had something to do with an unexpected health crisis with one of the owners, and neither of their sons wanted or couldn't take over the business. I'm not exactly sure. I don't have any contact with the original tenants, but if you wanted to talk to the property owner, he might be able to give you a better explanation," Yvonne suggested.

Noelle nodded. She wasn't interested in finding out the exact reason, but she wanted to make sure it wasn't because the business failed or the customers around the area weren't as receptive to having businesses in the area.

"What about the tables and the bookshelf over there? Why did they just leave them? It looks like they left a few other things." Noelle noticed as she continued to walk around.

"Yeah, there is a refrigerator in the back too. I think it still works, but I don't know. The dishwasher is broken, and the stove is pretty old, so both would probably have to be replaced. But if you are considering opening a coffee shop, I'm not sure if you would need a stove. Maybe you would, but I would assume coffee makers are much more important," Yvonne added.

"Ovens can be used in coffee shops for food, especially if they serve fresh bagels and muffins. I'm not sure if I want to go that route, but I need to keep that as an option," Noelle replied, still looking around the store. She walked toward the kitchen swing door and pushed it open. It was totally dark inside, and when she tried to turn on the lights, she saw a few sparks flying. Noelle rushed back out of the kitchen, worried.

"Why are there no open stores in this mini mall? I mean, I can understand there being one or two vacancies, but why is there…five or six empty stores? That's almost unbelievable." Noelle shook her head.

"It's like a catch-22 here. The problem is that nobody wants to open a new business as there isn't already a business here. I don't know all the stories, but I do know that two of the business owners retired and moved out of state. They had nobody to take over, so they just closed their businesses. I'm not sure what happened to the fourth…or fifth store. I think there were only four businesses together at the same time. Listen, I know this is a huge commitment, but I truly believe that this place will thrive again. All this mini mall needs is one brave and bold business owner to take a risk. I believe that person is you." Yvonne replied sincerely as she saw some potential within Noelle but was also hopeful to finally be able to lease the store to someone for the first time in almost seven years.

Noelle didn't say anything as she walked toward the bathroom and opened the door. The bathroom looked cleaner than the rest of the store. Everything looked like it was in order. She closed the bathroom door and walked back toward Yvonne.

"So how much is this place?" Noelle asked, trying to pretend like she wanted to barter. She thought it would be a good way to increase her business savvy.

"I don't have the exact figures, but I can tell you that besides being able to keep all the furniture left in the store, the rent is less than half of market value," Yvonne replied.

Noelle's mouth dropped. She was not expecting to hear that at all. "What do you mean less than half of market value? That is almost a steal. Is there anything else wrong with the store?" Noelle became suspicious.

"No, there is nothing wrong with the store nor the building. Since the store hasn't been occupied for over six years, you'll probably need basic maintenance for electricity, plumbing, and gas. That's in addition to the thorough cleaning the store desperately needs, but remember, you are saving over half in rent per month. It's perfect because you already have all the outlets for the additional appliances, which you will need, and you have the chairs and tables for customers to sit and enjoy their coffee or tea and even a counter where customers can place and pick up their orders. Personally, this is literally like finding a needle in a haystack. If I were you, I would think hard before passing up on this because you may never find something like this again," Yvonne warned her.

Noelle stood there on pins and needles. On the one hand, she wanted to just walk away, but on the other hand, this was almost too good to be true. Was this an actual sign that maybe this was her career path…to open up her own business? Noelle walked toward the window, staring out into the parking lot, thinking very hard for a few minutes before walking back to Yvonne and extending her hand.

"You have a deal," Noelle said nervously, acting on impulse.

Yvonne's face lit up. "Oh, that's fantastic! Okay, I won't be in the office this weekend, but are you available on Monday to come in and sign some paperwork and get the keys? I also need two months' rent, but if that's a little difficult, I'm sure I can renegotiate for maybe a month and a half rent or even less." Yvonne was really trying to make sure Noelle didn't change her mind.

"Can you give me an idea how much two months compared to a month and a half would be?" Noelle asked, trying to do some minor calculations in her head.

"Not off the top of my head, but if you want, you can call the office. Flora, the office assistant, is great. I will do some calculations when I get back to the office later and leave some notes for Flora. You can call her on the weekend and also to make an appointment for

Monday so you can sign the papers and get the keys." Yvonne seemed more excited than Noelle.

Noelle was in shock. She couldn't believe what she had just agreed to do. "Okay, great, I will give the office a call this weekend," Noelle replied, still stunned at what she just did. It almost felt surreal at this point.

"Okay, great. Well, I have to get going. My next appointment is over forty minutes away, and I want to try and miss the rush hour traffic," Yvonne replied, walking toward the door.

"Oh, okay. Well then, you better get going. Actually, I think I need to get going too. So many things to do in so little time." Noelle smiled as she walked out of the front door. Yvonne shut off the lights and locked the door behind them.

"Congratulations, and you made a very wise choice. You will not regret this! I will see you on Monday. Have a great weekend!" Yvonne yelled as she rushed toward her luxury sedan.

She watched Yvonne get back into her car and quickly drive away. Noelle got into her car and looked over at the little paper with the address. The address sounded familiar, and after thinking about it for a few minutes, it finally hit her. She was literally down the street from Romano's. She was ten minutes from her house. There was no other explanation for this except kismet.

Chapter 12

Noelle sat at the kitchen table surrounded by a few piles of several different-colored papers. Each color was placed into a separate pile. She had three different-colored pens and was making notes on different pages in different colors. To an outsider, it looked like an absolute mess, but there seemed to be a method to her madness. Noelle took a break as she sat back on the kitchen chair to stretch her arms while reaching back to tighten her ponytail. She pushed up the sleeves of her long-sleeved pale pink shirt before reaching past the paperwork to take another sip of her now lukewarm coffee. Noelle sighed when looking back at the paperwork, but as soon as she heard footsteps walking toward the kitchen, she tensed up. She tried to pull all the papers together so that nobody could see what she was working on. Chris walked through the doorway wearing his long-sleeved neon-orange work shirt and an old pair of jeans and his work boots, darting straight toward the refrigerator.

"Noelle, what's up with you? Mom will blow a small fuse if she sees that mess of yours on the kitchen table," Chris warned as he took the orange juice carton out of the refrigerator and shook it to see how much was left. He opened the top and started to drink.

"Chris, if Mom sees you doing that…," Noelle warned.

"Relax, it's almost empty. I'm just making some room in the refrigerator for her. I think she's going grocery shopping tomorrow.

I wonder what's for dinner tonight." Chris stuck his head back into the refrigerator.

"I think Mom said to order takeout. I was thinking pizza but maybe hamburgers. I'll eat whatever you want to eat. I'm not really picky," Noelle said agreeably while still trying to hide all her paperwork.

Chris gave her a strange look. "You almost always fight me on what to order for takeout. You've been like that since I babysat you when you were still in middle school, and we argued about ordering pizza or subs or whatever. Now all of a sudden, you don't care? What's up? This is not like you," Chris replied suspiciously.

Noelle shrugged her shoulders casually. "No reason. I just don't have the extra time to just worry about fighting over something trivial," Noelle remarked, looking straight at her brother.

Chris took a plate of leftover sausage and peppers out of the refrigerator, removing the tinfoil and placing it into the microwave. "Noelle, what's really going on? Is it being unemployed? I mean, if being unemployed is making you this weird, then I'll go ask my boss if they have any secretarial jobs available. Or is it graduate school? You know, maybe you should have just stopped after your bachelor's. More school may have just made you weirder," Chris replied, taking the plate of sausage and peppers out of the microwave and walking toward the kitchen table to start eating.

"That's not true. There's nothing wrong with having a master's degree. In fact, it might help me find a new job one day," Noelle replied, trying to avoid eye contact.

"Really? Because with the way you seem to be going, it doesn't appear to be helping you that much. You're beginning to look like a lost cause," Chris replied before taking a bite of his sausage and peppers.

Noelle wasn't amused. "So why are you home so early? Got into another fight with someone?" Noelle shouted back then tried to soften her expression to keep their conversation from escalating into an argument.

Chris raised his eyebrows but didn't get mad. "Actually, the job was done early. Spenser and I left after lunch. A couple of the older guys stayed a little longer to clean up, but they said we could leave," Chris replied calmly.

"That's a little unusual, isn't it? I mean, you always seem to be working late," Noelle asked casually.

"It depends. When I was working on bigger projects like the hotel renovation last year, yeah, we were constantly working overtime. Part of it was because we ran into more problems than expected, and they needed the hotel finished by a certain date. The overtime with that job was great." Chris's smile grew large.

"Then what are you doing now?" Noelle asked curiously.

"Smaller odd jobs until a bigger project shows up. My boss said something about an entire house renovation, which might start at the end of October or early November, but I'm not sure. Why are you asking all these questions? You never seemed interested before," Chris pointed out.

Noelle looked at him blankly. "Well, maybe I just want to know what's going on in my brother's life," Noelle said cautiously.

"Come on, tell me another story. You are trying to find out about me and Ally. Listen, I had Mom on my case the past month to the point where I'm avoiding Mom altogether." Chris's face was tensing up.

"Relax, I'm not asking about what's up with you two. That's between you and Ally. I'm not getting in the middle. I know it's more complicated than it appears," Noelle replied, trying to remain neutral.

Chris relaxed a little bit. "Thanks, sis," Chris said quickly.

"You are probably the only person who didn't say I overplan everything. I think a lot of people have also been annoying me lately," Noelle replied, gently shaking her head.

"Yeah, sure, you could relax a bit more and stop trying to plan everything out, but maybe it works for you. I think that might be one of the reasons you have problems with dating though," Chris interjected.

Noelle gave her brother a dirty look. "Please I don't want to think about my nonexistent love life right now. I have so many other things on my mind." Noelle took a deep breath.

"Yeah, like this paperwork mess. I mean, what is this? Several different-colored papers, different-colored pens, highlighters, sticky notes, and paper clips. What is this anyway? Schoolwork?" Chris picked up one of the straggler pink pieces of paper. Noelle quickly tried to reach across the table but just missed her brother picking up the paper. She started to panic a little bit. He sat there with a smirk on his face, which calmly faded as his eyes grew wide.

"Chris, can I have my paper back, please?" Noelle pleaded.

"I may not be a business major, but I know what a lease agreement looks like. What do you need a lease agreement for? Seriously, you are unemployed, and you are moving out? What has happened to you? The old Noelle wouldn't even have considered the idea of moving out. I think you need a job or a boyfriend or both." Chris had a perplexed look on his face.

Noelle rolled her eyes. "It's not for an apartment. It's a lease agreement for a store," Noelle replied reluctantly.

"For a store? What is that, like a cheap loft? You college kids really are a different type of breed. Is this some sort of early midlife crisis?" Chris shook his head as he continued to look at the paper.

Noelle's face grew long. "I'm not moving out. The lease is for a store…for my…for my…business." Noelle stumbled over the words. She wasn't ready to tell anyone just yet because she was still in shock that she had actually signed the lease to open a store.

"You don't have a business. Seriously, is this like an early April Fool's Day joke?" Chris burst out laughing, thinking his sister was joking.

Noelle sat still, looking at her brother very seriously. "What's so funny?" Noelle demanded, looking like a wounded bird.

"Come on, Noelle. You are very smart and could run a business successfully, but you are not bold or brazen enough to make that kind of step forward, especially in your situation. You are still in graduate school, and you are currently unemployed. I mean, that is even more impulsive than I would ever consider doing. Don't get me wrong. I don't want a business, but I would have no problem taking that risk," Chris replied, wiping some tears away from his eyes from laughing so hard.

Noelle took a deep breath and let out a long sigh. "Well then, I must be the craziest, most impulsive person that you know," Noelle replied, looking nearly defeated.

Chris stopped laughing and started to look at his sister more seriously. "Wait, you are being serious? You really signed a lease for a store? What got you to make that kind of jump? I mean, that is totally uncharacteristic of you." Chris looked at his sister in awe.

"Truthfully? I'm still in shock that I did this, but I did. I have a project for school, and I guess I was starting to take it a little too seriously. But almost everywhere I went, there was something talking about opening a business or being a business owner, and even my professor asked if I was interested in opening a business. I kept trying to ignore everything and just focus on school, but after going out on a limb and contacting a realtor, I found an opportunity too good to pass up," Noelle started to explain.

Chris was still stunned. "Wait, you went to a realtor because of a school project?" Chris asked, a little bit confused.

"No…well, kind of. This current week, we are learning about locations for businesses, so I figured if I could see some real properties, that would really help me. Plus, it would help me with some of my figures for my business budget. I wasn't planning on actually leasing any of them, but asking a realtor for help was the best option because I could see properties that weren't available to everyone. It gave me the opportunity to gauge the real market," Noelle tried to explain.

"Then what happened? I mean, you just said that you weren't planning on signing anything," Chris demanded, still stunned from his sister's announcement.

"The last place I looked at was almost too good to be true. Yes, it needs some electrical and plumbing work and probably a little bit of carpentry work, but it was an old luncheonette. I got the furniture that was left there, and the rent is less than half the market value. In addition, the store is already set up to serve food and drinks. All I would need to do are some minor adjustments, but I think it might work. I can't even believe that I'm saying all this." Noelle looked at her brother, nearly mystified.

"Are you really serious about this? I mean, opening a business is a huge commitment. Where are you going to get the money for this?" Chris asked earnestly.

Noelle sighed again. "Well, my car fund. I had been saving since I first started working, and now…well, I can't drive it, but it is an investment." Noelle shrugged her shoulders.

"You really are serious. Wow, this is like a brand-new Noelle—bold and limitless. I hope this doesn't mean I'm going to turn into the old you and be afraid to color outside of the lines." Chris shivered.

"Don't worry, Chris. There is no way that is possible." Noelle smirked.

"So where is the store?" Chris asked curiously.

"It's off Main Street. There's a parking lot on the right side driving toward our house…well, Mom and Dad's house…and at the end of the parking lot is a small strip mall," Noelle replied quickly.

"Wait, I think I remember that mini mall. I used to pass that parking lot with Dad when I would go with him to the locksmith. It was maybe a few blocks before the locksmith. I don't remember what was in there, but that's a long time ago. What other businesses are there?" Chris asked.

Noelle lowered her eyes. "There are no other businesses. The four of them left for a variety of reasons, but it had nothing to do with the area or the property owner. A lot of the business owners were older, so they retired, and nobody was there to take over. You think I'm crazy or stupid, don't you?" Noelle asked while putting her head in her hands.

"Neither. I think this is really ambitious and definitely outside of your comfort zone, but one thing I know about you is that you are rational and nonimpulsive by nature. If you thought this was the best thing to do, then maybe it really is the best thing to do. So I support you," Chris replied genuinely.

Noelle smiled. "Thanks, Chris. I really appreciate your support. Now I just need to find an electrician and a plumber," Noelle groaned as she looked back at her messy array of paperwork.

"I can help with that. I know a lot of people in the business, and you know pretty much nothing about home and building repairs. I don't want you to get swindled. I don't even think you know how to change a light bulb—" Chris started to reply before his sister interrupted him.

"I can change a light bulb, but I get your point. I would be totally in over my head, and you're right. I don't know anything about this stuff. Any help you can give me, I would appreciate it. But please, Chris, don't mention anything to Mom and Dad yet. I need to sort some stuff out before I talk to them. I doubt Mom and Dad would be as understanding and accommodating as you are," Noelle pleaded.

"Come on, Mom and Dad wouldn't react that way. They know you aren't irrational or impulsive. They know you're nothing like me. They might be shocked. I know I still am. But I can't see them saying anything against this." Chris tried to reason with his sister.

"Do you remember when I was looking at graduate schools out of state and both Mom and Dad convinced me that it was a better idea to stay here? I eventually gave up pursuing that idea because they were never very welcoming to it in the first place," Noelle recalled.

"That was different. You were going to live off on your own in a different state with no friends or family around. Not to mention the amount of money that you would have spent on attending school out of state. I think Mom and Dad were just trying to help you see the more practical side," Chris defended their parents.

"I spent months carefully researching graduate business programs until I found that specific one, and I also researched scholarships and grants to help pay for everything. This is not the same. I had a class project, went to look around at properties, and the next week, ended up signing a lease for a store. That's not more impulsive?" Noelle demanded.

Chris thought for a moment and then nodded in agreement. "Oh, okay, maybe you have a point, but you will eventually have to tell them. For the meantime, I'm not saying anything," Chris relented.

"Thank you, Chris." Noelle's eyes showed gratitude toward her brother.

"So what do you need? A plumber and an electrician? Okay, I'll check some of my contacts, and I'll let you know. I might just give them your phone number, so if you see a strange number, answer it, okay?" Chris instructed his sister.

"Yes, both and maybe a carpenter or two. Do you think anyone would consider a college student discount?" Noelle smiled.

Chris shook his head as he went to put his dirty plate into the dishwasher. He turned back toward her. "What about HVAC?" Chris asked.

Noelle looked at him blankly. "Huh?" Noelle wasn't sure what he was talking about.

Chris shook his head, understanding the mention of HVAC in addition to everything else was a little too much for his sister to handle at that moment. "Okay, plumber and electrician. I will see what I can do, but I have to go. I promised Spenser that I would help him fix his uncle's back door. It really needed to be replaced a while ago, but he refused. Now he has no choice," Chris replied, standing in the doorway, looking back toward his sister.

"Tell Spenser I said hi. How's his mom doing?" Noelle asked thoughtfully.

"I guess she's doing okay. She has her days, but she was out driving and grocery shopping last week, so I guess that's a good thing. But I'll tell Spenser you said hi and you were asking. I'll check that stuff out for you and let you know soon. Keep your cell phone on. See you later, sis," Chris muttered out as he walked out of the kitchen, down the hallway, and out the front door.

Noelle sat there for a moment still trying to grasp everything that was going on but somehow was feeling more adjusted to this huge change in her plans. Sometimes the best things aren't planned. They're experienced like an open doorway to step through to a new chapter. Noelle was ready for the next chapter to begin, no matter how daunting or unexpected it would be.

Chapter 13

Ring…ring…ring…

"Hello," Noelle quickly picked up her cell phone, cupping her mouth and the bottom of the cell phone so nobody could hear her conversation.

"Noelle, where are you? Dereck will be here around two thirty. That's in about twenty minutes," Chris *insisted* impatiently.

Noelle winced. "Chris, Val stopped over because she had some free time in between clients. I can't just kick her out. She'll get suspicious," Noelle replied anxiously.

"It figures that *she* would throw a wrench into your plans. Just tell her that you have to meet someone for something important. You need to be here to talk to Dereck so you have an idea of what is going on," Chris reminded her.

Noelle nodded even though she knew Chris couldn't see anything. "She has a name—it's Valerie. Don't worry. Hopefully, she'll be ready to leave soon. I'll see you soon, Chris," Noelle said before hanging up.

Valerie walked into the living room from the hallway with a bright smile across her face. "Guess what? I have no more appointments today! They are all canceled, and I don't have to call anyone until after dinner. Can you believe that?" Valerie replied, looking excited.

Noelle's face fell. She was one of the worst liars out there, but she needed to figure out how to get Valerie to leave and be able to meet her brother within the next twenty or so minutes.

"That's really great that you stopped by to see me. I mean, we don't really get to see each other as often as when we were in high school. We definitely need to start meeting up for pizza or something more often…of course, working around your schedule because I know how busy you are," Noelle suggested a little nervously.

"Why not today? It doesn't look like you are doing anything, and I know you don't have any class today. You really don't go out much except if you are going to school and for that two-week nightmarish mistake of a job. So maybe we can go to the mall and go clothes shopping and maybe even grab dinner at the mall. I haven't eaten in the food court for months. I wonder if they opened any new places to buy food from," Valerie pondered while still smiling and readjusting her pale-yellow dolman sweater over her dark jeans.

Noelle stood there nervously, quickly trying to figure out a way to get out of this. "Wow, that's almost like getting a day off without asking for it. You must be so excited! Since you have some extra time, why don't you use that time to catch up on sleep or even to get yourself ready for your busy holiday rush? Or maybe go visit someone. How's Lachlan doing? I know you are always saying you don't get to see him enough. You don't need to waste your extra time on me. I'm sure you have much more important things to do," Noelle rambled on cheerfully.

Valerie appeared caught off guard by her friend's response. Her bright smile started to fade. "Umm…he's working all day today. He doesn't even have time to talk on the phone. I would be wasting my time going to see him. Besides, I always go to visit him on the weekends…well, every other weekend. You already know that. I usually tell you when I'm meeting him for dinner and a movie," Valerie replied, a little suspicious of her friend's behavior.

Noelle tried to play it off as nothing serious. "Oh, that's right. I'm sorry. I guess graduate school has really started turning my mind into a big cluttered forgetful mess. How's Brynn? You haven't really talked about her in a little while. I mean, you always used to talk about her like she was family. After all, she's been your best friend since first grade. You're always mentioning how much you want to go visit her and her new baby, but you just don't have enough time," Noelle suggested, still rambling nervously.

Valerie's eyebrows rose as she was starting to become even more suspicious of Noelle's odd behavior. "You mean little EJ? Yeah, I only saw him at his Christening. They live in Pennsylvania. It would take me half a day to get there, plus it's kind of cramped until they find a new home," Valerie replied quickly.

"Oh?" Noelle asked intriguingly.

"Yeah, I just spoke to my cousin Eddy, and they are expecting their second child in the spring…" Valerie's voice trailed off. She was becoming annoyed with Noelle.

"Well, that's great news! I'm sure EJ will be thrilled to have a little brother or sister. How about Maya? You are always talking to her every week on the phone. Didn't you grow up together? I'm sure she would love to have you stop by to visit her," Noelle suggested, almost seeming desperate.

Valerie scrunched her eyebrows tightly together. Her smile completely faded as she pursed her lips tightly. "You mean my cousin Mayalen, who now lives in Tennessee? I'm definitely not able to make that trip in a day. Okay, Noelle, what is going on? It's like you are desperately trying to get rid of me," Valerie demanded.

Noelle sighed because she knew she had to be more direct. "I'm sorry, Val, but I actually have to get going. I have to meet Chris. We are working on something together." Noelle was struggling to make eye contact as though she was hiding something.

"Sure, I have nothing to do. Even if Chris is there, I'll just ignore him." Valerie laughed.

Noelle tried to take her keys out of her purse without giving Valerie the idea of coming with her. "I don't really want to see another war between you and Chris. Sometimes it's easier to just keep you two apart. It adds to my stress level." Noelle sighed.

"Well, I am capable of handling being around him. It's your brother who always seems to start something with me. It's like he really enjoys getting under my skin. I really feel sorry for any girlfriend he ever had. I doubt him and Lachlan would get along." Valerie smirked.

"Yeah, I don't think your boyfriend has much of a reason to meet Chris. So the best thing would be to stay away, and you will keep your peace...*and sanity*," Noelle said nervously while trying to get Valerie to walk out of the house.

Valerie was already becoming extremely suspicious at this point. "Okay, Noelle, what is really going on? I have known you for far too long. You wouldn't just try to get rid of me that quickly unless you are trying to hide something. It's not my birthday or any other holiday coming up, so what's up?" Valerie demanded, putting her hands on her hips.

Noelle's eyes lowered. She knew she was going to have to spill the beans sooner or later, so she figured she might as well try to be honest. "All right, I will tell you only if you promise to keep your mouth shut about everything," Noelle demanded.

Valerie was a little taken aback by her friend's change in demeanor. "Oh, okay, so what's up?" Valerie asked, a little bewildered.

"I'll drive, and I'll explain it to you on the way there. Don't worry. It's not a far drive." Noelle motioned for Valerie to leave the house so she could close and lock the front door.

Noelle walked toward her visibly aging but dependable car parked in the driveway. She quickly opened the driver's side door and rushed inside to start the car. Valerie took her time getting into the car, taking a seat, and getting settled before closing the door. She put her large beige canvas bag on the floor near her feet as Noelle quickly sped out of the driveway. Valerie jerked back in her seat while she put on her seat belt.

"What are you doing? Training to be a race car driver?" Valerie scolded.

"I'm running late. I am supposed to be at the store at two thirty," Noelle replied, trying to keep her focus on the road.

"Store? Are you and Chris buying something? A Christmas present for your parents?" Valerie asked, a little perplexed.

Noelle slowed her car down as she was approaching a red light. "No, *my store*. I have to be at *my store*. Chris is there waiting for me.

I'm supposed to be getting some estimates on work that needs to be done," Noelle said seriously.

Valerie's mouth almost dropped to the floor. "Your store? As in opening your own business? Really? When did this start? I mean, you told me a month ago that no way on earth would you even consider the idea of being a business owner," Valerie interjected.

"Yeah, well, that was before my dozen failed job interviews, a couple dozen more no responses, and then finally getting fired a second time in less than a month. No, this was not what I was expecting, but I feel like this is the right decision. Please don't ask me to explain," Noelle continued to focus on the road to make sure that she didn't miss the entrance into the parking lot. She pulled up in front of the store where she saw Chris's truck parked near the front door while he was waiting outside by himself. Noelle parked the car and then dug through her purse to get the store keys out. Valerie didn't say anything as she watched her friend rush out of the car and slam the driver's side door closed. Valerie picked up her bag and closed the passenger door, walking toward the front entrance.

Chris looked pretty calm until he looked over and saw Valerie walking toward them. "Really, Noelle, you couldn't leave her behind?" Chris asked agitatedly.

"Isn't the circus looking for one of their clowns? You should probably get back to work before you miss your next show," Valerie replied sarcastically. Chris gave her a sarcastic smile.

"Sure...if you let me borrow your large, very ugly clown bag. I need somewhere to put my costume." Chris laughed. Valerie became incensed.

"Isn't there some traffic you could be playing in or some sharks you could be swimming with?" Valerie replied sarcastically. Chris's face tensed up. Noelle managed to interrupt her brother before he was able to respond.

"Chris, Val, don't make me give you two a time-out," Noelle snapped as she managed to open the door.

Chris rushed inside and walked toward the front window. Valerie walked into the store, heading straight back toward the front counter. She took out a tissue to wipe off some of the dust before placing her canvas bag down.

"Val, just stay over here, far away from Chris. He won't bother you, but don't bother him either." Noelle looked stressed but tried to remain calm.

"Sure, I'll just look around. Do you have any cleaning supplies? I can do some dusting for you," Valerie offered.

"No, I was going to do that this weekend. Just look around and tell me what you think. I need to be with Chris and the plumber to discuss a few things," Noelle explained.

Valerie nodded and started to walk toward the large mahogany bookshelf near the front of the store against the wall. Noelle walked back toward her brother.

"Guess I made it just in time," Noelle joked.

"You had to bring her? I mean, I don't care if you want to tell her about the store, but she's probably the friend I like the least," Chris groaned.

"Chris, she's not going to bother you. That also means that you don't bother her either, okay?" Noelle scolded gently. She was starting to feel more like a parent to her brother and friend than a peer. If only she could figure out what could get them to stop fighting.

Noelle looked ahead out the large front windows and saw a big white van with black lettering and some graphics on the side. Because of the angle, Noelle couldn't read anything but assumed that this must be the plumber. She saw a very slender and tall darkly tanned male get out of the driver's side, quickly followed by a shorter chubbier redheaded male exiting from the passenger's side.

"Chris, I thought you said there was only one plumber?" Noelle inquired.

"Maybe that's his coworker. I haven't seen Dereck in a few years, and we only worked on a couple of smaller projects together. I think one project might have been with his uncle too. I've met a lot of people over the years. It's hard to keep track of everyone," Chris mumbled as he marveled at how many years he had actually been working since high school.

"Yo, Chris!" the taller man said in a soft accent after opening the front door.

Chris's face lit up. He reached over to give him a hug. "Dereck! Gee, it feels like years since I've last seen you. How is everything going?" Chris asked happily.

"Not bad. Uncle Louie is good, still out there working five to six days a week. We hired Seamus a couple of years ago so that my uncle could stay in the office more and relax. Well, that didn't quite work out. The only thing that did happen was business nearly doubling." Dereck smiled. "How about you? How's Ally?" Chris's face suddenly changed. Dereck could read between the lines.

"Not working out the way that I thought it would, but how is Maryse doing? And Regis?" Chris asked, trying to remember.

"Regis just turned three a couple of months ago. Maryse is good. She's working as an RN, so her mom watches Regis when he's not in day care," Dereck carried on the short conversation.

"Oh, Dereck, this is my sister, Noelle. This is her store…well, her future business," Chris said proudly.

"It's a pleasure to meet you." Dereck smiled genuinely.

Noelle smiled as she thought she detected a slightly familiar accent from him. "Do you mind if I ask? Do you speak French?" Noelle asked a little nervously for fear of embarrassing herself if she was wrong.

"Well - my family speaks Creole and some French. We're Haitian. My wife speaks Creole and fluent French, but she was raised in Québec. How did you notice an accent? Most don't notice anything," Dereck asked curiously.

"Oh, you just remind me a little of when our uncle speaks. We're part French," Noelle replied, trying to keep herself from sounding too boring.

"Wow, I had no idea you were French. Chris never mentioned anything. Bro, I could talk to you en francais then," Dereck replied excitedly.

Chris shook his head adamantly. "Not unless you want the conversation to end before it starts." Chris laughed.

"Come on, Chris. You have to know something," Dereck encouraged his friend. Noelle started laughing.

"He's just being coy, aren't you, Christian?" Noelle teased him in an almost perfect French accent.

"All right…enough clowning around for the moment. We have the plumbing to check out. We're wasting time, and time is money," Chris insisted. Dereck and Noelle looked at each other and smirked. Seamus looked over at Dereck before clearing his throat.

Dereck suddenly realized that Seamus was standing right next to them, making him feel embarrassed that he almost forgot to introduce his coworker to everyone. "This is Seamus. He's the other plumber who works with us," Dereck explained.

"Nice to meet you," Noelle replied.

"Is this really that large of a job that you needed two to check everything out?" Chris asked, concerned.

"No, but Seamus has a lot of experience working with older pipes. So sometimes he can spot something that I will miss. I'd rather be overly prepared," Dereck assured him. Chris nodded.

"Sure, whatever you think. I don't know anything about this stuff. That's why Chris is helping me." Noelle looked overwhelmed.

"Just a few questions. How old is the building? How long since anyone occupied this place?" Seamus asked seriously. His thick Scottish accent made it a little difficult to understand him clearly.

"How old is the building? I'm not sure. I think the whole strip mall was built in the early 1970s. This store, which was a luncheonette, was last occupied in '99 or 2000. I'm not really sure off the top of my head, but it's been at least six years," Noelle blurted out nervously. Seamus nodded.

"Well, Seamus and I will take a look around and check some stuff out, and then we'll talk afterward. Chris, do you want to tag along?" Dereck asked. Chris nodded and followed the two of them into the kitchen. Noelle walked toward Valerie.

"You know, Noelle, I just had a great idea! Please hear me out before you say anything," Valerie suggested with an excited expression on her face.

"Um…sure," Noelle said, not sure what to expect.

"Well, how about I agree to decorate your store? You know I am an interior decorator, and this would be a new challenge for me. I have decorated various rooms around houses and even a few condos, but I have no businesses in my portfolio. Your store could help me expand my business and hopefully get me away from the party and event planning and back to my first love of interior decorating!" Valerie exclaimed, looking around the store with a bright smile.

Noelle couldn't believe the excitement her friend had for wanting to decorate her store—the same place that needed a lot of work before an opening date could even be considered.

"How are you going to be able to balance another project? You are already booked pretty heavily for the next few months. Did you finally decide to hire an assistant or any extra help?" Noelle asked seriously.

Valerie shook her head nonchalantly. "I am managing just fine. I've been doing it on my own for a while since I started my business, and I'm still fine. Maybe a little sleep-deprived for a couple of months a year, but it's worth it. So what do you say?" Valerie asked, still excited about the proposition.

Noelle lowered her eyes. "Val, I don't mind if you want to make my store look 'pretty,' but I can't really afford the additional expenses. I mean, I have no idea how much the electrician or plumber are going to cost yet, and that's not including replacing any of the appliances. It wouldn't be fair not to pay you something for your hard work." Noelle sighed.

"Listen, consider it a gift from me to you. I would need you to purchase the materials, but I will give you the wholesale price, and I won't charge for any of the work," Valerie insisted.

Noelle couldn't pass up the opportunity to have her coffee shop look professional with the help from an interior decorator, but she still wasn't sure if it was feasible. The unknown expenses for the store were really making Noelle uncomfortable because she was unable to plan anything.

"I don't mind you using my store for your portfolio, but I also don't want to take up any of your extra time. Don't you start getting busy soon?" Noelle asked.

"Yeah, my busy season is from early to mid-October until mid-January, but I usually don't start picking up steam until early November. Don't worry. It's not like you need this done within the next couple of weeks. We can start to discuss the preliminaries now and then start to really get to work after the New Year. It does take time to order and receive materials," Valerie replied insistently.

Noelle started to soften a little bit. "What do you have in mind?" Noelle looked over to her friend.

"How about…neutrals for the walls and then maybe a border around the top of the walls. I know you don't like any bright or bold colors, so neutrals would be best, but do you have any colors you like besides pink?" Valerie asked hopefully, shifting her glance between the back wall and Noelle.

"No, I don't like anything loud and bold. My favorite color is pink, but I also like purple. However, that would make this place look like a dollhouse. I absolutely would not want that," Noelle insisted.

Valerie smirked. "Great, I'm not a fan of pink at all, so that's a relief. We could try a light lavender or periwinkle as a contrast against the neutrals. But it really needs to be bright enough to stand out. If it's too pale, it might blend altogether and look bland," Valerie insisted, moving her hands in the air as though she was painting the air.

Noelle tried to follow her, but she was getting lost. Noelle knew the basics about interior decorating from all their conversations over the years but had still no real grasp about all of it. "Okay, I trust your judgment. I would like a small section devoted to students to be able to study or work on group projects. Maybe a love seat or a small couch with a couple of chairs that could be known as a type of college corner," Noelle requested.

Valerie nodded. "Sure, I would just have to do some measuring and then look around at my vendors, but we could do something for students. Maybe even a small sign that says Quiet or Studying or something like that." Valerie took out a small notebook from her large canvas bag and started jotting down notes.

Noelle quickly lost her attention when she heard the kitchen door swing open and Chris talking with Dereck and Seamus. Noelle walked toward the three of them to find out what was going on.

"Well, it looks pretty good, but I think the faucet needs to be replaced. It looks kind of old. I'm gonna guess that it's the original," Dereck said.

"So what do you think I should do?" Noelle asked nervously.

"It will need to be replaced and possibly one of the pipes under the sink. There was a bucket under the sink, so we can assume that there might have been a leak at some point. Then again, it might have just been there for cleaning. We really won't know until the water is fully turned back on," Dereck replied.

Noelle's eyes lowered. "Yeah, I was told that the pipes needed to be checked before the water can be turned back on in case there are any cracks or leaks. Maybe they said something else, but I was too overwhelmed to understand or remember everything." Noelle looked flustered.

"Noelle, don't worry. From what we've seen, everything looks okay. I wouldn't worry too much. We just need to take a look at the bathroom, and then we can get going today. For all the repairs, it probably wouldn't take more than a day…two at most…to finish everything," Dereck reassured her.

Noelle felt a little bit of the tension begin to ease up. Seamus walked toward the bathroom door and stood outside while he made some small notes on his hand. Noelle noticed instantly and looked over at him strangely.

"Is he writing on his wrist? We do have paper if he needs it," Noelle suggested.

Dereck laughed. "There's a method to his madness. I don't get it, but it's been working so far, so I'm not messing with what he's doing." Dereck laughed. "Okay, guess we just need to look at the bathroom. Come on, Chris." Dereck motioned to Chris to follow him.

Noelle nodded as she watched Chris walk toward Seamus, and the three of them started talking outside the closed bathroom door. Noelle started walking back toward Valerie to further discuss possible options for decorating her store when a huge crash sent a jolt right through her. Initially, Noelle thought it was a car backfiring outside or a tire blowing out, but when a second louder crash occurred, she knew something was definitely wrong. Chris jumped at the sound of the second crash, and he was not an easily rattled person. Noelle could feel the blood drain from her face while her knees started to feel weak. This had to be a nightmare scenario playing out in her head. It couldn't be real. To her chagrin, it was as real as it could get. She was terrified about turning around and heading toward the bathroom but knew she would have to eventually. Valerie looked up from her binder with a concerned look because the noises were loud enough for her to lose her chain of thought. Noelle shook her head in disbelief while she quietly headed back toward the bathroom door.

"Wh-wh-what was that?" Noelle managed to mutter out.

"My professional opinion, a big crash," Seamus replied flatly.

Noelle wasn't amused, but Chris managed to crack a smile for stating the obvious.

"We don't know. I'll have to go in there and check it out," Dereck offered.

"Oh no, Maryse would have my head if something happened to you. Besides, I worked in situations like this all the time. Remember the apartment building?" Seamus shivered. As he walked closer to the bathroom, gently placing his ear near the door, proceeding to open it, a third crash made him jump back and quickly pull the door shut. Dereck and Chris looked at each other while Seamus stared at the door. Chris immediately searched in his tool belt and took out a small flashlight.

"Here, take this." Chris handed Seamus the flashlight.

Seamus slowly opened the door again and walked a few steps into the bathroom before walking back out as more of the ceiling began to fall on him. Seamus brushed off some of the debris from his arms and a little from his wild red hair. "I can't go back in there without a hard hat and probably better shoes. It looks like the whole ceiling collapsed. My guess, an old leak from a cracked pipe," Seamus explained.

"How did this happen? I looked at the bathroom a couple of times before, and it was fine." Noelle was stunned and started to feel sick.

"Sometimes small leaks are around for years and are ignored because nobody really pays attention to them. What happens with a crack? It becomes bigger over time. Just be happy it happened now and not after you opened and there was a customer inside," Seamus warned.

Noelle knew he was right, but this entire scenario was nothing she expected, not even in her most pessimistic expectations.

"So what is next?" Chris asked on behalf of his sister since Noelle was still at a loss for words over this whole situation.

"Well, looks like the debris knocked out the electricity too. So you will need an electrician to come, plus probably some carpenters, but I don't know anything else except plumbing, so that's as far as I go," Seamus explained flatly.

"Javy was supposed to come by next week, but I can ask if he can stop by tomorrow and then give an opinion about everything. Looks like you're getting your electric and plumbing done together, sis." Chris shrugged.

"What can I say? Do what needs to be done. I can't have the bathroom stay like that, and I need electricity and water to even consider opening up one day." Noelle sighed out loud.

"Okay, I'll call Javy later, and I'll give him your phone number too. Do you want me to have him call you too?" Chris asked Dereck.

"No, not necessary. We can speak to him in person, but I think before anything else, this place needs to be cleaned up. Seamus and I have a big job tomorrow, but we'll be available all next week," Dereck replied, looking seriously at Chris and Noelle.

Noelle was half-paying attention but not saying too much.

"I would offer to help clean up with one of my friends, but the dangling wires are kind of making me uneasy. Last thing I want to do is get electrocuted on my day off." Chris was trying to make a joke out of this situation. Noelle failed to find any humor but was too distressed to even think about yelling or getting angry.

Noelle walked toward the front window to get away from the bathroom to think. Valerie looked over at her friend but chose to leave her alone knowing she needed some space. Noelle knew there was nothing she could do now. She already signed the lease and committed to this, so she needed to follow through no matter how stressful or nauseating the results might be at the moment. The only bright side was the possibility of the solution being in Professor Summerfield's class. At least his stories made her laugh, something she was longing for at that very moment because she was no longer in the fantasy phase of being a business owner. It was now the reality phase—one Noelle had to learn to readjust to one way or another.

Chapter 14

"For homework tonight, I want you to answer questions 1–5, and please try to answer questions 6–10 on the next page," Professor Devi-Smith announced as she wrote them on the blackboard. She was greeted by a wave of groans. She turned around to face the class.

"Do we have to turn all ten questions in?" Rowena whined.

"Only questions 1 to 5 are to be typed and handed in next week for grading. But I want you to complete questions 6 through 10 because your midterm is coming up in a couple of weeks, and it will help you become more prepared. Next week, I will spend half of the class teaching and the other half as a review. The following week, which is the nineteenth, is Part I of your midterm. That will be in class. We'll talk about that more next week. Does anyone have any questions?" Professor Devi-Smith asked, looking around the room at gloomy faces slowly packing up their books to leave.

"Professor, you said Part I is in two weeks? When is Part II?" Jeff asked, a little confused.

"Part I is the in-class part of the midterm. It will consist of multiple choice, short answers, and fill in the blanks. Part II is essay questions. That will be due the following week. I used to give both in class, but some students require much longer to write, so I thought this was a fair compromise. There are no group essays, and everyone must work alone. If anyone is caught working together, those parties will receive a zero for that second part and potentially fail the midterm. I would think very hard before considering doing that," Professor Devi-Smith warned.

"Can we use the textbook?" Sally asked nervously.

"Yes, you can use it to support your answer, but remember to cite everything. If there is nothing else, you may leave. Everyone, have a great weekend and see you next week." Professor Devi-Smith smiled.

Keisha quickly threw her books into her schoolbag while Noelle seemed to be taking her time.

"Hey, are you okay?" Keisha asked.

"Yeah, just been a long couple of weeks, and I think this class makes me want to fall asleep. I hope I didn't say that too loud," Noelle said quietly.

Sally walked over and rolled her eyes. "You guys ready for midterms?" Sally joked.

"I think I'm more looking forward to getting stuck in a blizzard," Noelle replied sarcastically.

"Noelle, you need to go home and get some rest. Of course, so do I." Keisha laughed.

"Yeah, you're right. So where are you two parked?" Noelle put her sweater jacket on while throwing her schoolbag over her shoulder.

"Lot 3A," Sally and Keisha replied together. The two of them laughed.

Noelle's eyes lowered. "I'm in Lot 7A again, closest I could get," Noelle muttered out. "It's okay. We can walk out of the building together," Noelle suggested.

"Okay, cool," Keisha and Sally said in unison.

The three of them walked out of the classroom and made a left to start walking down the long hallway toward the end of the building.

"So what do you guys think about the midterm? I'm scared about this class. She's been grading my homework assignments really hard." Sally sighed.

"Mine too! I heard she was a hard grader, but I didn't think this hard. I mean, this is hard material, but maybe we're not used to this," Keisha suggested.

"Well, Tuesday night's class is almost like a television show some days, so I don't think we anticipated this semester at all," Sally joked. Keisha laughed. Noelle was quiet.

"Noelle, is everything okay? You've been quiet all class, and you looked like you were going to fall asleep," Sally asked, concerned.

"Yeah, I've been up late doing some research. I guess I got a little bit more into school this semester than I realized," Noelle joked.

"This semester is definitely giving me a run for my money. I actually thought about only taking one class this semester, but I wanted to finally graduate. Maybe I should have listened to myself. Working full-time and traveling so far for both school and work is really getting to me," Keisha admitted.

"Take care of yourself, Keisha. When I was an undergrad, I was working full-time as an assistant manager, who had a manager who didn't do much, and I was taking five classes. I got so sick at the end of the semester I said I would not do that again," Noelle explained.

"Did you sleep?" Sally asked.

"Working in a coffee shop, I loaded up on caffeine almost every day. Some weeks I was working seven days a week. The only time I had a day off from either work or school was a federal holiday or bad weather. It's not worth it." Noelle sighed.

"Don't get discouraged. I'm sure you make the best coffee out of any of your family or friends," Keisha teased.

Noelle smirked. "I guess you can say that. All my friends and family like it when I make coffee. My mom even prefers it when I set up the coffeepot the night before. So yeah, I spent several years learning how to make a superb cup of coffee," Noelle joked.

"Maybe you should open your own business," Sally suggested randomly.

Noelle froze in her tracks, and her mind became blank. She knew that she needed to reply but couldn't tell either of them just how accurate that statement was. "Well, I have one for intro to entrepreneurship, so I guess that counts." Noelle laughed nervously.

"The future is open to all possibilities. Listen, if it's meant to be, it will work out one way or another," Keisha said confidently.

The three of them got to the end of the building, and Noelle pushed the door open.

"Well, I'm tired, so I'm going to head home now," Keisha said, making a right toward Lot 3A.

"Yeah, I'm going with you. I'm parked there too. Noelle, will you be okay walking to your car alone? I can drop you off at your car if you want," Sally suggested.

Noelle smiled. "Thanks, but I'm okay. I've walked to my car alone before. You two have a long commute home, so you better get going. Be careful. I'll see you two next week." Noelle waved as she merged off onto the left path that led straight to Lot 7A. Noelle was so tired that she couldn't think too much except that she needed to get back to her car and drive home so she could take care of some more stuff for the store and her business.

As she approached her car, she could see something flashing in her bag. She figured it was her cell phone but didn't bother to check who was calling. Noelle unlocked her car and threw her bag in and took a seat. She sat there for a moment, putting her head back on the headrest and slowly closing her eyes for a moment, but then quickly jumped up as she was afraid of falling asleep. She started up the car and quickly drove home.

As she approached her house, she could see a flash from her schoolbag again. She decided to take a look at who called her. It was Paige. Noelle took her schoolbag out before closing and locking the car door and walking up to the house to unlock the front door. When she got inside, she saw all the lights were off except for in the kitchen. It looked like her parents were upstairs. Noelle took off her coat and hung it up in the closet and left her schoolbag near the foot of the stairs. She took her phone out of her bag and took it into the kitchen. There was a pot on the stove and a note from her mom.

> I made soup tonight and left it out for you. Take what you want.
>
> Love,
> Mom

Noelle took out a bowl from the cabinet, poured some soup into the bowl, and grabbed a spoon from the drawer before taking a seat at the kitchen table. She took a spoonful of soup before calling Paige back.

"Hello," Paige asked.

"Hi, Paige, I'm just calling you back." Noelle sounded very tired on the phone.

"Hi, Noelle, I'm sorry it's taken me a little while to get back to you. I did receive your message. I'm so happy that you finally got a job. How is everything going?" Paige asked, upbeat.

"Well, in the matter of three weeks since I've spoken to you, I managed to find a job and then get fired from the same job." Noelle sighed as she took another spoonful of soup.

"Oh no, fired from a second job in a month? It's so sad because you tried so hard to find something. Now you are dealing with that. Have you thought about maybe taking a break from looking for a job or even working?" Paige asked, trying to sound compassionate.

"Yeah, that was almost like a sign…to stop trying to look for a job. So I ended up with an alternative solution," Noelle started.

"Oh, what is it? I hope that it brings better luck," Paige replied hopefully.

"Paige, you wouldn't believe me if I told you. All I can say is that I really decided to really think outside of the box this time." Noelle sighed.

"Well, what is it?" Paige asked curiously.

"Well, I finally took a leap of faith and decided to try thinking outside of the box. I signed a lease to open a store. I'm opening a coffee shop," Noelle started to explain while Paige interrupted her.

"You're opening your own business? That's fantastic! Where is it? Do you have a name?" Paige was so excited by the news.

"No name yet. It's my last concern, but the store is local, only about fifteen minutes away. Right now, I'm in the early stages of getting the store ready. When the plumber was there last week checking out everything, the bathroom ceiling collapsed. I don't want to get into it. So I need the electrician and the plumber to work together. Thankfully, my brother and his friend said they would take care of the carpentry work, like I even understand what that means. I'm a business major." Noelle sighed.

"That's rough. I hope it's not as serious as it sounds." Paige tried to sound optimistic but came off as more doubtful.

"I really don't know. It's definitely an additional expense that I wasn't anticipating in dealing with, but I have to do what I have to do. I want to know the extent of damage before everything is finished, but all I can say is that thankfully this didn't happen after I opened the store. A customer could have been in there." Noelle's voice dropped from the mounting stress from everything.

"Yeah, that sounds like a blessing in disguise. Sometimes obstacles hit you when you are trying to move forward, but it's really just trying to toughen you up. Well, that's what my grandmother would say," Paige said encouragingly.

"I'm trying to think of it as a blessing in disguise. I guess what makes this feel even worse is that I'm starting midterms soon, and my brain feels so scattered. I mean, I have so much work due and so much stress because my classes give an incredible amount of work, and one is really tough. And when I leave class, I can't relax. I have to worry about my new impulsive venture collapsing before my eyes." Noelle sounded like she wanted to cry.

"Noelle, it may seem rough right now, but if this really is the right path for you, then it will work out. I know that's easier to say than to hear or especially believe, but you have to hang in there. You made it this far. You should hang in there to see how everything will come together later on. Besides, I'm super excited about the idea of one of my closest friends not only opening her own business but one that I will love to frequent often." Paige was trying to cheer her friend up.

Noelle sat there for a moment staring at her soup and then realizing that maybe Paige was right. Not to let the smaller things get to her but take things as they come, allowing them to make her stronger and braver. "Thanks, Paige. I think that may be exactly what I needed to hear," Noelle replied calmly, a small smile forming on her face.

Chapter 15

Noelle opened her eyes to the bright sunlight pouring in through her pale-pink curtains onto her face. She rubbed her eyes and stretched her arms up before sitting up in her bed, looking to see what time it was—after 10:00 a.m. She was so excited because this was the longest she had slept in months, and for a brief moment, it made her feel more energetic and hopeful. Jumping out of bed, she grabbed her pink bathrobe and put on her fluffy pink bunny slippers. She opened her bedroom door and started to wander down the stairs toward the kitchen to the smell of freshly made pancakes.

Noelle walked toward the coffeepot and poured herself a cup of coffee. The coffee tasted a little stale, as though it had been sitting out for a little while. She didn't care and poured some milk into her cup anyway. When she sat down at the kitchen table, she took the unused plate and fork left nearby, next to the large tinfoil-covered plate in the middle of the table. She removed the tinfoil, took a couple of pancakes, poured some syrup all over them, and began to eat. As she was about to take another bite, loud yelling poured through the front door.

"Sis! Sis!" Chris yelled while running into the house and slamming the front door behind him.

"What is it? I'm right here, not ten thousand feet away." Noelle winced as she held her ears.

"Sorry, been talking loudly the last couple of days. Are you busy? Oooh, pancakes." Chris replied as his mouth started to water. He walked toward the counter to take a plate from the cabinet and a fork from the drawer before taking a seat at the kitchen table.

"Chris, please, I'm having a pretty good morning so far. I managed to finish all my midterms, and I'm still here, even though I wasn't sure if I would make it through all of them. If you have any bad news, don't say anything. This is one time I will be happy with not knowing anything," Noelle instructed.

"Total pessimist, aren't you?" Chris scolded his sister as he took a few pancakes and placed them on his plate. He reached for the syrup to pour it all over his pancakes. Noelle looked in amazement at her thirty-two-year-old brother pouring syrup like a little kid.

"I'm not a pessimist…maybe a little cynical, but I'm just realistic. Remember, I got tons of calls, in between trying to study and work on projects for school, about this needing to be fixed and that needing to be fixed or replaced or updated. I swear half of the wiring in the store must have been replaced," Noelle groaned.

"It wasn't half. You did need a few outlets replaced, but a couple were completely dead. Javy said that's not completely unusual in a business. He did suggest a new electrical box, but it was to update the box, not because it wasn't working." Chris tried to reason with his sister.

Noelle's eyes widened. "Chris, Dereck told me how much needed to be replaced in the bathroom. It basically seemed like starting all over with a brand-new bathroom. I didn't sign up for this." Noelle sighed.

"Noelle, you're being a little bit overdramatic. It wasn't that bad. Yeah, you did need a couple of new pipes in the ceiling and the toilet, vanity, mirror, and some wall tiles replaced, but it could have been worse. At least the walls didn't collapse," Chris explained calmly.

Noelle looked at her brother in disbelief. "How can you be so cavalier about all this? Have you seen how much everything is going to cost? This is definitely more than my original budget. Maybe I should start playing the lottery," Noelle replied, visibly anxious. She took another sip of her coffee.

"Can't make money if you don't spend money," Chris reminded her.

Noelle gave him a strange look. "What does that have to do with anything? Spending money on a business to provide a product or service really isn't the same as inadvertently renovating an entire store. I hope this doesn't become a money pit. I hope I know what I got myself into." Noelle's voice trailed off. She didn't want to think or talk about this anymore.

"You know what you need? You need to get out of the house for a little bit…something to cheer you up. It's a beautiful autumn day outside. Come on, I have a couple of errands to run, and I wouldn't mind you coming with me." Chris was trying to cheer up his sister.

Noelle lowered her eyes and reluctantly nodded. She finished the rest of her pancakes and her coffee before getting up to put everything in the dishwasher. "I'll go upstairs and change. I'll be down soon."

Noelle walked out of the kitchen through the small hallway and up the stairs. She rushed into her room and tried to figure out what she wanted to wear. She decided on a pair of jeans and a yellow turtleneck and a beige cardigan that fell past her waist. She put on a pair of her most comfortable sneakers and grabbed her purse before closing her bedroom door behind her. Chris was already waiting at the bottom of the stairs.

"Chris, that was fast," Noelle commented, walking down the stairs.

"Mom's pancakes are like butter. Sometimes I wish she caved and opened her own restaurant, even if it was just breakfast foods," Chris replied longingly.

Noelle scrunched her face as she walked toward the hall closet to get her hooded black coat. "That's never going to happen," Noelle said flatly as she pulled her purse over her shoulder.

"Are you ready? You don't need your keys. I'll bring you back when I'm done," Chris told her calmly.

Noelle thought it was bizarre how calm her brother had been acting that morning. It seemed a little out of character.

"Ready?" Chris asked as he opened the front door. Noelle nodded and walked out of the house and toward her brother's truck. He closed and locked the door before walking toward his truck. He got in but forgot to unlock the passenger door. Noelle glared at her brother from the passenger's side window.

"Can you open the door?" Noelle asked impatiently through the passenger's side window, hoping this wasn't another one of her brother's practical jokes.

Chris shrugged as he couldn't understand what his sister was saying with the engine revving but quickly assumed her door was still locked. He unlocked the door, and Noelle climbed in.

"I know that fresh air is supposed to make a person feel better, but standing out there almost freezing in the bitter late October air is a little different than I had in mind," Noelle replied, trying to refrain from appearing too overtly sarcastic.

Chris smirked as he put his truck in reverse to pull out of the driveway. "Sorry, sis. I'm more used to driving by myself," Chris admitted while pulling out into the street.

"Don't you go to work with Spenser sometimes?" Noelle asked.

"Occasionally, if it's really far, we take turns driving. But I don't have to worry about opening the passenger's door because Spenser either climbs in through the back window or unlocks the door himself. He does the same thing with his own car. Spenser looks like a calm guy, but he's kind of a maverick." Chris laughed as he slowed down at the first red light.

"What about Ally? Didn't you used to go out with her in your truck?" Noelle asked before she realized she went into forbidden territory.

Chris took a deep breath before answering. "She hated the truck. She complained since I first bought it, but she always needed me to open the passenger door for her. I didn't mind opening the door for her at first, but after a while, it was starting to feel like I was more of a caretaker than a boyfriend. Maybe the age difference was starting to show cracks," Chris surmised.

Noelle nodded, listening to everything her brother was saying, but it gave her a totally different perspective of Chris's past relationship. There really was much more to the story than anyone knew about, and Noelle was not going to pry any further unless Chris offered. She glanced over at her brother for a moment before leaning her head on the passenger's side window and gazing outside.

"It's a beautiful autumn day. You were right. The sky is completely cloudless with a bright deep-blue background to all the colorful autumn leaves. Thanks for asking me to go out this morning. I guess you're right. I've been in the house too much. I've had so much work from midterms and then the store and then...," Noelle replied, shifting her gaze through the windshield at all the trees with an array of colors at different stages of autumn foliage.

"Do you mind if we make a quick stop at the convenience store? I need to grab some coffee and maybe a snack. Do you want something? I'm sure you want coffee," Chris asked as he pulled into the small parking lot of a local convenience store.

"Sure, medium...no sugar and some type of dairy—milk, cream, skim milk—I don't care," Noelle replied casually.

"Don't you usually like some autumn blend thing or something weird like that? Pumpkin pie spice? Pumpkin apple?" Chris asked, rolling his eyes playfully.

"Pumpkin pie or apple spice is better than your raspberry concoction," Noelle teased as her brother jumped out of the truck and walked toward the front door of the store.

Noelle sat in the truck with the window open. The breeze was cool, but the sun beating down on the dashboard made it feel hot inside. Noelle started to daydream about when the semester would finally be over, and she would be able to just sleep late and not have to worry about multiple-part midterms and final projects that could make or break her final grade. She was so out of it; she didn't notice when her brother came out of the convenience store with a tray of coffee and plastic bag full of snacks. He put the bag of snacks in the back seat while he reached over the front seat to hand his sister the tray of coffee. Noelle took it and counted five coffees. She was baffled because there were only two of them in the truck. As Chris closed the back door and got into the driver's seat, she looked at him, confused.

"Chris, I know math wasn't your favorite subject, but two people usually doesn't equal five coffees." Noelle pursed her lips.

Chris sat back in his seat for a moment before looking back at his sister with a smile. "That's because it's for five people—you and me, Spenser, Kirby, and Cesar," Chris replied calmly.

Noelle was bewildered. She couldn't understand how the other three guys fit into this equation. "Wait, where are we going? We aren't going to run some errands for you, are we?" Noelle asked, starting to shake off her confusion.

"Yeah, we're going to take a look at your store. It's been a couple of weeks since you've been there. Thought you might want to take a look at the progress." Chris turned the key in the ignition, putting the truck in reverse to back out of the parking lot onto the road.

Noelle pondered what she had just heard as though her mind was working in slow motion. It took a moment to sink in for Noelle. She had that horrible image of a disaster zone cemented in her mind and couldn't think about anything else. The short drive from the convenience store to the mini mall was pretty quiet as Chris was focusing on not missing the entrance of the parking lot again. Noelle started to realize that despite taking a leap of faith in going to open her own store, she still had been trying to plan everything. The bathroom was just one example of something that she couldn't control because it wasn't planned, and it was throwing her off even more. Although this was a huge step in the right direction, Noelle realized she needed to work on some things in the future if she ever expected to be successful at a risky venture.

Chris pulled his truck up to the mini mall and parked right across from the front windows. Noelle couldn't put her finger on it, but it seemed as though they looked different than they did the last time she was there. Perhaps it was because she was looking at them from the opposite direction and not competing with the sun for a clear view of anything. Before her brother got out of the truck, he turned to his sister.

"I wanted to mention this before I forget. I spoke to Javy, and neither of us are experts, but I think you need a new refrigerator. The outlet behind the refrigerator was dead. It's one of the several that were replaced, but even after trying to plug it back in, there was a grinding noise, and I noticed a small puddle in the back. In layman's terms, that's not good," Chris said calmly.

Noelle sat there expressionless. She wasn't happy to hear about that, but what was she going to do? "Yvonne, the realtor, said that refrigerator might be at least ten or fifteen years old. She didn't say anything, but hearing the dishwasher was broken, I figured that the refrigerator was probably broken too. It's like starting from scratch." Noelle couldn't help but laugh at this point.

"Noelle, look at the bright side. Better to find all this out now rather than later on. You don't want your refrigerator to go kaput when you have hundreds of dollars of dairy products in there and everything spoils," Chris warned.

Noelle nodded. "Well, you're the expert. Where do I go?" Noelle asked, trying not to sound too snarky.

"There's a company. They deal with industrial-sized refrigeration units. They also do repairs. They might also have freezers and other stuff for businesses, but yeah, their name is RetroFreeze Coolers," Chris replied while pulling out his cell phone from his pocket to check for any missed calls.

"RetroFreeze Coolers…sounds like a second-rate beverage company," Noelle replied, getting out of the truck, trying not to laugh.

"Noelle, they are a real company, and they are well-known. They have been around for a while," Chris explained.

"Okay, I'll take the number, and I'll give them a call. I just hope this isn't going to cost too much." Noelle sighed.

"I think they allow financing, but you can talk that stuff out with them," Chris replied quickly while taking the bag of snacks from the back seat before slamming the driver's door shut.

Noelle got out of the passenger's side, being able to balance herself and the coffee tray without dropping anything. She felt proud of herself for a moment. It almost felt symbolic that no matter how challenging it felt or looked, Noelle had the ability to keep it together and keep going forward. Her brother walked up first to the front door and opened it, waiting a moment for his sister to get there, and then moved to the side to let her go in before him. As Noelle walked through the doorway, she stared in disbelief as she almost didn't recognize the store at all. She just stood there almost frozen. Chris walked up behind her and tapped on her right shoulder.

"What do you think so far?" Chris asked proudly.

"It is almost unrecognizable. What did you guys do? It's only been a little more than two weeks," Noelle replied, still stunned.

Chris nudged her to place the coffee tray on the card table that was set up near the front window. "I found this in the garage…and three chairs. There's a couple of stains on it from something, but it's still in pretty good shape, and nobody was using it, so I figured it would be good to keep here. That way, if anyone wants to eat or drink anything or if you need to read or do some weird paperwork, you have a place to do everything," Chris explained.

Noelle placed the coffee tray down on the table and looked at the tops, assuming that the one in the middle with a purple *N* was for Noelle. "Thanks, Chris. I didn't even think about having a table or chairs. I think I couldn't get past all the dust and dirt. It looks almost spotless now," Noelle remarked, still amazed.

"Well, the bookshelf and the chairs and table are still in desperate need of being polished. That wasn't necessary right now, so we pushed them off toward the back wall. The bookshelf can't be moved as Spenser and I learned they bolted it into the floor or cemented it or something. It won't move, so for some reason, it needs to stay there, but honestly, with the way the store is set up, I don't think you have anywhere else to place it," Chris explained.

"What about the cleaning? Who cleaned? I feel terrible. I should have been here to help clean up the store," Noelle commented while avoiding eye contact and admiring the newly polished floor.

"Don't worry about it. There wasn't much you could have done until everything was repaired. Spenser and Cesar helped with the cleaning. They both volunteered their last couple of weekends. I needed some extra help to clean up the bathroom before Dereck, Seamus, and Javy could start working. It was actually Cesar who suggested cleaning up the place a little bit because it would make it easier to work if we could tell the difference between dust, dirt, and corrosion," Chris explained.

Noelle noticed Cesar walking toward the table. He was short and husky with a crew cut, the same one he had kept since his days in the military.

"Cesar, thank you. I don't know how to repay you," Noelle replied gratefully.

"*No hay problema.* You needed some help, and I had some free time. Besides, I owed Chris a favor from a few years ago. Is this my coffee?" Cesar asked. His attention flowed back and forth between Noelle, Chris, and the table with the tray of coffees.

"You could take any coffee except the one on the right—that one is mine. Oh, the bag on the table has some snacks in there," Chris started to explain.

Cesar rummaged through the plastic bag and took out a package of powdered doughnuts. "Ah, my favorite. Thanks, bro!" Cesar exclaimed, walking over to the front counter with his coffee and doughnuts to take a break.

"What kind of favor?" Noelle asked curiously.

Chris shrugged. "It's a long story. I'll explain another time. But it worked out in my favor too because I met my current boss through that job. Everything happens for a reason…," Chris explained.

Before Noelle could ask anything else, she became distracted as she saw a familiar face walking toward the card table to grab a coffee.

"Hey, Kirby, hands off. You have your own coffee," Chris warned, grabbing the coffee on the right side of the tray.

Kirby brushed his shaggy light-brown hair off his face. "All right, it's all yours. Gee, Chris, it's only coffee. What's in it anyway?" Kirby asked, pulling up his tool belt.

"It's raspberry cream and amaretto," Chris replied, carefully guarding his coffee.

Kirby backed up and gave him a strange look. "Sounds delicious, but you know what? I'm gonna let you have that one all to yourself. Hey, Noelle, great place. Don't forget to let us know when the grand opening will be." Kirby smiled brightly while taking his coffee and a prepackaged muffin over to the front counter near Cesar.

Noelle looked over at her brother. "I haven't seen Kirby in years. I almost didn't recognize him. Didn't he move to Upstate New York?" Noelle asked curiously.

Chris nodded. "Yeah, he got a better job offer, plus I think he has some family upstate. He still comes down every so often, but it seemed to be perfect timing. He called me a couple of weeks ago to see if I could hang out, and I told him I was helping you, so he asked if he could help," Chris replied while taking a sip of his coffee. Noelle could smell the combination of raspberry and amaretto and couldn't understand how her brother liked it so much.

"Noelle," a familiar voice called out to her. It was Spenser. He was of average height with strawberry-blond hair, blue eyes, and lightly tanned skin.

"Spenser, how are you? How's your mom?" Noelle smiled.

"My mom is doing pretty good. She's got some bad days here and there, but the new medicine seems to be working. I'm doing well. I usually don't work on the weekends, but when Chris told me it was for you, I said okay…if she gives me a discount on coffee when I come in. Just kidding." Spenser laughed.

"It seems like I already have a list growing of future customers," Noelle joked.

"Who doesn't like coffee? If they don't, it's okay, more for us." Spenser laughed.

"I haven't even started really thinking what will be on the menu, but I'm thinking I'll probably have tea and hot chocolate too," Noelle added.

"Great! My mom loves tea. I think so does my girlfriend, even though she tells me she likes coffee. Anyway, I told my mom about your store, and she wants to go to your grand opening, so keep us informed when you pick a date. I'm going to grab my coffee before it gets too cold." Spenser walked toward the small card table and picked up a coffee and a small package of doughnuts out of the bag and went over by the other two guys.

"So what do you think, sis?" Chris asked excitedly.

"I can't believe so many people are asking me for an opening date…" Noelle trailed off, hoping that her parents wouldn't find out about her store before she was ready to say anything to them.

"I meant about the store," Chris asked, taking another sip of his coffee.

"I really can't believe this is the same store, all in two weeks… wow." Noelle was still in awe.

"Well, you haven't seen the best part," Chris hinted, motioning toward the bathroom.

Noelle looked at the bathroom door and started to feel light-headed. "And I was having such a good time so far…" Noelle trailed off.

Chris got her to follow him toward the bathroom. He made sure her eyes were closed before he opened the door. Closing the eyes wasn't a problem for Noelle; it was whether or not she wanted to open them back up when the door was opened. Chris slowly opened the bathroom door, and she took a deep breath before opening her eyes and looking inside. Total amazement.

"Chris," Noelle said, stunned.

"Looks different, right? Well, it took about a whole day to clean up the mess. Javy had to turn off the power because there were some live wires dangling. I like living dangerously, but that was a little too much for me," Chris joked.

"But it looks like nothing happened. The only thing…blue toilet, sink, and vanity? I don't remember ordering blue. I thought I said white or whatever color was in there before…ecru?" Noelle tried hard to remember.

"Well, Dereck's uncle had the toilet and vanity with sink in storage. It was specially ordered for a customer, but then they changed their mind. They still got the work done, but they wanted a different color, so nobody wanted a blue bathroom set. They gave you a great discount on it, and it's all brand-new. I know it looks a little strange, but there is some blue in the wall tiles, plus having a blue bathroom makes it unique," Chris explained. He looked over at his sister's face.

"Yeah, a blue bathroom is definitely unique, but I'm starting to like it. Thanks, Chris. And if you see Dereck and Seamus, thank them too," Noelle exclaimed, still looking around the bathroom in amazement.

"I think Dereck will be stopping by in a week or so with a replacement piece for the pipe under the sink in the kitchen. They had to order it because it was out of stock. Dereck said it would take maybe twenty or thirty minutes to replace that piece. He'll call you to let you know which day he'll stop by. Don't worry. He knows you have class a couple of nights a week, so it will probably be early," Chris explained.

"That's fine. I'll just bring some homework or something while I wait. I should probably spend more time here…to get used to being here." Noelle turned to her brother and smiled happily.

"Okay, are you ready? I'm going to drop you back home because I need to come back here and do some more work with the guys." Chris jingled his keys in his front-right pocket.

"Yeah, I have to get back because I have some calculations for the store and some homework, and yes, I have to call RetroFreeze Coolers or something," Noelle replied as her brother glanced over at his sister. He started walking out of the store and waved to the guys.

"Hey, I gotta drop my sister home. Do you want me to bring back anything?" Chris asked randomly.

"Yeah, lunch!" Kirby yelled playfully.

Chris nodded as he walked out. Noelle waved to the guys before following her brother toward the truck. He remembered to make sure the truck was unlocked this time so Noelle wouldn't be stuck out in the cold.

"Chris, lemme pay for lunch for them. They have worked so hard," Noelle offered.

"I'll pay for it today, and you can pay me back. I'll probably get them meat lover's pizza and some drinks," Chris thought out loud.

"Okay, sounds good. Please don't forget," Noelle pleaded with her brother because she really wanted to do something nice for the three of them.

"Oh, while I'm thinking of it, lemme give you the phone number. Get your phone out." Chris waited until Noelle had her phone in front of her. "RetroFreeze Coolers is 201-555-3000. I guess they have specific extensions or whatever, but this is their main line," Chris replied, putting his phone back in the cupholder.

"Thanks. Are you sure they are legitimate? I'm not going to end up ordering cases of soda," Noelle joked.

Chris grimaced. "They are a real company. They are in the phone book if you don't believe me. I doubt you can order soda there. They don't sell beverages, at least not that I'm aware of." Chris shrugged.

"Sorry, Chris. This is just so overwhelming that sometimes I just need to make a joke to make sure I don't lose it. I really have to thank you for taking me here today. It renewed my hope that this wasn't the worst idea…opening my own business," Noelle confided.

"I understand. We all take risks at some point. It just works out better for some. You have your flaws. Yes, I know I'm far from perfect too, but being irresponsible and impulsive is not one of yours. Kind of cool that you're going to be a business owner." Chris smiled as he put the key into the ignition to turn on the truck.

"Yeah, definitely the last thing I ever thought, but life is full of surprises," Noelle remarked.

Chris quickly put his truck into reverse to turn around and drive out of the parking lot back onto Main Street to take his sister back to their parents' home.

Chapter 16

Noelle stumbled through the front door of her store with her schoolbag on her right arm and thermos in her left hand. She placed her schoolbag on an empty chair and her thermos on the card table. Noelle took off her hooded black peacoat and placed it on the back of the chair. Despite wearing a pullover white Fair Isle sweater over a navy turtleneck, it still felt chilly in the store. She knew that looking at the heating and cooling system would probably be next on her list, but for the moment, she was going to have to get a small electric heater so that nobody would freeze. Noelle looked around the store for a moment before glancing over at her school bag and taking a seat at the card table next to the front window. She knew that there was so much to do for school and for the store, but she was really feeling a lack of motivation to do anything. She couldn't figure out if she was extra tired because of lingering effects from midterms or because she really didn't want to be in the store that day. It seemed as though every time something was going right, something else would not work out. This was starting to feel like a real-life roller-coaster ride.

Noelle called RetroFreeze Coolers the same evening Chris dropped her back home after checking out her store. Being a little bit reluctant at first, she was pleasantly surprised that the conversation went really well, and they seemed to be very friendly and helpful. RetroFreeze Coolers sent Jackson, a technician, to the store a couple of days later to look at the refrigerator. Noelle's fears came to reality as the refrigerator was nonrepairable. With the help of Jackson, she was able to pick out a new refrigerator in stainless steel and an upgraded model. She was even more excited when they allowed her to finance it. When it arrived the following Monday, it was working fine. Jackson had plugged it into the outlet, calibrated it, and checked the internal temperature. She thought everything was fine, except when she went to the store a couple of days later, the temperature was wrong, and it wouldn't allow her to change it. Defective was the first thing she thought. *Can things get worse?* Noelle immediately called RetroFreeze Coolers the same day, and they agreed to send a technician—most likely Jackson—back to the store to check everything out. She was hoping it was a fluke, but her fears sometimes got the better of her and made her believe this was bad luck.

Noelle looked out the front window of the store into the parking lot, waiting for the RetroFreeze Coolers van to show up. She looked down at her watch and saw it was after two in the afternoon. She went to check the time against the clock in the store to make sure it was right and quickly realized that the clock was not working. It had been 7:35 since the day she first stepped into the store. Another thing to add to her list of things to do or fix or replace. The list seemed to be growing longer by the day, not leaving her a lot of room for spending money on beverages that she wanted to serve at her coffee shop. But Noelle couldn't worry about how much all the repairs were going to cost because if the store wasn't completely repaired and functioning, *it wouldn't pass inspection, couldn't open, and then there would be no customers.* That was what she kept telling herself every time she would get too discouraged. She brushed it off and took out a resealable bag of mini homemade apple cinnamon muffins and her textbook to try and get some reading done in the meantime while she waited. While taking another sip from her thermos, her phone began to ring. Initially, she thought it was RetroFreeze Coolers, but then she looked down and saw it was Sally.

"Hey, Sally, what's up?" Noelle asked while taking another sip of her coffee and taking a mini muffin out of the resealable bag.

"Hi, Noelle, how are you doing? I am on my lunch break. I finally had a chance to look over my midterm from financial management. I am going to try to make some corrections for a higher grade. I can't believe I got a C-. I studied so hard. I'm worried about the essays." Sally sounded deflated.

"I think our professor said she'll have them graded by the end of the week. Something about a lot of students handed them in right before they were due so she couldn't really grade any early," Noelle replied, taking another sip of her coffee.

"How did you do?" Sally asked curiously.

"Not as good as I wanted to. I got a B-. It's not terrible, but I think I spend more time with our other class and the project," Noelle suggested, leaving out the fact that a lot of her spare time had gone to her new business venture.

"B- is still better than a C-. Maybe a master's in business wasn't the best idea," Sally confessed.

"Sally, it's only one grade in one class. I wouldn't worry too much. During my undergraduate, I got a C or a C+ in accounting, and I'm a business major, so don't worry. You're in the master's program for a reason, and besides, you are almost finished. Hang in there, at least I have to remind myself all the time." Noelle laughed anxiously.

"Noelle, I don't think you need to worry. You are definitely business-minded. How many times have you explained things to me during group sessions in class? Well, Tuesday night is kind of like a hit or miss," Sally joked.

"Yeah, it feels like I'm stepping into the studio of a game show. I wonder if he was a comedian before he started teaching," Noelle wondered out loud.

"I don't know, but he did say that he's been consulting for over three decades and started teaching about a decade ago. Maybe when he was in high school or college?" Sally suggested.

Noelle started laughing. "Anything is possible…" Noelle trailed off.

"Thanks for the laugh. It really cheered me up. Unfortunately, I gotta run. Lunch is just about over. I will text you sometime over the weekend, and see you in class next week," Sally replied, about to hang up the phone.

"Sounds good. Talk to you soon," Noelle replied before hanging up. She looked down at her textbook and didn't want to read or study anything. She really just wanted to take a day off from everything, but it didn't seem to be working out like that just yet.

Noelle continued to routinely look out the front window and look down at her watch, waiting impatiently for RetroFreeze Coolers to finally show up at the store so she could go home and rest. All she saw seemed to be every other car but the one she was looking for. There was one car pulling into the parking lot to make a U-turn, another car stopping near the front of the building and the driver took out a map as though he was lost, and a third car with a woman who looked to be fighting with her boyfriend. Noelle was trying very hard to ignore that woman's argument, but she was screaming so loud it could be heard halfway across the parking lot. It was moments like these that Noelle was thankful to be single. Although Noelle had never personally experienced a fight like that, she had plenty of memories of Chris and Ally getting into screaming matches. As much as she missed talking to her, with each passing day, it was becoming clearer that Chris and Ally were better off apart and finding someone new. She tried to shake those memories out her mind so she could clear her head to try to focus on studying.

Noelle took another mini muffin, quickly eating it, and then taking another sip from her now lukewarm coffee. She glanced down once more to double-check what her homework assignment was when she caught something flashing out of the corner of her right eye. She looked up and saw a black sedan pull up in front of the store. Noelle was confused because she didn't know anyone with a luxury sedan and definitely wasn't expecting anyone else except for RetroFreeze Coolers. They had a company van, not a company car. She hoped it wasn't some type of loiterer or some other headache to deal with. For a brief moment, she wondered if that was Jackson just driving a different car, but she distinctly remembered him saying he preferred to drive bigger vehicles like vans and trucks. Then she saw the driver, and he looked absolutely nothing like the towering Jackson at six-seven. This stranger was no more than five-nine and was slender with light-brown hair. He wore a hooded light-blue jacket with something written on the back that she could barely see, a blue dress shirt, and a pair of jeans and what looked like sneakers on his feet. This was obviously not the same type of clothing that Jackson, the technician, was wearing or probably any other technician would wear. The guy walked up to the front door with a small toolbox in one hand and a light-blue hard hat in the other and pulled it open, slowly looking around for someone.

"Noelle?" The guy looked over at her sitting down.

She got up and walked toward him. "Yes, who are you? You definitely don't look like Jackson," Noelle replied suspiciously.

The guy was a little taken aback by her harsh introduction. "Oh, I'm not Jackson. I'm Matt. I'm here to check out your refrigerator. I'm sorry, I'm not really sure what's wrong. Maureen only told me that the temperature is broken?" Matt said quickly. His piercing baby-blue eyes caught the sunlight from the window. Noelle couldn't help but notice that he was kind of cute even if she still didn't trust him.

"Okay, Matt, where is Jackson? How do I even know you are qualified to take care of this problem? I don't know you." Noelle crossed her arms across her chest.

Matt shook his head and cracked a smile. "I can assure you I'm qualified," Matt replied confidently.

"Jackson's been working for RetroFreeze Coolers for over ten years. I never even heard of you. I can't afford to make a mistake. This refrigerator is still being financed!" Noelle protested.

Matt remained extremely calm. He handed her his business card. Noelle grabbed onto it very tightly but didn't bother to read it.

"I'm not a technician. I'm an engineer, but if you prefer Jackson to come back, I can leave." Matt smirked.

Noelle could feel her cheeks burning from embarrassment. It seemed that whenever she would take a stand, it would somehow bite her in the butt. "Oh, so you are kind of like an upgrade?" Noelle asked sheepishly.

"Yeah, you could say that. So what's the problem?" Matt asked with a sort of told-you-so look on his face.

"When it was first set up, the refrigerator was fine. Now the temperature is not working. I don't know. Maybe it's broken or maybe defective. It's just my luck." Noelle started getting upset.

"Noelle, calm down. I'll go check it out. Is it through that door?" Matt asked, pointing to the kitchen swing door. Noelle nodded, and Matt quickly walked through the door and disappeared.

She walked back toward the card table and took a seat. She had almost forgotten that she still had his business card in her hand. She placed it on the table to take a look at it.

RetroFreeze Coolers
Mechanical Engineering
Matthew D. Cervenka
MCervanka@RetroFreezeCoolers.com
(201-555-3000) Ext: 6371

Noelle stared in disbelief as she needed to reread the business card again. She couldn't believe it. It was Matt! Matt Cervenka, her huge high school crush. Although he looked a little bit different, he was still very cute. She wondered if he had any idea who she was or if he remembered her at all. He must have seen her last name on the invoice, but then again, maybe he didn't remember her name. She knew that they had been out of high school for nearly a decade and that she had changed a lot since they graduated. Noelle felt like she was sitting on pins and needles until Matt emerged from the kitchen. She pretended to be reading and drinking some of her now cold coffee when he emerged nearly twenty minutes later. She perked up right away and walked toward Matt. He took off his hard hat to expose his loose light-brown curls, brushing his hand through it.

"So?" Noelle asked, looking nervously.

Matt looked at her a little strangely. "It just needed to be recalibrated, not a big deal. Maybe it wasn't calibrated right, but Jackson's pretty good, so maybe it was just a fluke. Stranger things have happened. It's all fixed now. You shouldn't have any problems," Matt said, zippering up his hooded sweatshirt.

"Thanks, Matt. Wait, do you remember me?" Noelle blurted out.

Matt looked at her a little strangely. "Am I supposed to? Have we met? If we have, I'm sorry, I'm drawing a blank." Matt shrugged.

"St. Genevieve's class of '97. It's Noelle…Noelle DeGarmo," Noelle explained nervously.

Matt sat there for a moment with a blank expression on his face. Then he looked over at her, squinting his eyes to try and remember. After a few moments, his eyes widened as though he finally remembered. "Noelle from homeroom? I didn't recognize you at all. I mean, you've changed, in a good way, but you look so different," Matt stammered a little bit.

Noelle cracked a smile as she took that as compliment. "Well, I am like ninety pounds lighter than I was in high school. It's still a challenge to keep the weight off, but I've been working hard at it," Noelle said confidently.

"I don't remember you being that heavy, but then again, I don't remember too much from high school either. I think I used to study too much," Matt joked.

"Matt, you were supersmart. You were in the honors program and ranked in, like, the top 10 percent of our class. You worked really hard in school and got all those scholarships. There's nothing wrong with working hard," Noelle encouraged him.

"Yeah, but there is a problem when your priorities are out of order. I kind of learned that the hard way…" Matt trailed off.

"Yeah, I can kind of relate to that one too." Noelle thought she understood what he was talking about but wasn't sure.

"So this is your place? Your store? What are you opening?" Matt asked, pretty intrigued.

"Yeah, I'm a new business owner. I'm trying to get everything together, so I am hoping to open in the spring, but we'll see how everything works out. It's definitely more expensive than I initially thought," Noelle replied with a sense of fatigue mixed into her words.

"I can imagine. What type of business? I'm assuming food because of the refrigerator," Matt surmised.

"Yeah, it's going to be a coffee shop, and no, I don't have a name yet. That's usually the first question that everyone asks me," Noelle replied flatly.

"That's amazing! Takes a lot of hard work and determination to open a business. I doubt that I could ever try something like that," Matt replied humbly.

"You were really smart. I'm sure you could have done anything you wanted to do." Noelle was inadvertently flirting with him, but he didn't pick up on any of it.

"I like to fix things and understand how they work. Business is a totally different realm. Remember senior year when we took economics? You helped me through that class. I did pretty well because I had strong math skills, but the business concepts were a little confusing for me. You seemed to have a much better grasp at it," Matt replied thoughtfully.

Noelle could feel her cheeks reddening but didn't want him to see, so she tried to raise the collar of her sweater. "When I started high school, I wanted to be a journalist or a literature major, but after a couple of years and taking that aptitude test sophomore year, I started shifting toward business. When I started college, I declared business as my major first semester and never looked back. Opening a business was definitely not in the original plan, but I can't say that I regret it. It's just something that was totally unexpected." Noelle was trying to avoid eye contact because she could feel she would be staring at him just a little bit too long.

"I can tell you that this wasn't my plan in life either, but I actually like my job. I don't know if I'm going to stay here for my whole career, but I'm not planning on leaving. I like living in New Jersey, and my family is here, plus my job was really accommodating when I was going to graduate school. They're a good company," Matt said contently.

"Oh yeah, I'm in my second-to-last semester of graduate school. I hope to be graduating in the spring, and then right after graduation, the store will probably open. Maybe earlier if things work out quicker, but I am trying not to plan as much because overplanning kind of got me into this situation..." Noelle trailed off.

"What do you mean?" Matt asked attentively.

"Oh, it's nothing. I think sleep deprivation is getting to me on some days. So much studying and running to the store and then so little time to do everything else," Noelle replied honestly.

"Yeah, I work five days a week, but I am usually on call on Saturdays, and I will go into work. So I really only have Sundays off unless there is a holiday or I need to take a sick day," Matt replied calmly but almost looked a little bit embarrassed about something. Noelle just couldn't figure out what it was.

"So are you usually around the area, or is this just a special trip?" Noelle was trying to keep the conversation going.

"Um...I'm usually in the office, but I get sent out pretty much anywhere in the area. I tend to go more into New York though...," Matt started to trail off.

"Do you live in New York?" Noelle asked curiously.

"No, but I still have family in that area, so I'm pretty comfortable driving there," Matt replied, almost looking like a cross between nervous and bored.

"Oh, I used to work in New York. I was the manager of Janlene's. I obviously am not working there anymore." Noelle tried to make a joke.

Matt cracked a smile but didn't laugh. "I don't think I know that place, but maybe I did stop there at one time or another..." Matt's voice started to trail off again.

"Well, thanks for fixing my refrigerator. If you are in the area, you can always stop by and say hi. I might even have some snacks. I take food with me if I have to stay here for a longer period of time. I can't leave, and I doubt I can get delivery from anywhere," Noelle muttered out loud.

"You can try to order pizza or something. As long as you have an address, just ask them. You never know. Anyway, it was great to see you again, but I have to get going. I have a couple more stops before going back to the office today," Matt replied.

"Oh, sure, thanks again. I really appreciate it. It was great catching up." Noelle just kept talking as Matt smiled and walked out the door back toward his black sedan.

For some reason, even after all this time, seeing him again seemed to rekindle those feelings of her crush on him from high school. It was completely crazy that out of all people she bumped into, it was Matt. Maybe this was a sign to expect the unexpected.

Chapter 17

"Good evening, class," Professor Summerfield announced as he walked quickly into the classroom toward the front desk. He placed the same beat-up leather bag on the desk as he looked around the classroom to see who was there. "Where is everyone?" Professor Summerfield looked around, a little perplexed, as the class was nearly half empty for the first week of November.

"Maybe they thought Halloween came late or Thanksgiving came early?" Jeff joked. Owen snickered.

"Maybe those students need to get a new calendar," Professor Summerfield replied, retaining his usual deadpan.

"I think there was a bad accident. I don't know what happened, but I heard on the radio that traffic was backed up for miles!" Rowena yelled out.

"Thank you for letting me know. So in light of that info, I'll wait a few more minutes before we begin. How was everyone's weekend?" Professor Summerfield asked while taking a seat behind the desk.

"All right," a few students replied.

"Please try to keep the excitement to yourselves. I can barely handle it," Professor Summerfield replied dryly. A few students started cracking up at his reaction.

"Did you ever work as a comedian? Because you're hilarious," Orlando asked, slouching back in his chair.

"No, I actually don't think I have ever even thought about that type of career, but if I need something to do after retirement, I might embark on something new. Thanks for the suggestion." Professor Summerfield cracked a smile. "Does anyone have any questions about previous material or anything else related to the class?"

Keisha raised her hand. "Professor, did you finish grading our exams? I'm curious what grade I got," Keisha asked timidly.

"Well, I have a few exams left to finish grading. I should have them for you for next week, but I do have most grades in my grade book, so you can see me after class if you're really curious. I don't like to give your midterms back until I have all of them graded. That includes the essays. I will say that overall, everyone did well. I think the class average was a B or a B+," Professor Summerfield replied, nodding with approval.

"Oh, that's great to hear. I was really worried about some of the short-answer questions." Kendall looked relieved.

"As long as you fully answer the question and are able to support your answers, then you should receive full credit. I'm not expecting complex or intricate answers. I only need to know that you know the basics of business ownership and entrepreneurship. That is the point of this class," Professor Summerfield explained.

"What about our final projects? The weekly assignments are getting harder, and it's starting to get more complicated," Fallon whined softly.

"The final projects are just a compilation of the weekly assignments. It's the ten steps of opening a business, from brainstorming to preparing for your grand opening. Of course, this is a classroom, so everything is theoretical. In real life, things don't always go so smoothly. I'm not looking for perfection, but if you have questions, you can ask during class or see me after class or during office hours," Professor Summerfield replied.

"Okay, I'm just worried about answering one of the assignments incorrectly and then putting the incorrect information into my project. I know how vital these assignments are," Fallon explained, still looking pretty anxious.

"That's why I grade your weekly assignments and give you feedback. Most of you are catching on well, but if there is something that is confusing or unclear, feel free to ask me. You can even ask a fellow classmate. A few of your classmates have done exceptionally well so far. Okay, so after the ten homework assignments are completed, there will be one class to ask any last-minute questions before presentations. The last two weeks of class, I think that would be the first two weeks of December, the whole class will be putting their entire projects together to present to the class. You can bring visuals. In fact, I would encourage it. It doesn't have to be complex, maybe a drawing of what you imagine your business to look like or a sample of one or two of your products. For example, one semester, a student wanted to open a bakery, so she brought in some sample pastries. I think she made some homemade cupcakes and doughnuts. The class definitely appreciated the free food samples." Professor Summerfield cracked a smile on his typically serious face.

"Professor? I chose a car detailing business. Can I bring in a scale model car with some potential designs?" Jeff asked.

"That would be a great idea. I will leave it up to all of you to decide what would be best for your presentation, but if you have any questions, just stop by my office or see me after class. Nothing overly complicated and not extremely long either. The presentation shouldn't be more than ten or fifteen minutes maximum. I will not take off if you run a little bit over, but I will take off if it's too short," Professor Summerfield explained.

"What is too short?" Rowena asked as her face was tensing up.

"There is no specific time, but if it's under five minutes, I would consider either speaking a little slower or adding more information. You should have ample information from ten weeks of working on this. Okay, if there are no other questions, I guess we can start the new lesson." Professor Summerfield got up and turned toward the blackboard as a few students wandered in.

"Sorry, Professor, there was a bad accident. Some of us took the scenic route to get here," Amanda apologized as she took a seat.

"It's okay. We are just about to start today's lesson," Professor Summerfield replied while turning around to face the blackboard. He started writing something on the blackboard, but the way his body was angled made it difficult for any of the students to read anything. He moved away from the blackboard for the students to read a few words.

"Choosing a business name? Wasn't this part of the first week's assignment?" Kendall asked.

"No, the name and the business idea were not the same assignment. A lot of students decided to give their business name with the initial business idea, but several students still haven't. So for those who have already done this, it will be an extra easy week. I just need you to write an explanation as to where and how you came up with that name. That includes spelling and pronunciation," Professor Summerfield explained.

Noelle looked down on her notebook as she realized this had been the one weekly lesson she was trying to avoid because she still had absolutely no idea what to name her business—either the real or the fake one.

Rowena raised her hand. "Can we choose a name that isn't in English? My family is Welsh and Irish. I thought about something in Gaelic or Welsh," Rowena asked.

"I want you to think about it like this. If you were really opening your business today, could your future customers pronounce it, spell it, and remember it? If there is a 'no' or 'possibly no' to any of those questions, then I would consider something else. That being said, for this class, I will be a little more flexible with the names. If you picked a name in Welsh and explain in your paper how to properly pronounce it and what it means, then it's okay. Does that clarify everything?" Professor Summerfield looked at Rowena. She nodded as she made a note in her notebook.

"Thank you, Professor," Rowena replied after she put down her pen.

"Okay, just one more thing. You have to remember that your name needs to reflect your business. There also needs to be some sort of relationship between the name and your type of business. For example, you wouldn't want to name your auto body shop Turbo Dancing in the Wind or your shoe store Fresh Morning Java Brew. Is everyone following me? If there aren't any other questions, I want you to break up into your groups. I'll be walking around if you have any questions," Professor Summerfield explained.

Keisha and Sally looked at each other and quickly got into a group without Noelle noticing the desks moved.

"Hey, guys, do you have a name for your businesses? I picked a corny name—the Reading Center. It's memorable, but I think it's kind of bland," Sally complained.

"I think it's a great name. I mean, isn't that what your business is, helping students to learn to read better? At least that's how I remember you explaining it," Keisha chimed in.

Sally nodded.

"I'm still debating a name for my business. I thought about a Family Place, but I really don't know. My boyfriend gave me a couple of suggestions, but I wasn't really thrilled. I think he's more excited about this project than I am." Keisha laughed.

"What about you, Noelle?" Sally asked.

Noelle lowered her eyes. "Absolutely no idea. I have really struggled with this part. My brother gave me the corny suggestion of Joyeux Noël, which is Merry Christmas in French. I said no way. I do not want my coffee shop to appear as a seasonal place. I don't even like the idea of using my first name for my business," Noelle confessed.

"My business? Wow, Noelle, you are really taking to this project," Keisha said encouragingly.

Noelle's eyes opened wide as she didn't realize that she had said that and needed to carefully guard her words from slipping out and saying anything else about her *real* store.

"There's nothing wrong with using your first name. I mean, Noelle's Coffee Shoppe with an extra *p* and *e*, or maybe you can use the example that the professor gave. What was it…Morning Brewery or something? Maybe Fresh Morning Brewery," Sally suggested, struggling to remember.

"I never really liked the idea of using my first name. I personally think it takes away from the business. As for my brother, I think he's being funny because I have been teased since I was young about my name. I still get random people to start singing Christmas carols because of my first name. It was funny when I was a child, not so much now." Noelle sighed.

"How is everyone doing here?" Professor Summerfield asked, walking up to their group.

"I think I'm going with the Reading Center. It's corny, but it's the point of my business and easy to remember," Sally explained.

"Are you opening a tutoring center? It's not a bad name. It's related and easy to remember. What about the rest of the group?" Professor Summerfield nodded approvingly.

"I have been kind of in a toss-up because I started leaning toward the name a Family Place, but I also wanted to include that it has bilingual services. I guess I'm kind of stuck," Keisha admitted.

"What type of business are you opening?" Professor Summerfield asked, drawing a blank.

"A family health-care business, but I'm focusing on family health and nutrition. I guess like a wellness center," Keisha explained.

Professor Summerfield stood there for a moment, thinking. "How about using Family Place but then using the Spanish translation underneath it? I'm sorry, I don't know what that would be in Spanish, but that might help show to your customers that you offer bilingual services. You could also choose a Family Place and then, in smaller print, include that you offer bilingual services. It's your choice how you want to do it, but either way is okay with me." Professor Summerfield nodded approvingly. Keisha smiled as she made some notes in her notebook.

Noelle sat there with her eyes down as she felt totally unprepared for this day in class. "I am really struggling with finding a name," Noelle blurted out before their professor could ask her anything.

"Noelle, it's only a name. Yes, it's important to your business, but for the sake of this class project, it doesn't have to be perfect. In real life, it's a different story, but this is for a class project—nothing too complicated. You could just call it Noelle's Café or even borrow one of my examples from today's lesson. I think I have Fresh Java Brew or Morning Java Brew as an example." Professor Summerfield tried to put her mind at ease.

Noelle smiled and nodded as their professor walked off toward another group.

"You are really struggling with this?" Keisha noted.

"Yeah, it's so strange. I thought naming a business would be easy, but then again, I have spent so much time with everything else I guess I haven't really had time to think about it. I should be okay for next week. It's only a name, right?" Noelle asked nonchalantly.

"Yeah, it's not a big deal," Sally added, taking out her pen to jot down a few more notes in her notebook.

Noelle wrote something in her notebook with a contented smile plastered across her face. She was trying so hard to downplay the significance of naming a business to her professor or her friends and classmates. It might not seem important in the classroom, as once this semester is over, nobody would remember what she did or what she named her business. However, this was much bigger. The name wasn't just to get through an assignment. This was a part of her future, her career, her investment, and she really felt she only had one chance to get it right.

Chapter 18

"Wow, this place is bigger than I expected." Paige looked around in amazement as she slowly stepped through the doorway.

Noelle took her key out of the door's lock and carefully placed it back into her purse. "Yeah, even the realtor said that the size was deceiving. It's much bigger inside than it appears from the outside." Noelle walked toward the counter to place her purse down and a small box of cleaning supplies.

Paige placed the tray of two hot drinks down on the counter. "I got one hot chocolate and one hot tea. I thought I would shake things up a little bit. That and there really wasn't any coffee left. Must have been a busy morning at the convenience store. I really can't wait until your store opens." Paige shrugged as she took the cup of hot tea for herself.

"Oh, great! I wanted hot chocolate. You must have read my mind." Noelle excitedly walked back toward the counter.

"Great minds think alike! Does Valerie know what you are doing with this place? I know she's an interior decorator, so maybe she could give you some pointers," Paige asked while taking a sip from her cup of hot tea.

Noelle lowered her eyes. "Actually, Val offered to help decorate the store in return for allowing her to use my store in her portfolio. We started talking about some ideas, but she hasn't been back here to discuss anything else in person. Honestly, I haven't even spoken to her since. The last time I spoke to her was right before she was leaving to meet Lachlan for their sixth-month anniversary dinner. She told me that she would be back really late and had to be out early the next day meeting with clients and finishing up details at some venues, but then she just disappeared. I waited a few days and then sent her a few text messages. All I got back were very short cryptic responses. That's not at all like Val. She's never cryptic," Noelle replied, still confused about her friend's behavior.

Paige rolled her eyes. "Valerie's definitely not cryptic. At least that's no how I would describe her. But honestly, you might be overreacting. I mean, this is the start of her busy season. Perhaps this year, she's a little bit busier than she was last year. Think about it. So are you. Try not to overanalyze anything," Paige reassured her.

Noelle stood there for a moment before nodding slowly in agreement. However, her eyes said something completely different. "You're probably right. I mean, she did say after she started planning Halloween and Thanksgiving parties that her client list had grown by a lot." Noelle paused for a moment. "But it still seems unlike Valerie. I mean, even when she's really busy, she would always take a moment to send a text message or make a quick phone call. I can't tell you how many times she would be texting her closest cousins or even her best friend from elementary school. I don't know. Something seems off." Noelle sighed.

"Did you two have an argument or a disagreement?" Paige asked randomly.

Noelle shook her head. "No, the last conversation I had with her was normal. In fact, that was probably the happiest that I had seen her in a long time. I think she really likes Lachlan. I think you're right. I'm reading too deeply into this. We're both really busy. When Valerie gets some free time, she'll let me know. Sometimes I forget how much more time-consuming the party and event planning can be in addition to being an interior decorator." Noelle sighed.

"Isn't that kind of like two different careers?" Paige asked, taking a sip from her tea.

"If I remember correctly, she said she majored in interior decorating and then minored in event planning. Besides, making her appear a little more unique, Val mentioned something about using event planning to earn extra money around the holidays. Who would have ever figured that her backup plan would turn out to be the center of her business?" Noelle pondered.

Paige looked at her and smirked. "If there is anyone who understands life not working out just as planned or expected, it would be you." Paige gave Noelle an encouraging look.

Noelle laughed. "I couldn't have dreamed up the past few months if I tried," Noelle joked while Paige reached into her bag and pulled out a package of unopened oatmeal raisin cookies.

"I almost forgot these. When I went grocery shopping, they were on sale, so I bought two packages. Enjoy." Paige smiled while opening the package and taking out a cookie. Then Noelle reached in and took a cookie. She hesitated before taking a bite.

"I feel bad because you bought the drinks and the snacks, and you're spending your day off to help me do some cleaning. When I start to actually get a paycheck again, I owe you dinner," Noelle promised.

"I would settle for a discount on coffee after you open." Paige smiled brightly.

Noelle laughed. "So far, I have several people asking for coffee discounts. I'm starting to become suspicious if people are helping me because they want to or because they think they can get some freebies." Noelle gave a playful look.

"Well, I really do want to help you, but with the amount of coffee I buy per week, a discount would make a significant difference to my weekly budget." Paige tried to remain serious but burst out laughing.

Noelle nodded with a smile. "I'm glad I can help you out with that." Noelle rolled her eyes playfully. "Oh, before I forget. The plumber is stopping by today to replace a pipe in the kitchen under the sink. It shouldn't take more than twenty minutes, he told me, but just in case you see a stranger walking into the store, it's okay." Noelle took a sip of her hot chocolate.

"Oh, wow, was this the wrong day to come and clean up? I don't want to inconvenience you. I know you have your hands full with everything," Paige asked, feeling a little guilty.

"No, not at all. It shouldn't make a difference. I had to be here anyway to let him into the store, but I have been a little off with my days since midterms. I don't know. This semester has really thrown me for a loop so far," Noelle explained, rubbing her temples. Noelle turned her head and looked out the front windows to see Seamus exiting the company van. He had a small toolbox and an elbow-shaped white pipe in the other hand. He walked toward the front door, and Noelle pushed it open for him.

"Hello, Noelle. Sorry it took longer than we told you. Apparently, the part was on back order. Anyway, here it is. It shouldn't take more than ten or twenty minutes to change it," Seamus said in his thick Scottish accent. Little did Noelle know, Seamus had definitely caught the attention of Paige, who was trying to make herself appear inconspicuous.

"Hi, Seamus. Where is Dereck? I thought he said he was stopping by. It doesn't matter either way, just a little surprised," Noelle rambled on, trying not to insult Seamus.

"Yeah, Dereck told me that he was going to stop by, then he got tied up with a problem. His uncle is with him. Some flooding problem in a basement apartment. Not sure what happened…something about construction mishap." Seamus shrugged.

"That sounds horrible." Noelle's mouth dropped.

"Yeah, so it's right through the kitchen door?" Seamus asked quickly. Noelle nodded, and he walked straight through into the kitchen.

Paige waited until he was in the kitchen to say something. "Noelle, he's really cute. Do you know if he's seeing anyone?" Paige sounded like a teenage girl on her first crush.

Noelle looked at her a little strangely. "I know he's not married because Dereck was teasing him about being a bachelor, but I don't know much about him except he's Scottish," Noelle replied while watching her friend's eyes glaze over in a dreamy state.

"I know. Isn't that accent cute? My mother's parents were from Scotland. Well, my grandmother was born there, but my grandfather used to go back to visit. They were buried back in Scotland," Paige muttered.

"I always thought you were English descent, at least that's what you told me your last name Walcott originates from," Noelle asked curiously.

"Yeah, but my mom's maiden name was Kinnaird. That's Scottish," Paige informed her.

"Cool. Learn something new every day," Noelle replied casually.

"That's what my grandfather used to say, 'A new day, a new lesson,'" Paige replied, taking an oatmeal cookie from the package.

"That's a good philosophy. Maybe we should start cleaning so you aren't stuck here all afternoon. You should enjoy some of your day off," Noelle suggested.

Paige nodded as she grabbed a small red rag out of the box on the counter and walked toward the bookshelf with a can of furniture polish. Noelle walked over to one of the small tables and started to clean the top before she was startled by a loud voice.

"Noelle," Seamus called out in his Scottish accent.

Noelle dropped the rag on the table and walked toward Seamus. Paige stopped cleaning and carefully made her way toward the counter to be closer to them.

"Everything is finished. The piece fits perfectly, and you should be good now," Seamus replied.

"How much do I owe you?" Noelle walked toward her purse.

Seamus shook his head. "Nothing. If Chris was here, he would have even been able to do it for you. Anyway, you should be completely set with everything. If you have any other questions, give either me or Dereck a call. We'll stop by. Good luck with everything," Seamus replied flatly.

"Thanks, Seamus. I appreciate it," Noelle replied. Paige seemed to appear out of nowhere, standing right behind her. Noelle had to bite her lip to keep from laughing, watching the unusual behavior of her friend.

"It's no problem. It's my job." Seamus looked over at Paige.

"Seamus, I would like you to meet one of my friends. Her name is Paige," Noelle introduced them.

"Hello." Seamus extended his hand but with a strange look on his face as Paige's face turned bright red. It was almost as if he couldn't understand why she popped out of nowhere to introduce herself to a total stranger.

"Seamus, I'm assuming by your accent that you're Scottish? I'm half Scottish. My grandparents came from Scotland. Well, my grandmother was born there, and my grandfather used to travel back and forth a lot. They were both buried there," Paige muttered out nervously.

Seamus couldn't help but crack a smile at Paige's behavior as he didn't meet too many people that were interested in his heritage. "Yeah, I don't meet too many Scottish people around here. What is your family name?" Seamus asked, being friendly.

Noelle decided to sneak away toward the bookshelf to continue cleaning, giving them some privacy. She could hear the two of them carrying on a short yet friendly conversation. A few minutes later, the front door opened, and Seamus left while Paige walked back toward Noelle.

"So did you two have a nice conversation?" Noelle smirked.

"He's really nice. He comes off as kind of brutish and unfriendly, but when he found out that one of my grandparents was from the same area that his parents are from, we decided to exchange phone numbers. Well, I kind of nudged it because I said I would like to visit one day and it will help to know someone who's actually familiar with the area." Paige smiled.

Noelle couldn't keep herself from giggling. "You sound like a teenager," Noelle joked.

"No, I don't. Well, maybe a little bit. I don't know. I guess it's been a long time since I met a guy whom I really liked. Maybe I forgot how to flirt the right way?" Paige laughed.

"I don't think that is something that you forget to do. The only thing is maybe remembering to remain low-key. You were pretty out in the open today." Noelle laughed.

Paige blushed. "Oh well, at least I have his phone number. If he doesn't like me like that, it's not a bad thing. At least I know someone who could show me around Scotland one day or suggest a great tour guide." Paige shrugged her shoulders.

"Doesn't hurt to know people. I have a couple of distant cousins in Southern France who agreed to be my tour guides if I ever went to visit. We'll see, maybe on my honeymoon. Then again, that's a little bit too ambitious." Noelle sighed.

"Noelle, you really have to stop being so hard on yourself. I've been single for a while too. It doesn't mean that there isn't a guy out there for you. Hang in there. I think you're becoming too cynical," Paige warned her.

"Yeah, despite the unexplainable sequence of events that led me to being a new business owner, I still tend to be pretty cynical about things not working out. Maybe it's a defense mechanism?" Noelle inquired.

Paige shook her head. "Okay, no self-analyzing today. The shelves aren't going to dust themselves. Let's get back to work so we're not here all night," Paige instructed, picking up the other rag and quickly going back to dusting. Noelle smiled, nodded, and picked up the other rag to continue cleaning the bookshelf a little faster than before.

Chapter 19

Noelle pulled in front of her house, letting out a huge yawn before putting her car into park. She sat there for a moment, almost too tired to move, but knew she needed to go inside so she could eat dinner and get some sleep. The attempt at trying to balance all her schoolwork and keeping the store an open secret was starting to wear on her. She knew there was only a few more weeks of school left, and then she could finally rest and then maybe tell her parents about her new venture. Noelle was hoping by that time, the store would be closer to being ready to open and her parents would be less likely to overreact, at least that was how Noelle felt. It was a wonder if Noelle's hesitation was really about fearing how her parents would react to everything or if it was some sort of shame for not succeeding in her original plan.

Noelle quickly climbed out of the driver's side of the car to walk around to the other side to grab her schoolbag and thermos in the cupholder. She slammed the car door shut and walked up to the front of the house and quickly got her house key out to unlock the front door. She tried to be as quiet as she could because she knew her parents were probably sleeping. Noelle placed her schoolbag near the steps, taking out her cell phone and bringing it with her into the kitchen. She saw a large pot on the stove but no note from her mother. Noelle lifted up the lid and smelled her mother's homemade chicken and vegetable stew. It was definitely a family favorite because even her veggie-hating brother would eat it without complaint. She put some into a bowl and placed it into the microwave while she placed the pot away in the refrigerator while taking out a bottle of apple juice. When the microwave went off, she brought the juice bottle and the bowl of stew to the kitchen table for a late dinner.

As Noelle started to eat, she started to think about Paige and her crush Seamus. She marveled at the timing of how Paige and Seamus, who wasn't originally supposed to be at the store, ended up there together on the same day and at the same time. This was enough for somewhat-cynical Noelle, who experienced her own unexplainable chain of events, to actually start to believe in fate. Things seemed to be working out for both of her closest friends with everything else starting to fall into place. Valerie's business had been flourishing, and now she found Lachlan, and things were getting serious. Paige might not be at her dream job, but she was making the most of it, but then she found Seamus. Noelle wondered if this was a sign that good things could be coming soon to her too. If there was anything that Noelle had learned over the past few months, it was that everything could change in the blink of an eye. There is no amount of preparation for some things no matter how hard someone tries to prepare. She glanced down at the table and saw her cell phone ringing.

"Hello?" Noelle answered her phone, not recognizing the number. The connection was so bad that the call was disconnected. Noelle shrugged her shoulders and went back to eating. A few minutes later, the phone rang again. This time, it was another phone number she didn't recognize.

"Hello?" Noelle asked again. She could hear whimpering in the background. The voice sounded familiar, but she couldn't tell who it was on the other side.

"Noelle…it's Paige." Paige barely managed to get it out.

Noelle dropped her spoon in her bowl of stew. "What is it, Paige? Are you okay? Did you just try to call me?" Noelle started to feel her anxiety levels starting to increase.

"Yes…I tried from the pay phone, but the reception was so bad it just disconnected. I'm calling you from Prue's, my brother's girlfriend's phone. I'm in the hospital…" Paige trailed off, trying to compose herself enough to communicate.

"What happened? Are you okay?" Noelle asked.

"I'm here with Prue. She took my brother to the hospital after dinner. He was complaining about abdominal pain, and now they are doing a bunch of tests. He's on antibiotics. They might need to perform surgery. He looks terrible." Paige started crying again.

"Paige, are you okay?" Noelle didn't know what to say as she was completely stunned by the news.

"I'm…I'm…I really don't know. I'm scared, Noelle. I can't even bear the thought of losing Kenny. He's really all I have left." Paige started crying.

Noelle wished she knew what to say to comfort her friend, but her mind was coming up empty. "Prue is with you now? Is she able to stay with you?" Noelle asked, concerned.

"Yes." Paige's voice sounded muffled.

"Good. I don't want you to be alone. Please keep me informed about what is going on. I'll keep you in my prayers. If you need anything, you can call me anytime," Noelle replied, trying to keep her friend calm.

"Thanks, Noelle. I gotta go. The doctor wants to talk to us. I'll talk to you soon." Paige's voice was still muffled, barely making it audible enough for Noelle to comprehend.

"Okay," Noelle managed to get in before Paige hung up. She dropped the phone on the table and sat there almost completely frozen from the news she had just heard. It amazed and scared her how quickly her friend could go from being happy and excited about the future and now barely able to hold herself together. It seemed that since Noelle got fired from Janlene's in August that everything started spiraling out of control. As soon as things started to appear as though they were working out, another curveball or obstacle would drop out of nowhere. There was no way to prevent or prepare for any of it. This semester…this season…had turned out to be one of the most challenging that she had ever had to face. It wasn't just the additional academic rigor in school but also the intense feeling of her whole life being shaken up, making her feel very uncomfortable and sometimes helpless. Some days, it felt like there were endless opportunities on the horizon, while other days felt like her worst nightmare. The only thing she could do now was to admit she couldn't plan or control everything and just accept things as they were and find a way to continue moving forward anyway.

Chapter 20

The past few days almost felt like a whirlwind. Noelle waited anxiously for Paige to let her know how her brother was doing. She tried to keep her phone as close to her as possible for any updates on Kenny's condition but wasn't able to gather much information. The only thing that Noelle was able to decipher from the several brief text messages and phone calls was that Kenny was still in the ICU in critical condition. Noelle tried very hard to focus back onto her schoolwork and the store, but it was difficult because her heart really broke for Paige. If anything, it made Noelle just a little more appreciative of having her brother around to help her. Chris might have his flaws, but she couldn't even imagine going through anything even close to what Paige was experiencing with Kenny.

No matter how much Noelle might have felt terrible for Paige, there was only so much she could do and needed to turn her focus back toward her store and her demanding schoolwork. Although it was much easier to catch up with the reading and missing homework assignments, the store needed to be her main focus because it was much more multifaceted and time-consuming. There was so much left for her to take care of and finish before inspections and the eventual grand opening in late spring or early summer. That was why the lingering questions surrounding Valerie and decorating her store were weighing heavily on her mind. It had been over a month since she had spoken to Valerie and was starting to wonder if her friend was having second thoughts. Maybe Valerie was becoming too busy with her own business to help out, or maybe she just simply forgot all about it. Noelle wasn't upset about her friend being very busy, but she needed to know if Valerie was still available to help or not.

Just as Noelle was about to send a text message to Valerie because she couldn't wait any longer, Valerie sent her a text message out of the blue saying that she would be in the area Thursday evening and could stop by to discuss some details about the store. Noelle was relieved initially but also felt very aggravated. She didn't like missing class unless she was sick or in an emergency. However, Noelle really didn't have a choice and reluctantly agreed. To Noelle's chagrin, Valerie canceled at the last minute without an explanation and rescheduled for the following afternoon. Noelle had a lot of patience, but it was wearing very thin. Between the pressures from school and holding everything together with the store, she now had to rearrange her schedule for someone else, making everything much more difficult. She had to remind herself that Valerie was doing her a favor and needed to be gracious, but that didn't take away from her deepening frustration.

Noelle arrived early that Friday afternoon and sat down at the little card table in front of the store window, placing her thermos full of hot chocolate and her "store notebook" on top. She marked off a small section near the back of the notebook for the interior decorating to make sure she had her own guidelines to follow in case Valerie disappeared again for a couple of weeks or even months. She wasn't happy thinking like that, but she needed to plan ahead so she wouldn't be stranded. Noelle was visibly annoyed as she jotted some notes down in her notebook, but she was trying very hard to remain calm. The last thing she wanted to do was get into a fight. But anything can happen when patience is short, and tempers start flaring.

Noelle turned her head to look out the front window as she watched Valerie's car pull up in front of the store. Valerie parked a couple of spaces away from Noelle and hurried out of the car with the same beige canvas bag full of samples and supplies. Noelle got up to open the front door while Valerie rushed inside.

"It's freezing out there," Valerie remarked nonchalantly while shaking a few snow flurries off her winter coat sleeves.

Noelle was trying to keep her aggravation under control, but Valerie's complete disregard for standing her up the previous night without an explanation or an apology was getting under her skin. Noelle took a deep breath to calm down. "Yeah, I put the small electric heater on to take the chill out of the store. It's already starting to feel warmer in here." Noelle stopped before she could say anything else.

Valerie took off her coat and placed her bag on the folding chair nonchalantly. "Oh, great, it's better than nothing. At least I can walk around with my coat off. When are you planning on getting the heating and air-conditioning looked at? Because this really isn't practical," Valerie replied sarcastically.

Noelle was really trying to keep herself calm, but Valerie was already pushing her buttons. Valerie could be very direct, but she was rarely—if ever—thoughtless or inconsiderate.

"Well, I'm working on it. I can only get so much done at a time. I'm still working on other things, such as decorating the store," Noelle snapped back. She didn't even realize that her tone had grown a little sharp, but she didn't care either.

Valerie turned to her with a stern look. "Well, that's why I am here today. Now I can stay a couple of hours at most, but I have a few other clients I need to meet with, and I cannot afford to miss those appointments. Oh, sorry about last night. I had a couple of appointments I couldn't miss either," Valerie replied condescendingly.

Noelle crossed her arms and narrowed her eyes with a sarcastic smile across her face. "Well…let's get started, then. I wouldn't want to keep you from anything important," Noelle replied a bit snarkily. Valerie's face grew tense.

"What is that supposed to mean? You know that I am doing you a real favor by coming here and helping you for free. You should be grateful," Valerie snapped back. Her eyes narrowed.

"Wait just a minute, Valerie. It was you who suggested and offered to work for only the cost of supplies. If it was up to me, I would have worked something out with you so you would get paid something. Is that what's up with you? Is it about money? If that's what's wrong, we can sit down right now and discuss some numbers. I have some paper and pens on the table," Noelle replied, motioning toward the card table.

"Oh, I see. Now that you realize what type of strain I'm under, you feel guilty?" Valerie rolled her eyes as she tugged at the sleeves of her bronze satin dress jacket. "So to make yourself feel better… now you want to offer to pay me! Amazing how this thought never even popped in your head a couple of months ago!" Valerie's voice grew louder.

Noelle was a little taken aback by her friend's growing resentment. "Is this why you disappeared for over a month? Because you were mad that I didn't force you to take payment for helping me? I don't buy that crap at all! I know you for far too long. Come on, Val. We've been friends since high school, and all of a sudden, you disappear, and when you reappear, you act like I'm the enemy. What is going on with you? I wouldn't have agreed to allow you to help if I knew you would be reacting like this," Noelle asked sternly but with a hint of compassion. She wanted to try and diffuse the growing tension, but it seemed to be backfiring.

"What's wrong with me? What's wrong with me? You have some nerve! I mean, what do you do all week? Go to class a couple of nights a week and then stop by the store occasionally to check on the work that your brother or one of his friends is helping you with? I mean, what a great life! You don't know anything about what building a business really takes! I have busted my butt for over five years to build up my business—nights without sleep, months without a day off, or even a couple of years without a vacation. I never thought I would see you become so spoiled and lazy! Definitely not the Noelle I knew from years ago!" Valerie yelled.

The anger ran very deep, and Noelle could feel it cut right through her. She had no idea what set Valerie off but was still determined to figure out what was going on. "Spoiled? Lazy? Valerie, what are you talking about? I have always worked very hard, and I'm working harder now than I ever have worked before. I never once insinuated that you didn't work very hard to get to where you are now.

173

I know the sacrifices you made and without any handouts. If this is from something that Chris said, just ignore him like I do. Sometimes he speaks before his brain can react," Noelle said, trying to make a small joke, hoping that would cool things off, and yet again, it only backfired.

"This has nothing to do with Chris. I could care less about him. I'm not talking about him. This is about you!" Valerie yelled.

That cut Noelle very deeply. She fought back a few tears before she managed a response. "I didn't say a word when you said the only time you were available was Thursday night when I had class. No, I really didn't want to miss class, but I did because I knew you were going out of your way and your schedule is way busier than mine. Then all I get after wasting three hours alone was a cryptic text message that you were on your way home and had to reschedule for this afternoon because it was *better for you*. I wasted a whole evening sitting here for nothing! I can't afford to miss any class time. I can't afford to fall behind in anything! And if you really think that I don't do anything, then why do I have such big black circles under my eyes? I haven't been sleeping much because I have so much to take care of in a short amount of time!" Noelle started yelling. Her face became bright red with anger.

"Nobody told you to go through with this. You chose to open your own business. So if things aren't working out, then that's your problem, nobody else's. It's part of the risk," Valerie shouted back.

Noelle looked at her friend in disbelief. She took a huge risk by stepping out of her comfort zone, which already made her feel uneasy, but now she also needed to worry about her entire savings account being depleted before she even finished all of the maintenance and repair work around the store. "Where is all this coming from? This isn't you," Noelle exclaimed. Her facial expression was a combination of anger and hurt.

"Who said this isn't who I am? If you really have a problem with me, maybe we need to reevaluate the idea of being friends! I have been the same since high school, and it never bothered you before. Maybe you're the one that changed!" Valerie shouted back coldly.

Noelle could feel her eyes misting up again. "I have never seen you behave like this, even around people you don't like," Noelle argued, still trying to remain somewhat calm.

"This is all me. If you can't accept me for who I am, then I have no room for you either! Listen, I don't have time for this. I have a business to run and clients to see. I'm leaving!" Valerie shouted as she ran to pick up her large canvas bag and stormed out through the front door of the store.

Noelle didn't have a chance to get another word in edgewise, but judging by the look on Valerie's face, it wouldn't have done much anyway. Valerie slammed her car door shut and quickly flew out of the parking lot back onto Main Street.

Noelle and Valerie had their small disagreements in the past, but nothing ever escalated into an actual argument. Usually, they were both able to maintain composure and respected each other's opinions. Sometimes they would even laugh about it afterward. Despite Valerie's strong personality and blunt responses, she rarely stayed angry and almost never held a grudge. Unfortunately, the Valerie that Noelle saw today seemed to be a completely different person—someone she had never seen before. And it made Noelle question who the real Valerie was—something she never thought she would do.

For a moment, after calming down, Noelle wondered if she had done or said something over the past couple of months that made Valerie react so terribly. She took a seat down on the same folding chair and looked back out the front window, wondering if Valerie would return after cooling off. So many feelings were flowing around in her head and in her heart. Her one friend was watching her brother fight for his life, while the other friend was trying to blame and vilify her for accepting help from others with the store. Was this all part of growing up? Or did all this happen to expose the true colors of those around her? The last three months felt like a dramatic, nightmarish roller-coaster ride, and Noelle couldn't wait to get off. She took a few minutes to gather her thoughts together before getting up and looking around to see if there was any other cleaning left to do before leaving to go back home.

Chapter 21

Noelle pulled into parking lot 7A a little after 5:00 p.m. She knew she arrived extra early before class but had very little motivation to get out of the car and socialize with other classmates. Ever since the blowout argument with Valerie last week, Noelle just hadn't felt the same. In addition, she still hadn't heard anything from Paige about her brother. Even though that meant Kenny hadn't gotten worse, it also meant he hadn't gotten any better. At that moment, she almost felt like she had no one to talk to. It was true she had her friends Sally and Keisha from class, but both lived far away and had jobs and boyfriends and really didn't have the extra time to spend with her. Noelle wasn't angry; she was just feeling lonely at that moment. She laid her head back on the headrest when a noise coming from her purse startled her. She reached over and saw the missed phone call. It was Matt—definitely the last person she thought would call her. The phone rang again.

"Hello," Noelle answered excitedly.

"Hi, Noelle, it's Matt. How's everything going? I haven't been around the area to stop by your store, and you haven't called for anything, so I'm assuming everything is good?" Matt asked inquisitively.

Noelle got quiet for a second. "Yeah, Matt, everything with the store is doing great, but…" Noelle trailed off, not wanting to unload all her problems on her old friend.

"Noelle, what's wrong? Are you okay? I hope graduate school didn't swallow you up," Matt replied, trying to make a joke.

"I'm okay. I really don't want to bother you," Noelle replied hesitantly.

"If you need to talk, I'm here. Isn't that what friends are for? Do you remember junior year when I was so excited about being on the varsity baseball team? I thought I was a shoo-in, and then I ended up only making junior varsity. I complained all homeroom and even into English class, but you sat there and listened to me, so maybe this is a very late payback," Matt joked.

Noelle couldn't help but smile. "Well, the brother of one of my closest friends is in the hospital. I'm not sure what happened, but he got really sick, and now he's in the ICU. I feel so bad for Paige, but I don't want to bother her because she's going through so much. What makes it even worse is that she doesn't have her parents here," Noelle started.

"Oh, do they live in another state?" Matt asked.

"No, they passed away when she was in high school. So her brother being that sick is really hitting her harder. I wish I knew what to do." Noelle sounded kind of helpless.

"Oh, that's terrible to hear. I hope he makes a full recovery. All you can do is let Paige know you are there for her. She'll reach out when she's ready," Matt assured her.

"Thanks. That makes me feel a little more at ease. Now for my other friend…" Noelle sighed.

"What's wrong with the second friend?" Matt asked cautiously.

"I really have no idea. When I saw her in late September, she was really happy and looking forward to the holiday season and my new business venture. She even offered to help decorate my store. It felt so cool to have an actual professional interior decorator working in my store! Then she disappeared for a month and a half and then reappeared out of nowhere totally different," Noelle continued before Matt interrupted her.

"Wait… Why did she disappear?" Matt asked suspiciously.

"Oh, she owns her own interior decorating and party planning business. Even though she has clients throughout the year, the holiday season is her busiest. Despite being really busy during the fall, I would always hear back from her from time to time, even if it's only a text message. But this year, almost nothing but a couple of cryptic and cold words. I just assumed that she was extra busy, but my instincts say something is not right," Noelle confided.

"Did you try to talk to her? Ask her if everything is okay?" Matt inquired.

"Yeah, I tried multiple times, but we ended up getting into a huge argument. Every time I tried to ask her what was wrong, I hit more roadblocks with her, and she continued to throw insults back at me. Maybe agreeing to have a friend work on my store wasn't such a good idea," Noelle answered honestly.

"Maybe it's not you. Maybe it's something going on in her life. Maybe the holidays are extra stressful?" Matt suggested.

"Yeah, I was thinking something similar, but she wouldn't open up and say anything. It all went back to me." Noelle sighed.

"Even if there was some type of miscommunication between the two of you that made your friend upset, you can't blame yourself for all this. Maybe there is something that she needs to work out alone. I wish I could give you better advice, but that is a truly bizarre situation," Matt exclaimed.

"I know. That's why I think it bothers me so much more. Maybe we both just need some time to cool off before we try to work things out. I've been friends with Valerie for so long…I don't want to lose her friendship." Noelle's voice started to trail off as she felt a tickle in her throat.

"Things have a way of working themselves out. That's corny, I know, but my mom usually says that. It really came in handy when school didn't work out the way that I had hoped it would," Matt started.

"What do you mean? Didn't you graduate from some prestigious engineering school in New England?" Noelle inquired.

Matt was quiet for a couple of seconds. "Yeah, I got accepted into the Northeast Watterfjord Valley Institute and even got some scholarships, which helped, but the school wasn't the right choice for me. As much as I excelled in high school, I really struggled after I got there. I started drowning in all the schoolwork and pushed myself to study and work harder. Well, that gave me pneumonia. I couldn't finish the semester, so I withdrew, but if I stayed, I probably would have failed something. Believe it or not, I ended up in a local community college for a couple of semesters before transferring to a state school," Matt replied, kind of melancholic.

"Oh, Matt, I'm sorry to hear that, but you know, it doesn't matter which school you attend or graduate from. It's what you do with your degree. I think you are making a big impact in a lot of people's lives," Noelle tried to encourage him.

"It's okay. It actually worked out for the best. I am in New Jersey near my family, and that's where I want to stay. I guess I just needed to spread my wings a little bit to see where I really belonged," Matt joked.

Noelle laughed right along with him even though she didn't find it that funny. "I feel the same. I'm okay relocating, but I still want to be close enough to my family," Noelle agreed.

"Oh, sorry to cut this short, but I have to get running. I have a few things to do before I get home tonight, and I'm sure you have class or something." Matt sounded a little bit rushed.

"I'm in my car in the parking lot of school." Noelle laughed.

"Good luck tonight and hope everything else works out too. I'll talk to you soon," Matt quickly replied, getting off the phone.

Noelle sat there for a moment still holding the phone in her hand even though the call was disconnected. She still couldn't believe it, but Matt had called her out of all people! Did that mean that maybe there was a possibility he might like her too? But she knew in reality that he was just an old high school crush who found his way back into her life. Noelle didn't want to look deeper into anything he said or did for fear of being disappointed or hurt again. As of right now, their relationship was no more than old high school friends working together professionally.

Noelle threw her phone into her bag and grabbed her thermos out of the car before slamming the driver's door shut. She looked up from her schoolbag and thought that the campus looked a little desolate with only a few students walking around. It seemed a little unusual, but Noelle shrugged it off as nothing significant and walked quickly toward Delaney Hall, where both of her graduate classes were held. She pulled the side door open and looked around, also noticing only a few students, making the building seem empty. She wondered if some students started their Thanksgiving break a little early but then realized it was probably heavier-than-normal traffic heading toward school because of the upcoming holidays. She started to walk up the stairs toward the third floor where her Thursday night class was located. She had the option of also taking the elevator, but it was often not working or very slow; the stairs just seemed like a better choice. She didn't mind Delaney Hall, but she preferred attending her Tuesday-night class much more. The Tuesday-night classroom was on the first floor, with more windows, and near the side door for a quick exit back toward the parking lot. The only thing she preferred in the Thursday-night classroom was the brand-new chalkboards, which made it much easier to read than the ones in her Tuesday-night class. When she got to the classroom door on the third floor, she was stunned to see barely any other students.

"Where is everyone?" Noelle asked out loud.

"You're guess is as good as mine," Orlando replied, looking at his watch and comparing it to the clock in the classroom.

"I hope this isn't Thanksgiving." Noelle started to wonder off in her thoughts.

"It's not Thanksgiving. It's the week before. Yeah, this is strange. Was class canceled?" Sally asked, looking around, a little confused.

"I'm starting to think that, and you know what, I'm going to head home. It's ten to six, and nobody is here. I still have a ton of work to catch up on. Between this and Tuesday night's class, I feel like I'm a full-time student," Orlando commented, throwing his notebook into his book bag and swinging it over his left shoulder.

"I know exactly how you feel. Yeah, I think I'm going to leave if nobody shows up in the next five to ten minutes, but if the professor does show up, I'll let her know you were here, Orlando," Sally offered.

"Thanks. Have a Happy Thanksgiving since we don't have any classes next week." Orlando smiled at both of them while walking out of the classroom.

"Happy Thanksgiving," Sally and Noelle replied as Orlando left the classroom.

Sally turned to Noelle. "I think there's no class today. My friend told me earlier that her class was canceled today too because her professor is sick. I wonder if something is going around school. It looks pretty empty today," Sally commented at the eeriness of the darkly lit rooms.

"You know what? Let's just leave. If there really was class tonight, at least the professor would have shown up by now," Noelle surmised. Sally nodded while Noelle took a sip from her thermos.

Just as they were exiting the classroom, an older woman with silvery-grayish hair and a pair of pink plastic eyeglasses attached to a gold chain around her neck walked up to the classroom door. She reached down to put her eyeglasses on to make sure she was putting up the sign on the right door and then quickly walked away without saying a word. Sally walked toward the sign and nodded to Noelle before walking away.

"Class is canceled for tonight, so I guess this means I get some extra sleep," Sally remarked while looking at all the empty classrooms down the hallway.

"I'm probably going to just do some homework. That will be my whole weekend," Noelle muttered gently.

Sally stopped for a moment and turned to Noelle. "Really? That's all you are doing this weekend? So you have no other plans?" Sally asked curiously.

Noelle scrunched her eyebrows. "What am I supposed to do? Finals are coming up soon," Noelle argued.

"Listen, I don't know if you are up for this or not, but Jimmy's cousin is coming in for the week. We were going to take him out for dinner this weekend on Saturday if you want to come." Sally looked hopeful.

"What are you talking about?" Noelle asked directly.

"Well, it'll be awkward being a third wheel," Sally replied sheepishly.

"Are you trying to set me up on a blind date? I don't know." Noelle didn't appear interested.

"Not exactly. It's just to sit and talk to him. Listen, there is nothing at all expected. He lives in Connecticut, so there is no expectation to date him or anything. It's just a night out for fun. Come on, Noelle, when do you go out? I mean, all I ever hear you talk about is studying or searching for a job or helping your brother with some afterwork projects. When do you have some time for yourself?" Sally inquired.

Noelle tried to avoid eye contact because she knew that Sally was right, but at the same time, she needed to worry about her store, which nobody still knew about. "I don't know." Noelle hesitated.

"How about if I ask Keisha and her boyfriend? I would like to meet Gil because Keisha talks about him all the time. I feel like I know him already. At least you'll have me and Keisha there if things don't work out well. He's a nice guy but kind of quiet. He works in HVAC," Sally replied quickly, hoping that Noelle would change her mind.

Noelle thought for a moment but eventually relented. "Oh, okay. What time on Saturday?" Noelle asked.

"I would say between seven thirty and eight p.m., but I will call you tomorrow with all the details," Sally replied excitedly.

"So what is his name? You know I would like to know what to call him," Noelle replied, trying not to sound too disappointed. Even if Noelle thought Jimmy's cousin was nice, she still had many mixed feelings emanating from all of her previous bad blind date experiences and her small crush on Matt.

"Wilder," Sally replied quickly.

Noelle froze for a moment before cracking a smile. "Wilder? Is that really his name or some weird nickname?" Noelle was a little stunned but tried not to laugh for fear of insulting Sally or Jimmy.

"No, that's his real name. I know it sounds a little strange. I think it's his mother's maiden name, but I don't really know. Either way, he's still a nice guy. When they were growing up, some of the cousins used to call him Wil, so he might still respond to that name," Sally replied, trying to make this more enticing for Noelle.

They walked down the stairs to the first floor and walked through the long hallway until they reached the back exit heading toward the parking lots.

"I am glad that I got to see you tonight so I was able to ask you in person, but I drove all the way here for almost nothing," Sally whined while cracking a smile.

"Yeah, I'm lucky I only live about twenty minutes away, and I was out running errands anyway." Noelle shrugged.

"Which parking lot is your car in?" Sally asked.

"I'm in Lot 7A," Noelle explained.

"Why? You should be trying to find a spot in Lot 3A like Keisha and I usually do. I know sometimes you need to drive around, but students are usually leaving by five thirty or five forty, so there is still time," Sally explained as she pushed the back door open to go outside.

"I think it's become habit. I can't guarantee when I can get here unless I need to be here at a specific time. It depends on when I leave. Sometimes if I leave too late and get stuck in traffic, I could end up here close to class time. So I just go to the parking lot that I assume I'm going to find a parking space in." Noelle shrugged.

"Noelle, maybe you need to take a risk. Be a little daring and search in another parking lot." Sally laughed.

"Yeah, I think my life needs something to really spice it up," Noelle joked, trying to hide her real feelings. She was thankful that Sally didn't notice the expression on her face.

"Okay, I will call Keisha later and ask if she and Gil are available. I will call you tomorrow with all the details. I'm so excited to be hanging out with all of you! Anyway, see you Saturday!" Sally waved as she embarked on her walk toward Lot 3A.

Noelle took her time walking back toward her car in Lot 7A. She spent the whole time pondering if she had made the right decision to go on another blind date. Noelle never really had much luck with dating, but her blind dates always seemed to turn out for the worst—her last blind date being a complete disaster. Her date arrived very late because he didn't have a car, spent the whole time talking about his video game collection, and then left her with the bill because he *forgot* his wallet at home. It was times like those that really made her appreciate being single, but then she would find herself thinking about Matt and start to second guess those feelings. As of right now, she had no idea if Matt was really interested in her and being shy about it or if it was wishful thinking on her part, but she was hoping to find out real soon.

Chapter 22

Noelle stood in front of her full-length mirror as she clicked her silver loop earrings into her left and then right ears. She stood up straight to make sure her outfit was smooth and nothing was sticking up. She smoothed out her black dress jacket and made sure her pale-pink dress blouse was lying flat around her collar. Noelle was so nervous not because she was being set up on a blind date but because it had been so long since she had gone out and had some fun. If it wasn't for Paige and Valerie, she probably wouldn't have had any social life. She didn't know what to think about Jimmy's cousin, but the idea that Wilder was trained in HVAC definitely got her attention. Of course, she would not want to date someone just to get some free work done, but maybe he was an honest guy who wouldn't try to rip her off. Chris said he was going to keep looking for someone from his contacts, but between his full-time construction job and all his spare time working at the store, he didn't have much time left over. Although she hadn't always been the closest to her brother, words really couldn't express the appreciation she held for everything he did. The most important thing was that he still managed to keep quiet about the store until Noelle was ready to come clean to their parents. The only thing she had to worry about now was making sure she didn't accidentally spill the beans while she was out with her friends. She walked back toward her closet to pick out a pair of black kitten heels, then walked over to her bedroom door to grab her matching black purse, shutting the door behind her.

Noelle walked very slowly down the stairs as she was afraid of falling because it had been a long time since she wore anything except sneakers or ballet flats. She made a slight left to continue walking down the short hallway toward the kitchen. Her mother was in the kitchen baking another cake, turning her head when she heard the gentle tapping of shoes on the hardwood floor.

"Noelle, why are you all dressed up?" her mother asked, slightly intrigued.

"Sally asked if I wanted to go out tonight with her and a few friends. It's only at a diner. I forgot what she called it, but I have the address," Noelle replied calmly as she nervously moved her hand over her hair to make sure her frizzy curls weren't sticking up.

Her mother had to look at her daughter again because she wasn't used to seeing her with eye shadow and lip gloss. "I'm so happy to hear about you going out. You always seem to be either at school or searching for a job and, the rest of the time, in your room. Life isn't all about work. Sometimes you need to just enjoy life. Besides, if you want to find someone…" Her mother mentioned nonchalantly.

Noelle rolled her eyes. "I'm not going out to meet a guy. I'm going out to not think about schoolwork." Noelle cracked a smile.

"Have fun. I know I don't know Sally, but tell her hi." Her mother smiled.

"You know Keisha, don't you?" Noelle asked curiously.

"I haven't met her, but you did talk about her a lot, so I guess you can tell her hi too." Her mother went back to checking her cake.

Noelle turned around and walked back down the hallway to grab her black coat out of the closet and her car keys off the small hallway table. She walked out the front door without saying another word. As soon as she stepped outside, she felt a bitter chill in the air, quickly bolting toward her car parked in front of the house. She turned the heater on as soon as she started the car while she rubbed her hands together to warm them up. Even though she always said she would buy gloves, it would always slip her mind. She pulled out a small piece of paper with the name and address of the place where she was meeting everyone. She didn't remember ever being there but had passed that route several times when she was commuting between New York and New Jersey as the manager of Janlene's.

Noelle put her signal on and quickly pulled onto the street when it was clear. It was pretty slow for a Saturday night. She figured that maybe people were getting ready for traveling or holiday plans for the following week and didn't think twice about it. The whole drive from her home toward Chez Lulu was very nostalgic. She remembered the first time she drove that route to Janlene's for her first interview and that no matter how worried she was, she felt calm, almost as though she knew that was the place where she was meant to be working. Throughout the past three months, she had experienced an array of emotions, from anger to hope to disappointment to inspiration to betrayal, but was finally finding some sort of peace. Noelle might not have asked for this to happen, but with each passing day, she was becoming more grateful for the new direction her life was taking because it was helping her to see that sometimes thinking outside of the box could bring more hope and joy than trying to remain comfortable.

As she reached the parking lot of Chez Lulu, she looked around to see if she saw Sally's car or even Keisha's car. She wasn't sure if Keisha and Gil were coming but was still hopeful. Noelle didn't see anyone and decided to just sit in her car with the car running for a few minutes to see if maybe someone would show up soon. If not, she was going to bolt inside where at least she wouldn't be freezing out in the cold alone. After a couple of minutes, she saw a white compact sedan pull up beside her car. The car didn't look familiar, but the driver was instantly recognizable. It was Sally. Noelle turned her car off and quickly got out with her purse and had to consciously remind herself to lock the door since the automatic door locks didn't work all the time. Sally was standing on the sidewalk wearing a pair of jeans and a long-sleeved sienna-colored tunic under a goldish-colored peacoat.

"So glad you could make it!" Sally said, giving Noelle a hug.

Noelle hugged her back. "I think I needed a break from school and life. Even my mom was thrilled to hear I was going out," Noelle joked.

"Well, if she's like my mom, she's probably worried about you. My older sister was always out with people. I was more of a wallflower that was reading. That's probably why I ended up majoring in literature." Sally laughed. Noelle laughed too.

"I was a bookworm too…until graduate school." Noelle rolled her eyes.

"Yeah, hard to keep up with all the additional reading. Well, let's go inside. It's really cold out tonight." Sally rushed over to the front door and pulled it open and motioned for Noelle to go inside first. Noelle nodded and walked inside but waited for Sally before they went into the restaurant. Noelle looked around and tried to remember if she had ever stopped there for dinner or takeout, but nothing looked familiar. Sally walked up to the hostess and asked for a table.

"I need a table or maybe a booth for six people," Sally said loudly.

Noelle felt relieved because she knew that meant Keisha and Gil were planning on coming tonight.

"Well, there's like a twenty- or thirty-minute wait, but you can take a seat at the bar until your table is ready. We'll call you," the hostess, an older woman with a warm smile and reddish hair with silver streaks, answered.

"That sounds good. My name is Sally. Do you need my last name?" Sally asked hesitantly.

"If there's another Sally, then yes, but you could just give a letter if you want," the woman suggested.

"Sally O.," Sally replied quickly. The woman jotted her name down and nodded before they began walking toward the bar.

"I'm following you because I don't know this place at all. I do remember there being a smaller diner around here somewhere, but I hadn't been in there either, at least that I don't remember. I used to drive this route a lot when I was still manager of the coffee shop," Noelle said, looking around, trying to take everything in.

"This used to be Lulu's Diner. I used to come here with my sister when I first started college. We would go out once a week. Then the owners retired, and their children took over. The diner was still popular with locals but failed to get more attention. So the children wanted to try something different and turned it into a restaurant. They renamed it Chez Lulu to make it sound chicer. The food is a mixture of some of the classics and some new stuff. I'm sure you will find something that you will like." Sally smiled as she took a seat on one of the barstools. Noelle took a seat right next to her.

"What can I get you ladies tonight?" asked a good-looking young bartender. Noelle blushed a little bit but tried to act uninterested. Sally noticed and tried not to laugh.

"I'll just have a glass of the house white wine," Sally replied calmly.

"A margarita with sugar," Noelle replied quickly.

The bartender nodded and went to make their drinks.

"Somebody has a little crush," Sally teased. Noelle blushed slightly, but it wasn't visible under the dim lights.

"I barely noticed. I guess he's okay," Noelle said calmly, trying to play it off.

"Sure, whatever you say." Sally placed her hand over her mouth to keep herself from laughing too hard.

"Can I get you two anything else?" the bartender asked while placing their drinks down in front of them.

"No, I think we're okay. Thanks," Sally replied while Noelle was trying not to talk to avoid potentially embarrassing herself.

"My name is Cullen. Let me know if you need anything else. Enjoy," Cullen replied before turning his attention to other customers sitting at the bar, waiting for their drinks.

"Well, now you at least know what to call the cute bartender," Sally joked.

Noelle just rolled her eyes. "Okay, whatever," Noelle said while taking a sip of her margarita.

"I was able to get ahold of Keisha last night. She said that she and Gil should be free tonight and that they are going to try and make it. She said something about packing for a trip down south," Sally replied while taking a sip of her wine.

"Yeah, I think Keisha's aunt lives down in South Carolina, and usually, she goes with her mom and sister for the week of Thanksgiving. I guess this year Gil is finally tagging along," Noelle said casually.

"Oh, I wonder if some big announcement will come next year," Sally wondered.

Noelle shrugged her shoulders. "I really don't know. All she said was that she wanted to complete her master's degree before she wanted to talk about a serious commitment, but I know she's head over heels for Gil, so I wouldn't be surprised." Noelle took another sip of her margarita.

"Have you ever met Gil? I mean, he sounds really nice," Sally asked, trying to get some details about the mysterious guy.

Noelle smiled. "He's a good guy. I met him once briefly in the second semester of graduate school. Keisha's car was in the shop for some reason, and she didn't have a way to get to and from class, so Gil left work early and drove her to class and waited around until it was time for her to go home. He was very friendly and took the time to grade his students' papers. He's a high school teacher," Noelle recalled.

"Do you know what subject he teaches?" Sally asked curiously.

"I think he teaches Spanish, but you can ask him. He likes to talk about his job and his students. He's very outgoing," Noelle said, taking another sip from her drink. Noelle looked up, and her eyes widened at the sight of Keisha and Gil seemingly appearing out of nowhere. "Keisha? You must have mental telepathy. We were just talking about the two of you," Noelle replied, pleasantly surprised.

"Well, I hope it was only good things," Keisha teased.

"Yeah, I was just telling Sally when Gil drove you all the way to school when your car was being repaired and that he stayed there and graded papers," Noelle explained.

"Oh, my prince charming to the rescue! Yeah, my car was fine the night before, and then when I got up in the morning, it wouldn't start. I had to call out of work and take it to the auto body shop who said it was my ignition and I would have to wait two days to pick up my car. I could afford to miss a day or two of work since I never take time off, but I was so afraid of missing class. Here comes Gil to the rescue who said 'Sure, I'll take you' and then found an empty classroom to grade some papers. It almost felt like a repeat of what happened to your mom's car when we were in middle school—can't believe we've known each other for that long!" Keisha gushed. She looked up to her slender much taller boyfriend who was checking his cell phone, apparently missing all the conversation. She gently nudged him, and he looked up and smiled at Sally and Noelle.

"I'm Gil. Wait, I think I know you. Did we meet before?" Gil asked, looking over at Noelle. She nodded.

"Yes, I'm Noelle. We met that day you dropped Keisha off to class when her car was being repaired," Noelle reminded him.

Gil nodded with a big smile as though the memory came flooding back to him. "Yes, I'm sorry I didn't remember your name, but your face looks familiar. How is everything going?" Gil asked, being friendly.

"Same thing…different day." Noelle smirked.

"Ah, I definitely can relate to that. So that would make you Sally? Thanks for inviting us. I'm always asking Keisha about her friends from school, but since it's so far away, it's hard to hang out together," Gil continued to talk. It was evident that he could outtalk his girlfriend by a mile.

"Yes, I'm Sally. Well, I'm just glad that you two were able to show up tonight. Noelle tells me that you are a teacher. What subject do you teach?" Sally asked curiously.

Gil smiled. "High school Spanish. It has its moments, but it's definitely rewarding." Gil smiled.

Keisha turned to him and smiled. "Gil, don't be so modest. He is in charge of the Spanish Honor Society and teaches AP Spanish. They really love him there," Keisha said proudly while holding his hand tightly.

"They only gave me that class because nobody else wanted to teach it. I guess it helps that I'm a native Spanish speaker," Gil replied humbly.

"You're a great teacher! You have really helped with my Spanish, *mi corazón*," Keisha reached up to kiss him on the cheek.

Sally smiled as she thought they were really cute. Noelle was happy for them, but the mushiness was starting to get to her. Maybe being single for a while had made her a little bit bitter toward other couples, or maybe it was jealousy because that was something that she wanted for herself and just couldn't seem to find.

"Sally O.," a voice called seemingly out of nowhere.

Gil and Keisha looked at each other, and Noelle shrugged her shoulders.

"Sally O.?" Keisha asked.

"Oh yeah, that's me," Sally replied, getting up from her barstool.

"What does the *O* stand for?" Keisha asked.

"Overtired," Sally joked. Noelle and Keisha started laughing. Sally walked ahead of Noelle, Keisha, and Gil toward the hostess to see what was available.

"There's a booth available, but you'll have to await a little longer for a table," the hostess replied gently.

Sally nodded. "Sure, a booth is fine," Sally replied.

"Okay, she's going to take you to your booth," the hostess replied, pointing to a middle-aged waitress with bleached-blond hair.

Sally, Noelle, Gil, and Keisha followed the waitress toward the booth. Sally took a seat on one side and Noelle on the other side, and Keisha and Gil grabbed two chairs to sit at the end of the booth. They knew there wasn't enough room for six people at the booth without the extra chairs.

"I'm not your waitress, but if you want something to drink, I can get it for you. If not, you'll probably wait a few minutes. We're usually busy on the weekends, but it's extra busy tonight," the waitress explained.

"We're fine. Thank you," Sally replied. Gil and Keisha were too busy in their own conversation to pay attention.

"Enjoy your evening!" the waitress replied while walking away. Neither Sally nor Noelle was able to read her name off the name tag.

"I'm sorry, guys. I didn't expect it to be so busy this weekend." Sally sulked.

Gil laughed. "It's not a big deal. I guess it makes sense being the weekend before Thanksgiving." Gil shrugged his shoulders casually as though nothing bothered him.

Keisha sighed. "This is why I like to leave in the evening when we're going to travel to South Carolina. I want to avoid the traffic. We can leave after dinner on Sunday. Did you finish packing?" Keisha looked at Gil.

Gil smirked. "Um…well…I have another thing to do when I get home tonight." Gil laughed.

Keisha wasn't amused. "Gilberto, I need you to be ready tomorrow so we don't leave late. My aunt is expecting us for dinner on Monday evening. I don't want them to get a bad impression. What is going to happen when we visit the rest of my family in Grenada over the summer? We can't be late for the airplane!" Keisha exclaimed, getting upset.

Gil put his arm around her. "Relax, *mi amor*. Everything will be fine. I was up late the last couple of nights preparing assignments for the three days I won't be at work. Don't worry. I didn't forget. I wouldn't have taken the week off if I didn't want to be there," Gil said, smiling. Keisha smiled and rested her head on his shoulder.

"Keisha, don't feel bad. Jimmy is the same way. When we went to visit my parents for Christmas in New Mexico last year, he packed the morning our plane left. I was so upset, but he did get everything together…a little too close for my comfort," Sally admitted. Keisha laughed.

"I'm sure South Carolina doesn't get as much snow as we do in Jersey," Noelle commented, trying to be a part of the conversation.

"Oh, definitely not a lot of snow where my aunt lives. But I like going to visit because I think it's so quiet and peaceful. Sometimes I wonder about moving there," Keisha replied.

"Jimmy has gone there on vacation with his family a few times when he was growing up, and he said the same thing. Sometimes I think he wants to move there, but I know the truth is, he doesn't like shoveling snow," Sally started before she was interrupted by a thin blond male who leaned over and kissed her on the cheek. "Jimmy!" Sally's eyes widened as she exclaimed excitedly.

"We made it. The traffic was awful though," Jimmy said, sitting down next to Sally.

"Where's Wilder?" Sally looked around, confused.

"Oh, he got a phone call, so he's outside. I told him when he's done to come in and just look for us sitting down. He'll be fine," Jimmy reassured her.

"Jimmy, I would like you meet my friends, Keisha and Noelle. And this is Keisha's boyfriend, Gil." Sally slowly waved her hand around the table while introducing everyone.

"Oh, Sally talks about you two all the time. She says you helped her get through this semester with some ease and a sense of humor. Of course, that one professor sounds like a real comedian," Jimmy commented.

"He's more like a game show host, but not every class. He can be very serious, and best of all, we have learned a lot, but this final project really is a lot of work. I never realized how much work it is to open a business. I have a whole new respect for business owners because I couldn't do it," Sally interjected.

"I think a cross between a game show host and a comedian, but he really is a good professor, just a little unorthodox. Then again, he said the best way to teach this class was through a hands-on approach. I think he's right," Keisha added.

"Your class sounds cool! If I could take the class nonmatriculate, I would," Gil responded.

"What do you need a business course for? You're a high school teacher." Keisha looked perplexed.

"I don't care about that. I just think your final project is cool! You have full reign to pretty much be as creative as you want without the actual real-life commitment, plus your professor sounds like a real character," Gil replied enthusiastically.

Keisha thought it was cute that Gil was so interested in what was going on in her academic life but thought he didn't know just how much work was involved. Some nights, Keisha couldn't wait for the semester to be over. Noelle laughed as though she agreed with everyone else, but deep down, she knew it wasn't the same for her. This wasn't just a school project anymore; it was her future.

Noelle started to look around for Wilder to come and take a seat with all of them so she wouldn't feel like the fifth wheel anymore. Keisha and Gil were having a small conversation on their own, as well as Sally and Jimmy. It was making her feel a little bit uncomfortable; she was sticking out like a sore thumb. Then Jimmy looked up and began to look strangely at Noelle. Initially, she ignored it, but after a couple of minutes, it was starting to make her feel kind of weird and self-conscious. She looked over to Sally to start a conversation to prevent this situation from becoming awkward, but Jimmy said something before Noelle could gather her thoughts together.

"Do I know you? You look so incredibly familiar," Jimmy muttered inquisitively.

Noelle shrugged her shoulders. "I'm sorry. I don't know. Maybe I look like someone in one of your classes or an old coworker. I've gotten that a lot," Noelle replied, still a little confused and feeling uncomfortable.

"No, like you used to work somewhere I used to visit. Did you work at a grocery store or fast food or a coffee shop?" Jimmy inquired.

"I used to work at a couple of coffee shops. The last one was Janlene's," Noelle just randomly blurted out, not thinking much of it.

Jimmy's face lit up. "Janlene's? You were the manager, right? Wow, what happened? Why aren't you there anymore? You were the best manager they had," Jimmy replied a little too overenthusiastically.

Noelle was taken aback by his overzealous response. "Yeah, I worked there until they let me go a few months ago. Now I'm kind of in between jobs," Noelle replied solemnly.

"Sally, she was a great manager. The best! She could multitask, and she always made sure that my coffee was made the way I needed it to be. That's why I won't go back there. They are constantly making mistakes, and that last time, I got so sick. I was home all day." Jimmy turned to face Sally before turning back to Noelle. His face grew long with disappointment.

Noelle looked over at him, and a smile grew across her face. "Large hazelnut with an extra flavor shot, no sugar, and soy or coconut milk. You couldn't have any dairy, right? I remember you. I haven't seen you in a while. I'm sorry I don't remember everyone's name, but I do remember orders, especially regular customers." Noelle smiled at the familiar face.

"Yeah, well, sometimes I did like gingerbread around the holidays. I know I haven't been around since the spring because I didn't take any summer classes. I would usually stop at Janlene's on the way to college, but not anymore! Ever since you left, that place is a mess. They messed up my order more than once, but the last time, they gave me a cappuccino with regular milk. I'm never going back there. If you are working anywhere now or start working somewhere, please let Sally know. I will go there. I trust you to make my coffee," Jimmy said proudly.

Noelle blushed slightly as she didn't expect to hear such a glowing endorsement like that, but a part of her needed to hear it. Even though she had kept pushing forward with her store, there were still many lingering doubts about her ability to really run her own coffee shop. Jimmy's comment helped silence some of those doubts and put her a little more at ease. That discussion about coffee opened up a larger discussion between the five of them about different flavors and brew types. Noelle was starting to feel somewhat valuable as she was able to explain differences thoroughly and with ease. She wasn't feeling like a fifth wheel anymore.

While the five of them were talking, a tall guy in his early twenties wearing cargo pants and a black sweater with blue streaks in his dirty-blond hair walked up to the table.

"Hey, cuz. Hey, Sally," he said quietly, only making eye contact with his cousin.

"Wilder, what took you so long?" Jimmy asked, a little concerned.

Wilder shrugged his shoulders. "I had to take the phone call. I'm off now. Did you order dinner yet? I'm hungry," Wilder asked, taking a seat near Noelle.

"No, we are still waiting for the waitress. Everyone, this is my cousin Wilder. He's visiting from Connecticut for the week," Jimmy explained while introducing him to everyone.

"Wilder, sitting over there is Keisha and Gil, and sitting next to you is Noelle." Sally pointed out everyone to him while smiling.

Wilder looked around at everyone, waved, and nodded until he looked at Noelle. "Where's your guy? You seem to be the odd one out. Were you dumped or something?" Wilder asked bluntly.

Ordinarily, Noelle would have been offended, but she took what he said with a grain of salt. "Apparently, he's sitting right next to me, but you're late. Were you stuck in traffic or forgot how to use your cell phone?" Noelle smirked.

Wilder looked at her, confused, then looked back at Jimmy. "What's up with this one? Does she think she's my date or something? I don't think Peyton will be too happy to hear about that." Wilder grimaced.

Jimmy looked at his cousin, a little confused. "Who is Peyton?" Jimmy asked, leaning over the table to whisper to his cousin.

"Peyton is my girlfriend. We've been dating for several months. Oh, do you think that I can ask her to go ice skating with us on Friday? I mean, she would go nuts because she loves ice skating and wants to see all the decorations in the city," Wilder asked excitedly.

Noelle sat there motionless. Jimmy and Sally both looked a little bit embarrassed as they had inadvertently placed Noelle in an awkward position.

"Sure, she can meet us in the city. If anyone else wants to go, you are more than welcome to join us," Jimmy offered, looking around the table with a nervous smile.

"I'm sorry, we can't. We'll be in South Carolina until probably Saturday, but maybe we can do something after school is out for the semester," Keisha suggested. Sally nodded.

"I can't either. I have a weekend full of family stuff, but maybe Keisha's right. After the end of the semester would be a good time to plan something together," Noelle agreed.

Wilder turned to her. "Am I assuming you stay at home a lot with a bunch of cats?" Wilder asked, a bit persnickety.

Noelle bit her lip to keep from saying something really rude but still needed to defend herself. "That's only on Crazy Cat Lady Day, which is reserved for Monday afternoons and evenings. The rest of the week, I am just regular old Noelle," Noelle replied, smirking.

Wilder rolled his eyes. "Now I understand why you were sitting alone," Wilder replied, needing to get the last word in.

Noelle didn't even bother to respond because she didn't really want to get into an argument, but this was by far the worst blind date she had ever been on. At least the other guys that she was set up with were single. Although Noelle needed a day away from all her hard work, she was starting to wonder if she had agreed to a night out with friends or a night at the circus.

Chapter 23

"Good morning, sleepyhead," Noelle's mother joked while she watched her daughter stumble into the kitchen half asleep and yawning.

"Is there coffee?" Noelle asked, walking toward the coffeepot and reaching up to the cabinet to grab a mug to pour herself some coffee before taking a seat at the kitchen table. When she sat down, she accidentally grabbed the syrup bottle but quickly dropped it for the pitcher of milk before she could ruin her coffee.

"Were you up late last night? You came home late Saturday night and then spent almost the next whole day up in your room, except to come down for dinner, and then you barely spoke three words. I hope you are getting your much-needed rest," her mother asked, concerned.

Noelle took a sip of her coffee. "I got home around ten thirty on Saturday night, and then I was too wound up to sleep, so I decided to do some reading. Yesterday I worked on my final project. I don't have any class this week, so I need to be prepared for school when I go back next week. Finals are starting soon." Noelle took another sip of her coffee. She brushed some of her blond curls off her face.

"No class at all this week? Why?" her mother asked, kind of mystified.

"My classes are on Tuesday and Thursday, and since Thanksgiving is on a Thursday, class is obviously cancelled. Professor Summerfield used to have class on the Tuesday before Thanksgiving, but he said not enough students would show up for a regular lesson, so he turned it into a kind of study hall. Then he realized everyone could do the same thing from the comfort of their own home. He thought it was much more practical to cancel class," Noelle explained. She started to wake up a little bit and realized there was French toast on the table.

"Would you like me to get you a plate?" her mother asked while getting up from her chair. Before Noelle could answer, her mother had already placed a clean plate and fork in front of her. She reached over and took a couple of slices of French toast and poured a little syrup on them.

"Is there a special occasion? Usually, you don't make breakfast during the week unless it's a holiday or when Chris and I were growing up and we had a snow day," Noelle recalled. She took a bite of the first slice.

"The bread was about to expire, but I am also home today. I'm going to be cooking dinner for tonight but also starting to bake for Thanksgiving. I'm supposed to be working tomorrow and Wednesday, so I don't know when or even if I'll get to go grocery shopping this week…" Her mother trailed off but expected her daughter to read between the lines.

"Uh-huh, I see, you want me to go grocery shopping? Okay, I needed to get more computer paper anyway. I have a lot of stuff to print out for the end of the semester." Noelle sighed.

"You can get it at the grocery store with everything else," her mother reassured her.

"Okay, Mom, as soon as I finish eating, then I will get dressed and go to the grocery store," Noelle replied while taking another bite of her French toast.

Her mother got up and started putting some ingredients for baking on the kitchen table. Noelle knew this was her mother's subtle way of telling her to speed it up a little bit. She quickly finished up the rest of the French toast and the rest of the coffee before getting up to place everything into the dishwasher, rushing upstairs to get dressed. Noelle needed to get out of her pajamas and her pink fuzzy bunny slippers but really didn't feel like putting on jeans, so she opted to put on a pair of her university sweatpants and a matching sweatshirt with a pair of sneakers. She knew her pink fuzzy bunny slippers looked juvenile, but they were so comfortable that she didn't care. She pulled her curly blond hair back into a ponytail with the same few strands sticking out on the sides and then reached over to the hook on the wall to take her purse. She rushed back downstairs toward the kitchen and waited at the doorway. Her mother handed her the shopping list and a credit card. Noelle's mouth dropped as she saw how long it was.

"Mom, I thought maybe you needed a few items. This is more like sixty!" Noelle looked up at her mother with a stunned expression.

"Don't exaggerate. This isn't much more than my usual weekly shopping list, but remember, I have also included everything I need for Thanksgiving weekend. I do a lot of cooking in a few days," her mother reminded her.

Noelle pursed her lips. She thought this was going to be a short trip, but it looked like it would be a much longer one than expected. Noelle really wanted to get back home and rest a little bit before trying to tackle more of her final project. Somehow, her final project for BUS730 always seemed to mirror what was going on in her real future business, seemingly making her feel much more exhausted.

"Okay, okay. I will try to be back as soon as possible." Noelle looked down at the list again before stuffing the list and the credit card into her purse.

"I'll have something ready for lunch when you get home." Her mother smiled.

Noelle nodded as she walked to the closet to get her everyday black coat and threw it over her arm.

"Put your coat on. It's bitterly cold out there! Be careful, Noelle!" her mother yelled.

Noelle nodded while she took her car keys off the small table in the hallway, throwing her purse over her right shoulder.

As Noelle got outside, she realized her mom was right, but to maintain her independence, she wasn't going to put her coat on until she got into the car. Despite being an adult, Noelle would still resort to behaving like a teenager from time to time to rebel. She just didn't like to admit that her mother was right more often than not. She pondered if that was one of the reasons why she was hiding her new business from her parents up until now. Then again, Noelle had needed to prove to herself that she deserved to be the owner of her coffee shop. No matter how much reinforcement she received from those around her, which kept pushing her in that direction, she still wasn't completely convinced that this was the right decision. Noelle wasn't going to back out now because she made too much of an investment already, but she really didn't know what to expect going forward. That was one the of the scariest things for her—the unknown and the unplanned.

Noelle slowly pulled out of the driveway and was pleasantly surprised to see that no traffic was coming from either direction. She drove straight down the street toward the local shopping mall, which included the family's regular grocery store. Sometimes her mother would prefer to travel an extra fifteen or twenty minutes further away to another grocery store, which was twice the size and carried three times the number of items. Noelle wanted to make this experience as easy as possible, especially being the week of Thanksgiving, so she opted to go to the closer store. The parking lot was barely a third full, and she was able to get a parking space up close, near the front entrance. She wondered if this was a good sign that things would run smoothly today and without any unexpected curveballs.

Noelle parked her car and quickly got out, searching for a basket. She didn't see any around her car but saw plenty near the entrance of the grocery store. She took her coat with her knowing that she wouldn't be wearing it in the store but would probably need it when she was leaving. She checked a few grocery baskets before finding one without a squeaky wheel. She hated getting baskets with squeaky wheels because they would always end up going around in circles, making her shopping trip seem like it took three times as long. With the way everything was going in her life, she didn't have any extra time to spare for anything.

As soon as she entered the grocery store, she looked to the right where a small floral shop was located. Although it wasn't on the list, Noelle picked up a small bouquet of autumn-colored flowers for her mother. She thought they would look perfect on the dining room table. Right across from the floral shop was the produce section. Before Noelle went any further, she took her coat, purse, and shopping list, placing them in the top section of the basket, leaving the rest of the basket for just groceries.

Noelle proceeded toward the produce section and started to read down the list. "Five pounds of red apples, five pounds of potatoes, five pounds of sweet potatoes, five pounds of carrots, three pounds of green beans, five pounds of onions… Wow, Mom, who are you cooking for? The four of us don't and can't eat all that food," Noelle thought out loud. She proceeded to get the rest of the items on the list from the produce section, briefly glancing down at the basket, which was already a quarter filled up. She shook her head in disbelief before she pushed the basket forward toward the deli counter and took a number. She stood behind an older gentleman ordering a couple of different types of cheeses. Noelle was only half paying attention to everyone around her until someone called her number.

"Number 67," the woman behind the counter called. The woman had broad shoulders with a round face, and her brown hair was neatly tucked under her black hairnet.

Noelle looked for a name tag, but the print was too small to read from behind the counter. "Oh, hi, yeah…one pound of ham, one pound of Swiss cheese, and I think the last one is half a pound of roast beef." Noelle was squinting at the list to make sure. The woman behind the counter smiled and turned around to start preparing Noelle's order. While Noelle waited, she glanced over the rest of the grocery list, and her jaw dropped at how many more items she still needed to get.

A few minutes later, the woman came back with three separate packages.

"Wow, thank you. Have a Happy Thanksgiving." Noelle smiled as the woman behind the counter nodded and walked over to help another customer.

Noelle continued toward the next aisle, which was the cereal aisle. She looked at the list again to make sure she wasn't missing anything. "Honey nut toasted flakes? Wheat bran…" Noelle muttered out loud while she was looking at the shelves of cereal. She was in so much of a total daze she couldn't see that her basket bumped into the person in front of her. She heard a high-pitched wince. She lifted her head up to apologize but then saw who was pushing the other basket. "Ally?" Noelle yelled, surprised.

Ally looked at her with a sheepish smile. She seemed to be much different than she was a few months earlier but still wasn't as perky and enthusiastic as Noelle always remembered her being.

"Noelle, I wasn't expecting to see you here. Your mom must have sent you shopping for the holidays?" Ally said, cracking a smile, looking at Noelle's basket.

"Yeah, look at this. My mom asked me to go shopping for a few things, and then she gave me this." Noelle held up the list with all the items on it.

Ally started laughing. "One thing about your mom is, she could cook for an entire army. Nobody ever went hungry at your house, and we usually were sent home with care packages of food and desserts. Your mom really is a great cook and baker," Ally added happily with an underlying somberness in her voice.

"And she really enjoys it, but she is also so busy for the days leading up to Thanksgiving or even Christmas. I can't even try to get into the kitchen." Noelle rolled her eyes.

"Yeah, remember that one Christmas when we went to get a snack in the kitchen and you found some fresh baked gingerbread cookies and we both took a couple? When your mom saw us, she flipped out and chased us out of the kitchen and wouldn't let us back in, but those cookies were definitely worth the punishment." Ally tried to laugh, but there was a bit of anxiety and nervousness while reminiscing. Noelle laughed, not paying attention to how uncomfortable Ally was retelling the story. It looked very difficult for her.

"Yeah, those were some great memories. I'm sure they wouldn't mind you stopping by for the holidays," Noelle blurted out.

Ally's face lowered. "I have some wonderful memories with you and your parents around the holidays, but I think it's better to leave the memories I have intact and not ruin them. I think I really need to keep my distance…at least…until…Chris…" Ally's eyes became a little misty.

"Ally, I didn't mean anything bad by that. I just meant that you are always welcome at our house…at my parents' house. But I understand how difficult this all has been. I really thought after six years, you and Chris would have been planning a wedding, not breaking up," Noelle blurted out, not realizing it was probably better to have said nothing.

"Yeah, that's what I thought too. Years ago, I thought that I would be married by twenty-five. Well, that didn't quite work out, but I don't want to fight anymore. I don't want the roller-coaster relationship where we are good for a while and then back to unstable and volatile. I really don't want to be married with children in that type of relationship. We tried…I tried…and it's taken me a little while to figure out that maybe Chris and I aren't meant to be together. I can't change him, but maybe he doesn't need to be changed. He just needs someone who better understands him," Ally said calmly while fighting back the tears in her eyes. Even though Ally didn't say a word, it was obvious to Noelle how painful this had been for her.

"I really understand about things not working out as planned, but sometimes it's because there is a bigger reason, like something better is in the works," Noelle replied optimistically, trying to give Ally some hope.

"Well, you know what they say. When one door slams shut and locks, there's another door waiting to be opened." Ally grimaced. Noelle nodded in agreement but was certain that wasn't the way the old adage went.

"Other than that, how have you been? I tried to call you a couple of times to see how you were doing," Noelle asked sympathetically.

Ally took a deep breath. "I'm much better than I was. I know you called, but I just couldn't pick up the phone to talk to you. It wasn't anything personal. I needed space…lots of space. I needed to be away from Chris and everything and everyone that reminded me of him. I'm sorry, Noelle. It wasn't personal," Ally replied genuinely, rambling on a little bit while wiping a tear away from her left eye.

"Ally, I'm not mad at you. I was just worried. I was really worried that I lost a close friend in the process too." Noelle's eyes grew sad.

"Noelle, we can still be friends. I still need a little bit of time, but I still have your phone number, and I will be texting and calling to see how everything is going with you. Maybe you can come and visit me next summer and go to the beach. They have really nice beaches in South Jersey," Ally replied, trying to be hopeful.

Noelle seemed surprised. "South Jersey? When are you moving? When did this happen?" Noelle asked curiously yet a little stunned by the news.

Ally smiled. "Well, if there was any silver lining to any of this, it was repairing my relationship with my sister Jenny. I know we didn't always get along, but I think I didn't understand that losing our mom was just as painful for her. She just handled it differently than I did. When my mom was really sick, I would come home after school and help her to eat and take her medicine. Some days she was in so much pain she would start to cry. I would cry along with her. My sister, on the other hand, would fail classes and get into fights. It was no wonder she dropped out of high school," Ally explained.

Noelle looked at her compassionately. "That is good to hear. I mean, even last year, you would tell me that the only thing you and Jenny had in common was your last name. I guess that means there was a sort of silver lining," Noelle agreed but wanted to refrain from saying anything that might make Ally get upset again.

"Everything happens for a reason. She called me one day to just ask how I was doing, and I turned out to be crying over another argument I had with Chris, and she helped me through it. She had a few bad relationships and gave me good advice. Anyway, she has a full-time job and owns a little house down in Hyland Beach. She invited me to live with her and even said that she would support me while I go back to school. I didn't even mention that I wanted to go back to school. She just brought it up. It's almost like this is the way it's supposed to be," Ally surmised happily.

"Wow, that's like the other side of the state," Noelle replied, trying to hide her disappointment.

"Yeah, I know it's far, but I need a fresh start. I need a place where I have no memories with Chris so that I can really move on. No matter where I go here, I have some kind of memory with Chris, whether good or bad. I'll never be able to move forward. Besides, it's a good chance for me and Jenny to rebuild our relationship. I'm looking forward to that. I know that's what our mom would want." Ally smiled while momentarily looking up to the ceiling.

"I hope everything works out for you, Ally. I'm going to miss you." Noelle walked over and gave her a hug.

Ally smiled and hugged her back. "I think it will, but I'm sorry, Noelle. I really have to go. My aunt sent me to the grocery store for a few items so she could make some special desserts this Thanksgiving. We think Whitney is getting engaged, and Lucy just finished her master's in nutrition, so there are things to celebrate. Jenny can't make it up for Thanksgiving, but she'll be here for Christmas. She's going to help me pack, and we're going to travel back down together, almost like a road trip." Ally smiled as she walked back toward her basket.

"Have a Happy Thanksgiving! Good luck with everything, and don't forget to keep in touch." Noelle waved as she watched Ally push the basket out of the aisle.

"I will. Bye, Noelle." Ally turned to look at her once more before disappearing, walking around the bend at the end of the aisle.

Noelle stood there for a moment, overwhelmed by a bittersweet, melancholic feeling. The reality was finally sinking in that no amount of wishful thinking was going to change the fact that Chris and Ally were officially broken up and were never getting back together. Even though Noelle hoped that Ally would want to keep in contact, there was no way to say for sure it would happen. Ally was going off to start a new chapter in her life, and maybe there wouldn't be enough room left for old friends, including Noelle, who was like a sister, but she could always hope. The only thing Noelle could do now was hope that whoever Chris ended up with in the future would be just as close of a friend as Ally had been to her.

Noelle shook off those thoughts as she continued through the rest of the shopping list. She took a deep breath and started to push the basket toward another aisle. It was a good thing that the grocery store wasn't really busy; it would make it easier for her to complete all the shopping in a shorter amount of time. She took out her pen and tried to divide the shopping list into separate parts to speed up her shopping trip. First, she went to the bakery aisle for baking items, such as flour, sugar, confectionary sugar, cake mix (which confused her because her mother preferred to make everything from scratch), chocolate chips, almonds, walnuts, hazelnuts, and food coloring, to name a few items. She noticed autumn-shaped leaves and pumpkin sprinkles and put them in the cart too. Her mother didn't ask for them but could always use sprinkles for something.

Noelle then walked toward the drink aisle to get a case of water and a few bottles of soda, including ginger ale and sparkling apple cider. Next was the pasta aisle where she grabbed a couple of boxes of pasta, a couple of jars of spaghetti sauce, and a box of lasagna noodles. This made Noelle so happy because she knew her mother was going to make her traditional Thanksgiving lasagna probably that weekend. She continued going through the aisles picking up several more items (some were on the list and a few that were not), including crackers, pretzels, and potato chips. Although the potato chips looked like it was written in Chris's handwriting.

Noelle backtracked a little bit to go get the computer paper she needed before going to the meat section. She grabbed the family package of ground meat as well as the family package of hot sausages. Her mother also put down the family package of chicken breasts. She was a little puzzled with the chicken breasts because the family ate turkey for Thanksgiving, and her father already picked up a frozen turkey the previous week. Noelle shrugged it off and walked toward the dairy section. She got orange juice, then two dozen eggs, and two gallons of milk. She pondered for a moment whether or not the traditional holiday grocery shopping lists were that long or if her mother had added extra items this year. Then again, she never actually did the grocery shopping before the holidays; she would only pick up a few extra items that her mother needed or forgot to pick up.

Noelle continued down the same aisle and picked up a large sour cream and two packages of cream cheese. While looking for the best date, she noticed there was pumpkin-flavored cream cheese. Her mother didn't like to buy it because almost nobody ate it, but Noelle liked it and figured it would be delicious on some plain bagels. She figured her mother wouldn't be mad because it's seasonal and only available once a year. She continued to go down the same aisle now looking for some cheese. Noelle picked up the two blocks of white Vermont cheddar that was on the list and a sixteen-ounce package of shredded cheddar cheese. She was really curious about what her mother was planning on making for Thanksgiving. Then she went looking for mozzarella for the lasagna. No matter how hard she was looking, she couldn't find it, neither the blocks nor the shredded. She continued looking furiously around the cheese section and found nothing until she spoke out loud in frustration.

"Oh no, no mozzarella? Really? How is my mom going to make lasagna if there is no mozzarella?" Noelle sighed, becoming irritated.

"There are a couple left…over here. Better take what you can find, not many left," a female with a higher-pitched voice said from Noelle's left side. She turned and saw a young woman a couple of inches taller than her with long dirty-blond hair and glowing skin. She looked like a model or at least dressed like one with designer clothes, shoes, and a handbag.

"Thanks. I don't want to appear greedy, but I might take an extra one just in case," Noelle replied, almost feeling bad.

The young woman smirked. "If you don't take it, someone else surely will," she replied shortly but with a polite tone.

Noelle stood there looking at the mozzarella and decided to take two blocks and one bag of shredded because her mother didn't specify what she needed for the lasagna. Noelle put her head down to start marking off more items on the list and checking what else she needed when she heard a couple talking nearby.

"Mattie, what did your mom say she needed? Um…I don't really know what she's making. Maybe I've never eaten it," the young woman replied, staring at the cheese unsatisfactorily.

"Lauren, please don't call me that. You make me feel like I'm still in kindergarten. It's Matt," a very familiar voice spoke.

Noelle didn't want to be nosy but looked up and saw Matt standing with what looked like his girlfriend. He hadn't noticed her yet.

"What type of cheese does she need? I mean, I don't want to spend all day in the grocery store. I have a couple of meetings later on, and I don't want to be late for them," Lauren replied, a little snarky.

"It doesn't matter if I have to take a day off, but it you need to take any time off, it's the end of the world? Double standards," Matt replied, visibly irritated.

"Mattie, my job is more important. I mean, you can find an engineering job anywhere," Lauren replied, being a bit persnickety.

Matt was trying to keep his emotions in check, but his face told a different story. Noelle didn't want to be in the middle, so she managed to move her basket toward the other side of the aisle where the tea and coffee were located. She tried to block out their conversation, but it was becoming harder, especially since she wasn't prepared to see Matt with another female. Almost like watching her dreams get crushed for a second time.

"Who said my job isn't important? I happen to like what I do," Matt snapped back.

"Well, when you're in LA, you'll be doing the same job for twice the pay and half the work. I pulled some strings. You should be a shoo-in for a manager position." Lauren smiled as she went to lay her head on his shoulder.

Matt looked uninterested. "When is this supposed to happen?" Matt asked, still irritated.

"If you play your cards right, as early as the beginning of the new year," Lauren assured him.

Noelle couldn't contain her uneasiness and accidentally knocked over an entire stand of holiday herbal teas. She was very embarrassed, but it was worse because Matt turned his head and recognized her at once.

"Noelle?" Matt called out, surprised.

Noelle tried to ignore him while she went to clean up the boxes and put them back on the display. Matt walked toward the display stand to help her. Lauren crossed her arms and walked up the aisle toward the yogurt section.

"Matt, I'm okay. Go back to your girlfriend. I'm sure you need to spend more quality time together before you go to LA," Noelle blurted out in an emotional outburst, afterward realizing that probably wasn't the right thing to say, but she couldn't control herself.

Matt took a step back, a little confused by her behavior. "Noelle, you overheard us? What did you actually hear?" Matt asked suspiciously.

Noelle got up from the floor and looked him in the eye. "It amazes me. You told me that coming back to New Jersey after your time at the Watterferd Valley Institute didn't work out, made you realize you didn't want to go anywhere else. You wanted to be near your family and that this was home. LA is on the other side of the country. That's a little ways from New Jersey," Noelle yelled back. She could feel the tension growing between them, which she figured to be either frustration or jealousy. The way she felt at that moment looked more like the latter, and it was becoming obvious to Matt too.

"Noelle, is there something you would like to say to me?" Matt demanded.

"Yeah, your taste in females has never changed. They all look like models and appear just as shallow. I can't believe I was too blind to see how superficial and self-centered you could be. I always thought you were a genuinely nice guy…that's probably why I've liked you for so long," Noelle accidentally blurted out. Her face turned bright red with embarrassment.

Matt stood there for a moment calmly, but his facial features were starting to tense up. "How is it your business who I'm dating or what my type is? You sound like you're jealous, and if we're just friends, you have no reason to be," Matt scolded her.

"Maybe I'm just helping you to see something that you seem too blind and ignorant to realize…" Noelle replied, trying to keep her emotions in check.

Matt understood right away. "I think you're confused about our relationship. We're just friends, Noelle. We aren't dating. Now I'm wondering if we can continue being friends if you obviously don't seem to understand that," Matt scolded her.

Noelle felt those words like several little daggers digging into her heart. She tried to keep herself composed but felt like her heart was on her sleeve, ready to fall off or blow away. "I know we are only friends. I'm not trying to date you. If I was, I would have been trying to flirt with you the whole time!" Noelle shouted back.

"I have to wonder if every time you were nice or friendly to me, did you have an ulterior motive? Can I trust you?" Matt started to go off on a tangent.

"Matt, we've known each other for way over a decade. If you can't trust me by now, you'll never trust me. Besides, maybe I'm telling you things you don't want to hear about your personal life… about you…that you're not ready to accept. Humility is a good trait!" Noelle yelled back. Immediately she could see those words got very deep under Matt's skin.

"You have absolutely no right to judge me! I don't go around criticizing your love life or anyone you're dating. I have the right to make my own decisions and choose who I want. Maybe you just don't know me that well." Matt glared at her. The argument growing in intensity between them was causing onlookers to stop and stare. It didn't look like two friends having a disagreement but rather a couple hashing it out in the dairy aisle. Even Lauren noticed something wasn't kosher.

"The Matthew I knew would never trade his happiness for some extra sunshine and money. You have wanted to be an engineer since high school, and now you want to throw everything away for extra beach time?" Noelle asked, somewhat disgusted.

Matt's eyebrows lowered. "Well, you know what? Maybe you don't really know me at all, and apparently, I don't know you either!" Matt yelled.

His words stabbed Noelle with a dull, agonizing pain. She tried to keep herself from crying, but it was becoming more and more difficult. She was way too upset to manage a response and just walked away toward the bread aisle. Matt stood there for a moment staring at Noelle and waiting for her to turn around.

Lauren came up to him and gave him the dirtiest look. "Do you have something to tell me? That wasn't just some friendly argument, you pig!" Lauren yelled in his face.

"Not now, Lauren. Just go grab the cheese, and I'm taking you back home. I don't want to talk," Matt managed to get out.

"You get your own stupid cheese and enjoy Thanksgiving without me! I didn't want to spend time with your weird family anyway…and your annoying nephew!" Lauren yelled, storming away down the aisle.

Matt clenched his fists as he walked toward the cheese section to pick something up and hurried to check out of the store.

Noelle spent several minutes hanging out in the bread section, waiting for Matt and his girlfriend to leave the store. She did not want to see him again nor have any more interactions. She tried very hard to fight back the tears, but it was becoming harder to hide how her heart felt broken. She felt betrayed by someone she considered to be a real friend. Knowing that she couldn't spend the whole day in the grocery store, she quickly grabbed some bread, dinner rolls, and a package of sesame bagels to put in her basket. Not her first choice of plain bagels but better than nothing. Her thoughts started to wonder. Was everything she knew about Matt a lie? Was he really a nice guy, or was he a total fraud and a jerk the whole time? The reality of everything was starting to hit her hard and a little too much for her to handle at that moment. Looking for a quick distraction, she saw a sign for cakes and cookies on sale. She reached over for the double chocolate chip cookies with white chips and put them in the basket. Her mother would be angry about the store-bought cookies, but Noelle felt it would cheer her up after what she just went through. She pushed her basket into the first open checkout line. While starting to place the items on the conveyor belt, she frantically looked around to make sure she didn't see Matt or Lauren. The cashier smiled at Noelle but barely said a word. It was okay. Noelle really wasn't in a mood to talk to anybody. After she completed checking out and helping to pack the groceries, she pushed the carriage out of the store into the parking lot and quickly packed up all the groceries into her trunk before pushing the basket toward the sidewalk away from the cars. She took her coat and purse out of the front of the basket.

Noelle walked back toward her car and closed the driver's side door. Before she started the car, she just broke down in tears. She didn't understand why she was crying, but she felt like everything was starting to hit her at once, and Matt was the final straw that pushed her over the edge. Between Paige's brother getting so sick, then her argument with Valerie, and now her falling out with Matt—things appeared as though they could only get worse. Noelle reached into her purse for some tissues and tried very hard to dry her eyes and blow her nose so when she went back home, her mother wouldn't be asking too many questions. She didn't want to talk about Matt; she didn't even want to think about him. There was nothing else she could do at this point except push forward and focus on school and the store because that was all she could control.

Noelle took a couple of deep breaths and managed to get herself together before she turned the car on and started to pull out of the parking space. She rushed through the parking lot, turning back onto the road to go back home. She managed to calm down a little bit when she started driving back home, but she really hoped that she wasn't going to see either Matt or his girlfriend driving in either direction. When she arrived back at home, she pulled onto the right side of the double driveway behind her mother's car. She took another few deep breaths before grabbing her purse from the passenger's seat and pushing the driver's side door open. She ran toward the trunk of her car and started to take out as many bags as she could at a time. Her mother had left the front door unlocked, so Noelle just had to manage to open the front door without trying to get the key into the lock. She rushed into the house and placed them in the kitchen while putting her purse on the small table near the stairs before going back outside. Her mother was in the kitchen stirring a pot on the stove and quickly turned around to start putting the groceries away. Noelle left to go back to get more groceries from the trunk of her car, each time coming back into the kitchen and placing them on the floor, while her mother was putting everything away. Noelle went back and forth at least three more times before taking off her coat and taking a seat at the kitchen table.

"Is lunch ready? I'm thinking about taking my lunch upstairs so I can do double the amount of work. I have a lot to get done this week," Noelle said flatly. She was trying to keep her emotions under control so her mother wouldn't ask her anything. Her mother noticed that her daughter was in a much more somber mood than before leaving to go grocery shopping.

"I made you a sandwich. It's tuna fish with lettuce and tomato. It's in the refrigerator. Are you sure you want to eat upstairs?" her mother asked, appearing curious, but hid the fact she was really concerned.

"Yeah, Mom, I will be down for dinner. What is for dinner?" Noelle asked curiously, looking around the kitchen and walking over to help her mother put away the rest of the groceries.

"It's soup. I'm not telling which one because I want to surprise you. I'm sure you will like it. Well, okay, your sandwich is on the second shelf. I didn't make any coffee, but I boiled some hot water for tea. I felt like apple cinnamon tea." Her mother smiled, referring to the herbal tea she bought the previous week.

"Sounds good. I can take the tea and my sandwich upstairs." Noelle picked up her coat from the kitchen chair and walked down the hallway to hang it up in the closet. Her mother had already poured her a large cup of tea and placed it on the kitchen table.

"Store-bought cookies?" Her mother gave her daughter a playfully stern look.

Noelle couldn't help but crack a smile. "They were on sale, and I really like those. You don't make these cookies, at least I don't remember you ever making them," Noelle tried to justify her actions.

"That's because I have a hard time trying to find the white chocolate chips, but nobody except you really likes them. Maybe Chris would eat them, but he's not really picky unless it includes vegetables," her mother mumbled as she placed the packaged cookies on the kitchen table. Noelle grabbed the cookies and placed them under her arm while she walked toward the refrigerator to get her sandwich before going back to the kitchen table to get her tea.

"What time is dinner?" Noelle asked.

"Probably around five, maybe a little later. I'll call you when it's done," her mother replied with a concerned look on her face. Noelle didn't really pay attention, nodding and leaving the kitchen to go back upstairs to her room. Even though Noelle didn't say a word, her mother couldn't help but get the feeling that something else was going on with her daughter. Her mother noticed that she had been extra tired and more easily stressed out over the past few weeks but now just appeared completely drained and exhausted. Whatever was causing the change in her daughter, she hoped it would work itself out just in time for the holidays.

Chapter 24

Noelle ran to the window in her room at the sound of a car parking in front of the house. She was hoping it was Paige. She ran downstairs to the front door and pulled the curtain back from the right-side panel. She saw a slender redhead getting out of a car and walking across the grass toward the front door. (Noelle's dad didn't like anyone having to walk across the front lawn, so he planned on putting a walkway from the curb to the front porch, but it never seemed to work out.) Noelle stood anxiously near the front door as Paige approached it, making sure the door was open before Paige could ring the doorbell.

"Valet service?" Paige joked while she walked inside the house wearing her favorite plum-colored peacoat. Her purple canvas sneakers squeaked across the hardwood floor.

Noelle closed the front door and offered to take her coat. "No, I was just looking forward to talking to another human being. I have literally been upstairs most of yesterday and part of this morning. I have been working so hard to finish my project, and I have also ordered more equipment for my store. I don't know how I'm balancing all this together," Noelle explained without bringing up anything that happened on Monday at the grocery store.

Paige smiled gently. "If anyone can do this, you can. I'm glad I was able to come over," Paige replied while focusing on being able to unbutton her coat.

"I'm surprised Laurel gave you off right before Thanksgiving. Usually, she won't let you out early unless she's leaving to go somewhere. I think she should just set up a bed for you there," Noelle tried to make a joke to lighten the mood while hanging up Paige's coat in the hall closet. It had the inverse effect with Paige's face growing serious.

"I don't have to worry about Laurel anymore. She fired me," Paige said flatly.

Noelle's face froze, completely stunned by the news. "What?" Noelle managed to get out.

"Yeah, well, apparently, the fact that I chose my brother over coming in to do inventory was a dealbreaker for her. It was so strange, because the first couple of weeks after Kenny first got so sick and was in the ICU, Laurel was very understanding. She had no problem with me taking two weeks of my vacation time off. She even called a couple of times to see how Kenny was doing. I thought it was genuine, but now I wonder if it was all a facade. I don't think I will ever know the truth. At least I have rid myself of one headache. You know, as much as I really don't want to admit this, but Valerie was right. Laurel was a terrible boss," Paige explained, crossing her arms over her plum sweater vest. The sleeves of her lavender blouse pulled away from her wrists as her arms tightened around her chest.

"That's really awful. I guess the only thing that is a blessing is that Kenny is doing much better. How is he?" Noelle asked, concerned.

"He's home now. He can't do much, but he feels much better than he did. I think he's happy to be out of the hospital. Prue and I found out recently that Kenny had been having abdominal pains for a little while. He just didn't say anything. I was mad, but I didn't yell because I'm grateful I still have my brother." Paige's eyes misted up from the overwhelming emotion.

Noelle motioned to follow her into the kitchen. "Hungry? I ordered pizza. I think I ordered too much…three boxes…so I might send some home with you," Noelle joked while walking toward the cabinet to grab two plates and placing them on the counter to take two slices of pepperoni pizza out of the box. She handed one to Paige and took the other one over to the kitchen table where she was going to sit. Noelle's back was facing the wall while Paige was facing the doorway.

"I think my younger cousins will be very happy to see they got some pizza to eat for breakfast. Do you have anything to drink? I'm not picky…really anything." Paige looked around for a bottle of soda or water. Noelle nodded and got up to grab two bottles of soda from the pantry before heading back to the table.

"I'm sorry, all we have is lemon lime soda right now. I did go shopping for Thanksgiving, but my mom wants to save the unopened soda for Thanksgiving first. We're having company, just the neighbors though," Noelle kept talking.

"It's nice to have people over for the holidays. My aunt is cooking, so it's going to be my aunt, uncle, two younger cousins and their girlfriends, and me. I'm not sure about Kenny and Prue, but if I know my brother, he is going to try to go. Prue is working tonight, so if they do go, it'll be tomorrow morning," Paige explained while taking a bite of her pizza.

"What exactly happened to Kenny? I couldn't really get too much from your phone calls," Noelle asked, concerned. She took a bite of her pizza.

"I had no idea what was going on. I was too upset anyway. Prue was amazing because she was able to talk to the doctors when I was too upset and able to explain to me when I was totally confused. Basically, he had an abscess in his spleen. The doctors needed to remove it, but then he ended up septic." Paige started getting visibly upset talking about it.

"How could that happen? I mean, did he get injured, or did he get a virus or something? I'm sorry, you don't have to talk about it if you don't want to." Noelle felt guilty asking so many questions to her friend.

Paige nodded. "It's okay. We don't know. The doctors weren't sure either. One doctor suspected a virus attacked his spleen, another doctor suspected an injury to his abdomen or spleen, but nobody is sure, and it really wasn't important enough to waste time figuring it out. My brother's life was much more important," Paige explained, choking back some tears.

"The most important thing is that Kenny is doing much better, and he's going to make a full recovery. I felt bad that I wasn't there enough for you, but I really didn't know what to say or what to do. I kind of felt helpless…" Noelle trailed off.

"I know you are asking because you care. I knew you were there if I needed to talk to you. That's what matters. I think I needed some time alone. I had way too much going on." Paige sighed.

"When can he go back to work? I know he's like Chris, doesn't like to be home for too long," Noelle asked curiously. She took a couple more bites of her slice of pizza.

Paige hesitated. "Well, thankfully, Kenny will be okay, but I think he's going to need to find a new career. The doctor warned him that construction might not be in his future. I don't know why he said that, but I wonder if the doctor suspects something happened at a work site? Kenny is kind of in denial because he keeps talking about when he's going back to work in construction. Prue has been trying to talk him out of it, mentioning that there is a maintenance job available where she works. Kenny wasn't thrilled." Paige sighed.

Noelle looked at her friend sympathetically. "That's rough… changing careers overnight. It's a hard transition…" Noelle trailed off again. Her eyes wandered across the table toward the corner of the kitchen.

"What makes it worse is that Kenny has been working in construction since he was sixteen. He worked a couple of summers when he was off during high school, and then after graduating, he worked full-time. Kenny being able to work full-time allowed us to stay in the house so I could graduate high school," Paige started to explain but quickly trailed off because talking about her parents always made her terribly upset.

"That means he's been working in construction for almost half of his life. That's a long time. I know how that feels. I worked at coffee shops for almost a decade, and then I ended up on this path of business ownership…big transition." Noelle sighed.

"But you are still in the same field," Paige protested.

"Maybe so, but there is a big difference between working for someone else and running your own business. It helps that I'm in the same field, but I'm responsible for things now I didn't even know had to be done. I can't wait until the end of the semester." Noelle sighed as she leaned her head onto her right hand, propped up by her right arm.

"Kenny won't have a choice but to switch careers if he wants to protect his health. The only positive thing is that he owns his house, so he doesn't need to worry about a mortgage or rent. I hope he takes Prue's advice because he won't listen to me at all. I guess I'm too close and too emotional," Paige explained.

"That's probably what it is. It's good that you seem to be getting along with Prue so well. The only girlfriend I ever really liked was Ally. At first, I thought she was a little bit young for Chris, but she was friendly and would always go out of her way to see how I was doing or hang out with me. Some of his exes were nice, but a few were nasty, and I got into fights with them. Ally was a welcomed change. She was someone I could call a sister," Noelle explained.

"I guess it's official that they are not getting back together? You know, I didn't really know Ally. She seemed nice. But Chris and Ally never really seemed like they were matched right. I didn't want to say that then, possibly because I was still bitter because of Ian, but now I can say it's because something was off," Paige explained.

Noelle lowered her eyes and nodded. "Yeah, I think I used to turn a blind eye to a lot of their arguments thinking it was normal, but it really wasn't. Maybe I wanted it to work out with them so badly I was willing to ignore the obvious," Noelle admitted.

"You're only human. Besides, it's good that you got along with Ally. I'm sure if your friendship was strong enough, you can still rebuild your friendship, but she needs time. Remember when you met me? I was a year or two out of my relationship with Ian. I knew it was the right choice to split up, but it took a while before I could or would talk to any of our mutual friends from high school. It was too painful. Time does heal. I'm not even bitter anymore that Ian found someone else and got married and started a family. When I found out that he was involved with someone else, I knew that I made the right choice. Good thing it worked out for me to move to New Jersey to get away from everyone," Paige recalled.

"I bumped into Ally at the grocery store on Monday. I didn't tell anyone else, but she told me that she's moving to South Jersey. I guess it's a way to start over without any memory of Chris." Noelle shrugged.

"I was with Ian for over seven and a half years. Even when you know that a relationship is over, it's not easy to just go back to normal. Relocating may be the best thing for her right now. I know it was the best thing for me. I'm speaking from experience," Paige explained.

"I invited you over to try and cheer you up about your brother, and here you are trying to cheer me up about Chris and Ally. At least I have one friend I can still depend on…" Noelle's voice trailed off.

Paige looked baffled before taking a sip of her soda. "Although I'm not a huge fan of Valerie, I know she's definitely a close friend to you. Has she really gotten that busy this year?" Paige asked.

Noelle's face became serious. "We're not talking. We had a huge fight. She came to the store a couple of weeks ago and just started accusing me of being lazy and manipulating people into doing all the work for the store." Noelle shook her head.

Paige was stunned. "You have been sacrificing sleep to make sure everything is taken care of. You are always on the phone or at the store or calculating something. You work really hard. That does not sound like Valerie. Is something going on with her?" Paige asked, still stunned.

"She told me no, but deep down I believe there is more going on than she said. I can't force her to talk to me, but after what she said, I don't know if I want to talk to her right now. She really hurt my feelings. She's one of the last people I thought would say or do anything like that," Noelle replied, feeling betrayed.

"Maybe you two just need some space away from each other while you both cool off. Maybe she's extra busy this year, and it's too much stress for her to handle everything, not an excuse but a reason. Give her another chance to explain everything," Paige urged.

"I'm not throwing in the towel, but I'm still too angry to want to talk to her. But after being friends since freshman year of high school, it's so sad," Noelle replied, straightening herself up so her back was leaning against the kitchen chair.

"I don't know what to tell you, but maybe the space will help her to cool off. The holidays have a way of softening people's hearts and bringing people back together. Maybe I'm a softy because I believe in Christmas miracles." Paige smiled as she finished her first slice of pizza. Noelle shook her head with a smile.

"Do you want another slice of pizza?" Noelle asked, ready to get up.

"No, but coffee is always welcomed. Do you have any dessert? I know your mom is always baking around the holidays," Paige replied, looking around for some type of homemade pastry. Noelle got up to turn the coffeepot on, then she walked into the dining room and brought back a large plate of cookies, placing them in the middle of the kitchen table.

"Do you want some cookies? My mom has a plate of extras that she is *allowing* us to eat," Noelle replied, quickly getting up to grab two small dessert plates and two coffee mugs from the cabinet. She placed them down on the kitchen table before going back over to the refrigerator to get the pitcher of milk to bring back to the table.

"What kind of cookies are these?" Paige asked while carefully studying all of them.

Noelle stood there for a moment thinking before she started to point them out. "Okay, those are double chocolate chip, those are leaf-shaped sugar cookies with icing, those are cranberry oatmeal almonds, and I think those are apple spice. Oh, and the last ones are plain shortbread." Noelle stopped for a moment before nodding to make sure it was accurate.

"When does your mom have time to do all this?" Paige asked as she watched Noelle take the two coffee mugs back to the counter and pour some coffee into both of them before bringing them back to the table. Paige started to giggle as soon as Noelle sat down.

"I can't believe I did that. I should have just left the mugs on the counter. I really need to take a day off to rest." Noelle sighed.

Paige laughed. "It's okay. I've had those moments. I would usually call myself an airhead and just laugh it off. I think the lack of sleep from my last job really did more damage than I realized. My priorities were all messed up. I liked what I did, but I put my job over everything else. I missed holidays and events. I lost a couple of friends because I never had time to hang out anytime. I will not do that with my next job. I want balance, and I want a different type of boss," Paige declared while picking up one of the cookies.

"You are a hard worker and will make some employer very happy. It's Laurel's loss," Noelle reminded her.

Paige nodded while taking a bite of a cookie. "Yummy! These cookies are so good. I might want a goodie bag of cookies to take on the drive," Paige joked.

Noelle giggled. "Sure, take as many as you want. These are the extra cookies. My mom was baking all day Monday and part of Tuesday and then for a few hours this morning. I have no idea how she is able to do all this for the holidays. I mean, this is nothing. You've seen Christmas at my house." Noelle laughed.

"Yeah, I remember I think I came over for Christmas Eve when we first met at college, and I couldn't believe the amount of baked goods and food your mother made. It looked like a real holiday feast. It was like a bakery unloaded a truck full of treats at your house." Paige laughed while taking a second cookie.

"Yeah, it's been like that since I was little. My great-grandmother owned a bakery, and my grandmother used to help run it. My mom said she would enjoy making pastries with her grandmother, my great-grandmother. I guess she never really grew out of it. My aunt, on the other hand, total opposite. Can barely make cookies." Noelle laughed.

"Well, it sounds like the business thing runs in your family. Whatever happened to the bakery?" Paige asked while finishing her second cookie.

"Um…I'm not exactly sure. I think my great-grandmother decided to retire because of health reasons. My mom told me she suffered from bad arthritis when she got older. I think it was sold after my grandfather, my mother's father, got sick because my grandmother couldn't take care of my grandfather, her mother, and the business together," Noelle explained.

"That's too bad, but maybe you can start something new with your business. Maybe you can get your mother to bake for your coffee shop," Paige suggested.

Noelle rolled her eyes. "I think the moon will turn purple first, but you never know," Noelle replied cautiously optimistic.

"Anything is possible," Paige started to reply before looking down at her watch. "I'm sorry, I need to get going."

"Sure, I'll get the box of pizza ready for you. It will be like half plain and half pepperoni and sausage and peppers," Noelle explained while getting up to prepare the pizza for her friend.

"Do you have a plate or something I can put the extra cookies on that I'm taking with me?" Paige asked.

Noelle nodded and handed her a paper plate from on top of the refrigerator. "Sorry, we only have Easter and Halloween paper plates. I hope my mom picks some up for Christmas because these would look tacky at the Christmas Eve party." Noelle laughed. Paige finished placing several cookies from the larger plate onto the paper plate. Noelle handed her some tinfoil to put over them.

"Thanks. I think this is good. I hope I didn't take too much. These are just so good." Paige smiled while tightening the tinfoil over the paper plate.

"I will be sure to tell my mom when she gets home from work later. I'm sorry I can't give you any coffee. Nothing to hold it in." Noelle frowned.

Paige laughed and nodded. "It's okay. There's a convenience store on the way there that usually has fresh coffee, and they are opened late. I'll just stop there," Paige replied, getting up out of her seat.

The front door slammed open, and Noelle looked around the corner through the kitchen doorway to see who it was.

"Oh, hi, Dad. You actually beat Mom home tonight. There's some pizza in the kitchen for dinner," Noelle called out while she helped Paige get the paper plate full of cookies into a plastic bag, making them easier for her to carry.

The sound of work boots pounding on the hardwood floors echoed into the kitchen.

"Hello, Paige. It's been a while. How is everything?" Noelle's father asked, walking toward the box of pepperoni pizza on the counter.

"Hello, Mr. DeGarmo," Paige replied quickly to avoid getting into another discussion about her brother.

"Do you have plans for tomorrow? We always have room for one more," Mr. DeGarmo offered.

"Thank you so much. I will take a rain check, but I'm going to my aunt and uncle's house for Thanksgiving. Actually, I'm a little bit nervous. I have never driven up there by myself. It was usually my brother or my cousin driving, but this year, it's just me," Paige replied a little nervously.

"Where do your aunt and uncle live?" Mr. DeGarmo asked.

"Conway Creek," Paige replied, still a little anxious about the trip.

"I used to work up there for about five years when Noelle was in middle school and high school. I think I still remember the route pretty well. Could probably drive it in my sleep. There are a couple of ways to get there, but I always preferred 307," Mr. DeGarmo replied quickly.

"That's what I think Kenny, my brother, told me, but I got a little confused after that because he mentioned Route 23 or 223, and I never heard of that road. I have the directions printed out, but I'm in the car traveling alone." Paige sighed.

"It's actually NJ-323. Well, the way I used to go was to take Route 16W to NJ-307 southbound until you reach the exit for NJ-323. I don't know the number of the exit or what towns are on the exit, but I know it's NJ-323. You should be okay, but in case, gas stations are usually pretty good at giving directions, or you can always call Noelle, and I'll try to help you," Mr. DeGarmo replied calmly.

"Thank you so much! That sounds easy enough. Thank you, Mr. DeGarmo." Paige gleamed happily as she took her plastic bag with her plate of cookies. Noelle took the pizza box off the kitchen table for Paige.

"Happy Thanksgiving, Paige. Have a safe trip," Mr. DeGarmo replied while going to sit down and eat his dinner.

Noelle followed Paige into the hallway to grab her coat out of the closet. She held the pizza box and the bag of cookies until Paige put on her coat and buttoned it up.

"Thank you so much! I'm so glad I have a friend like you," Paige replied gratefully. Paige took her keys out her coat pocket and quickly walked out of the house toward her car. Noelle waited for a moment to make sure she got into her car safely and then walked back into the kitchen.

"Are you going to have some pizza?" her father asked.

"Paige and I ate earlier. I didn't know when to order the pizza, so I guess I ordered it too early and was all alone," Noelle replied, taking a seat to finish her coffee and take another cookie.

"Is this dessert?" her father asked excitedly, looking at the plate of cookies.

"Yeah, these are the extra cookies. Mom said we could eat these but can't touch anything else until tomorrow. I mean, look at all the desserts she made for just the six of us," Noelle replied, a little dumbfounded.

"What can I say?" her father muttered in between bites of pizza.

"Dad, I'm going upstairs. I have a lot of work to get done this weekend, and I want to try and not go to bed too late," Noelle replied, taking a few cookies on a napkin and grabbing her cup of coffee.

"Do what you have to do," her father replied nonchalantly while continuing to eat his dinner.

"Okay, I'll see you later." Noelle nodded as she walked out of the kitchen to go upstairs to her bedroom and work on more school assignments.

Chapter 25

"Everything was delicious," Mrs. Jankowski replied while taking the napkin off her lap and placing it on the table.
"Thank you, Marge. Would anyone care for dessert?" Mrs. DeGarmo asked while getting up and collecting a few of the dirty plates to take into the kitchen.

"Let me help you, Lorraine," Mrs. Jankowski offered as she got up and took the couple of remaining dirty plates left on the dining room table. Mr. DeGarmo and Mr. Jankowski snuck out of the dining room to head back into the living room to watch more football.

"Herbert, where are you going?" Mrs. Jankowski asked as she stood in front of the sink, ready to wash some dishes.

"Marge, we'll be right back. I just want to see the final score. The game should be over soon." Mr. Jankowski looked up at the clock in the kitchen.

"Probably about twenty minutes," Mr. DeGarmo chimed in calmly.

"We're going to start eating dessert without you, Charlie, if we're finished cleaning up and you're still watching football," Mrs. DeGarmo warned playfully.

"As long as you save me a slice of apple pie," Mr. DeGarmo said while giving his wife a kiss on the cheek.

Mrs. Jankowski smiled. "It's good to see that after all these years, you two are still happy together," Mrs. Jankowski replied, rolling up the sleeves of her long-sleeved navy floral pleated dress to start washing some of the pots and baking pans used for cooking Thanksgiving dinner. Mrs. DeGarmo stood on the side with a dish towel in her hands to dry everything. She rolled up the sleeves of her black velvet dress just to make sure she didn't get herself or her dress wet with any of the splashing water from the sink.

"You would never believe that Charlie and I couldn't stand each other when we first met. Oh, how we used to fight. I thought he was immature and weird. He thought I was obnoxious. I got along better with his brother Clem, but I thought he was a little strange too," Mrs. DeGarmo replied with a smile on her face.

"You and Charlie couldn't stand each other? That's so hard to believe," Mrs. Jankowski asked in between rinsing off dishes and placing them in the dish-drying rack.

"Oh yes, Charlie and I were a couple of years apart. We met in high school. I met him through my old best friend Lynda. Lynda was dating his old best friend Wayne. We went to a few football games together and got into such bad arguments that we had to be separated." Mrs. DeGarmo was laughing.

Mrs. Jankowski looked at her, a little surprised. "How in the world did you two end up together?" Mrs. Jankowski asked curiously.

"It's a long story, but when Wayne and Lynda started to have problems, we were kind of their go-to messengers. Charlie and I would exchange messages between the two of them. Long story short, Wayne and Lynda broke up, but then we started dating. Best thing that could have happened to us," Mrs. DeGarmo gushed.

"I met Herb when he was about to be shipped out to Korea. We were engaged after three days, and when he came back six months later, we got married. Some called us crazy, but we are still happily married over fifty years later." Mrs. Jankowski smiled warmly while reminiscing. Mrs. DeGarmo's eyes lowered.

"That's what I have always hoped for my children. I just want Chris and Noelle to find someone who will make them happy and they can grow old with. I really thought that Chris had found that with Ally." Mrs. DeGarmo's face lowered.

"Lorraine, have you forgotten about coming to me for advice when Chris and Ally couldn't seem to stop fighting? You thought that maybe Chris was not mature enough for a serious relationship because they would constantly go back and forth between getting along well and arguing. It's possible the arguments weren't because of immaturity but because they weren't really compatible," Mrs. Jankowski suggested. She started to wash a couple of the casserole dishes and placed them in the dish rack for Mrs. DeGarmo to hand dry them with a towel.

"Marge, I just want my children to be happy. Chris never seemed to have a problem meeting someone, but his relationships never seemed to work out. I was really starting to think that he doesn't want to get married. Meanwhile, Noelle, who wants to be married, can't seem to find anyone. I wish there was something I could do," Mrs. DeGarmo pleaded.

Mrs. Jankowski turned off the water and placed one of the pots into the dish rack to be hand dried. She turned her head to face Mrs. DeGarmo. "Lorraine, maybe you are putting too much pressure on them. Look what happened with you and Charlie. You weren't trying to meet anyone or even date, and everything just fell into place. You need to stop worrying. When the time is right, they will find someone. The last thing you want is for them to force something and they end up miserable," Mrs. Jankowski warned her.

"You're right. Thanks, Marge. You are always able to give me good advice," Mrs. DeGarmo replied, quickly pivoting to glance into the dining room. Noelle and Chris were still sitting and talking at the table.

"One last pot to wash out, then I guess we will start with getting ready for dessert?" Mrs. Jankowski suggested while looking up at the clock in the kitchen.

"I'm putting the coffeepot on right now. I'll ask Chris to check on Herb and Charlie." Mrs. DeGarmo turned toward the dining room doorway, watching Chris and Noelle carrying on a conversation. "Chris, can you check on your father and Mr. Jankowski and let them know that dessert is ready?"

"Sure, Mom!" Chris yelled as he got up from the dining room table. Noelle stayed seated, waiting for her mom to give her some instructions. Usually, she would be a little more ambitious, but she was feeling extra tired today.

"Noelle, can you set the table for dessert?" her mother yelled.

"Okay, sure, Mom," Noelle replied as she slowly got up out of her seat. She walked toward the corner hutch to move the dessert plates and coffee cups with saucers onto the table. She wasn't sure if her mom wanted her to set each place setting or just leave them there. Although she didn't feel like doing anything else, she pushed herself to set all six place settings for coffee and dessert. She quickly took a seat back down on her chair, facing the kitchen. Noelle wasn't even in the mood to really dress up as she was wearing flats with a long-sleeved puffy pink dress blouse and a pair of dark jeans. Her mother wasn't happy but didn't think it was worth having an argument over.

Mrs. Jankowski walked back into the dining room carrying a large plate of cookies on one hand—similar to the ones that Paige, Noelle, and her father ate the night before—and a freshly baked apple pie on the other hand. Mrs. DeGarmo followed into the dining room carrying what looked like a pumpkin spice pie and a cinnamon apple pound cake. Noelle's eyes looked a little glassy and fatigued.

"Noelle, are you okay? You look a little tired today," Mrs. Jankowski asked gently while placing the plate of cookies on the table.

Noelle smiled sheepishly. "Yeah, I think I stayed up too late last night working on schoolwork. Finals are going to start soon, so I have to be ready," Noelle explained while covering her mouth after yawning.

"It's almost over. All that hard work will pay off." Mrs. Jankowski smiled as she walked back into the kitchen to get the pitcher of milk for everyone's coffee.

"Noelle, did you get any sleep last night? When I came home, you were already upstairs in your room. I thought you were taking the night off, but I guess you were still working on more homework. I think you should relax tonight. You look a little flushed. I don't want you to get sick," her mother replied, worried.

"Today is Thanksgiving. I think I'm just going to take some time off and rest and maybe watch something on television, but tomorrow, I'm going back to finishing my project. These finals are driving me nuts. I think I need a day off from thinking," Noelle joked.

Her mother looked at her concerned before heading back into the kitchen to bring the carafe full of fresh coffee into the dining room. She looked out into the hallway, watching her son leaning against the living room doorframe.

"Chris…Chris…Chris!" his mother called out loudly.

Chris jumped up as he turned around to walk back toward the kitchen. "What's going on?" Chris asked, a little frazzled.

"Chris, what is taking so long? We're about to have dessert. I just made coffee. Everything is already in the dining room." His mother put her hands on her hips while looking out at her son standing in the hallway.

"It's almost over, really great game." Chris's face lit up as he turned back toward the living room to watch the rest of the game from the doorway. Mrs. DeGarmo and Mrs. Jankowski walked back into the dining room and took a seat.

"I guess we can either wait for everyone else or we can start early. In the least, I will start pouring some coffee." Mrs. DeGarmo took the carafe and started pouring coffee in everyone's cup.

Noelle reached over for the pitcher of milk to pour into her cup. She took a sip. It tasted a little bit off but figured it was because she was overtired. Chris rushed into the dining room and took a seat across from Noelle.

"Mom, no French vanilla cupcakes? Really?" Chris pretended to pout.

His mother shook her head and walked back into the kitchen to grab a plate full of cupcakes and placed them on the table. "I didn't forget that you asked for them. See, I am always listening." Their mother smiled as she took a seat near the head of the table where her husband was sitting during dinner.

"Where is everyone else?" Mrs. Jankowski asked while sitting across from Mrs. DeGarmo.

"Oh, they're watching the interviews after the game. I wasn't really interested. I saw the end of the game and the final score," Chris explained while picking up a French vanilla cupcake.

"How long will that be?" his mother demanded.

"Could be ten or twenty minutes. Sometimes with the sports highlights, maybe up to half an hour." Chris shrugged.

His mother looked very upset. "We're not waiting. They can have dessert when they finish watching TV," his mother replied, pouring herself and Mrs. Jankowski some coffee.

"You know, Noelle, I have the greatest idea. Now just hear me out. How about a television in the corner of your store with random sports games on? You could have football in the fall, baseball in the spring, and whatever sport in between. That way, you would be able to appease every one of your future customers. And you could even reach people who think reading and coffee alone are boring and pointless," Chris said proudly while pouring some milk into his coffee.

Noelle looked at him bizarrely. "Chris, are you serious? It's not a sports bar. It's a coffee shop. Thanks for the suggestion, but no," Noelle tried to talk lower so that nobody else could hear them.

"Come on, sis, I think it's a great idea. Isn't one thing about business bringing in more customers?" Chris asked, still smiling excitedly about his idea. His voice was louder than Noelle's voice but still too low for their mother or neighbor to hear them speaking.

Noelle shook her head adamantly. "No, Chris, it's not a sports bar. I am not opening a sports bar. I'm opening a coffee shop!" Noelle's voice rose much louder than she expected but just enough to make her mother and neighbor stop their conversation to look at Noelle. Her father and neighbor walked in and looked directly at Noelle. She froze as she realized everyone heard much more than she wanted.

"What is this about a coffee shop? Are you talking about that project for your business class? You said it was really hands-on," her father asked while taking a seat at the other end of the dining room table.

Noelle sat there for a moment, trying to think if she should try to cover this up or tell the truth. "Yes, I do have a project for intro to entrepreneurship," Noelle started to explain, hoping that would be enough to silence everyone. It wasn't.

"Why would Chris be making a suggestion for a school project?" her mother asked suspiciously. Chris lowered his eyes, realizing that this was the moment of truth.

"You know Chris," Noelle joked.

Her mother didn't find it funny, while her father was becoming suspicious of both Chris and her behaviors. "Noelle, Chris, what is going on here? If this is just a school project, then why the hesitancy. Why the secrecy?" their father asked.

Noelle and Chris looked at each other. Chris mouthed sorry. Noelle lowered her head and decided she needed to do this sooner or later.

"Yeah, I do have a school project to pretend to open my own business. I liked it so much, I decided to do it myself. I'm in the process of opening up my own coffee shop." Noelle smiled meekly.

"That's wonderful, Noelle! Congratulations," Mrs. Jankowski said, smiling.

Neither of Noelle's parents were amused nor appeared thrilled. Her mother especially looked upset.

"Noelle, could you please see me in the kitchen?" her mother demanded while getting up from the table and walking into the kitchen. Her father followed behind her. Noelle walked into the kitchen, and Chris remained seated, trying to distract the Jankowskis from what was occurring in the kitchen.

"Noelle Cassandra DeGarmo!" her mother shouted.

"You forgot my Confirmation name." Noelle smirked, trying to lighten the mood.

"This is not funny. What were you thinking? Opening a business is a lot of work. I should know. My mother and grandmother ran a bakery. Neither of them had school or any other responsibilities. How are you paying for this? This is not something that is cheap to do!" her mother exclaimed, very upset.

Her husband tried to calm her down. "Lorraine, there are worse things than opening a business. Let's ask Noelle what got her to decide to do this," he replied, turning his attention to his daughter.

"It wasn't that I woke up one day and said, 'Oh yeah, I want to spend a lot of money and start a business.' I was having so much trouble trying to find a job, and then this project came along. I got really into it, and before I knew it, I was put into a position way too good to be true. So I took a chance," Noelle explained. She coughed lightly because of a tickle in her throat.

"What type of opportunity?" her father asked calmly.

"I found a property through a realtor, which I was using to get an idea about property values for my project, and it was fully set up to be a coffee shop, plus it has a very discounted monthly rent. I couldn't say no to that," Noelle explained.

"Where is it located?" her father asked, remaining calm. Her mother had her arms angrily crossed over her chest.

"Off Main Street. It's literally ten or fifteen minutes from here. It was an old mini mall. Chris has been helping with some of the repairs. He has a lot of contacts from working in construction," Noelle explained.

Chris got up from the table and joined his sister in the kitchen. "Don't be mad at Noelle alone. I kept the secret too. At first, I thought it was crazy, but she's very serious about this, and the place is really starting to transform into something special. I'm proud of her," Chris defended his sister.

"So you were lying to us for how long? The whole semester? Noelle, it's one thing that you decided to take a risk like this, not the smartest during the semester, but it's another thing to do it completely behind our backs. What is the one thing that we taught you? Always be honest," her mother scolded her.

"You think that maybe the way you are reacting is one reason I didn't say anything to you sooner? That last thing I needed was to be condemned. I need support. This was a big step, and it was outside of my comfort zone," Noelle responded back, trying to remain respectful.

"How are you paying for this? If you took out more loans, we can't help you. There's still a mortgage on the house," her mother scolded.

Noelle rolled her eyes. "My car fund! Since I started working, I started saving money for a brand-new car, which I was hoping to purchase after graduation, but I thought that this was a much better investment. I'm not asking for any money. I want moral support." Noelle started coughing fiercely, and her throat became raspy. Her mother went to get her a bottle of water. Noelle took a sip as her mother looked at her face and put her hand against her forehead.

"Noelle, you feel warm. I think you should go upstairs and lie down. We can talk more about this later." Her mother's demeanor began to soften.

"But..." Noelle managed to get out, trying to defend herself.

"Noelle, go get some rest," her father urged gently. Noelle nodded and walked upstairs with her bottle of water.

"Maybe we should go," Mrs. Jankowski suggested. Her husband was right behind her.

"Are you sure?" Mrs. DeGarmo asked, a little disappointed.

"Yes, Lorraine. We're getting tired, and I think you look like you could use a little bit of rest too," Mrs. Jankowski replied softly.

"Okay, Marge, but at least let me prepare a couple of plates for you to take home," Mrs. DeGarmo offered, walking toward the kitchen table where there was a package of unused paper plates.

"Can I have one of those plates to take some dessert home?" Mr. Jankowski asked, looking back at the desserts on the dining room table. She nodded and handed him a paper plate.

"I'll take you home. I will go outside and warm up the truck," Chris offered, grabbing his keys off the key rack on the wall in the kitchen.

Mr. Jankowski came back into the kitchen with a plate full of cookies, two cupcakes, and a slice of pumpkin pie. Mrs. DeGarmo piled up food on two paper plates enough for two full meals for both of the Jankowskis, wrapped them in tinfoil, and placed them into a plastic bag. She walked back into the dining room and took a couple of slices of apple cinnamon pound cake and placed them on the plate of desserts before putting tinfoil over that plate and placing it into the same plastic bag. Mrs. DeGarmo held the bag while she followed the Jankowskis into the hallway to get their coats out of the closet. Mr. Jankowski got his coat on quickly, shook Mr. DeGarmo's hand, smiled, and waved at Mrs. DeGarmo and then walked outside to meet Chris in the truck.

"Thank you for coming." Mrs. DeGarmo smiled as Mrs. Jankowski buttoned up her coat.

"You're welcome. We're lucky to have neighbors like you. And you are lucky to have a daughter like Noelle. There are worse things than opening a business," Mrs. Jankowski reminded her. Mrs. DeGarmo nodded as she watched their neighbor walk out of the front door and toward Chris's truck parked in the driveway. A few minutes later, Chris slowly pulled out of the driveway to take the Jankowskis back home.

Mrs. DeGarmo looked at her husband. "Maybe she's right, Charlie. I mean, she opened a business, not like she dropped out of college and ran off to join the circus. Yeah, she was dishonest with us, but maybe I am overreacting," Mrs. DeGarmo conceded.

"Why did you become so upset? Was it your grandmother's bakery?" Mr. DeGarmo asked.

Mrs. DeGarmo turned to face the front window and began talking. "You mean Lucette's? I guess that's one of the reasons I never wanted to pursue my own restaurant—I always remember what happened to my grandmother. The bakery was sort of an unexpected dream come true for my grandmother. She loved baking so much that my grandparents' kitchen was filled with baked goods, from pies to cakes to cookies. It wasn't until my grandfather complained that he had no place to eat because the table and counters were filled up with too many baked goods everywhere that my grandmother decided to open up her own bakery. At first, things seemed to be going well. She had a steady group of customers, but then things started to become stagnant. My grandparents were still able to pay their bills, but the business was never lucrative. As much as my grandmother loved baking, I think the business started to really steal her joy of it. Baking was no longer something she *chose to do* but something she *had to do*.

Money started to become tight when my grandfather was injured and couldn't work anymore, making my grandmother the only income in the household. Everything seemed to get worse as my grandmother was not only running the bakery but also needed to take care of my grandfather and my aunt. Losing my aunt so young really devastated the whole family," Mrs. DeGarmo replied solemnly.

"You used to talk about your grandfather often, but I barely heard you talk about your aunt. Did you even know her?" Mr. DeGarmo asked sympathetically. His wife's face grew a little long.

"Aunt Eloise? No, she was barely a teenager when she passed away. My mom was a couple of years younger than her, and they were really close when they were growing up. My mom never really likes to talk about her sister. I think it's just too painful. My mom was pushed to help out in the bakery with the customers when my aunt became too sick to continue working," Mrs. DeGarmo replied somberly.

"Why did your family sell the business? All you ever told me was that your father was sick and that your mom thought it would be better to relocate, but it sounds like your grandmother really loved that bakery," Mr. DeGarmo inquired.

Mrs. DeGarmo thought for a few seconds while looking out the front window before turning back to face her husband and respond. "I don't know if my grandmother really loved the bakery at that point, but that was their only source of income, so there wasn't any other option at the time. My mom dropped out of high school to help my grandmother run the bakery. My grandmother would do almost all the baking herself while hiring a couple of part-time bakers around the holidays. My mom took care of the customers and the books, the business end. It just seemed like the right fit..." Mrs. DeGarmo trailed off.

"Plus, your mother can't bake to save her life. That cherry pie she made tasted like sugar-coated cardboard." Mr. DeGarmo smirked.

"Do not tell my mother that. She doesn't need another reason to dislike you," Mrs. DeGarmo instructed.

"It wouldn't matter because she doesn't like me anyway. I don't think she's a huge fan of Neil either." Mr. DeGarmo laughed.

"You know my mother. She's a very strong woman," Mrs. DeGarmo explained.

"Oh, that's what you call it." Mr. DeGarmo nodded, smirking. His wife shook her head before continuing to talk.

"Anyway, by the time my grandmother retired, she had horrible arthritis and her eyesight had deteriorated from reading all those fine-print recipes. My mother tried to take over the business completely but always had difficulty finding good bakers to work for them. It was very stressful. I think the added burden of having two young children, a sick mother, and a husband in the Air Force didn't help. The final straw was when my dad became very ill. My dad did get better a few months later, but at the time, my mom expected the worst. So she asked my grandmother for permission to sell the bakery, and my grandmother agreed. The business was sold, my grandmother passed away, and then we moved to New Jersey." Mrs. DeGarmo sighed.

"Why are you telling me all this?" Mr. DeGarmo asked attentively.

"I don't want Noelle to be impulsive with this. I don't want her to take something she really loves and end up hating it. I don't know if she understands everything that revolves around opening and running a business," Mrs. DeGarmo replied, worried.

"Lorraine, if I know anything, Noelle is not impulsive and is not irresponsible. She wouldn't be taking on something like this unless she believed it was the right thing to do. Now I'm not happy that she wasn't honest with us, but there's nothing we can do about it now. She told us the truth, and we have to try and help and support her the best we can," Mr. DeGarmo explained to his wife. She nodded.

"I guess you're right, Charlie. I just want to protect her from making a mistake. I've seen the negatives with this type of venture." Mrs. DeGarmo lowered her head.

"Noelle's a business major. Maybe that might work to her advantage. We won't know unless she gives this an actual try," Mr. DeGarmo explained.

"Maybe you're right, but there are too many factors involved with whether a business is a success or a failure. I guess all we can do is support what she is doing. Right now, I think I'm more concerned about her health. She didn't look well all day today, and now she's flushed and has a raspy voice. I hope she's not getting sick," Mrs. DeGarmo replied, concerned. "It doesn't matter how hard Noelle is working in school or preparing her business to be successful when opened, if she doesn't have her health, nothing else will matter."

Chapter 26

"Hi, Mom. How is Noelle feeling?" Chris asked, picking up the phone and leaning against the store counter. He reached over to take a drink from his coffee cup. His mother sighed.

"After a very long battle with her, I finally got her to go to the doctor's office today," his mother replied, frustrated.

"She probably didn't think she was really sick. She's been running low on sleep for weeks," Chris explained while taking another sip of his coffee.

"I just wish she would have told me and your father earlier. Opening a business is a huge responsibility. This is probably why she is so sick," his mother replied, very upset.

"It doesn't matter now, does it? Everyone knows, and the store is starting to come together. The dishwasher arrived this morning, and I have a two-hour window for the stove to arrive this afternoon," Chris replied flatly.

"Well, that's some good news. I'll have to tell Noelle later when she comes down to eat and take her medicine. She's resting right now," his mother replied calmly.

"What did the doctors say?" Chris asked again, very concerned.

"Well, your sister did have a mild fever the last couple of days, but now it's over 102. She has a severe sinus infection and strep throat. She can barely talk. She's on a couple of different medications, but the doctor said she should be okay. He told her she needed to get lots of rest and drink lots of fluids. So I'm making soup all week for Noelle. Don't worry. I'll make something different for the rest of us, but you might be eating a lot of soup this week," his mother warned.

Chris shrugged his shoulders. "It doesn't matter. The worst thing is, I'll order something for takeout this week. Right now, you just need to worry about Noelle. She needs to get better and get her strength up," Chris exclaimed.

"Oh, Chris, can you do me a favor? I need a few things at the grocery store that I haven't been able to go and pick up. I really didn't want to leave your sister alone," his mother confessed.

Chris winced because he knew what *a few things* usually entailed. "Go ahead," Chris said as he took out a small piece of paper and a pen.

"Orange juice, honey, two boxes of ice pops, and the family-sized package of chicken thighs," his mother replied quickly.

Chris was surprised that it really was a short list. "What type of ice pops?" Chris wondered while still staring at the short grocery list.

"I don't know, but I know Noelle prefers grape-flavored," his mother replied casually.

"Okay, sure, Mom. I have to finish a few things up here while I'm waiting for the stove, and then I can leave. I'll let you know when I'm about to leave. But if Noelle isn't up to be here next week when the HVAC guy comes, Dad will have to take the day off because I can't take another day off from work," Chris replied adamantly.

"I'm sure your father will not have a problem, but knowing your sister, she won't want to stay stuck in the house that long," his mother joked nervously.

"Yeah, that sounds like Noelle. Anyway, I gotta go, Mom. The sooner I get done here, the sooner I can leave," Chris replied, ready to hang up the phone.

"Okay, dinner will be ready around five o'clock. If you come home later, it will be on the stove, keeping warm," his mother replied quickly before getting ready to hang up the phone.

Chris rolled up his neon-orange work shirt and took a piece of sandpaper out of his toolbox on the counter to try and smooth out the new window frame near the front of the store. Chris stopped for a moment to go back toward the small card table and turned on the small battery-operated radio. It wasn't the best quality, but it worked well and kept the store from being too quiet. He managed to find one station that came in clear enough to listen to—an oldies rock station. Not his favorite but still better than sitting in silence. Chris became so engrossed in what he was doing that he didn't notice a car pull up in front of the store. A woman got out of the car and tried to quietly close her car door before walking toward the entrance of the store. Chris had put a bell on top of the front door a couple of weeks earlier so Noelle could hear whenever someone entered the store. He was unfazed when he heard the front doorbell ringing.

"We are not buying or looking at any junk that you have to sell. Thanks, and have a great day!" Chris shouted while still smoothing out the window frame, not even bothering to look up to see who was there. After a couple of minutes of not hearing the bell ring again, Chris looked up and dropped his sandpaper in surprise.

"Hi, Chris," Valerie said uncharacteristically calm. Her eyes lowered. She appeared pretty somber.

"Valerie, what are you doing here?" Chris asked, still surprised but not thrilled to see her.

"I was hoping to talk to Noelle. Is she here? I can wait if she is out or coming back later. I have some free time today, and I felt like this was too important to keep avoiding. Well, I really should have done this sooner." Valerie tugged nervously on the sleeves of her yellow sweater while struggling to maintain eye contact with Chris.

"She's not here. She won't be coming in today either," Chris replied coldly. He didn't know what happened between Valerie and his sister, but he knew there was some type of falling out.

Valerie's eyes lowered. "Oh, I see. I'm sure she's still mad at me. After all, I can't blame her. I really was totally out of line, being inconsiderate and cruel, not much of a friend. I said some things I shouldn't have said. I thought about calling her many times to apologize, but I didn't think she would want to talk and thought maybe talking in person would be better. Maybe I was wrong to come here,"

Valerie rambled on while she looked down at her yellow-and-white canvas sneakers before starting to pivot back toward the front door.

Chris stood there for a moment, hesitating whether or not to say anything. "Wait, Valerie. Noelle isn't here because she's very sick. She has a fever and a sinus infection. She's been working herself to the bone for weeks," Chris explained, his face very serious. He could see the shame written all over Valerie's face.

Valerie's golden-hazel eyes widened. "Oh no," Valerie replied, stunned and concerned.

"She's been trying to balance everything with the store and keeping up with her assignments. If she wasn't doing schoolwork, she was on the phone with a vendor or a repairman. I'm not sure how much she was sleeping, if she was even sleeping, but she really wore herself down." Chris glared over at Valerie.

Valerie took a seat in one of the open folding chairs and lowered her head. "Noelle was right. I couldn't do it all by myself. I needed to hire an assistant. I needed to get some extra help because I was burning the candle at both ends and then some, and my business started to suffer because of it," Valerie started. "You know, when I first met Noelle, I didn't think that our friendship would really go beyond high school. Now she's become one of my closest friends." Valerie sighed as her eyes kept fixated on the floor.

"If this is the way you treat your friends, I would hate to see how you treat your enemies," Chris replied sardonically.

Valerie gave him a dirty look. "Well, Chris, you don't fit into either category, so you don't need to worry about that." Valerie snickered.

Chris leaned against the counter near his cup of coffee, folding his arms across his chest. "It's not like I'm crying any tears over here about that. The only reason I even talk to you is because you are good, or at least were good friends with my sister," Chris replied smugly.

That response rubbed Valerie the wrong way. "I forgot I was talking to Mr. Perfect who has never had a disagreement or an argument that caused you to lose friends or a relationship to break up! Well, guess what? Life happens, and relationships are always changing! Brynn, my best friend since elementary school, was like a sister to me until she got married, then we started to grow apart. I didn't think that could ever happen. Then again, I thought everything was going great with Lachlan until he dumped me—" Valerie cut herself off, realizing she was going off on a wild tangent.

Chris knew something was up with Valerie. He hesitated for a moment, wanting to say something snarky to defend himself but decided to bite his tongue. "It sounds like this goes a lot deeper than your business or Brynn or Noelle," Chris replied calmly, still staring at her seriously.

Valerie shrugged her shoulders. "I don't know… Maybe it's a combination of a lot of things, but why should I talk to you?" Valerie asked suspiciously.

"Who else is here to talk to? Unless you think that the front counter, the garbage can, or the bookshelf can give you undivided attention or advice, then it looks like you're stuck with me," Chris replied smugly.

Valerie grimaced as she didn't want to talk to him but knew she had no other option at the moment. At least he wasn't a total stranger. "I don't know. When I first started my business in my parents' garage, I was limited to clients around Pineville Park. Now it's grown into several counties in New Jersey and a couple in New York. I don't mind driving or even the long days working with clients, but it's getting to be too much for one person. I'm getting burned out. Of course, it didn't help that my now ex-boyfriend decided to dump me after six months with no warning signs. I mean, why would a guy do that?" Valerie replied, looking up at Chris with tears in her eyes.

Chris's facial expression started to soften. He took a seat on the folding chair across from her. "Well…you are probably the most obnoxious person I have ever met, not to mention that you are a loudmouth who always has an opinion that nobody really cares about…" Chris started to reply.

Valerie's face hardened as she glared at him. "Thanks a lot. What a way to kick me when I'm down." Valerie sneered.

Chris's face softened further. "I didn't finish. Which, of course, is nothing new with you… Been doing that to me since I first met you, but whatever. You might be all those things, but you also have some redeeming qualities. I know you are a genuine friend to my sister. I know you and Noelle have your differences, but you were always there when she really needed a friend. I remember you getting up early without being asked on a Saturday morning for our grandmother's funeral because you knew how hard Noelle was taking it and wanted to be there for her. That's one reason I was totally puzzled when I heard you two had a falling out," Chris replied, looking over at Valerie suspiciously.

Valerie stayed quiet for a moment before responding. "I really liked your grandmother. I mean, your grandmother was always nice to me. She loved to tell stories, and they were funny. I really don't know what it is to grow up with grandparents because my father's parents passed away before I was born, and my mother's parents live in Spain, so I only really see them for special occasions. Besides, my Basque is pretty bad. They probably wouldn't understand me." Valerie paused for a moment. "You know reminiscing about all those wonderful memories has really started to cheer me up. Most of my conversations lately haven't gone so well. Honestly, I think this is one of the best conversations I've had in weeks. I haven't really been myself. I've been short with a lot of people around me lately," Valerie replied honestly.

Chris looked over at her blankly. "Um…uh-uh…well, considering you haven't said anything overtly obnoxious or rude or resorted to calling me some juvenile insult, I guess this has been a successful conversation," Chris responded sarcastically.

Valerie's eyes narrowed as her aggravation was already growing with him. He always knew how to get under her skin without even trying. "Have you ever looked at yourself? I mean, you come off as rude and obnoxious. I've known you for way too long, and I can see you haven't changed much." Valerie scowled.

Chris took a deep breath while slouching back in the folding chair. "Yeah, those are probably two words overused by a few of my ex-girlfriends. Maybe I deserved it. Maybe they really couldn't accept my personality. I've always been like this. Maybe a little rough around the edges, but this is who I am," Chris replied nonchalantly.

Valerie nodded. She couldn't believe she actually could relate to something he said. "Yeah, that's pretty much what I said to Lachlan right after he decided to break up with me. He told me that I was too outspoken and direct, and that was embarrassing to him. It's like he would have felt better if I just kept my mouth shut. Maybe I should be more like my sister Cristina or Noelle and just stay quiet more often," Valerie remarked.

Chris sat there for a moment and pretended to think hard while a small smile grew on his face. "Quiet? Yeah, even our first time meeting left me with a lasting impressing of an unforgettably gigantic headache! You've never been quiet unless you count the one time you had laryngitis, and I think it's because you went to a football game and was screaming all evening, at least that's what I remember." Chris laughed.

Valerie wiped a tear away from her right eye as a small smile grew on her face. "Yeah, that's right. Noelle and I were juniors in high school, and my cousin Eddy had just gotten tickets to see a college football game. I asked Noelle, but she wasn't interested. I don't think she likes sports at all. Anyway, my cousins Eddy and Jon were so angry at the calls all night that I started to yell along with them. I learned a lot about football that night. I actually like it more than soccer now, and I grew up watching soccer," Valerie explained.

Chris's eyes widened in intrigue. "I didn't know you liked football. That's probably my favorite sport too. I've been watching football with my dad since I was in elementary school." Chris's face eased up a little bit. Even Valerie seemed a little more relaxed.

"That's why I don't understand what the problem is with starting a new relationship. I like sports. I'm low maintenance. I have no problem meeting guys or getting asked out on dates, but trying to keep a relationship going seems to elude me. I had one year-and-half relationship in high school and a three-year relationship in college, and now I struggle to make it to at least six months. Maybe my family is right. I should be more like my sisters because both of them are already happily married with families. But with the way I'm going now, it might be easier to just superglue the next guy to me or quit dating completely." Valerie let out a loud sigh.

Chris nodded slightly. "Most relationships I had were very short, maybe a dozen dates over a few months. Ally was the longest relationship I ever had. I had one other relationship last about a year and a half when I was in my late teens or early twenties. Her name was Kathleen. Of course, she probably got tired of dealing with my inability to keep a job. So much potential and yet I seemed to lack the maturity and self-control to keep a job and get myself together." Chris shrugged his shoulders.

"What do you mean *your inability to keep a job*? Since I met you, the one thing I actually could respect was that you were not lazy. I thought that was your only redeeming quality—good work ethic," Valerie remarked suspiciously.

Chris nodded. "Yeah, I guess Noelle forgot to mention that. I guess you also don't know that I went to St. Genevieve's for freshman year." Chris slouched back in his chair.

Valerie looked at him, surprised. "Noelle told me you went to a vo-tech because you couldn't stand wearing uniforms for another year," Valerie replied suspiciously.

"I'm the one who picked out St. Genevieve's High School. They had a great wrestling team and a decent football team. The uniforms were ugly though." Chris laughed.

"Yeah, plum purple, mustard yellow, and beige plaid skirts and pants with a purple cardigan or purple sweater vest, not a great combination." Valerie laughed. Chris chuckled.

"As much as the uniforms were hideous, it was more that I was a bit of a slacker in school. I never really was studious, but in high school, I fell behind quickly, and it really affected my grades and prevented me from being on sports teams. I don't think my parents wanted to spend all that money for me to just slack off, so I transferred sophomore year. I chose a vo-tech to learn a trade, not having a particular interest but finding a real knack for carpentry, which led me to luckily being hired by D'airelle-Seeland Premium Construction right after graduation," Chris admitted. Chris suddenly noticed the sunlight illuminating the golden flecks in Valerie's almond-shaped eyes as she continued to stare at him in bewilderment.

"Do you mean you worked for Darelle-Seeland? That's a huge company and a lot of room for promotions. My cousin has been working with them for over fifteen years. He loves working there. He's even been promoted a few times into management," Valerie explained.

Chris shook his head with a look of shame scrawled across his face. "Yeah, well, as an eighteen-year-old, I was hotheaded and defiant. I got myself fired after six months. By some miracle, I was able to find another good job with another well-known construction company. That lasted about a year, maybe a year and a half. I was considered a great carpenter with potential, but I still had the same bad attitude and was very difficult to work with. Eventually, management got tired of my attitude, and I got fired from there too. That's around the time Kathleen dumped me. At that point, I was pretty much unhirable, and my parents were disappointed and probably grateful they still had Noelle—the hardworking and polite honors student. I enrolled in trade school to earn a certificate in carpentry while picking up small, odd jobs anywhere I could. I was trying everything to make myself marketable. That's actually how I met Ally. I was hired to fix her uncle's back deck," Chris explained.

Valerie sat there for a moment, a little surprised at how much he had opened up to her in one sitting considering they could barely carry on a normal conversation for the thirteen years they had known each other.

"Wow, I had no idea. I guess I understand how you feel though. I seemed to be overshadowed by my older sisters. Cristina was a gifted athlete with several varsity letters, and Loreya was very studious and attended a semiprestigious university on a generous scholarship. I was a complete klutz and pretty much a B and C+ student. I was also the only daughter in remedial classes, math and chemistry, while both of my sisters had a couple of honors and AP classes. I think that's why my parents tried so hard for me to find a job and work during high school, thinking it would make me more responsible and a better student, but I kept getting fired from most of them. The truth was, I had no interest in working. I just wanted to spend my spare time working on set designs for school and learning all about the latest fashion and decorating trends. When I chose to go to an out-of-state private college, my parents were upset because they thought it was irresponsible, but it was for what I wanted to do—be an interior decorator. Now I'm an event party planner with a couple of bathroom makeovers a year. Don't get me wrong. My parents are proud of how hard I've worked to build up my own business, but now I'm in danger of losing some of what I worked so hard for. Chris, I lost over 20 percent revenue compared to last year. I'm in the red. I can't even tell anyone else this. I have no idea why I'm telling you." Valerie sighed.

Chris thought for a moment of what to say. "But how? I don't understand... Noelle always tells me how busy you get every year. This isn't all because of that guy, is it?" Chris asked, a bit perplexed.

Valerie shook her head. "No, but Lachlan definitely didn't help anything. I mean, I really liked him, and I really tried to make that relationship work, but I guess he just wasn't as committed. The frustrating part is that I didn't see it coming. Lachlan would always use his job as an excuse not to drive up to see me because he was on call and couldn't go too far away from where he lived. That's why I was always driving to see him in South Jersey. I actually thought he would have at least taken the day off for our anniversary. I couldn't even get him to do that! I spent a lot of money on a glow-in-the-dark, waterproof watch for him, and all I got was a lousy dinner!" Valerie's voice grew louder as her face tensed up.

Chris shrugged his shoulders. "Sounds like anniversaries don't bring either of us any luck. My relationship with Ally started to totally collapse right after our sixth-year anniversary. Sometimes I would forget the exact date and that would make her really upset but never like she was the last time. I had no idea what was wrong, but to try and make it up to her, I took her out to the same restaurant where we had our first official date. That only gave temporary relief, because the real reason she was upset was, I didn't buy a ring to propose. We talked about marriage one day, but nothing specific, and it really was the last thing on my mind. I just had a lot of doubt and confusion," Chris replied honestly.

Valerie sat there for a moment, thinking of what to say next. "Oh, were you unsure about getting married, or were you unsure about getting married to Ally?" Valerie asked.

Chris sat there for a moment, thinking. "Maybe you're right. Things were up and down with Ally. Sometimes we would be good, and then we would be bad and volatile. It's nothing against Ally. She's a good person, but sometimes things just felt so out of sync, like we didn't belong. Maybe it's really me, and I'm meant to stay single." Chris shrugged.

"Things weren't perfect with Lachlan either, but I think I was so busy with work and my family and friends here that I didn't really pay attention to the little things going wrong, like when he almost missed my birthday this summer. I guess it's hard for me to admit, but I let my guard down with this one. I had no idea that it would affect me so badly. My business also started off slower than usual this year with some regular clients either downsizing or canceling their holidays parties. I guess I became so distracted with everything else going on in my life that my business started to suffer. I missed some appointments or double-scheduled others, which caused some angry clients to yell at me. I would yell back, which only made it worse. Some long-standing, loyal now ex-clients wrote negative reviews against me while I got myself blacklisted with some potential future clients. I really made a mess out of things. I could lose my business, and my love life is a mess. Maybe I am destined to stay single. It's disheartening to think I may never find someone, but I also worked way too hard to watch everything go down the drain. I hope I at least get to keep my business going." Valerie looked as though part of her spirit had been crushed.

Chris nodded. "Guess we got two things in common," Chris replied flatly.

Valerie looked at him strangely. "Huh?" Valerie asked with a puzzled look on her face.

"We both like football and both think we're meant to be single. But you'll probably meet someone else. I'm probably gonna end up single. I'm thirty-two and still living in my parents' basement." Chris laughed.

"Wow, you're getting old." Valerie laughed.

Chris playfully stuck his tongue out at her. "You're my sister's age, so you aren't too far behind." Chris smirked.

"Some days I feel older than you, so I guess we're even with that too." Valerie shrugged. Her tears were starting to fade away to reveal a genuine smile.

"You know, that guy Lachlan or whatever, he probably did you a favor. Yeah, I know being dumped feels crappy, but now you are free to meet someone better, a guy who will appreciate all of you, even your very charming personality." Chris smirked as he started to get up from his chair. He pivoted back toward the counter to take another drink from his coffee cup.

Valerie lowered her head as she didn't want him to see her blushing, something she never in her wildest dreams thought would happen around Chris. That day, she saw a different side to him and strangely was interested in maybe seeing this side a little more often. Valerie started to daydream a little bit before she glanced down at her watch and jumped out of her chair.

"Chris, I'm sorry, I don't mean to be rude, but I have to get going. I have an appointment in about thirty minutes, and I don't want to be late," Valerie stood up and threw her beige canvas bag over her shoulder while pushing the folding chair under the card table.

"I understand. I'll tell Noelle you stopped by, but I think you should call her when she feels better," Chris suggested calmly.

Valerie nodded. "Yes, I'll send her a text message. She's probably not up to talking. Um…thanks, Chris. Wow, two words I never thought I would be saying together, but thank you. Talking to you today really helped." Valerie smiled genuinely.

"This time will be on the house, but next time, there will be a charge. I do charge on a sliding scale, but my rates don't come cheap." Chris chuckled. "But seriously, just don't tell anyone about me being mushy or sensitive. It's going to change people's perception of me. You know I need to uphold my tough-guy image," Chris said proudly as he picked up a piece of sandpaper to go back to sanding the window frames.

Valerie bit her lip to keep from laughing too loudly. "Sure, whatever you say, *stud muffin*." Valerie laughed while rolling her eyes.

Chris puffed up his chest while walking toward the window frame to start sanding again. "From now on, you can refer to me as stud muffin or Chris or whatever you feel like, but I kind of like stud muffin." Chris couldn't keep himself from laughing.

Valerie nodded before heading toward the front door. She actually found herself laughing with Chris rather than at him.

"See you later." Valerie looked over to Chris before pushing the door open and walking out toward her car.

He pretended to continue sanding for a few minutes but was really watching out of the front window to make sure she got into her car and left the parking lot safely. He found himself staring at her just a little bit longer than he had realized. The strangest thing was realizing he had a smile on his face. Two words he never thought would be together in a sentence—*smile* and *Valerie*. He shook his head adamantly to get that thought out of his head and went back to work sanding.

Chapter 27

"Good morning, Noelle. How are you feeling today?" her mother greeted her from the kitchen table while she was drinking her morning cup of coffee and reading the newspaper. Noelle walked toward the counter and poured herself a cup of coffee, opening the refrigerator to pour some milk into her cup. She walked back toward the kitchen table and took a seat, taking a sip of her coffee.

"Coffee…I can actually taste it! Everything tasted like cardboard for like a week…well, whatever I was able to swallow. I guess I must have been very sick," Noelle relented.

Her mother gave her a stern look. "Yes, you were burning the candle at both ends. Noelle, why didn't you tell us sooner? We could have tried to help you. That is a lot to take on by yourself. Remember, you're still finishing up your degree." Her mother sighed.

"Mom, maybe the timing looked to be all wrong, but everything seemed to be falling into place. If you think about it, the business should be opening around the time that I finish graduate school. At least I know that I will have a job." Noelle laughed nervously.

"Maybe so, but if you don't take care of yourself and your health, it won't matter. Noelle, you have always been very hardworking and have accomplished so much, but this is very different. Just remember that," her mother replied sternly. Her mother started to soften on the idea of Noelle running her own business but was still taking longer than her husband.

"You're right. I have learned some things the hard way through this process, but I have worked so hard and come so far. You should really go with Dad and Chris to see the store. I think you will like it," Noelle replied, trying to get on her mom's good side.

"When is the HVAC guy coming to check the system? I think you said he was stopping by this week," her mother asked while walking toward the counter to pour herself another cup of coffee.

Noelle nodded. "Wednesday, I think, but I told them if he can't make it to reschedule for Friday because I have class on Thursday. I'm not going to try and overextend myself right now, especially with finals coming up," Noelle replied a little anxiously. She glanced toward the middle of the table and noticed a big plate covered in tinfoil. Her mother took out a plate from the cabinet and placed it in front of her daughter while she took a seat on the other side of the table with her cup of coffee.

"Thanks, Mom." Noelle's face lit up while she took a few pancakes with her fork and placed them on her plate while pouring some syrup on top of them.

"So what do you have planned for today? I hope you aren't planning on going back to your old routine," her mother warned.

"No, but I do have to go to the store today. I am expecting the coffeepots. I ordered two, and Valerie said she *might* stop by the store. She did say she wanted to help 'decorate' my store to make it look captivating to my future customers," Noelle replied cautiously.

Her mother's face tensed up. "Noelle, take it easy. You just got over being sick for over a week. I don't want to see you get a relapse," her mother warned.

"Don't worry. I will be dressing warmly, and I have the heater in the store. If you are really worried, I can bring some hot tea with me," Noelle replied, looking up after finishing her pancakes.

"You shouldn't be gone that long, at least you better not be gone that long." Her mother looked at her sternly.

"Don't worry. I'll be back by lunchtime. The delivery guy said the coffeepots will arrive between ten and twelve," Noelle replied while she placed her empty dish and cup into the dishwasher. She walked out of the kitchen into the small hallway and opened the hallway closet.

"Please be careful and take your coat!" her mother yelled as Noelle stood in front of the hallway closet near the front door. She took out a puffy pink jacket with a hood. It wasn't really her first choice, but after being so sick, she figured she should be more cautious than not by wearing a heavier coat. She grabbed her purse and keys off the small hallway table and walked out of the house toward her car.

The drive to the store was quiet and seemed shorter than usual. It seemed as though every light was green while she was driving, and there was barely any traffic. Noelle wondered, looking around, at why there were not as many cars and thought maybe because of work and school. This was the first time that she had been unemployed around the holidays since she was a senior in high school. It was giving her a chance to see things that she had missed before. Then again, the entire semester had really been like looking at everything through a new lens, one that better fit Noelle and her vision for her future. It still seemed so unbelievable that one event could have caused all these changes in such a short amount of time and placed her on a completely different trajectory. However, this was the path she knew she belonged on; she just didn't realize it until she was on it because she spent all her time trying to plan rather than experience and learn and, most importantly, to really live.

When she arrived at the store, Valerie was already waiting in her car. Noelle was a little bit surprised because she didn't expect Valerie for another hour or two. She quickly parked her car and rushed out, running toward the front door to unlock the door, put the lights on, and turn the mini electric heater on. Besides getting over being so sick, she didn't want the store to be too cold for anyone else. Noelle barely turned around to put her purse down when she heard the bell ring to notify her that Valerie entered the store.

"Hey, Noelle. How are you feeling?" Valerie asked calmly while walking to the front counter where Noelle was standing with her coat still zippered all the way toward her chin.

"Better. I have my voice back, and food doesn't taste like cardboard anymore. I was so happy that I was actually able to taste my coffee this morning! It's the little things," Noelle joked.

Valerie smiled. "Yeah, you're right it is the little things. Listen, I just want to apologize again. I had no idea that you were even sick until Chris told me. I'm so sorry that I took everything out on you. You didn't deserve any of that. I should have told you what was really going on with me. I know you asked me what was going on, but I thought I could hold everything together. I just made a mess out of everything." Valerie sighed.

Noelle gave her an encouraging look. "Val, it's okay. You've already apologized. Yeah, I was pretty upset with you, but after you told me what was really going on, I completely understood. I just wish you would've told me everything sooner. I mean, I thought everything was going well with you and Lachlan. Then again, I dated Grant, so I may not be exactly an expert on relationships," Noelle replied, starting to slowly unzip her jacket as she could feel the store starting to warm up.

"Grant? Haven't heard that name in a long time. Yeah, that was a total loser, trying to date you, his ex, and another girl all at the same time. He actually tried to push the blame on you and the ex-girlfriend. Whatever happened to him?" Valerie asked disgustedly.

"No idea. I heard from one of his friends that he transferred to another college, and a mutual acquaintance told me that he dropped out of college, never graduated, and moved out of state. I honestly don't really care. I do owe his ex-girlfriend some gratitude for being bold enough to call me up and tell me what was going on. Of course, I didn't believe her at first, but it at least planted some doubts in my head. Made it easier to dump him later on." Noelle smirked.

"You know, Grant and Lachlan might get along if they hung out together. Lachlan could be really charming and kind, which is what really threw me off when everything fell apart. I was really angry at myself because for some reason, I really got blindsided by him. I guess the truth was I really cared about him more than he cared about me, and I made it too easy for him. He always had some type of excuse, and I just shrugged it off. The next guy I date, I won't make it so easy," Valerie exclaimed adamantly.

Noelle could feel the store was much warmer, and she decided to take off her coat. She was wearing a hooded light-blue-and-gray Faire Isle sweater with a heavy navy turtleneck underneath. "Maybe it would be easier if you found someone who lived around here. Not making excuses for your ex, but…" Noelle suggested.

"You're right. Long distance is not going to work, especially with my business being in North Jersey. But it's not just about the distance. It's also the thoughtfulness of surprising me every once in a while with something special. With Lachlan, even the phone calls became routine. No surprise calls or text messages. I knew down to the minute when I would hear from him. He also never brought me any gifts, except that piece-of-junk necklace for my birthday that broke after a couple of weeks, never remembering to get me a replacement." Valerie grimaced.

"The right guy is out there…somewhere," Noelle replied encouragingly.

Valerie lowered her eyes. "I have bigger things to worry about than dating. I'm in the red this year." Valerie shook her head, ashamed.

Noelle's eyes widened in surprise. "What? How are you in the red? What happened? I mean, I thought that business was doing well and that you were expanding because you were booking more and more holiday events," Noelle asked, still pretty surprised. "Wait, does this have anything to do with Lachlan? It's not worth it to lose any business over him. Maybe you should have taken the watch back for a refund," Noelle instructed.

Valerie smirked. "Yeah, you're right. I should have. I spent all that money on an expensive glow-in-the-dark, waterproof watch, and all I got was a cheap, lousy dinner! As much as I'm still angry, he is not the sole reason why I am struggling this year," Valerie started to respond.

"What do you mean? Nobody wants to decorate for the holidays like before? Or is it that you really can't keep up with everything on your own?" Noelle asked seriously.

"Well, yes and no…not exactly…but sort of. Noelle, you were right. I need an assistant. I really didn't believe that I needed extra help because I started my business all on my own and continued to do everything on my own. Other than my parents letting me use their garage, I didn't ask nor want any other help. I was afraid hiring an outsider would cause me to jeopardize what I worked so hard at building up. I couldn't afford to throw away almost five years of hard work. This year started off a little slow with a few of my regular clients either modifying or canceling their holiday parties, which was a loss of revenue for me. It wasn't what I expected, but I figured I would make it up by booking more events for around Christmas and Hanukah, but that didn't happen. That's one reason why I asked about using your store in my portfolio, to help expand my client base. I was already really struggling to book extra clients. I just didn't want to say anything. I needed to take any client or potential client who needed an event planned. That's why I was supposed to meet potential clients early the day after that crappy anniversary dinner. Eventually, I did start to get a little busy, but I handled everything wrong. I missed appointments, forgot to call some clients back, and even double-booked several clients. I had a few clients who were understanding and knew something was wrong, while others told me to lose their phone number. I even had potential new clients hang up on me or just tell me to leave them alone and never come back. I not only lost business, but I also lost clientele. It's all my fault." Valerie felt deflated.

Noelle smiled warmly at her friend. "That's why you were so short about the topic of money and working for *free*. Honestly, I never did feel comfortable with you doing all that work for free, so I am going to pay you something. It will definitely be less than your normal fee, but it will be something. We can discuss numbers after the holidays," Noelle insisted.

Valerie smiled gratefully. "Thank you. You really don't have to do that, but I'm not going to lie. The extra income will help. However, the right thing to do is to continue with our original agreement because I would feel guilty for going back on my word. I don't feel that I have the right to ask you to pay me after I already told you I would do the work for practically nothing," Valerie admitted humbly.

"You're not reneging on your agreement. I should have insisted on paying you something when you first offered," Noelle asserted.

Valerie smiled. "Let's go over some of the details so I know what to order for your store. I have at least a couple of hours to spare before I go to my next appointment. Mary had to reschedule for this afternoon because of a doctor's appointment. She's a sweet older woman who hires me to decorate her house every year for Christmas. This year, she also asked me to go Christmas shopping too. She makes the best homemade oatmeal raisin cookies and will make sure that there is a big plate of fresh cookies waiting for me when I go over to decorate later," Valerie replied with a dreamy look on her face thinking about the cookies.

"Sounds delicious. Homemade is always best, but then I get to have almost everything homemade because of my mom. I can't even begin to tell you how much flour my mom buys around the holidays. My dad joked about putting a mill in the backyard." Noelle laughed.

"Your mom is a fabulous baker. Her marble brownies are the best in the world." Valerie's face lit up at the thought of the brownies.

Noelle laughed. "I sometimes think that you only come over to just eat my mom's food and desserts. Oh, speaking of coming over, my mom wants to know if you would like to come over for our annual Christmas Eve dinner. My mom's already talking about making even more food and desserts than previous years. I already asked Paige, but she said she can't make it because she'll be spending the holidays with her family. Do you think you can make it?" Noelle asked eagerly yet a little disappointed about Paige.

"Noelle, you know that I love your mom's desserts, but both of my sisters and their families are coming over for Christmas Eve. Usually, they come over later, but this year, they want to come in the afternoon. I guess they are worried because my nephews are so young and need their sleep. If anything changes, I'll let you know," Valerie explained, looking a little disappointed.

Noelle nodded understandably. "Don't worry. Family is important. I'm sure we'll be having some leftovers, so you can always come over sometime during Christmas week. My mom is already hinting at me to stay away from my store for a week, but it's almost impossible to just forget about this place…still so much to do." Noelle looked around a little anxiously.

"You need to try and relax. I know how you feel. When I first started off, I used to look at my pathetic collection of decorations, and now I have two full storage lockers and a full stockroom at my office. You'll get there. Hey, have you considered asking your mom to bake for your store? I'm sure her treats would be a real hit with the customers, and it would take care of one of your problems, trying to find a vender to supply baked goods," Valerie suggested.

"Well, maybe next time I have a conversation with my mom, I will ask her again, but she's still getting over not finding out about the store until a couple of weeks ago." Noelle sighed.

Valerie looked at her, a little confused. "Is your mom really still mad at you? I mean, I understand she's upset you weren't honest with them and did it all behind their backs, but you are so far into this now," Valerie replied, still puzzled.

"My mom is starting to warm up to the idea. She's still a little hesitant, but I think she mellowed a little bit because of how sick I got. She realized if anything, I have been working very hard and am taking this seriously. My dad, on the other hand, is totally supportive. In fact, he is coming back here Saturday with Chris to check everything out. They even offered to make sure the dishwasher and stove are hooked up and working properly. I have no idea how to connect the gas correctly, and I really don't want to make any mistakes," Noelle replied a little nervously.

Valerie looked casually down at her watch. "We should probably start going over some of the details. Okay, I remember you said neutrals, which is okay. I think beige or eggshell or ecru would be good. I don't remember which one you mentioned, but it's going to look too dull with just neutrals, so you need a color to contrast with it. I did look at different shades of pink and purple, and honestly, it would make the store look like a real-life dollhouse. At least from my professional opinion," Valerie replied, rushing toward her canvas bag to pull out a special smaller binder marked Noelle's Store.

"Oh, I get my own binder! I feel so special," Noelle teased.

"Yeah, it just makes it easier for me. I don't want to mix up anything for your store with other clients' files. You are special because this is the first business I am using my interior decorating skills for. I'm actually kind of excited to see how this all turns out. I didn't even get to do any offices or businesses when I was in college with my internships. This is all new and exciting." Valerie gleamed as she clicked her pen to start writing.

"I've been trying to imagine the store when it's all finished, and I can't quite do it yet, but it's starting to feel so real. I'm actually getting excited about the grand opening next year." Noelle smiled brightly.

"So I do remember you mentioning something about wanting a place for students to be able to study or work on projects. I contacted a vendor about chairs and love seats. I don't have the estimates on hand. They're at the office, but it would be cheaper to order a set rather than one piece. If the measurements I have written down are accurate, you do have enough room. We would just have to angle the pieces," Valerie explained.

"Okay, so what colors?" Noelle asked while looking into her binder.

"There are five colors currently offered. You can order a different or special color, but it will cost more. I wouldn't go that route…just my suggestion. I was thinking eggshell or beige," Valerie suggested.

Noelle shook her head. "Too light. One of the coffee shops, Coffee-n-Cookies, had off-white and beige furniture, and it was full of coffee stains. What made it worse was, I think they were leather. I tried to clean them up because it bothered me, but it only made it look worse. I want a darker color," Noelle insisted.

Valerie looked perplexed. "I wouldn't go with black…too harsh for this store. Maybe if there was no lighting, the dark furniture might work, but I really don't like dark colors like that. It looks depressing," Valerie explained while looking over at the bare corner near the wall where the couch and chairs were meant to go.

"What colors are available?" Noelle demanded, looking over at the empty corner, trying to imagine the corner fully furnished.

"Off the top of my head? Black, beige or eggshell, red [it looks like fire-engine red], lime green, and navy," Valerie recalled, squinting her eyes toward the ceiling as though that would help her memory.

"How about navy? I mean, I have a blue bathroom, so it would kind of match. Plus, the navy would give some color to the store instead of just bland neutrals," Noelle insisted.

"Blue bathroom?" Valerie looked at her, confused.

"Yeah, remember the disaster when the ceiling caved in and destroyed everything? Well, I needed a whole new bathroom set. Dereck's uncle had a blue porcelain toilet and sink with a matching mirror. I think the frame is blue too. It was ordered a while ago and then canceled, and nobody else wanted it, so he gave me a really good price. It's like blue jay, not my first choice, but it really has started to grow on me," Noelle answered quickly.

"Remind me to check out the bathroom before I leave. Okay, so I'll order the navy love seat and matching chairs after the holidays and probably won't get it until sometime in February or March. Oh, I did see an electric sign in one of my vendor catalogues. I think it says College Corner or Study Corner, something like that. But come to think of it, it's neon blue. That's the only color it comes in. The navy furniture might be a perfect choice for you," Valerie explained.

"I really like the idea about the sign. I actually think it's going to look cool. Now the only other thing I need to figure out is what to do with the bookshelf. I thought about selling prepackaged coffee there, but I'm not sure. I thought about coffee mugs with my store name and logo on them. Then I thought maybe board games or books for anyone who comes into the store and wants to sit and enjoy their coffee," Noelle replied, staring at the bookshelf.

"I like the idea of coffee mugs and maybe thermoses with your store name. You still have no idea what to name the store?" Valerie asked curiously.

Noelle's face dropped. "I am really pulling a blank with this one. I don't understand how it is so difficult to come up with a name. How did you come up with the name for your business?" Noelle asked curiously.

"Izar's Designs and Party Events? It was nothing spectacular. I just took my middle name and put it with what I wanted to do—design. I know, very original, but it works," Valerie replied.

"Cassandra's Coffee? No way. I don't even like my middle name." Noelle shivered.

"You're going to have to come up with something eventually, but don't go crazy looking for it. When you find the right name, you will know," Valerie reassured her.

Noelle shrugged, then looked at the front door slowly opening with a slender redhead carrying a tray of what looked like coffee and a plastic bag around her arm.

"I was in the neighborhood, and I thought I would see if you were here, Noelle. I brought hot drinks and some snacks," Paige said, walking through the front door and placing the tray of coffee down on the card table along with the bag.

"Three coffees? Do you have mental telepathy?" Noelle teased, referring to Valerie being there also.

Paige looked down at the tray while taking off her plum peacoat. "Well, I guess unconsciously I counted Chris in too, but it worked out great because Valerie is here. How is everyone doing? How are you feeling, Noelle?" Paige asked cheerfully.

"Feeling much better thankfully." Noelle smiled.

"That was really weird because you seemed fine when I saw you right before Thanksgiving. It must have come on fast." Paige picked up the tray of coffees and walked toward Valerie and Noelle.

"I was feeling tired, and my sinuses were starting to bother me, but I thought it was the change in weather. I had no idea I was really sick, but I shouldn't have ignored it either. Don't worry. Everyone, including my brother, yelled at me to take better care of myself," Noelle replied, picking up the cup marked peppermint. Noelle looked at both Paige and Valerie to see if they approved.

"Enjoy it," Valerie replied calmly.

Paige looked at her for a moment strangely as that was very calm and unlike Valerie's normal snarky responses. "Val, is everything okay? You seem unusually laid-back today," Paige asked suspiciously.

Valerie laughed. "Yeah, I think things are better than they have been. Maybe I'm trying a new persona…a new me," Valerie responded confidently.

Paige bit her lip to keep from laughing because she wasn't sure if Valerie was serious or not. Noelle took a sip from her coffee before rushing to answer her cell phone buried in her coat pocket.

"Hello? Yes, this is she," Noelle responded as she started to motion to her friends that she needed to step away for a few minutes while she took her coffee with her. Paige and Valerie leaned over on the counter.

"I wonder who that is," Paige wondered, watching Noelle walk toward the other side of the store near the bathroom door.

"Maybe it's about the shipment she's supposed to get today. I think she ordered a coffeepot. I can't keep tract. My own job keeps me busy enough." Valerie turned and leaned against the counter.

"Running a business must really be exhausting," Paige acknowledged while taking a sip from her coffee.

"I should know. Of course, nobody can do it alone. That's probably why I am swamped," Valerie started explaining.

Paige gave her a perplexed look. "Do you have an assistant or a receptionist? Does anyone help you with your event planning?" Paige asked curiously.

"It's just me and my computer and phone in my office. I usually do everything myself, but for the bigger events, I will hire some workers to help. I usually get college students who are looking to make a little extra money. I have a few workers who come back annually, but most are usually brand-new every year. I've been pretty lucky so far because they are always punctual, hardworking, and responsible," Valerie explained.

"Do you need any help this year? I would work to help you set up any event or party for the holidays," Paige offered, trying to remain hopeful at the distant possibility of a job.

Valerie shook her head. "I'm sorry, I am all set for the rest of the year. I think even for the New Year's Gala, I have enough staff. Wait, Laurel will let you take the day off to help me decorate for a holiday party? I doubt that." Valerie rolled her eyes.

Paige's face grew serious. "I'm not working for Laurel anymore. She fired me. Like I said to Noelle, I couldn't believe I'm saying this, but you were right about Laurel. How did you know?" Paige inquired.

"It's because the way you described Laurel reminded me a lot of one of my old bosses from a college internship. I worked as an intern, and I loved my job and some of the clients, but I was doing all the work and receiving almost no credit. I would look the other way because I thought that it would negatively affect my job search after graduation, but after receiving no credit for the guest bedroom I spent weeks working on, I lost my temper. I got fired and listed as unhirable by that company. I was fortunate enough to be in good enough standing with my college that they helped me find another internship. So what did she fire you for?" Valerie looked at Paige calmly.

"I had a choice to come in and do inventory or stay with my brother who was in ICU, not much of an option," Paige replied seriously.

"Ouch, that's harsh. I didn't see that one coming. I'm so sorry to hear that. How is your brother doing?" Valerie asked compassionately.

Paige was a little taken aback by Valerie's very calm and friendly demeanor toward her. "He's doing much better. Still has a long road ahead, but he's going to be okay. I made so many mistakes. I stayed at a job way too long because I became comfortable. It was a steady paycheck with constant overtime, but I also had almost no time off, and I missed so many parties and holidays and lost friends. The trade-off wasn't worth it. I have no problem working hard, but my job will not become my life again," Paige announced confidently.

"That's a great attitude. What exactly did you do at your past job?" Valerie asked casually.

"Oh, I answered phones, scheduled appointments, organized the office, took care of inventory, which included both paper and computer files, and occasionally met with clients. Oh, I also had to learn about antiques, so I'm not great, but I have a pretty sizable knowledge of them." Paige stood there thinking as though she missed something.

Valerie's eyes widened, and she turned to Paige. "Can I ask your opinion on something? So Noelle and I can't seem to agree on what type of border for the store. I think maybe geometric designs. She wants something plain. I know the colors would be beige or eggshell and probably navy or blue. I'm drawing a blank, and Noelle is pretty adamant," Valerie asked, looking over at Paige thinking.

"How about something in theme with the store? I mean, this is a coffee shop, so why not coffee cups and maybe tea bags? I guess you could use beige or pale gold with navy and light blue. The contrast might help it to pop out more." Paige stood staring at the wall where the border would be placed.

Valerie was mildly impressed. "Listen, Paige, maybe this is a crazy idea, but how would you like to come work for me? I can't give you the same pay, but you will get benefits and vacation time. The only thing is, no vacation from September through mid-January unless it's an emergency," Valerie replied seriously.

Paige stood there stunned yet excited about the offer. "Are you serious?" Paige asked skeptically.

"Yes, surprisingly, I think so. You need a job, and I need an assistant, and you seem to have just about everything I'm looking for. So what do you say?" Valerie asked, extending her hand toward Paige's hand.

Paige's eyes widened in excitement. "Yes! This is like an early Christmas present. Valerie, you have no idea how much this means to me. If I didn't find a job by next month, I would have to give up my apartment because I wouldn't be able to afford it," Paige exclaimed gratefully. She skipped the handshake and gave her a hug.

Valerie was a little taken aback by the hug, especially since she's never been the most affectionate, but let it slide this time. "Great. You can start after New Year's. I have one event on the first or second weekend in January. You won't be working at the event, but you will be coming with me to see how the whole process works. Okay, I have a system, and I don't change from the system unless I need a backup plan. We'll get into all that after you start. Please don't make me regret this," Valerie explained while trying to shrug off a few doubts.

"I promise you will not regret this at all! Thank you so much, Valerie!" Paige replied excitedly.

"I hope you're right. Okay, it's a deal." Valerie extended her hand again toward Paige. Paige reciprocated the handshake. Noelle had just gotten off the phone when she saw the two of them shaking hands.

"What in the world did I miss?" Noelle asked, almost stunned.

"Meet Valerie's new personal assistant!" Paige said excitedly. "I have a job!"

Valerie sighed deeply with a look of growing regret over her face, wondering if her good mood and desperation pushed her to make a rash decision.

"Great! You needed help, and you need a job. Looks like things are working out just in time for the holidays." Noelle smiled excitedly. Valerie smiled sheepishly but didn't say a word.

"Hey, Noelle, what do you think about a navy-and-plum or navy-and-indigo color scheme?" Paige asked curiously.

Noelle walked toward the table with the small box of doughnuts. "Why not add a disco ball and some strobe lights while you are at it?" Noelle replied sarcastically.

"Looks like a no," Valerie answered cautiously.

"Yup, it's a no way. Keep trying. In the meantime, let's eat the doughnuts before they get stale." Noelle opened the box and started to look at which one she wanted. Paige and Valerie walked toward the card table with the box of doughnuts.

"Well, at least we know one thing. You are definitely feeling better." Valerie smiled.

Noelle lit up as she bit into a vanilla cream doughnut, and Paige just couldn't stop laughing at the expression on Valerie's face. Noelle looked at Valerie before turning to Paige and smirking.

"I can see this is going to be an interesting business partnership," Noelle joked.

"Opposites attract." Paige laughed. Valerie rolled her eyes in typical fashion, but instead of some snarky remark, she just joined in with the laughter too.

Chapter 28

"Thank you, Jeff. That was one of the most interesting presentations that I think I have ever seen. It will definitely be one that I won't forget anytime soon," Professor Summerfield said, looking a little bit bewildered from his seat in the front row. Several students clapped as Jeff finished his presentation, and a couple of students chuckled at what their professor had just said.

"No prob, Professor. I always aim to please. If I actually open my business one day, I will paint neon racing stripes down the sides of your car free of charge," Jeff said while smiling proudly on the way back to his seat. Professor Summerfield stared blankly toward the blackboard, saying more without speaking a word.

"Okay, so I think that we are almost done. There is one more presentation. Noelle…is Noelle here tonight?" Professor Summerfield asked while looking around.

"Yes, Professor, I'm here," Noelle replied while walking to the front of the classroom. She put up her trifold white poster board on the professor's desk and made sure it opened as wide as possible for everyone to see. "Can everyone see the poster board?" Noelle asked, pivoting between her classmates and the poster board.

"Yeah!" a few students yelled back.

Noelle nodded in acknowledgment and walked back toward the side of the professor's desk to get out of the way. She took out her pack of note cards from her navy sweater pocket and looked up at the class. Her hands trembled slightly. "Okay, so good evening, everyone. My business plan…my business idea was…is…a coffee shop. Now personally, I thought this might be a little easier for me because I had worked in a few coffee shops over the past few years and learned a lot of the ins and outs of the business. However, it wasn't exactly what I had expected. I was used to cleaning out the coffeepots and espresso machines, making sure everything was stocked up while still taking care of customers, to name a few responsibilities. Now I needed to focus on the location of the building…my store…my business, make sure all the equipment was working properly, pay the bills including rent and utilities, apply and receive proper licensing… I think you all get the point," Noelle started rambling with her hands trembling slightly more as her nervousness grew. Professor Summerfield raised his hand. Noelle called on him.

"Did you notice a difference between working in a coffee shop with a different owner as compared to starting your own coffee shop?" Professor Summerfield inquired while sitting almost completely still with his classic poker face.

"You mean if I thought it was harder or easier than working for someone else? Well, yes and no," Noelle started to explain, seemingly a little loss for words despite having the note cards in front of her.

Professor Summerfield tried to help her out a little bit. "Could you explain what you meant?" Professor Summerfield asked, still sitting almost emotionless.

Noelle took a moment to collect her thoughts. "Well, initially, I didn't think it would be that much different. I thought it would just be an expansion of the responsibilities I had as a manager. I was wrong. Besides the obvious additional responsibilities of paying the bills and making sure the store is completely staffed, I didn't calculate in the lease or rent, utilities, salaries, and making sure there is enough money to replace any piece of equipment that wasn't working properly. I didn't realize just how much I really didn't know. In addition to that, I didn't realize how much the owner can play a role in the atmosphere or environment of the business. I used to think that was simply the fault of the manager and the rest of the employees, but it's a combination. A business really is an intricate collaboration of many different things. Tremendous learning experience," Noelle replied, a little calmer and more relaxed.

Kendall raised her hand. "Was the initial $50,000 allocated enough for your business?" Kendall asked inquisitively.

Noelle noticed their professor was continuing to sit almost emotionless, making her feel a little self-conscious. She was afraid her nervousness might have been perceived as unpreparedness. "Before I really started to do research, it seemed like more than enough money. Then I factored in all the equipment, maintenance for the store, unexpected emergency repairs, and rent without calculating in coffee or anything else I needed or wanted to serve at my store and realized just how expensive it can be to open a business. So I did need to look into taking out business loans to cover the difference," Noelle explained.

"How much more would you have needed to open the coffee shop? Well, just the estimated amount," Kendall asked curiously.

Noelle stood there for a moment trying to think of an answer, but she really didn't know the amount off the top of her head. "Um, I don't really know exactly because I didn't finish calculating all the necessities with all possible expenses. It would have taken me forever…well, way past the end of the semester, but I think it was somewhere like double the initial allocated funds. Does that answer your question?" Noelle replied, seemingly looking more confident and at ease.

"Yes, thank you." Kendall nodded before turning her attention to their professor.

"Noelle, would you like to share about what happened to the bathroom in your store? That purely *hypothetical situation*," Professor Summerfield asked flatly.

Noelle wasn't expecting to answer anything relating to the bathroom catastrophe. She almost regretted adding it into her project at that moment. Her face became red from embarrassment; she quickly puffed up her cheeks to keep herself from laughing nervously. "Um… well, you know, I really got into this project and wanted to see how things were at a worst-case scenario. I like to try and carefully plan things out, but it was a challenge for me because some things cannot be anticipated. I automatically thought about the one client you helped who had started a business, had all the finances in order, and then needed a brand-new roof because of a nor'easter hitting it two weeks before the grand opening," Noelle explained.

Professor Summerfield smiled. "I'm glad that my stories are having an impact, but please share with the class your situation," Professor Summerfield nudged.

Noelle nodded. "So in my store, I was going through the estimates for basic maintenance and repairs when the bathroom ceiling collapsed. That is horrifying. Try hear…uh…I mean imagine…try imagining something like that happening. In my situation, the bathroom ceiling collapse caused massive damage to the bathroom, including cracking the toilet and breaking the sink. I'm not a plumber or a maintenance worker or a janitor or anything like that, so I would have no idea what would cause it, but a common cause could be a cracked pipe, which can cause leaks in the ceiling. So afterward, I needed to calculate how much more it would cost to repair the bathroom. I had two different amounts calculated to cover the damage listed on my project: one was for just replacing all the bathroom furnishings, and the second one included repairing structural damage. The second one actually made me want to cry," Noelle admitted.

Rowena raised her hand. "Why did you choose the bathroom to have an unexpected catastrophe and not another part of the store? Was there something that inspired you, or was it random? Did you read about a similar situation?" Rowena asked curiously.

Noelle froze for a second as she needed to come up with a good and believable response. "Um…I think it was more by chance…randomly chosen. Who really thinks this stuff can happen?" Noelle was hoping that response was enough to prevent any other questions.

Keisha raised her hand, and for a moment, Noelle was afraid that it would be related to a question she wasn't prepared to answer either.

"Does your business have a name?" Keisha asked curiously.

A smile grew across Noelle's face as she felt relieved. "Oh, sorry, I should have probably mentioned that when I first started my presentation. So the name is nothing special and probably kind of corny but easy to remember and pronounce. It's *My Little Coffee Shoppe*," Noelle replied, looking around the classroom.

"Very original." Orlando laughed.

Noelle nodded. "Yeah, I don't think I would recommend something that dull, but for the sake of time and that it was for a school project, I really couldn't think of anything else that wasn't too complicated. And I did not want to name the store after myself. That's just a personal preferential thing," Noelle explained, looking around at the class for any other questions.

"Thank you, Noelle," Professor Summerfield replied, getting up out of his seat in the front row.

Noelle nodded and closed up her trifold poster board and took it back to her seat, placing it in the back of the row. The class applauded as Noelle went to sit back down. Professor Summerfield went back to his desk in front of the class.

"Professor, would you mind if I left a little bit early?" Fallon asked while starting to put her books away. He nodded.

"So if nobody has any other questions about the semester or the final exam or project, then you are free to go. Remember, the take-home final exam is due by Friday in my mailbox at school. If there are concerns, please come see me after class. If that's it, hope everyone has a very Merry Christmas, Happy Hanukah, happy holidays, happy winter break!" Professor Summerfield replied, smiling.

Many of the students shouted back to him the same thing while hurrying to pack up their bags. Noelle was slowly starting to get her stuff together by placing everything in her schoolbag. Keisha walked up to Noelle and placed a small present on top of her desk. Noelle glanced down with a look of surprise.

"Hey, Noelle, just a little something to say Merry Christmas, and I'm glad we're friends. Gil even helped me pick it out. He really likes you and Sally." Keisha gave Noelle a hug.

"You didn't have to get me anything. Thank you, and tell Gil thank you too. Maybe we can get together over the winter break and go out," Noelle suggested as she picked up the small present from the desk.

"Yeah, but no Wilder. He's weird," Keisha started saying before she saw Sally walk up behind them. "Sorry, Sally," Keisha tried to explain.

Sally nodded her head and smiled. "I'm so sorry, Noelle. I've been meaning to call you, but you were out and so sick. I just wanted to apologize for putting you in that position. I had no idea he had a girlfriend. Jimmy had no idea either." Sally looked remorseful.

Noelle laughed. "It's okay. When I saw the look on your faces, I knew you had no idea. If anything, this is definitely a unique experience and a great future ice breaker." Noelle laughed.

Sally looked relieved. Sally turned to face Keisha. "Don't worry about it, Keisha. Jimmy and Wilder ended up having a small fight after everyone left. On the bright side, Peyton, his girlfriend, is very nice. She seems to be a good influence on him because when Wilder started getting rude, she gave it back to him. Jimmy likes her. He would still like to hang out again with both of you and Gil," Sally replied to both of them.

"Oh, before I forget, this is for you. Gil and I picked it out together. I'm sorry to have to run, but I have a really early meeting tomorrow at work," Keisha said, pulling her schoolbag over her shoulder.

"Are you going to be in class on Thursday?" Sally asked.

"Did our professor say it was mandatory?" Keisha asked nervously.

"No, she said we can come and drop off our take-home exams in class or stay to talk or ask questions, but Thursday isn't required. Only last week for the first part of the final. I feel kind of bad. I think missing two weeks really affected her syllabus," Noelle added.

"I think having two weeks off in a row made me lose motivation to go back to class." Sally laughed. Keisha laughed.

"Okay, good luck with the rest of the semester and have a very Merry Christmas." Keisha smiled as she rushed out of the classroom door.

Sally looked at Noelle. "I feel so bad I didn't get her anything. She didn't have to do this," Sally lowered her eyes.

"I know, but she's really thoughtful like that. I remember one semester she remembered that I said I was running late and probably wouldn't get to eat a real dinner. So when she stopped to get herself dinner, she picked up an extra hamburger for me. Maybe we can do something for her birthday next year. I think she's turning thirty in March," Noelle suggested.

"That's a great idea, but we need to talk about this again because I will forget. March is too far away, and I'm still on finals." Sally shook her head and laughed. She looked down at her watch and started to button up her coat.

"I gotta get going. I promised Jimmy I would meet him for a late dinner. He's still taking finals, but he's done with class for the semester," Sally replied, reaching over to give Noelle a hug.

"Tell my favorite customer I said hi," Noelle joked.

"He's still asking me if you found a job working somewhere. Even if you decided to open your own business, he will reroute his morning commute just to go there. I said I doubt she's opening her own business, but I'll let her know," Sally joked before walking toward the doorway. "Oh, if I don't talk to you before the holidays, have a very Merry Christmas. Hope it's extra special." Sally turned to walk out of the classroom as Noelle waved bye.

Noelle had to laugh because Sally had no idea how much closer to reality that comment from Jimmy really was. She shrugged it off and was about to leave when her professor called out to her.

"Noelle, do you have a moment?" Professor Summerfield asked, looking up from his desk. A couple of students had moved off to the side of the desk toward the window to have a conversation. Noelle was a little nervous because she had no idea why the professor would want to talk to her. She walked up to his desk.

"Yes?" Noelle seemed a little bit nervous and confused. She started to think something was wrong with her presentation or final project. That caused her extra anxiety as she worked so hard on everything.

"Noelle, your presentation was very thorough. In fact, it almost appeared realistic," Professor Summerfield remarked as though he suspected something.

Noelle tried to avoid eye contact. "I take my work really seriously, and I wanted to make sure that this was as authentic as I could get it be," Noelle answered back quickly.

He smirked. "Noelle, I've been consulting for over thirty-five years. I know hypothetical versus reality. Your presentation was almost as real as I've ever seen. Your figures are even exact to the penny with some of the expenses. The only question I have is, Did you plan on opening a business prior to this class, or was it more spontaneous?" Professor Summerfield asked calmly.

Noelle put her head down. "Professor, is this going to affect my grade? I didn't mention anything because I thought it would have negatively impacted my presentation or my final grade." Noelle sighed.

"Why would any of that negatively impact your grade? I'm grading you on what you do in the classroom. This class is only meant to give you the tools to prepare you for real life. Your grade in real life is the wisdom you acquire from your successes and failures," Professor Summerfield replied succinctly.

"Truthfully, opening a business was probably one of the last things on my mind when I started this class. Then through a series of bizarre events, I kind of was led to spontaneously sign a lease agreement for a store. It's been hard, but thankfully, I had this class to fall back on. I learned a lot, and it really was perfect timing because I don't think I would have been able to go this far without this class or your very entertaining stories," Noelle answered honestly.

"How far are you in the process?" Professor Summerfield asked curiously.

"I've started buying and replacing equipment and appliances. I also just got the HVAC checked out. It can be overwhelming somedays. The bathroom really threw me for a loop. Yes, that really did happen." Noelle sighed.

"I think that was my last clue. You wanted to say 'hear,' not 'imagine.' There were too many details in your weekly assignment for you to just make that up," Professor Summerfield explained.

"I had nightmares from that incident. I think it would have been different if I could have anticipated it, but some things really are out of our control. The only silver lining is, I found out that two pipes in the ceiling needed to be replaced. Thankfully, it happened before the store opened," Noelle explained.

"If you have any questions about the rest of the process or need any help, please reach out. I'm not on campus as much over winter break because I don't teach during that time, but you can email me. I'm getting better at responding. Or you can stop by my office in the spring, and I'll help you through the final steps of the process," Professor Summerfield offered.

Noelle's face lit up. "Thank you so much. I think I'm okay, but I definitely welcome any help because I want to make sure I do everything right the first time," Noelle explained.

"Well, good luck with everything and hope to see you in the spring. Oh, and if you happen to have an extra invitation for your grand opening…" Professor Summerfield smirked.

Noelle nodded and waved as she rushed out of the classroom with less than a handful of students left, still talking among themselves or waiting to speak with their professor. Noelle walked down the hallway very quicky, excited about getting to her car to go home. Her semester was almost fully complete, only needing to stop by on Thursday to hand in the second part of her final exam for her other class. She couldn't help but continue to marvel at what Professor Summerfield had said to her. How did he know about her store? Maybe it was true that her project and presentation were a little too lifelike, but maybe it was also his own personal experience working with new business owners. It was ironic that a failed entrepreneur actually turned out to be such an asset to other people starting their own businesses. It only means that everyone has a purpose, no matter how unconventional and unexpected that purpose may be. The only other thing that seemed to puzzle her a little bit was everyone's added excitement about the upcoming holidays. It's not that she minded anyone telling her "Merry Christmas" or that it was unusual to hear around this time of the year, but somehow, it just felt different. It sounded different. Almost as if everyone knew something special was about to happen over the holidays. All she could do now was sit back and look forward to whatever would be coming next in her life.

Chapter 29

"Come on, what is taking so long to load?" Noelle asked while sitting impatiently, tapping her fingers angrily on her desk, waiting for the college portal website to finally load on her laptop. She had been trying to access the online portal for her college all morning and even into part of the afternoon. It seemed as though every time she tried to log on, it would either time out or it would simply kick her off. Noelle was getting very frustrated. She thought that taking smaller breaks to go do things like eating breakfast and getting changed out of her pajamas into a pair of jeans and a long-sleeved navy shirt with a large iridescent snowman stitched on the front would be sufficient time for her to be able to log on. Noelle wondered if the Internet connection in the house wasn't working, or worse yet, her laptop needed to be replaced. She didn't want to spend the whole day on her laptop because there were hundreds of things to do around the house to prepare for the annual family Christmas Eve dinner. However, she felt like until her semester was officially over, she couldn't do anything else because she would be constantly thinking about her grades and GPA. Noelle was starting to think this was going to be a very long day. Finally, after trying to log on dozens of times, the portal finally let her log in. She immediately clicked on her grades for the fall semester.

BUS 760 (Financial Management): B+
BUS 730 (Intro to Entrepreneurship): A

When Noelle saw her grades, she was so excited that she jumped up and spilled the rest of her coffee on her jeans, bolted out of her room, and ran downstairs. Her mother noticed her daughter running down the stairs and into the kitchen.

"What is going on?" her mother asked, surprised by her daughter's strange behavior.

"I finally feel like the semester is over! I got my grades. I got a B+ in financial management and an A in intro to entrepreneurship. This semester felt like it was going to burn me out, but I made it, and now it's over!" Noelle's face lit up as she raised her arms in the air to celebrate.

"Now one more semester and you will finally have your master's degree," her mother commented proudly.

"Mom, I don't want to think about more homework or projects right now. My brain needs a break. Plus, any extra energy needs to go straight toward the store." Noelle calmed down as she watched her mother take a freshly baked cake out of the oven.

"Is it really necessary to do anything for your store this week? I was hoping you could just relax and enjoy the holidays," her mother replied, looking at her daughter disappointingly.

"No, I won't have any more deliveries until after New Year's. The HVAC guy took care of whatever he needed to do, so I now have heat in the store. I did need a new thermostat, but that wasn't a big deal. Now I don't have to worry about taking that electric heater all over. For the time being, it was better than nothing." Noelle shrugged.

"I know you are going to be really busy going forward. Just remember to take a breather every so often," her mother reminded her.

"Yeah, don't worry, Mom. I have learned my lesson from this semester. It's still going to be a little bit of a crunch, but I'll remember to take it easier next semester. That's all too far away right now to focus on. I still need to finish putting up the Christmas decorations. Where is Chris? I hope he brings the Christmas tree today," Noelle asked, looking back toward the front door.

"Your father and I have talked about getting an artificial tree for next year. He's going to take a look at sales after the holidays. The real trees are pretty, but it's getting to be too much work," her mother replied, glancing up at her daughter still standing in the doorway.

"And I think we would be able to enjoy having an artificial tree up longer than a real one. Things were different when Chris and I were growing up." Noelle looked back at her mother taking what looked like a pound cake out of the cake pan. "Mom, what is that? Please tell me that's not for Christmas too," Noelle pleaded as her mother would make them wait to eat any of the treats until their Christmas Eve dinner party.

"It's kind of a new recipe or a different take on an older recipe. It's caramel apple pound cake. Instead of making it apple cinnamon, I made it caramel apple. The caramel is homemade. Took me all morning to do this. Since it's a new recipe, I'm making it just for us to try out. I know that you, your brother, and your father will tell me the truth. If it's good, I will make it next year for the holidays." Her mother placed the cake on a dish and left it on the table to cool before she added the glaze.

"It looks and smells really good. I'm sure it's delicious. Anyway, I'll be in the living room going through the Christmas decorations," Noelle said while pivoting back into the hallway going toward the living room.

After arriving at the living room doorway, she looked around at the stacks of boxes of Christmas decorations. She sighed and mumbled something under her breath before taking a seat on the couch, pulling one of the smaller boxes near her feet. She slowly opened the box and began to take a few smaller ornaments out, placing them on the coffee table before she was rudely interrupted by the sound of the doorbell.

"Noelle, can you get that? I'm busy in here. I have to start preparing dinner!" her mother yelled from the kitchen.

Noelle grumbled before she got up and answered the front door. When she opened the door, she was shocked at who was standing on the other side.

"Kayla? Justin?" Noelle exclaimed as she reached over to give her two younger cousins a big hug.

"We're so glad to see you, cousin!" Kayla, Noelle's look-alike cousin, exclaimed while still standing in the doorway. Both Noelle and Kayla resembled their moms in appearance with their blond hair, blue eyes, and diamond shaped faces with dimples in both cheeks.

Justin walked past his sister into the house, taking off his coat and throwing it over his left arm. "Yum, what's for dinner?" Justin asked, looking at the kitchen.

"That's probably the cake you're smelling. My mom just took it out of the oven a little while ago," Noelle explained. Justin stood against the banister while holding his coat and continuing to stare into the kitchen.

"Can I take your coat, Justin?" Noelle asked, noticing he was totally distracted. Justin handed his coat to his cousin to hang up before he wandered off toward the kitchen.

"Smells delicious, Aunt Lorraine," Justin exclaimed, taking a whiff of the freshly baked pound cake she was taking into the dining room.

"Justin? What are you doing here? Where are your sister and parents?" his Aunt Lorraine asked while looking into the hallway at her daughter and niece talking near the closet. She walked over to greet her niece.

"Aunt Lorraine! Where is Uncle Charlie?" Kayla exclaimed while giving her aunt a big hug.

"Uncle Charlie is still working. Where are your parents?" her Aunt Lorraine asked, looking up and seeing her sister and brother-in-law standing in the doorway, wiping off some snowflakes from their coat sleeves. Lorraine was a few inches shorter, a little heavier, and had a few more gray hairs than her older sister, but there was no mistaking they were related.

"Louise." Lorraine walked up to her sister and gave her a big hug.

"Lorraine! It's so good to see you. I hope we aren't barging in. We wanted to surprise you, but our flight was delayed because of a snowstorm. We didn't arrive here until three or four this morning," Louise replied to her sister.

"Three or four this morning?" Lorraine asked, motioning to Noelle to come over to help with their coats.

"Is this my new job, coat checker?" Noelle asked, trying to make a joke. Her aunt and uncle laughed, but her mother didn't find it funny. Noelle just rolled her eyes and went to hang up their coats in the hallway closet.

"Yeah, this was kind of a last-minute trip. The snowstorm wasn't even in the forecast…guess that's one of the wonders of traveling in the winter. I know I mentioned to you a few weeks ago about the possibility of coming to visit over the summer, but things changed, and we decided to do something a little more spontaneous," Louise replied.

"Well, that is wonderful! How long are you staying?" Lorraine asked excitedly.

Louise looked over at her husband and then back to her sister. "I think until either the third or the fourth of January, so through the holidays. Justin is even more excited because he misses an extra day or two of school," Louise replied, looking sternly at her son.

"It's fine with me." Justin smiled as he walked into the living room to take a seat.

"Do you have plans for dinner? You are all welcome to stay here. I'm making pot roast with mashed potatoes and glazed carrots," Lorraine replied, still smiling from the unexpected visit.

"Only if you allow me to help you," Louise insisted.

"I think I might even have an extra matching apron." Lorraine referred to her festive reindeer apron.

Louise laughed. "What do you think, kids?" Louise asked her children.

"The reindeer needs more Christmas lights around its antlers," Justin replied quickly.

"I was thinking a little less." Louise sighed as she followed her sister into the kitchen.

"Uncle Neil, would you like something to drink?" Noelle asked.

"Oh no, I'm fine. I can help with your Christmas tree if you want. I'm usually adjusting the tree to make sure it's standing straight. This year, we only have a wreath on the door and a small artificial tree on the table. It wasn't really worth buying a real tree since we were leaving before Christmas and won't be back until after New Year's," Uncle Neil replied, walking into the living room to take a seat near his son.

"We still don't have our tree. Chris is supposed to pick it up soon." Noelle was interrupted by the loud sound of an engine revving outside.

"What's that noise?" Justin asked, looking at the door, trying to figure out where that noise was coming from.

Noelle rolled her eyes. "That would be my brother's truck." Noelle sighed.

"That thing sounds cool!" Justin got excited and rushed out the front door.

"Brothers." Kayla rolled her eyes. Noelle couldn't help but laugh.

"Dad, come help us. Chris got a tree. It's huge!" Justin ran back toward the front door. Noelle's uncle shook his head while walking outside without his coat on. Louise and Lorraine were so busy in the kitchen preparing dinner and blasting Christmas songs on the radio while trying to sing along that they didn't notice anything going on outside. Kayla and Noelle couldn't help but laugh, watching their moms in the kitchen.

"Does your mom usually do that?" Kayla asked.

"Sometimes when she's baking all day, she'll start humming some Christmas songs. I think it helps keep her in the Christmas spirit, especially since she does a lot of cooking and baking for days." Noelle walked toward the opened box near the couch and started to take out more Christmas decorations.

"At least your mom bakes. The only thing my mom bakes is cupcakes and sometimes a layered cake with icing. I missed Aunt Lorraine's baking extravaganza." Kayla smiled brightly.

Noelle couldn't help but laugh. "I've never heard it described like that, but that's a great way to describe it. *Aunt Lorraine's Baking Extravaganza*. I'm going to have to borrow that one, especially since she does this for several holidays. It just seems like it more around Christmas because she does the most amount of baking now," Noelle replied, glancing back into the kitchen from the doorway, watching her mother and aunt still having a great time singing and laughing.

"Sometimes I wish I had a sister. I mean, I love my brother, but we are so different." Kayla sighed.

"You want to talk about different? Look at me and Chris." Noelle laughed while being interrupted by her brother and cousin bringing in the Christmas tree into the house. It was a very large Douglas fir. Everyone could smell the strong aroma of the Christmas tree throughout the house. Noelle and Kayla watched their brothers carry the tree toward the back of the living room near the picture window and placing it on the opposite side away from the fireplace.

"What do you think, Uncle Neil?" Chris asked, taking a step back and looking at it admiringly.

"A little crooked," Uncle Neil replied quickly.

Chris walked back toward the tree and helped straighten it up a little bit with Justin on the other side helping him. "How about this?" Chris asked while still holding the tree and looking back toward his uncle.

"Much better," his Uncle Neil replied. Louise and her sister walked up to the doorway.

"Oh, Chris, what a nice tree. How did you manage to get it so full so close to Christmas?" his mother asked.

"I know the guy that runs the Christmas tree lot and asked him to put it aside for me about a week ago. I knew if I waited too long, I would end up with a straggly little tree." Chris smiled proudly while admiring the tree some more.

"I was worried you were going to bring it really late and make me stay up all night." Noelle breathed a sigh of relief.

"Come on, sis. I wouldn't do that to you. At least not again. That and Mom pretty much told me to get a nice tree and bring it earlier this year or else… I took that as a direct order." Chris laughed nervously.

"Thanks, Chris. I appreciate it." Noelle nodded.

"Well, I'm going to start putting the lights up outside. I know I should have probably done this a couple of weeks ago, but sometimes there's not enough hours in a day," Chris mumbled as he started to walk out the front door.

"Yo, Chris, need some help?" Justin ran after his cousin.

"Maybe you two will need some help. I'll come too," Uncle Neil replied while putting his coat back on and walking out the front door after his son and nephew. Kayla and Noelle looked at each other.

"Justin usually doesn't like decorating at home. He's usually too busy reading," Kayla joked.

"Hey, nothing wrong with reading. I read a lot. I would always make room to read a new book or a short story in my spare time. Of course, by graduate school, even I started to get a little burned out," Noelle admitted.

"I never liked reading, unless it's a computer manual. That's probably why I take care of all the computer problems at home," Kayla joked.

"Better than me. I can't seem to do much more than check email and type up an assignment for class. Then again, I'm much more interested in business than computers," Noelle replied, opening up a second box of ornaments. Kayla was standing in the doorway looking at the opened box of Christmas ornaments.

"Kayla, can you do me a favor? Can you go and get some water for the tree? I think in the bathroom downstairs there's a small watering can…um…under the sink. Just fill it up so you can water the tree. I know that's usually something I forget to do," Noelle admitted.

"Sure." Kayla nodded excitedly and ran down the hallway toward the kitchen.

Noelle could hear Kayla talking to her mother and aunt before coming back toward the living room with a glass of water. Noelle looked at her, a little confused.

"Aunt Lorraine gave me a glass of water to use to fill up the tree. She said she keeps it under the sink for the tree. Anyway, dinner will be ready in about twenty minutes. She said we should probably let the guys know soon so they don't get lost outside. I know my dad could get too engrossed and then totally forget about everything else," Kayla said before walking through the living room toward the picture window where the Christmas tree was set up to give the tree some water. Noelle waited for her cousin to finish giving water to the tree.

"Kayla, I'll go outside to get everyone. You can stay here and finish going through one of the smaller boxes if you want. I'll be busy going through the rest of the boxes and decorating the tree tonight," Noelle replied, placing a few ornaments down on a chair in the living room. She knew it was getting cooler but didn't bother taking her jacket, something her mother would have yelled at her even if she was only standing on the porch, especially after being so sick only a couple of weeks earlier. She saw her father and Uncle Neil talking and pointing to the front of the house, while Chris and Justin were bringing boxes out of the shed.

"Chris, Justin, Mom said that dinner will be ready in like twenty minutes, so you should probably start getting ready to come back inside. I'll put the rest of the outside lights on because it's starting to get dark, but please don't be late. You know how Mom gets," Noelle warned her brother.

Chris nodded. "Sure. We'll put the boxes down on the patio, and then we'll be inside. I think we're going to decorate the back of the house first and then work around until we get to the front porch last. At least Dad said he wanted to decorate the deck this year," Chris explained.

"Chris, I have nothing to really do this week, so I can come over tomorrow and the day after and help with putting up the lights. It would be fun. Can't do much in a hotel room." Justin sighed.

"Sure. I don't have a problem. Just ask your parents. I'm not working until after Christmas," Chris replied.

Noelle looked at him, puzzled. She pulled the sleeves of her shirt over her hands to keep them warm. "You have almost a week off?" Noelle asked, starting to shiver from the bitterly cool winds blowing from both directions. She wrapped her arms around her chest to try and keep warm.

"Yes, I don't work on weekends unless it's overtime, and Christmas is on a Monday, so I have that off, but we'll talk about it later. Get back in the house before you get sick again!" Chris yelled.

Noelle nodded and ran back into the house. She slammed the door shut and started to rub her hands together, hoping to warm herself up faster. After a couple of minutes, she was able to stop shivering and walked back into the living room where her cousin was slowly going through a box of decorations.

"How are you doing over there?" Noelle asked Kayla, taking a seat next to her on the couch.

"You have a lot of stuff. I guess our moms really are different. My mom is not as sentimental. It looks like Aunt Lorraine saves almost everything from you and Chris." Kayla marveled as she looked at some of Chris and Noelle's handmade Christmas ornaments.

"Sometimes a little too sentimental. She keeps everything. I wouldn't mind throwing away or donating some stuff to make room." Noelle sighed.

"Nothing wrong with being sentimental. Maybe you might be the same way when you get married and have children," Kayla reminded her.

Noelle almost burst out laughing. "Yeah, I don't see that happening anytime soon. I think I'm going to be more like your mom and get married older." Noelle sighed gently.

"I think our moms are different. My mom said Aunt Lorraine wanted to get married young, and she was already engaged after high school, while my mom wanted to have a career and make money. She wasn't against marriage or children. Just wasn't as interested. When she met my dad, she had no expectations. They just fell in love pretty quickly." Kayla smiled as she stared at one of the handmade ornaments.

"You can't really plan this kind of stuff. I mean, you can have aspirations, but love always finds you when you aren't looking for it. If it was up to me, I wouldn't be single, but things didn't work out that way." Noelle sighed again.

"Maybe you needed to finish college before the right guy can find you, so you'll have more time to spend with him rather than studying," Kayla suggested.

Noelle gave her cousin a hug. "Thanks, Kayla. So how is everything going with you and school? What are your plans?" Noelle asked curiously.

"Well, I'm at a community college right now, and I'm on track to graduate this spring. I took classes last summer to catch up, and I'm registered for sixteen credits in the spring. Not happy about so much work, but I'm almost there. Then I'm planning on transferring to a four-year school. Actually, I was going to ask you about your school, if I can get a short tour. I've been thinking about going to school in New Jersey or Pennsylvania. I want to be closer to you and the rest of the family," Kayla explained.

"What about your brother and parents? Do you really want to move that far away from them? Noelle asked.

Kayla shook her head. "No, of course not. I would miss my family very much, even my annoying younger brother, but I miss it back east and you, cuzzie." Kayla smiled brightly.

"Don't worry. Things will work out, but sure, I'll take you around after Christmas just to give you an idea what the campus looks like. We could even go shopping or out to lunch afterward," Noelle suggested.

"Sounds great!" Kayla yelled excitedly.

Aunt Louise walked around the corner of the living room and tapped on the doorframe to get their attention. "Kayla, Noelle, dinner is just about ready. Did you tell the guys?" she asked, looking around at all the boxes of decorations, most of them still unpacked. "How much did you get through?" Aunt Louise asked Noelle and her daughter.

"I don't even think we got through a third of them." Noelle looked down.

"Well, I can stay over, and we can work on this until really late," Kayla suggested, "you know, like a sleepover."

"How about you come back tomorrow with your brother and you can both help finish decorating?" Kayla's mom suggested with a stern expression. Kayla understood what that meant and shrugged it off, but the look of disappointment was all over her face.

"Chris and Justin said they were putting some boxes down on the back patio, but they were waiting for Dad and Uncle Neil to finish whatever they were doing," Noelle answered her aunt.

Aunt Louise rolled her eyes. "If your father is anything like your uncle, it will be at least another forty minutes," Aunt Louise replied, looking very frustrated. She started to walk back toward the kitchen to finish setting the dining room table for dinner when the front door slammed open.

Chris and Justin plowed through and shook off their snowflake-covered coats. Chris didn't want to hang up his coat in the closet, so he hung it over the banister—something his mother never liked. Justin followed his cousin's actions. Chris looked into the living room at his sister and cousin.

"Isn't dinner ready? Wow, what were you two doing? It looks like you barely went through any boxes or did any decorating," Chris teased while looking at only a few boxes opened and the Christmas tree still completely bare. Noelle playfully stuck her tongue out at her brother while Justin and Kayla laughed at their cousins' behavior.

"A lot more decorations than I remember. I can't even find what box has the garland or Christmas lights. It's going to be a long few days." Noelle sighed.

"That's because every year, it seems like we increase the number of boxes of Christmas decorations but decrease the amount of space. Maybe it might be time to start sorting through them," Chris suggested.

"Yeah, suggest that one to Mom," Noelle sneered.

"Um…I'll let you take care of that one." Chris chuckled.

"Whatever. Um…where's Dad and Uncle Neil? Aren't they supposed to be coming inside with the two of you?" Noelle asked curiously.

"They both said in a few minutes, but that was several minutes ago. As soon as Dad got home, he saw Uncle Neil, and they have been discussing Christmas lights and the back deck." Chris shrugged his shoulders.

"It probably means they are checking all the lights right now. At least that's what my dad usually means," Justin suggested. Kayla nodded her head in agreement.

"Right now?" Chris asked, giving his cousin a baffled look.

"Yeah, when Dad starts something, he likes to try and finish it. Is Uncle Charlie like that too?" Kayla asked. Chris and Noelle looked at each other and sighed.

"You know what, Chris, you better go out and make sure you bring back Dad and Uncle Neil, and the three of us will take a seat in the dining room and try to keep both Mom and Aunt Louise from losing their temper," Noelle instructed.

"Yeah, 'cause if we're late for dinner, Mom will fly off the handle. She's always a little more uptight around Christmas," Chris warned while looking directly at his sister.

Noelle nodded. "Oh, okay, come on, Justin and Kayla. We're going to try to distract our moms while Chris goes to retrieve our dads before they get lost outside," Noelle replied, motioning to her younger cousins to follow her toward the kitchen while Chris nodded and walked back outside the front door to bring his dad and uncle back into the house to eat dinner.

Chapter 30

"Noelle!" Mrs. DeGarmo called from the bottom of the stairs. "Noelle, I really need you to come downstairs. Your aunt and uncle and cousins are already here. Everyone else will be arriving shortly."

Noelle quickly finished pulling half of her hair into a hair clip before walking toward her bedroom door and opening it. "Be right there!" Noelle yelled back while she adjusted her scalloped, cap-sleeved cream-colored lace dress before reaching over her bed and picking up her black cashmere cardigan to put on. She double-checked her hair in her full-length wall mirror. Her shoulder-length very curly blond hair was pulled half up in a silver hair clip encrusted with several colorful faux jewels. Noelle gently applied some light-pink eye shadow and some pink lip gloss. She didn't care if the eye shadow enhanced her blue eyes or not; her favorite color was pink and always would be. She walked toward her closet and stepped into a pair of black patent leather pumps before walking back toward the other side of her room. She closed the door behind her and quickly walked down the stairs toward the kitchen door. She saw her Aunt Louise and her mother walking back and forth in the kitchen as though they were running out of time to do everything.

"Merry Christmas, Aunt Louise." Noelle smiled while standing in the middle of the doorway. Her aunt was wearing a long-sleeved indigo silk blouse with light-gray pants and light-gray pumps. Her very short curly blond hair was adorned with a small sparkly silver barrette.

"Merry Christmas, Noelle," her aunt said, giving her a big smile.

"Is everyone in the living room?" Noelle asked, looking around the hallway and kitchen.

"I think your father and uncle are on the deck admiring their hard work with all the lights and decorations. Kayla was fixing some of the garland on the tree. She said it looked crooked. Justin was in the living room trying to find something to watch on TV. He was complaining because you have a better selection of channels here than in the hotel." Her Aunt Louise shook her head.

"He's welcomed to watch TV over here, as long as my parents don't mind, but I can lend him some books to read. I remember how much Justin loves to read, just like his older cousin." Noelle smiled.

Her Aunt Louise smiled. "That would be a great idea. Sometimes your uncle and I can't seem to pry the book away from him. It's no wonder he's taking accelerated English classes. Oh, but no mushy romance books. Justin just had to read *Romeo and Juliet* and complained the whole time." Her aunt laughed.

"I'm not really a fan of mushy romantic books either, but I was lucky when I was reading Shakespeare, my teacher chose Hamlet," Noelle replied, trying to stand up straight even though her feet were already starting to hurt from wearing heels.

Her mother looked over at her from the counter near the stove. "Noelle, when Mrs. Jankowski arrives, please ask her to come in the kitchen and help. I think an extra set of hands wouldn't hurt. I'm not used to preparing dinner for this many people." Noelle's mother sighed as she carried two empty casserole dishes over to the kitchen table. Her mother rolled up the sleeves of her shimmery white-and-silver sweater. Even though she was wearing the same apron with dancing reindeer decorated with Christmas lights to protect her clothing, she was still afraid of spilling something on herself.

"Mom, how many people did you invite this year? Usually, it's around fourteen or fifteen people, and that's a busier holiday," Noelle asked suspiciously, raising her eyebrows.

Her mother looked up at her while trying to start placing the sweet potatoes and mini marshmallows into one of the casserole dishes. "I'm not sure, but as of right now, it's already over twenty. I think we're not all going to fit in the dining room, so eating arrangements will be a little different this year. Don't worry. Everyone will have a place to sit and eat, and there will be more than enough food," her mother reassured her daughter.

Noelle's eyes widened as she realized this was going to be a little more hectic than previous years, but this was out of her hands, so she was going to go with the flow. Noelle saw her Aunt Louise opening the oven to baste the turkey while her mother was trying to continue preparing two casserole dishes simultaneously. She didn't want to bother them anymore.

"Mom, Aunt Louise, I'm going to the living room. If you need anything, just yell down the hall," Noelle offered while pivoting toward the hallway leading to the living room.

"Actually, you could bring a couple of trays of appetizers into the living room. It's getting closer to two, so the guests will start arriving soon." Her mother walked toward the refrigerator and pulled out two separate small serving trays. One with cheese slices and crackers, and the other with a variety of veggies and salad dressing. Noelle reached out her arms to hold the trays steady while walking through the hallway toward the doorway of the living room.

As she approached the doorway, Kayla ran to help her by taking one of the trays. Justin was on the couch changing the channels, completely unaware of anything around him.

"Thank you, Kayla. Merry Christmas! I love your dress. It matches your eyes." Noelle smiled brightly as she placed the second appetizer tray on the coffee table.

"Merry Christmas! Thank you. When I went shopping before we left Idaho, I saw this in the store, and I just couldn't forget about it. I'm not usually a fan of shimmery dresses, but this just caught my attention, and I was even able to find matching silver flats! I guess this was meant to be my dress," Kayla replied excitedly.

"Yes, when something is meant to be yours, it will be," Noelle replied philosophically.

Justin noticed the appetizers right in front of him. "Yum, food!" Justin grabbed a couple of crackers and a couple of slices of cheese before noticing his cousin and sister talking. "Oh, Merry Christmas, Noelle." Justin wiped a few crumbs of crackers off his navy dress pants, hoping that nobody would notice.

"Justin, do you want something to drink with your food?" Noelle asked, watching her cousin grabbing more cheese and crackers off the tray.

"He needs a plate or a napkin more," Kayla teased.

Justin gave his sister a dirty look. "No, thanks, Noelle. I think I'll wait a little bit. At least until Chris comes to watch some football. Where is he anyway?" Justin asked, looking around the living room. Kayla shrugged her shoulders and shook her head.

"You know, that's a great question," Noelle replied, looking around the living room and hallway for her brother. When the front door slammed open, Noelle rushed over thinking that it was Chris, but it was her father and Uncle Neil. Both of them took off their coats pretty quickly and hung them up in the hall closet. Noelle's father was wearing a pair of gray dress pants, a white dress shirt, a light-gray V-neck dress sweater, and a Christmas-themed tie. Her uncle was dressed similarly to his son Justin—navy dress pants, light-blue dress shirt, and an argyle beige-and-blue dress sweater.

"Hi, Dad, Uncle Neil. Have either of you seen Chris? He seems to have disappeared," Noelle asked, a little worried.

"I don't know. Maybe your mother asked him to run a last-minute errand for her," her father suggested.

"I think I heard something about going to pick up the liquor, but I thought he was going yesterday to do that," her Uncle Neil recalled.

Before Noelle's father could say anything, everyone was distracted by the sound of a revving truck engine. Chris jumped out of the driver's side of his truck and grabbed a paper bag with handles in one hand and a case of beer in the other hand. He rushed toward the back of the house and placed everything on the back deck near the sliding door. He ran back around the house a few minutes later, opening and rushing through the front door.

"Sorry, the line at the liquor store was insane. I knew I should have gone earlier," Chris apologized while trying to catch his breath.

"I thought you were going yesterday," his father demanded.

"I wanted to, but I wasn't free until after dinner, and by then, the store was already closed, so I said I would go early this morning. I left a couple of hours ago. Like I said, the lines were absolutely insane. The good thing is, I was able to get everything Mom asked for. It's on the back deck right outside the sliding door," Chris explained while rolling up the sleeves of his navy sweatshirt.

"Go get ready. The guests will be arriving soon," his father instructed sternly. Chris nodded and ran toward the door to his basement apartment. Noelle's father and uncle walked into the kitchen to grab the liquor off the back deck. Kayla grabbed a couple of appetizers from the tray on the coffee table before walking toward her cousin.

"So now what do we do?" Kayla asked.

"I guess just wait, but maybe one of us should check if there are any more appetizers," Noelle started saying before her mother interrupted her from the kitchen.

"Noelle, Kayla, there are more appetizers in the kitchen!" Noelle's mother yelled.

Noelle rolled her eyes. "I'll go get the appetizers, and you can set up the small card table in the leaving room. It should be leaning against the wall in the hallway. Chris was supposed to bring it upstairs yesterday. If you need more space, there are a few TV dinner trays next to the bookshelf to set up. I really don't want to use them for appetizers because we may need them when people start eating dinner," Noelle instructed as she walked back toward the kitchen.

Kayla walked out into the hallway to grab the card table and take it back into the living room. She just managed to set it up near the wall next to the bookshelf when Noelle got back into the living room with two trays of hot appetizers—stuffed mushrooms and mini hot dogs in mini rolls. Kayla took the dish towels off her cousin's shoulder to place under the trays of hot appetizers.

"Is that everything?" Kayla asked.

"No, there are two more trays. I think one is hot and one is cold," Noelle replied quickly.

"I'll get them. Just stay here and rest, and I guess answer the doorbell if it rings," Kayla joked.

Noelle rolled her eyes at her cousin before trying to arrange everything on the card table to make sure there was enough room for all four trays and still had room for paper plates and napkins. When her cousin came back a few minutes later with two trays of appetizers—another tray of cheese and crackers with pepperoni slices and a tray of mini cheese pizza bagels—Noelle helped her to arrange the last two appetizer trays on the card table.

"Oh, we still need the paper plates and the napkins for the appetizers. Where are the guests going to be able to keep their food, in their hands?" Noelle asked a little anxiously.

Kayla laughed. "Well, they can always do what Justin does—pile them in his hand until he runs out of room."

"Sounds like something Chris would do." Noelle smirked.

"One of us needs to get the paper plates and napkins," Kayla started explaining before the doorbell rang. "I'll get them, and you can answer the front door."

Noelle sighed when she turned to open the door while Kayla walked back toward the kitchen. "Valerie?" Noelle asked, surprised to see her friend.

Valerie wore a winter-white turtleneck sweaterdress with dark-brown leather boots and a matching dark-brown dress coat. She wore golden-bronze eye shadow, which accented the golden flecks in her eyes. Her lip gloss was a light plum. The colors complemented the golden tones of her complexion.

"Yeah, I'm sorry. Is it bad timing or something? When my sisters told my parents they wouldn't be able to make it until tomorrow, my mom postponed Christmas dinner, so I had nothing to do. I got dressed a little bit early. I was afraid of showing up too early. Am I too early?" Valerie looked a little nervous for fear of imposing on her friend and her family.

"Don't be silly. Even if you were early, my mom would still be thrilled that you stopped by," Noelle replied, smiling while backing up to allow her friend inside the house.

"Thanks! I feel relieved that I'm not imposing. When is everyone going to start showing up? Where is Chris?" Valerie asked, looking around.

Noelle was caught off guard by the last question. "Did you just ask about Chris…as in Chris, my brother? The guests, family and friends, should be arriving shortly. My mom told everyone to be here around two or two thirty," Noelle asked suspiciously yet calmly.

Valerie relented. "Yeah, I figured it's the holidays, and maybe I need to be a little more charitable. Besides, I think I realized that the more I fight with your brother, the more tension I bring into your life, negatively affecting our friendship," Valerie replied sincerely.

"Wow, I'm going to take this as an early Christmas present." Noelle was thrilled to hear that but wasn't totally convinced that Chris and Valerie could manage to be civil around each other all the time. Kayla heard some talking before inquisitively approaching her cousin.

"Oh, Valerie, this is my younger cousin Kayla. She's visiting from Idaho with her family for the holidays," Noelle explained.

Valerie stopped and stared at both of them for a moment. "Oh, wow, you two could pass for twins. I know you said your cousin resembled you, but I didn't think she was your look-alike." Valerie looked stunned.

Kayla laughed. "Yeah, most people who see Noelle's picture ask if she's my sister, and I'm like no, she's my cousin. Nobody believes me. I'm like whatever." Kayla laughed. "Anyway, would anyone want something to drink? I'm going to get a soda." Kayla started to pivot toward the kitchen.

"Sure, regular is good. Thanks." Valerie smiled while Kayla turned around to get the drinks from the kitchen.

"There are appetizers in the living room. I don't think there is anything to watch on TV because my dad, uncle, and cousin are looking for some sports game to watch. Probably a football game." Noelle rolled her eyes.

Valerie laughed. "That reminds me of my nineteenth birthday. I was dating Jack for about six months, and the soccer semifinals were on TV. I thought my family were big soccer fans, but they were nothing in comparison to Jack and his family. Although I did get a birthday gift, most of that birthday was spent watching a soccer match. Probably the most boring birthday of all time. I don't even think Jack noticed I fell sleep." Valerie rolled her eyes and laughed.

"Jack from college?" Noelle asked, trying to remember.

"Yeah…my longest relationship, we were on and off throughout junior year, so about almost three years together. He was a really good guy. My family loved him too. Well, he was Basque-descent like me, but that wasn't the only reason they loved him. He liked to watch soccer with my dad, would always bring my mom's favorite flowers when he came over for dinner, and even helped Cristina's boyfriend, now husband, fix his truck. But honestly, I don't think we were really compatible long-term. Then again, we were so young. I sometimes wonder if I did things differently and ended up staying in Connecticut." Valerie looked away, pondering.

Noelle nodded as though she understood. "Yeah, I sometimes think the same thing about Cody. I know we were only together like seven or eight months, but maybe I should have considered pushing to pursue a long-term relationship. Maybe I would be married now," Noelle pondered thoughtfully.

Valerie looked at her, perplexed. "I thought it was Cody who told you he preferred to break up so things didn't get too complicated," Valerie inquired.

"Well, kind of. I actually think it was kind of mutual. Cody said he preferred to try not to hurt me or get hurt himself. He was in the reserves, but when he would be on active duty, we could have been separated from each other for several months at a time. I guess he wasn't sure about a long-distance relationship. I don't think I really was either. He told me if I really wanted to try and make it work, he was more than willing to try. I guess I chickened out. It was really overwhelming. He was my first relationship and my first love. It was hard to tell if I really wanted to be with him or if I couldn't let go.

In the least, I have some good memories." Noelle smiled while she reminisced.

"Where would you be if you ended up with Cody? You might not even be in Jersey, let alone finishing graduate school or starting your own business. I guess I can say the same thing about Jack. If I stayed with him, maybe I wouldn't have my own business, and that is definitely something I wouldn't want to give up for anyone. I guess if either of them were meant to end up with us, they would have found their way back into our lives one way or another," Valerie replied confidently.

"Well, maybe we should get out of the past and start focusing on the present," Noelle remarked quickly.

Valerie nodded. "You're right. Oh, thanks, Kayla." Valerie held her hand out as Kayla approached with her soda.

"No problem. I think it's getting a little bit warm in the house. Maybe it's all the cooking in the kitchen. I had to really try to dodge getting hit by trays or pots to make it toward the cups and soda. Does Aunt Lorraine put this together every year?" Kayla asked while taking a sip from her soda.

Noelle took a deep breath. "And every other holiday that includes dinner and a dessert. I really think my mom missed her calling," Noelle laughed. Valerie was about to suggest also baking for the coffee shop when Noelle turned and gave her a look not to say anything.

"Well, it was nice meeting you, Valerie, but I need to take a seat before I spill soda all over my brand-new dress." Kayla smiled while walking back toward the living room.

"Your family doesn't know about the coffee shop?" Valerie asked in a loud whisper.

"Not yet. My parents and Chris know. Eventually, I will tell everyone else, but I'm not ready. Besides, I don't want to take away from the holidays to just talk about me," Noelle whispered back. Valerie nodded as though she understood.

"Maybe I should take a seat too. I'm afraid of spilling something on this sweaterdress. I love this color but am always afraid of wearing it." Valerie walked into the living room with her soda.

Noelle stood up in the doorway waiting for the doorbell to ring again, because somehow, this had been designated as her job. To pass the time, Noelle's mind started to run away with her, and she started to daydream. Being distracted only made her jump even higher when she was startled by the cellar door flying open. Noelle stared in amazement as she almost didn't recognize her own brother. Chris stepped out in a pair of navy dress pants and a dressy blue V-neck sweater with a white dress shirt underneath.

"Chris, I almost didn't recognize you. Wait, are you wearing cologne too? I didn't even know you owned any cologne," Noelle said, stunned.

Chris smiled nervously. "Noelle, of course I own cologne. It's called eau de construction worker," Chris joked.

Noelle shook her head. "Only you would say that." Noelle rolled her eyes and laughed.

"Come on. Of course I own cologne. I just don't wear it very often. It's usually only for special occasions, just like I don't always dress up, but sometimes I have to step out of my comfort zone and be a little different. It's like growing up." Chris smiled. "Hi, Valerie." Chris smiled sheepishly as Valerie walked up behind Noelle.

"Wow, Chris, is that really you? You clean up very nicely. Until today, I didn't think you owned any dress pants. I've only ever seen you wear cargo pants or jeans." Valerie laughed nervously as she felt a little awkward being around him now. That was a totally new and very strange feeling for her.

"I can't wear my work shirt and ripped jeans everywhere. I have to shake it up sometimes," Chris joked.

"That didn't seem to stop you before," Valerie replied quickly before realizing what she had said.

Chris bit his lip from saying something really rude, but a part of him really couldn't help it. "Very nice dress, Valerie, but I think there's something a little off. Isn't your eye shadow supposed to match your dress? I guess that would mean that you're mismatched, and you did it all wrong. Better luck next time!" Chris replied sarcastically.

Valerie crossed her arms angrily. "Amazing. You can dress up and look so classy, but then you open your mouth and ruin it," Valerie sneered as she walked back into the living room.

"Out of all people, you had to pick her as a friend?" Chris grumbled while he walked into the living room looking for some appetizers. Noelle shook her head but couldn't help laughing to herself. No matter how much those two argued with each other, it started to appear as though they didn't dislike each other as much as it seemed.

Noelle heard the doorbell ring again, so she walked toward the front door to open it up. She was greeted by warm smiles from several familiar faces.

"Merry Christmas," Noelle greeted the people behind the front door.

"Merry Christmas, Noelle." Mrs. Jankowski smiled.

"How did you get here? I know you and Mr. Jankowski really don't drive much," Noelle inquired, walking backward to let them inside. The Jankowskis were followed by two more adults and two young children. One woman with strawberry-blond hair looked familiar.

"Hi, Noelle, do you remember me? I haven't been up here in a few years," the woman asked.

Noelle squinted at her as though the woman looked familiar but couldn't place her face or name. "I'm sorry. I'm drawing a blank," Noelle replied, a little embarrassed.

"I'm Caroline, the Jankowski's daughter. I know you haven't seen me in several years, but we were able to both get time off this week and wanted to surprise my parents," Caroline replied while unbuttoning her coat and moving out of the way for her husband and children to walk into the house.

"Oh, Caroline, it's so nice to see you. It has been a long time." Noelle smiled, pleasantly surprised.

"This is my husband, Bill. This little blondie is our son Logan, and this little firecracker redhead is Vivian," Caroline introduced her family while Noelle started to take everyone's coat to hang it up in the closet.

"Mommy, my name is Vivian," Vivian explained while staring at her mother with her big bright blue eyes. Caroline picked up her daughter and brushed her curly red bangs off her face.

"She is extra excited about Santa coming tonight, right, Vivian?" Caroline explained to Noelle before turning her attention back to her daughter. Vivian was already struggling to get down, so her mother placed her feet on the ground while helping to take her coat off.

"She's adorable. How old is she?" Noelle asked while smiling and watching Vivian energetically wandering around the hallway.

"Logan is seven, and Vivian just turned four a couple of months ago," Caroline explained while her husband helped their son take his coat off and gave it to Noelle to hang up. Vivian ran over to her grandma and gave her a hug. Since neither Mr. nor Mrs. Jankowski was very tall, it was much easier for her to give them a hug.

"I am four and three months," Vivian corrected her mother. Everyone laughed, but Vivian didn't bother to pay attention.

"Noelle, dear, does your mother need any help in the kitchen?" Mrs. Jankowski asked.

"Actually, I think my mom would appreciate any help that anyone wants to offer. She's in there with my Aunt Louise, and they have been busy all morning cooking and preparing food," Noelle replied. Mrs. Jankowski smiled as she walked back toward the kitchen.

"Bill, can you take Vivian and Logan with you into the living room to maybe watch TV? Then I can go into the kitchen to help," Caroline asked, looking at her husband.

Vivian shook her head adamantly. "I don't want to watch TV," Vivian replied, crossing her arms.

Caroline sighed as her husband waited by the doorway of the living room holding Logan's hand. Kayla noticed the commotion going on in the hallway and decided to try and help. She walked toward Vivian and knelt down to eye level.

"What is your name?" Kayla asked gently, watching Vivian twirl her puffy-sleeved red-and-green plaid dress back and forth.

"I'm Vivian. Who are you?" Vivian asked bluntly. Caroline shook her head feeling embarrassed, and Noelle bit her lip to keep from laughing.

"My name is Kayla. Are you excited about seeing Santa tonight?" Kayla asked.

"She has been nonstop talking about Santa and Christmas trees for the past month." Caroline laughed.

"I wanna see Santa, but Mommy says no." Vivian's face grew long.

"Santa isn't here. He's at the North Pole, really busy, but I can show you the Christmas tree. Your mommy says that you like Christmas trees." Kayla was trying to cheer Vivian up.

Caroline knelt down near her daughter. "Vivian, would you like to tell Kayla all about what you asked Santa for this year?" Caroline asked gently.

Vivian nodded while grabbing Kayla's hand.

"She also likes any Christmas books or poems you can find. She loves being read too," Caroline suggested.

"There are a few books on the third shelf of the bookcase, Christmas stories and poems for children. One of those books was my favorite growing up," Noelle suggested to Kayla.

"Come on, Kayla, hurry up," Vivian started pulling Kayla toward the living room.

Caroline laughed as she looked at Noelle. "Thank your cousin for me." Caroline smiled gratefully.

"How did you know Kayla is my cousin?" Noelle asked curiously.

"I know you don't have a sister. It's the resemblance. You two could pass for sisters. I'll be in the kitchen helping anywhere I can." Caroline smiled while she walked down the hallway into the kitchen.

Noelle stood at the living room doorway with a grateful smile growing across her face. Initially being upset about all the extra guests this Christmas Eve, Noelle had started to change her opinion. Watching Logan and especially Vivian made her think about when she was growing up with Chris and eagerly waiting for Santa to come and visit. It might not have lasted, but those were some of the happiest memories she had and looked forward to one day sharing them with her children. Noelle glanced into the living room watching several people having conversations, watching television, or snacking on some appetizers. She then looked over toward the corner of the room near the card table and saw what looked like Chris and Valerie having a civil conversation and even laughing. She shook her head as those two were becoming like the weather, at least this was a step forward rather than the constant fighting and insults dished out at each other. Maybe one day they would be able to figure out how to get along all the time. Noelle started to turn around to check the door when her cousin Justin popped up behind her.

"There's someone at the door for you," Justin said nonchalantly as he walked back into the living room to get another appetizer and take a seat on the couch.

Noelle looked baffled. She slowly walked up to the front door and opened it to find Matt standing on the other side. That was probably one of the last people she expected to see. She felt very conflicted because a part of her wasn't interested in seeing him at all as her facial expression and body language tensed up quickly. However, there was a small part of her that felt some joy in seeing him again.

"Hi, Noelle, can we talk?" Matt asked, putting his hands into his coat pockets.

Noelle hesitated for a moment but then nodded as she went back inside to grab her coat from the hallway closet. She walked toward the front door and stepped outside, closing the door behind them. She figured if Chris and Valerie could try to be civil, she could too with Matt.

"So?" Noelle asked while crossing her arms over her chest.

"Wouldn't it be a little warmer inside?" Matt suggested. His sparkling blue eyes glistened in the light snow as a few snowflakes fell on the end of his Greco-Roman nose.

Noelle, unamused, shook her head no. "I don't think my family and friends need to hear our conversation. What are you doing here? Isn't Lauren the supermodel preparing to drag you off to LA?" Noelle asked, kind of snarky.

Matt grimaced. "Lauren is back in LA without me, and she's not coming back. That display in the grocery store seemed to really be the final nail in the coffin for the relationship," Matt admitted.

Noelle looked at him, perplexed. "What are you talking about?" Noelle asked suspiciously.

"Things already weren't going that great between me and Lauren. We actually had a small argument before you knocked over the whole display of herbal teas. I think the argument between you and me in the dairy aisle was the breaking point, and it got more than just the other customers' attention. Lauren noticed too, and she got pretty upset. She accused me of being dishonest and hiding things from her," Matt started to explain before Noelle interrupted.

"What would she think you were being dishonest about? On the other hand, I can think of a few things that I can question about you." Noelle's face remained stern.

Matt took a moment before trying to answer. "Like what? Are you talking about moving to LA? That was never my idea. That was completely Lauren's plan, but I didn't put up enough resistance until I was backed up against a wall. I told her I preferred to stay on the East Coast, but she probably thought she could persuade me to change my mind. I guess I thought she wasn't serious, or I got too comfortable in that relationship. Honestly, my family really didn't like her, and they were very happy and relieved she didn't come to Thanksgiving dinner. I guess that was a clear sign it was time to move on," Matt explained.

"So why did you come here? By the way, how did you get my address?" Noelle asked defensively.

Matt took a deep breath. "Well, all of your information was on the invoice in your file. I know, I probably went over the line, but I needed to talk to you in person. Besides, I thought if I tried to call you on the phone, you wouldn't answer or just hang up," Matt relented.

"Looking at the invoice was actually kind of clever, especially since you did do work for my store." Noelle cracked a smile.

Matt let out a light chuckle. "I needed to talk to you in person. I wanted to apologize. I kind of overreacted in the grocery store. You may have said some things that got under my skin, but I might have deserved it. Listen, Noelle. In high school, the one thing that I could say about you was that you were genuine. You told me things I needed to hear even if I really didn't want to, and I really valued your friendship because of that reason. I have a feeling that if I was more open and honest with you about everything, we wouldn't have gotten into a fight," Matt replied honestly but struggling a little bit to keep eye contact.

Noelle wasn't quite sure what he was implying, but she felt hopeful. Even the possibility that Matt was interested in her was more than she expected to hear. "Where do we go from here?" Noelle asked, trying to remain calm. Matt looked at her a little confused as he had no idea what she was implying.

"Huh? I don't mind continuing to talk, but can we go inside now? It's getting pretty cold outside, and it's starting to snow," Matt almost pleaded, digging his hands deeper into his coat pockets.

Noelle nodded and opened the front door. Matt followed quickly behind her. Noelle walked toward the closet before quickly taking off her coat. She went to hang her coat up before turning to take Matt's coat from him. He slowly took off his charcoal wool dress coat, handing it over to Noelle and revealing his navy dress pants, a dark-blue dress shirt, a navy V-neck dress sweater, and a silver-and-gray striped tie.

"I guess blue is your favorite color?" Noelle teased while looking at what he was wearing.

"Actually, no. I don't mind blue, but I think my favorite color is gray," Matt replied, glancing down at his tie.

Noelle couldn't keep from laughing. "You really are the adventurous type," Noelle teased.

Matt shrugged his shoulders before turning his head toward the living room to listen to what was playing on the TV. "Is that football?" Matt's eyes grew large.

Noelle shook her head in disbelief. Matt rushed into the living room to take a seat on the couch. She didn't have much time to be upset as the doorbell rang again, and Noelle turned around to answer it.

"Joyeux Noël!" her uncle Clem exclaimed in his native French accent. Noelle was shocked to see her uncle and aunt standing right behind the door.

"Joyeux Noël, Oncle Clem et Tante Corrine! Merry Christmas, Uncle Clem and Aunt Corrine!" Noelle replied back with a pretty good French accent. "Where are CJ and Colton?" Noelle asked, looking around for her cousins.

"Right here, cousin! Do you need glasses?" CJ teased her while brushing his left hand through his light-blond hair.

"Merry Christmas, Noelle," Colton said quietly. Colton was a little taller than his brother but much quieter and shier. He felt pretty comfortable around family but always took him longer to warm up to strangers.

"Come in…come in. Does my dad know you were coming?" Noelle asked curiously.

"I know your mom knows, but I'm not sure about your dad. I think she wanted to surprise him," her Uncle Clem explained.

"Is there anything to eat? Even a snack? I'm kind of hungry," Colton asked quietly. It was loud enough for everyone else to hear him, but compared to the rest of his family, Colton was barely louder than a little mouse. CJ laughed at his younger brother.

"It must be the hockey player appetite. Burns off everything he eats and then wants to eat more. I swear if he continues to play as well as he does, he will have a chance of at least going semipro," CJ said proudly while putting his arm around his younger brother. Colton didn't say much, handing his coat over to Noelle to hang up and then wandering into the living room to search for a snack or appetizer until dinner was served.

"Does your mom need any help?" her Aunt Corrine asked while adjusting her knee-length navy-blue velvet dress with matching heels. She looked like she was more ready for a fancy party rather than a family holiday dinner.

"You know, I think my mom will appreciate any help that you can give. She's in the kitchen with my Aunt Louise and our neighbors." Noelle directed her Aunt Corrine toward the kitchen doorway.

"Where is Chris?" CJ asked while fixing his light-blue V-neck dress sweater. He was neatly dressed but looked as though he wasn't very comfortable, indicating he didn't get dressed up much outside a few occasions.

"He should be in the living room, I think, watching football." Noelle shrugged her shoulders.

Her Uncle Clem handed CJ two plastic bags filled with presents in various sizes to place under the tree. Her uncle was so preoccupied with making sure his son took all of the presents into the living room that he forgot he was still wearing his coat.

Noelle's father was distracted by the voices in the hallway and turned his head to see what was going on. A bright smile formed across his face.

"Clément!" Noelle's father yelled in a strong French accent from the couch. He got up from the couch and walked into the hallway to give his brother a big hug.

"Joyeux Noël, Charles!" Clem hugged his brother back. Noelle looked embarrassed as her uncle and father were starting to speak French, which very few guests and family could understand.

"Merry Christmas, Clem! How were you able to come for Christmas? You said you almost never can get off from work, especially around the holidays," Charles inquired.

"This year, as a different type of Christmas bonus, we were given a whole week off with pay. They decided to close the office through New Year's. It was a real gift," Clem replied, finally taking off his coat.

"Yes, Clem, take off your coat so you can stay awhile. Listen, a bunch of us are watching the game in the living room. You can take a seat on the couch. I'm going to grab a beer. Want one?" Charles asked his brother.

"Oui, merci, mon frère," Clem replied happily. Clem walked into the living room to take a seat on the couch while Charles walked into the kitchen to grab two beers.

Noelle went to take a seat on the stairs to continue watching the door for anyone else to show up. She barely got a chance to sit down before the doorbell rang again. Noelle sighed, hoping this would be the last guest. She quickly opened the front door.

"Merry Christmas, Noelle," Spenser greeted her with a hug. Noelle smiled as she moved backward to allow both Spenser and his girlfriend into the house.

"Merry Christmas, Spenser, and…" Noelle greeted them but didn't know his girlfriend's name.

"Amelia. Very nice to meet you. Spenser has told me all about your coffee shop opening next year. That is so exciting! I'm always looking for a great place for a latte and to read one of my books. Maybe when it gets warmer, Spenser's mom might want to get out too." Amelia smiled while looking where to place her coat. Noelle opened the hall closet and hung up both Spenser and Amelia's coats.

"How is your mom doing?" Noelle asked Spenser.

"She's doing pretty well. I think the weather is affecting some of her symptoms, but she wanted to come out today. I didn't want her to, so my brother and his girlfriend are at home with her. I promised to take some desserts back home," Spenser replied, quickly looking around for Chris.

"I'm sure there will be more than enough to take home. My mom will probably be sending some food home too." Noelle smiled as she watched Spenser and Amelia walk into the living room. She looked at the living room and saw it was becoming crowded and could see that almost all the appetizer trays were empty. Noelle glanced into the kitchen and saw everyone walking back and forth around the kitchen, performing different tasks. She was hoping that dinner would be served soon because it was starting to feel overcrowded. She never remembered Christmas Eve dinner this packed, but then again, there were unexpected guests who arrived. Of course, all surprises were very welcomed, including Matt, even though she still wasn't sure what all this meant.

Noelle walked down the hallway to ask about dinner. "Mom," Noelle asked while hugging the doorframe, "how much longer for dinner?"

Her mother glanced up at her and responded in a rushed tone. "Probably another twenty or thirty minutes. Is anyone getting restless? We still have some pretzels and chips to put out," her mother offered.

"Lorraine, where do you want me to put this?" Mrs. Jankowski asked while carrying a casserole dish.

"On the dining room table. There should be enough pot holders to put underneath," Noelle's mother responded.

"Just keep doing whatever you're doing. Someone will be out soon to announce when dinner will be ready," her mother said, rushing back to check on something cooking on the stove.

Noelle lowered her eyes and walked back toward the front door, taking a seat on the stairs. "Yeah, opening the front door and taking people's coats. Gee, if I knew I was so good at this, I would have skipped the headache of opening my own business and worked as a coat check girl somewhere," Noelle mumbled very agitatedly to herself. She looked up and saw a familiar face.

"Hey, Noelle, want some company? It's getting a little bit stuffy in the living room. I don't remember so many people, or maybe I thought your living room was larger," Valerie pondered.

"No, we have more people this year. I mean, it's great. I haven't seen some of our relatives in a long time, but it is getting kind of crowded. I'm just hoping nobody else stops by." Noelle sighed. Before she could even turn her head back toward Valerie, the doorbell rang again. Noelle sighed and rolled her eyes before slowly getting up to answer the front door. She was hoping this would be the last time she would have to open the front door.

"Grandma?" Noelle replied as her mouth dropped open.

"Well, are you going to let me inside, or are you going to let me freeze? I may be Canadian, but it doesn't mean I like to stand out in the snow," her grandmother replied powerfully in her French-Canadian accent. Valerie backed up to allow Noelle to step back to give her grandmother room to step inside the house.

"How are you doing, *ma chérie*? It's so good to see you!" her grandmother announced in her French-Canadian accent while giving her a hug. She looked over at Valerie standing behind them. "And you must be..." Noelle's grandmother demanded.

Valerie seemed a little nervous and fought quickly to gather some words together. "I'm Valerie. I'm a good friend of Noelle. We've been friends since high school," Valerie explained with a nervous smile.

Chris rushed out of the living room at the sound of voices in the hallway. "Grandma! It's so good to see you," Chris said as he gave his grandmother a big hug.

"Christian, where is that girlfriend of yours? The skinny one with the squeaky voice?" his grandmother demanded.

Chris drew a blank before realizing that she was talking about Ally. "You mean Ally? Um—well... you see..." Chris stammered nervously while trying to avoid eye contact with his grandmother.

"Christian Xavier Sébastien, what is so difficult to answer, whether you are together or broken up?" his grandmother demanded. Although Valerie wanted to laugh, she also felt sorry for him for being scolded like that in front of everyone.

"*S'il te plait*, Grandma. You are embarrassing me," Chris replied as his face reddened with embarrassment.

Valerie hesitated for a moment while gently biting her lower lip before interjecting.

"Well, Christian, if you don't want to be embarrassed, then stop acting childish," Valerie stated firmly. Chris and Noelle's grandmother looked over at Valerie with a smile and a look of approval.

"I like this one. Valérie, *n'est-ce pas*? Christian, meet Valérie. She's a good match for you," his grandmother insisted. Both Chris and Valerie were speechless.

"Um, we're just friends...well, acquaintances...distant acquaintances," Chris asserted.

"Don't be foolish." His grandmother looked at him and shook her head. She took off her coat and went to hang it up in the closet by herself.

"Hey, Chris, you're missing some of the best plays of the whole game!" Matt yelled while rushing out of the living room to get Chris to come back. Noelle and Chris's grandmother looked at Matt with a smirk.

"I don't remember you at any of the other family parties," their grandmother commented harshly.

Matt looked a little embarrassed and struggled for a moment to find the right words. "Um...I'm...well...I'm an old friend of Noelle's from high school," Matt managed to mutter out.

Their grandmother looked at Noelle and then back to Matt before turning back to Noelle. "He's cute, Noelle, but doesn't seem to be that bright," their grandmother replied harshly before heading off toward the kitchen to see her daughters.

Noelle walked over to Matt, her cheeks burning with embarrassment. "I'm so sorry, Matt. I had no idea she was coming. I would have tried to prepare you a little bit," Noelle replied anxiously.

"Your grandmother really is a force to reckon with. Until today, I thought my Great-Aunt Shirley was blunt. I think your grandmother wins hands down," Matt replied, still a little bit frazzled.

"And to think this is her being mellow." Noelle sighed. Matt lowered his eyes as he was at a loss for words.

Chris turned to Valerie to try and remedy what his grandmother had said to them. "Look, Valerie…" Chris started to speak but was unable to look her in the eyes because of feeling uncomfortable and awkward.

"Listen, Chris, we can call a truce for Noelle's sake. Okay, maybe even go as far and call each other distant acquaintances or something. I'm cool with that. But as far as you and me together—as in dating—in a relationship, not gonna happen! I would much rather walk on a bunch of rusted nails before even contemplating dating you!" Valerie stated firmly.

Chris's eyes narrowed. "Great! I'm not even sure if I would want to go as far as calling you an acquaintance. Maybe more like an unavoidable person! As for dating you, which would never happen, I would rather walk on pieces of charred broken glass that sliced up my feet and got infected. That would be much less painful!" Chris retorted angrily.

Valerie's face reddened with anger. "Great! We're in agreement!" Valerie shouted as she started to walk off toward the living room. Chris shook his head angrily and walked off in the opposite direction.

Matt looked at them bizarrely and then back toward Noelle. "What's up with those two? They were getting along great in the living room, and now they want to fight like cats and dogs?" Matt asked, a bit perplexed.

"Welcome to my life. Going on thirteen years of this," Noelle groaned. Matt gave her a sympathetic look. She turned her head to hear voices coming from the kitchen and then getting louder. It was her mother, aunt, and grandmother all standing together.

"What an amazing Christmas this year! My sister and her family made a special visit to celebrate the holidays with us. Then my brother-in-law and his family chose to spend the holidays visiting us. They both haven't been back here in over a decade! This is truly a joyous Christmas," Noelle's mother beamed. Noelle's aunt and her uncle looked at each other, seemingly communicating without using any words. Her aunt walked toward her uncle so that everyone in the living room could see and hear them.

"Mama, Lorraine, Neil and I have some big news. Neil has been offered a promotion with a generous pay raise, which also involves a relocation. That's why we came here for Christmas. We wanted to keep it a secret, but I think it's easier to just tell everyone. We're moving back east!" Noelle's aunt exclaimed.

Noelle's mother's eyes filled with tears of joy upon hearing the news. "When are you moving back?" Noelle's mother almost couldn't contain her happiness, tears streaming down the cheeks of her diamond-shaped face.

"Neil will be moving back around the end of April or beginning of May to start his new position, but we won't be moving until June because Kayla is graduating from community college and Justin is graduating from high school," Noelle's aunt replied.

Lorraine went to give her sister a hug. Noelle was stunned by the announcement as her cousin Kayla walked up to her.

"Kayla, is that why you were asking about going to see my college?" Noelle asked.

"Yeah, I was trying to think of a clever way of asking about the campus so I can apply without actually giving too much away. I almost slipped up a few times. It was so tough keeping this one in." Kayla pretended to wipe some sweat away from her forehead. Noelle gave her younger cousin a big hug.

"Kayla, we have a spare bedroom that you can stay at if you decide to attend college in New Jersey. You are always welcome here," her Aunt Lorraine replied.

"Thank you, Aunt Lorraine. I might take you up on that offer, but let's see if I get accepted first," Kayla replied, uncertain.

"Don't doubt yourself. If I did, I wouldn't have—" Noelle cut herself off before sharing her big open secret.

"Well, since everyone is sharing surprises, guess it's my turn," Louise and Lorraine's mother replied. Louise and Lorraine looked at each other in total confusion.

"What are you talking about, Mom?" Louise asked, thinking it was referring to not being able to visit Idaho anymore.

"I'm not getting any younger, and my friends and neighbors are all moving away to be closer to their families, or they are passing away, so I think it's time that I take the next step. Next year, I'm getting an apartment here, and it's going to be permanent. I have so many things to look forward to—my grandchildren *eventually* getting married but also my dear hardworking granddaughter Noelle who has decided to follow in the footsteps of her great-grandmother Mathilde in opening her own business," her grandmother proudly announced.

Noelle's face dropped as she wasn't planning or expecting to mention anything yet.

Noelle's mother expanded on what her mother started announcing. "I'm not sure if Noelle was ready to share this with everyone, but I think the cat is out of the bag. Noelle is not only graduating with her master's degree in the spring, but she is also in the initial stages of opening her own coffee shop next year. It will be a very busy spring semester for her, but after seeing how hard she worked this semester, I know she will come out successful. We want everyone to know just how proud of her we are." Noelle's mother fought back a few more tears of joy.

Noelle was initially mortified, but after hearing several friends and relatives shout "Good luck" and "Congratulations," she started to feel more at ease.

Her mother and aunt went back into the kitchen to continue preparing everything for dinner. Noelle's grandmother approached her before following her daughters toward the kitchen.

"Just remember, *whatever you have on the menu to always serve a little bit of café au lait*. That was something that my mother, your great-grandmother, would always say." Her grandmother smiled before heading back to the kitchen.

Noelle stood there thinking, almost completely lost in thought. It looked as though she had a eureka-type moment from the look on her face. She was so preoccupied with her own thoughts that she barely noticed her mother stepping out of the kitchen into the hallway to announce dinner being ready.

"Since this year there are a few more people than usual, we will be doing more of a buffet style. I need everyone to form a line to go into the kitchen to get their food. You can sit anywhere you would like. There is a little bit of room in the dining room and kitchen, and there are tables and TV dinner stands in the living room. And as my mother would always say, bon appétit." Noelle's mother smiled as she walked back into the kitchen.

Everyone started slowly walking out of the living room to form a line down the hallway into the kitchen. As Noelle watched friends and family lining up and walking slowly toward the kitchen, she saw Chris and Valerie standing near each other in line and having a friendly conversation. The conversation appeared to start off friendly, but within minutes the conversation soured as Chris's face tensed up. Valerie crossed her arms and glared at him. Noelle just shrugged it off as trying to figure those two out was going to give her a big headache. She turned to her side and saw Matt standing right next to her.

"Are you waiting to get in line? Matt asked, looking at the long line and thinking about dinner. He was trying to slowly nudge her to walk over to the line with him.

"No, I'm just so struck by something my grandmother said to me. What do you think of the name Café au Lait for my coffee shop? For some reason, it kind of grabs at me, like it might be what I was looking for," Noelle replied as a smile started to grow across her face.

"Okay, sounds cool! We can talk about this in line while going to get food. I'm kind of getting hungry, and all that food smells incredible," Matt suggested.

"It's just too perfect, and it's just what Val told me, I would know when the right name found me," Noelle recalled, still smiling. She slowly followed Matt toward the end of the line walking toward the kitchen to get their dinner and sit down to eat.

The past few months might have been quite a real whirlwind, with so many things turning upside down or appearing to go in the wrong direction. However, everything managed to turn out better than Noelle could have ever planned or expected. She wouldn't change a thing because she ended up exactly where she was meant to be; all she needed was a little spark to ignite a change, pushing her in the right direction. With the holidays bringing lots of wonderful surprises for her and her family, Noelle could only feel really excited about all the possibilities that lay ahead for her in the New Year.

About the Author

Since she was a little girl, Arabella always had a very overactive imagination. She would invent new characters and stories, which she would quietly write down at the back of her notebook. As she grew older, Arabella gravitated toward writing poetry and some song lyrics. By college, she shifted away from creative writing altogether and delved more into the study of language—linguistics. It helped her to better understand not only her linguistically diverse family but also the deeper meaning of language and communication. Language can be much more than just being used for expression and communication but also to help inspire, to heal, and to bring people together. Even though Arabella thought that her creative writing hobby had completely faded away, a pen and paper (or a laptop) would always seem to find its way back to her. Just like the main character, Noelle, in her book, Arabella was confronted with two choices: to either remain content with the status quo or take a step out of her comfort zone. After some very careful thought, she placed her trust in God and took that leap of faith to complete her first novel. The first step in anything new may feel like the most daunting task, but with a little bit of faith and determination, anything is possible.

Printed in the USA
CPSIA information can be obtained
at www.ICGtesting.com
CBHW031354091024
15572CB00011B/223